Heart of STONE

THE STONE SERIES: BOOK ONE

USA TODAY BESTSELLING AUTHOR

DAKOTA WILLINK

PRAISE FOR THE STONE SERIES

"There's a new billionaire in town! Fans of Fifty Shades and Crossfire will devour this series!"

— After Fifty Shades Book Blog

"It's complex. It's dirty. And I relished every single detail. This series is going to my TBR again and again!"

— Not Your Moms Romance Blog

"This read demanded to be heard. It screamed escape from the everyday and gave me that something extra I was looking for."

— The Book Junkie Reads

"Hang on to your kindles! It's a wild ride!"

— Once Upon An Alpha

"A definite page turner with enticing romance scenes that will make you sweat even during those cold winter nights!"

— Redz World

"Alexander and Krystina are an absolute must read!"

— Tracie's Book Review

"I would gladly hand over my heart to Alexander Stone!"

— Crystal's Book World

Dakota Willink, LLC

This book is an original publication of Dakota Willink, LLC

Library of Congress Cataloging-in-Publication Data

eBook ISBN-13: 978-0-9971603-0-7
Paperback ISBN-13: 978-0-9971603-1-4
Paperback ISBN-13: 978-1-954817-10-4
Hardcover ISBN-13: 978-1-954817-04-3

BOOKS BY DAKOTA WILLINK

The Stone Series

(Billionaire Romantic Suspense)

Heart of Stone

Stepping Stone

Set In Stone

Wishing Stone

Breaking Stone

The Fade Into You Series

Untouched (New Adult Romance)

*Defined (*Second Chance Romance)

Endurance (Sports Romance)

Take Me Trilogy

(Billionaire Romantic Suspense)

Take Me Under

Take Me Darkly

Take Me Forever

Standalone Titles

The Sound of Silence

(Dark Romantic Thriller)

Please visit www.dakotawillink.com for more information.

HEART OF STONE

THE STONE SERIES: BOOK 1

DAKOTA WILLINK

DRAGONFLY INK PUBLISHING

"Do or do not. There is no try."

— YODA

1

Krystina

A tendril of curly brown hair came loose from my ponytail. I pushed the hair out of my eyes, wiped the sweat off my brow, and stood to view the masterpiece before me. Well, it wasn't really a masterpiece—it was a supermarket end cap. Plain and simple.

"Excellent work, Krys!"

I looked up to see my portly boss, Walter Roberts, walking toward me.

"Thanks, Mr. Roberts," I replied absently. I wiped the dust off my hands with my apron and scrutinized the display I had built.

God, I hate planograms.

"Oh, come now. Don't look at me like that," my boss said, noting the apparent irritation written all over my face. "I know you don't like to build displays copied from a diagram."

"I don't like the way the sides stick out into the aisle like this," I complained, pointing to the outsides of the end cap. "The display is okay, considering the fact it's only a bunch of canned green beans and cream of mushroom soup. It's the racking that bothers me. I think this upside-down pyramid design is a hazard."

"You know, if it were any other day, I would let you run away with your creativity. I just can't allow it today," Mr. Roberts said, vehemently shaking his head. Worry lines spread across his round face. "The potential investors will be here at one o'clock, and everything must be perfect. I have to play this by the book, Krys. I'm sorry, but there's too much at stake."

He placed a patient hand on my shoulder for reassurance, and I couldn't help but soften my sour disposition. I liked Mr. Roberts, and I didn't want to give him a hard time, especially considering all the stress he was under.

It was no secret that Wally's Grocery Store was in financial trouble. After the stock market hit bottom a few years back, most of the smaller grocers had to close their doors for good, leaving Duane Reade as the only real competitor. Wally's had stayed afloat, but they would need a strong investor if they hoped to remain open much longer. If I wanted a job, I needed to stick to the planograms—at least for today.

"I suppose you're right," I conceded.

"That's better!" he said after seeing my change in demeanor. He gave me a sharp pat on the shoulder. "I knew I could count on you, Krys. You'll be a manager before you know it!"

And with that, he was off to harass the employees in the other departments.

I laughed to myself as I cleaned up my work area. Mr. Roberts always cracked comments about promoting me, even though he was fully aware I would never take a management job here.

I enjoyed working at Wally's for the most part. My coworkers were great, and I got along well with my boss. I had given careful consideration to the many management offers Mr. Roberts had presented to me over the past few months. However, a manager position at Wally's just wasn't for me. And it certainly would not pay my bills. My college graduation six months ago didn't just mark the beginning of a new future; it was a reminder that my student loan bills would come due any day now. Unfortunately, my salary at Wally's wouldn't even put a dent in them.

While the job had suited me well during my college years, it was becoming monotonous. Build a display; take it down. Build another, take it down—the same repetitive duties, day in and day out. I longed to use my degree in marketing, wanting my passion for sales to impact the world of advertising. I wanted a real job—one that gave me satisfaction. And one that gave me a fatter paycheck. I couldn't continue to accept my stepfather's support, but the job opportunities in New York had been slim to none. When the stock market took a tank, it affected not only grocery stores. It impacted the entire world of business.

I sighed to myself as I made my way back to the break room to gather my belongings. It didn't do me any good to dwell on the fact jobs were scarce. I just needed to keep looking. But not today. I hadn't had an afternoon free in what seemed like ages, and I was looking forward to some quiet time. It was a beautiful day, unusually warm for the beginning of October, and I wanted to take advantage of the early shift. An afternoon in Central Park, reading a book amidst the changing foliage was just what I needed to unwind.

Thoughts of sunshine and autumn leaves played in my mind as I stepped up to my locker and began spinning the combination lock.

"Hey, Krys!" said an all too familiar voice.

I glanced up and caught the eye of Jim McNamara. I inwardly groaned as I tossed the contents of my locker into my oversized purse.

"Hi, Jim," I greeted with forced politeness. I knew what was bound to come next, and a knot of dread formed in my stomach. Jim was forever asking me out, and I didn't want to deal with his wounded puppy dog eyes when I turned him down—again. I was tired from a long shift, and I just wanted to clock out. I prayed that perhaps it would be my lucky day, and he'd leave me alone for once.

"Do you have any plans for tonight? How about joining me for a bite to eat?" he asked, always the tireless optimistic.

So predictable.

Apparently, lady luck was not going to cooperate with me.

Maybe if I don't answer him, he'll take the hint.

I turned back to my locker, pretending not to hear his invitation for dinner.

"So, what do you say? Dinner at the new taco joint down the street?" he eagerly asked, failing to acknowledge the fact I had been ignoring the invite.

I should know Jim better by now.

"I actually already have plans. I'm sorry," I apologized half-heartedly, pushing my locker door closed.

A part of me felt guilty for thinking of Jim as nothing but a nuisance. He was a nice guy, decent looking with sandy blond hair and that boy-next-door sort of face. Jim and I worked together at Wally's over the past three years, and I think he asked me out every day of the last two. He might have been a good catch if I had any interest in dating. Unfortunately, Jim understood none of the subtle clues I threw his way, and I didn't have the heart to be outright nasty to him. I'm usually great at avoiding him, so I cursed myself for not hearing him come into the break room in the first place.

"Oh, come on, Krys! You're always busy," he complained. When I turned to consider him, there it was—the sad puppy face. I had to force back the urge to roll my eyes.

Be nice.

"Another time maybe," I said, trying to wiggle my way out of the corner I was backed into—and I was, quite literally, in a corner. With a wall at my back, a row of lockers to my left, and a table to my right, I was essentially trapped. Jim stood in front of me, making a perfect box, blocking the way out of the break room.

"I'll tell you what—how about you pick the date and the time? I promise to make it worth your while," he said with a wink.

"I'll check my calendar and let you know," I lied.

It suddenly reminded me of a cartoon I saw as a kid, the one with the dog that had an angel on one shoulder and a devil on the other. The angel was lecturing me and shaking her finger in disapproval.

You shouldn't lead him on, Krystina. Why don't you just agree to have dinner with the nice boy?

I ignored the angel, slipped my way past Jim, and walked hastily toward the break room door. I knew I should have been straight with Jim a long time ago. Any other guy would have received a blunt, if not rude, refusal on their first attempt at asking me out, deterring any thoughts of asking me again. Jim just made it so hard—he was almost too nice of a guy.

"Check your schedule, and I'll catch up with you tomorrow," Jim cheerily called out to me.

I was sure he would, too.

Guilt gnawed at my conscience. Perhaps I was handling the situation with Jim entirely wrong, but I knew in my heart it was for the best. He didn't know about my past, and it was better he didn't. The last thing I wanted was his pity. Jim deserves a nice girl and not someone bitter like me.

"I'll catch you later, Jim."

I threw a dismissive wave over my shoulder and hurried out of the break room toward the front entrance of Wally's. I needed to get away quickly before he could pressure me any further.

As soon as I stepped out onto the streets of New York, I took a deep breath. The smell of hot dog vendors and car exhaust permeated the air while the passing traffic noise and people filled my ears. A siren from a police car sounded shrilly in the distance, adding to the constant rush of the city's organized chaos.

I stretched out my arms and shoulders, muscles stiff and sore from lugging canned vegetables all day. Fatigue set in as I walked away from Wally's. Working the early shift was great because I got to enjoy the afternoons. However, the early shift also meant a four in the morning wake-up call. My body screamed for caffeine. A stop at Café La Biga was definitely needed, especially if I wanted to stay awake long enough to enjoy the heatwave the city was experiencing so late in the year. I took my iPod from my purse, plugged the little earbuds into my ears, and began the short walk up 57th Street to my favorite coffee shop.

There was some minor construction up ahead on the sidewalk, and I had to move off the curb to avoid it. A few men in neon orange hard hats nodded my way appreciatively, then followed up with obnoxious wolf whistles. They reminded me of a news article I once read about the staggering number of times the average woman gets harassed when walking through the city.

I scowled at the men and resisted the urge to throw them an obscene hand gesture.

Pigs.

I quickly sidestepped the construction, turned up my iPod's volume, and hummed along to a song by Tokyo Police Club. It was an upbeat tune that added a little spring to my step, quickly warding off the irritation I endured over the city workers.

Feeling more relaxed, I did what I always do when I walked the streets of New York—I took in the surrounding sights. Since moving here over four years ago, I had yet to tire of the constant changes and the little surprises my city held in store for me every day. The sounds, the smells, and the energy could not compare to anyplace else.

While its sheer size may have been intimidating to me initially, I had quickly grown accustomed to the busy hustle and bustle and adapted accordingly. New York was a living being. It had its own pulse, a different beat than the rest of the world, and I loved living here more than I ever imagined possible.

I smelled the aroma of espresso and fresh pastries before I even rounded the corner onto 8th Avenue. Café La Biga was opened thirty-five years ago by an Italian couple, Maria and Angelo Gianfranco. The café was small, with a simple interior that the owners modeled after the original Café La Biga in Rome, Italy. Angelo frequently boasted that the café was the only place in New York to get an authentic Italian espresso. Whether it was true, I didn't know. That was not why I had become a regular of the cozy little coffee shop. I came because La Biga was an experience.

I opened the door to the café and heard the familiar sound of espresso beans being ground. Every one of the little two-person tables was occupied, with the local chatter almost drowning out the voice of Dean Martin playing over the speakers. Angelo was whistling behind the counter and tamping espresso grounds into a portafilter. He stopped to give me an enormous smile when he saw me walk up.

"Krys! *Ciao, bella*! Where have you been? We have not seen you in a long time!"

"It's only been two days, Angelo!" I laughed lightheartedly.

"Two days is too long to go without seeing your beautiful face," he joked in broken English. Angelo prepared my favorite drink without my asking—a cappuccino with two packets of raw sugar. The aging Italian had the memory of an elephant.

"I'm sorry. I've been busy with work and sending out resumes to different advertising companies. Plus, I worked the early shift yesterday and today. Unfortunately, you're not open at four in the morning," I pointed out with a regretful shrug of my shoulders. "Besides, don't feel too bad about not seeing me. I haven't seen my roommate in three days, and she lives with me!"

"You young people are always so busy—you never sit still!" he chided.

"Speaking of which, can you put my cap in a to-go cup? I have a date with a book in Central Park," I added with a grin.

"Bravo, bravo! It makes me happy to hear you are going out to enjoy this wonderful sunshine. You need to relax and enjoy life more often, *bella*. If I were a few years younger, I would show you how the Italians enjoy living," he said with a devilish wink and handed me my drink.

As if on cue, Maria came out of the backroom.

"Ah, stop it, you old fool! Leave the poor girl alone. She doesn't want to be bothered by you!" Angelo's wife quipped. Maria's eyes crinkled in the corners as she smiled at me. I walked over to the register and waited as she cashed me out.

"How are you, honey? You seem thin. You are working all the time," she scolded. "You need something to eat, yes?"

"I'm fine, Maria. No, thank you," I graciously declined, then sighed as she packaged up pastries for me, anyway. I mentally calculated the calories going into the bag. My hips didn't like the resulting sum. She left me with little choice but to pay for the cappuccino and the pastries I didn't need. As sweet as Maria was, she never understood the word 'no.'

I said my goodbyes to Maria and Angelo and left the café. My conversation with the shop owners reminded me I had to call Allyson, my roommate. I missed her. Our schedules had been so opposite lately, and I hadn't talked to my friend in days. It was a short walk to Central Park, and I decided to give her a call along the way.

I reached into my purse for my cell phone but had trouble locating it. After fishing around for a few minutes, I knew it wasn't there.

Damn!

In my mad dash to avoid Jim, I must have left it in my locker at Wally's. Frustrated over the time wasted, I turned around and headed back.

When I finally reached the front doors of Wally's, I hesitated before going in. I really didn't want to risk another run-in with Jim. On impulse, I yanked the ponytail out of my hair and shook out my curly mop.

Head down and face hidden. Maybe he won't see me.

I knew it was a long shot, so I superstitiously crossed my fingers before hurrying inside.

By some minor miracle, I managed to get to my locker, retrieve my phone, and leave the break room without being seen. As I was walking down aisle nine, I mentally congratulated myself for a successful stealth mission, even though I was still mildly aggravated that it had delayed my plans. Hopefully, it wasn't too late for the park.

I glanced down at my phone to check the time and saw I had a missed call from Allyson. Trying to remember what my friend had planned for that night, I began typing her a quick text to ask her—

WHAM!

Pain pierced through my skull in a ferocious blast, and stars dotted my vision. I grabbed my head with two hands to stop the clanging sound of metal reverberating through my eardrums. After a moment or two, I regained some sense of focus and stared directly at the metal racking of an end cap—the same end cap I had so carefully built that morning.

"Damn planogram!" I cursed.

My right eye was killing me, and I could already sense it swelling. I looked down at my shirt. Not only had I smacked my head, but my cappuccino had dumped all over the front of me. As my gaze traveled down to the floor, I saw my cell phone lying face down in a puddle of milk and espresso. I groaned.

Please don't let the screen be cracked!

I repeated the silent plea over and over again as I bent over to pick it up. Sure enough, the screen had shattered.

"Son of a bitch!" I swore out loud, looking at the spiderweb cracks on the glass.

Feeling more than just a little foolish, I looked around to make sure no one had seen my klutzy mishap.

Heat spread up my neck to my face in embarrassment when I saw Mr. Roberts, Jim McNamara, and a man in a suit standing about halfway down the aisle. They were all staring at me in shock over what had transpired.

Fantastic—I have an audience.

Then I did a double-take.

The third man was not just another ordinary guy in a suit. This man was attractive—very attractive. He was young, too. I guessed he wasn't a day over thirty, with an arresting face and perfectly chiseled square jawline. He was taller than the other two men, standing over six feet. He looked absolutely magnificent in his dark gray sport coat, white shirt, and solid black tie. His hair was wavy and almost black. It was cut longer, but not too long, with the dark ends just touching his collar.

Holy hell! No man should be allowed to look that good in a suit!

The sleeping devil on my shoulder woke up to take a peek. I

suddenly had a vision of running my hands through those silky dark waves, across the broad span of his shoulders...

"Oh, my! Are you okay?" Mr. Roberts' voice broke me from my reverie. The three men started walking in my direction. Mr. Roberts, alarmed over what happened, was running his hands over his thinning gray hair.

I caught the gaze of the man in the suit as he strode toward me with an air of confident grace. His stare was intense, intimidating almost, yet lines of concern spread across his flawlessly sculpted features. Speechless and embarrassed by my clumsiness, I took a step back.

Big mistake.

I slipped on the spilled drink and went down—hard. Now my head and my ass hurt. Mortified beyond all belief, I wanted to crawl into a hole and stay there forever.

This cannot possibly be happening. The hottest guy on the planet. Me sitting in a puddle of cappuccino. Un. Fucking. Believable.

I felt a warm hand on my shoulder, and I looked up. The suited man was gazing down at me with the most incredible pair of blue eyes I had ever seen. They were the color of cobalt blue, reserved and calculating as he regarded me. I didn't think eyes could be so vibrant. For a moment, I presumed he wore colored contacts. However, as I continued to stare, the depths of his eyes were endless and seemed to swallow me whole. The intensity of them sent a shiver up my spine, raising the hairs on the back of my neck.

He was definitely not wearing contacts.

Somewhere in the distance, I heard Mr. Roberts speaking again. "Did you hear me? I asked if you were okay? This is Mr. Stone. He's trying to help you up."

"Mr. Stone?" I asked, half in a daze. I couldn't tear my focus away from those astonishing deep blues.

"That's correct. And you might be?"

Stone's voice was smooth and confident as he lowered himself to a crouching position next to me. Running his hand down the side of my arm, he rested it near my elbow. I felt my pulse quicken at his sudden closeness and from the heat surging off of him in a palpable wave. He was just so there, radiating with power, eyes level with mine.

He repeated his question a second time, again asking me my name. All I could think of was the hand firmly present on my arm, warming my skin through the sleeve of my thin cotton shirt. His touch sparked an electric shock, igniting a presence in me I hadn't known existed. Butterflies twirled and danced in my stomach. I shook my head to collect my bearings and gave myself a quick reprimand.

Um, hello? He's asking you a question! Get a grip—he's just a guy in a suit for crying out loud!

"I'm K-Krys," I finally stammered out. I sounded like an idiot. I was sure of it. I fidgeted with my hands and licked my lips, my mouth suddenly feeling as dry as the Sahara Desert. A dangerous look flashed in Stone's eyes. It happened so fast, and I couldn't be sure if it were only my imagination.

"Krys? Is that short for something else?" He sounded displeased. Was there something wrong with my name?

When I didn't answer immediately, Jim responded for me. "It's short for Krystina. Krystina Cole."

It was hard to miss the expression of irritation on Stone's face as he slowly turned his head to consider Jim.

"Why, thank you, Mr. McNamara, for speaking on Miss Cole's behalf. However, I would have preferred to hear it from Miss Cole herself," he said curtly.

"Well, Miss Cole appears to have lost her voice," Jim retorted back, his voice dripping with sarcasm.

"Jim!" Mr. Roberts hissed.

Stone simply ignored both Jim and Mr. Roberts and turned back to me. He stood gracefully and held out his hand.

"Please, allow me to help you up," he offered.

I didn't know if I could stand, and not because of the fall I took. I was utterly mesmerized by this man. It was as if he had me under a spell, and I didn't trust my shaky legs.

I took hold of his outstretched hand and carefully moved to

stand up. His grip was firm as he pulled me to my feet. He reached his free arm around me, securing it against my lower back to balance me. His hold was steadfast, pinning me against his side, eyes never once wavering from mine. My cheeks flushed crimson, and those striking blues darkened. I felt my heart rate accelerate even faster as I returned his gaze. He was so close to me. I couldn't stop myself from breathing in his scent. It was a heady combination of sex and sin.

"I'm sure she could have gotten up on her own, you know," Jim said irritably, reminding me of my humiliating predicament. I blinked, clearing my clouded vision.

Ugh! Go away, Jim!

I wanted to grab one of the canned goods off the nearest shelf and throw it at Jim's skull.

Much to my disappointment, Stone slowly removed his arm from around my waist, took a step back, and released my hand. Once he was sure I was steady on my feet, he broke his gaze from mine and turned his head toward Jim. I could no longer see the expression on Stone's face, but it must have been intimidating. Jim seemed to cower visibly and took a few steps back.

Mr. Roberts, having noticed the tension on the verge of boiling over, made a loud show of clearing his throat and was quick to dismiss Jim to do some other task in the dairy department.

"But, Mr. Roberts, I was supposed to—" Jim started in protest.

"Jim, please go help Melanie. Now. She's alone in the department today, and I'm sure she could use a hand unloading the truck that just arrived," Mr. Robert ordered Jim sternly.

Jim looked in my direction, his face creased in a scowl, and stomped away. I couldn't care less about what Jim was supposed to do. I was still thunderstruck, having uttered only four words since setting my eyes on the daunting Mr. Stone. I was usually a chatterbox, but I was so taken by the man in front of me, I'd been stunned into silence. I forced myself to do a reality check.

Pull yourself together already!

I looked at the two remaining men. Mr. Roberts had a worried expression on his plump face. Stone, on the other hand, wore a look of amusement. I followed the direction of his stare and realized he had been looking down at my espresso-stained work shirt, wet and plastered to my torso.

Once again, I felt an embarrassing flush creep up my neck.

So, what? I fell—big deal. Accidents happen. Sure, I'm a stuttering idiot too, but that isn't my fault either. Nobody should be allowed to be as savagely gorgeous as he is. My reaction is just natural. I'm sure every woman he meets wants to jump his bones.

Jump his bones? Did I really just think that?

It was time to leave—and fast. I couldn't think straight. I didn't understand how this man could unnerve me so much. I couldn't even talk, let alone form a coherent thought. I only knew I was mortified and could no longer endure his penetrating stare.

I began to slowly back away, using caution, so I didn't slip again on the wet floor. Mr. Roberts was rambling on about terrible planograms and schematics that needed changing. Stone continued to watch me a moment longer before turning his attention back to Mr. Roberts. I took advantage of the distraction to make my escape, but not before chancing one more glance at the hypnotizing Mr. Stone.

He was looking at me again, a bad-boy smile curling up the edges of his lips. He held up his hand to silence Mr. Roberts.

"Have a good day, Miss Cole. I'll be seeing you soon."

He said it like it was a promise.

Then the realization struck me—he was the investor.

Alexander

I WATCHED HER WALK AWAY. ACTUALLY, RUN AWAY WOULD HAVE BEEN a more accurate description. I smiled to myself, intrigued by the very embarrassed yet delectable Miss Cole. Her pouty mouth, round chocolate-colored eyes, and ready blush made my dick twitch.

"I'm so sorry about that, Mr. Stone. Krystina and I were just discussing how the display needed changing. It just goes to show how much our vendors know about merchandising," the round man in front of me said with a nervous laugh.

"Yes, indeed," I murmured absently, my eyes still following the captivating young woman as she continued her way to the front doors of the supermarket chain. "Walter, tell me about that woman. I assume she's an employee?"

"Oh, yes. Krystina has worked here for years. Great eye for merchandising, that one does," Walter Roberts observed, following my gaze. "I hate the thought of losing her."

"Is she going somewhere?"

"Hopefully not, but I'm sure it won't be long before she lands herself a fancy marketing job," Roberts said regretfully.

"Marketing, you say?" I asked, turning my attention back to the store owner.

"Yes, I believe that was her major," he answered cautiously.

Roberts narrowed his eyes at me suspiciously.

Hmm... protective of her, are we?

I glanced back again, only to barely glimpse her tight jean-clad ass, as the front doors closed behind her. I wished I had more time to converse with her, but between her fall and the annoying store clerk, there had been little opportunity for talking before she took off.

That clerk... what was his name? Jim something or another?

I absently wondered if he was her boyfriend and was surprised to find that the possibility bothered me. I hoped he wasn't.

Walter Roberts cleared his throat annoyingly as if he were trying to remind me of the business at hand. It was no matter. I knew a wise investment when I saw it. There was no need to dawdle in the store any longer. After all, time was money. And while I had plenty of the latter, I was now pressed for time. If I stayed much longer, I wouldn't be able to catch up with Krystina Cole.

"I'll have my lawyers draw up a proposal, one I think you will find satisfactory. We can discuss things further at a later date," I shrugged off.

"Well, er...," Roberts faltered. "Mr. Stone, don't you want to see the rest of the store? Or perhaps some of our other locations?"

"No, I believe I've seen enough here to decide. I'll be in touch," I dismissed.

I left Walter Roberts gaping after me as I made my way to the front entrance. Pulling my cell out of my jacket pocket, I hit the number one on speed dial.

"Hale, did you see which way the brunette went?" I asked into the phone.

"Which brunette, sir? There must have been a hundred that walked by in the past thirty minutes," my security detail told me.

I pushed through the turnstile front doors of the grocery store and glanced back and forth down the street. There was no sign of her.

Damn it!

"Ah, forget it, Hale. I'm finished here. Bring the car around."

I'll catch up with you eventually, Miss Cole.

2

Krystina

By the time I got back to my apartment, it was after four o'clock. I mourned for the lost day of relaxing in the sunshine as I tossed my keys, purse, and cracked cell phone onto the corner table by the front door. I was bone-tired, and now it was too late in the day for reading in Central Park.

I contemplated taking my latest mystery novel to the nearby Washington Square but ended up deciding against it. At this time of the day, I knew the park would be filled with music from street performers. The chance of relaxing in quiet solitude would be slim to none. In fact, just the thought of going back out was exhausting. Curling up on the couch would have to do.

I kicked off my sneakers and looked around the apartment. After more than four years of residing in Gree[illegible]ch Village, I still wasn't entirely comfortable with the fifteen [illegible]dred square foot flat I lived in, even though the three-bedroo[illegible]it was more than spacious enough for Allyson and me.

We each had our own rooms and master [illegible]s, complete with custom vanities and heated marble floors. We[illegible]d turned the third bedroom into an office and added a sleepe[illegible]ofa for overnight guests. The arrangement worked out well whenever our friends or parents came for a weekend visit.

The place was truly beautiful, but I never felt like it was mine. Maybe if I were the one who paid the rent, I would feel differently. But then again, if my mother weren't so neurotic about my safety in New York City, I could have flat out refused my stepfather's extravagance and lived someplace within my budget. However, my mother didn't want me living in a tiny apartment in Brooklyn, which was all I could afford, and her lectures about crime in Brooklyn were endless.

Nevertheless, I drew the line there. I allowed Frank to pay the rent, but I refused to take the monthly stipend offered to me. I was perfectly capable of making my own money and buying my own food. My insistence on taking out student loans to pay for my college tuition was another huge battle with my mother, probably one of our biggest fights ever, but one I took satisfaction in winning.

My mother and I were like night and day. I was determined to make it in this world on my own. The sooner I could break free from my financial dependence on Frank, the better. My mother, on the other hand, seemed content just to be a rich man's wife. She could never understand why I wanted to do things independently, especially when Frank was always so willing to foot the bill.

Yet, as infuriating as she could be, I knew my mother's heart was in the right place. She worried about me and didn't want me to struggle like she had to for so many years, a fact Allyson was always good at pointing out. Allyson was the only one who was able to talk me down after a heated battle with my mother.

In fact, I wasn't sure if I could have managed to live here without Allyson, and I was thankful to have her as a roommate. She appreciated Frank's lavishing's more than I did and worked to make our apartment a place to call home.

I was absently thinking about where my friend might be tonight when the rumble in my stomach reminded me it was almost dinnertime. I flipped on the stereo and went into the kitchen. Thirty Seconds to Mars blared through the speakers as I opened the refrigerator to peruse the contents. I spotted last night's leftovers on the shelf. The thought of a glass of wine and leftover pasta had my mouth watering. I was hungry, but I was a sticky coffee mess and needed to shower first.

I closed the refrigerator and went over to our makeshift wine bar to pour a glass of Bully Hill Riesling. Sitting on the bar was a note from Allyson.

Hey you! I called your cell, but it went right to VM. Clear your schedule for tomorrow night. 7 PM. Dinner and drinks at Murphy's. I have news for you. Enjoy your wine! Love ya! — A

I smiled to myself as I swirled the sweet vintage around in my glass. My friend knew me too well. With the hubbub at Wally's over the potential investors, the past week had been a rough one. Allyson was right to assume I'd unwind with a bit of vino.

"Oh, Ally. I wish you were home tonight," I said aloud to myself, raising my glass in silent cheers to my friend.

I really wanted to talk to her about what had happened today with the sexy Mr. Stone. I felt like a complete idiot. I knew she would probably fall over laughing at my story, but then she'd pour us both a drink and reassure me I wasn't really a clumsy fool. Her laughter and assurances would have been the perfect medicine after such a mucked-up day.

I headed to the bathroom, glass in hand, wondering what news Allyson had for me. I turned on the shower and adjusted the water temperature before stripping off my jeans and cappuccino-stained shirt. When I faced the mirror, I was shocked at what I saw.

My eye wasn't just slightly swollen as I had initially thought it might be. It was turning a deep purple, with a small gash over my right eye. I peered closely in the mirror and tried to decide how much makeup I would need to cover up the bruise. I gingerly poked at the swollen eye for a minute before standing up to examine my reflection.

My hair was in complete disarray. I reached up to smooth out the unruly curls.

Just great. Blue Eyes got to see me rocking the Medusa look.

I turned to one side, then the other. My behind was sore, and I was surprised to see there wasn't any bruising. However, despite the fact I managed to escape any real damage to my rump, I still frowned at what I saw.

I really need to hit the gym.

A week off and I was already seeing and feeling the effects. My voluptuous behind wasn't going to fit into a size six much longer if I didn't get back into a routine. Some girls were just naturally skinny. Unfortunately, that wasn't me. I had to work at it.

My stomach rumbled yet again, reminding me to get moving.

I quickly showered, then went back to the kitchen to heat the leftover pasta. Once the microwave beeped, signaling the food was heated, I tiredly made my way into the living room with a steaming bowl of garlic pesto farfalle. I sat down on the couch and sank into the deep cushions, relishing the feeling of my weary bones settling as every muscle in my body began to relax for the first time that day.

Angelo's right. I have been working too much lately.

I leaned over to pick up my book from the coffee table and opened it to where I had it marked.

An hour later, I found myself staring at the words in front of me. I had only read five pages and had barely comprehended any of them. I couldn't concentrate at all on the text. Every time I started a new sentence, my focus would drift to a pair of piercing sapphire eyes. Eyes so powerful, just the thought of them had my stomach doing flips.

Who is the man with the blue eyes? Is he the investor?

If he was, hopefully, today's mishap didn't mess anything up for Wally's. I'd hate to be the reason for a potential investor to pull out. The memory of his promise to see me again echoed through my mind.

Why did he say that?

So many questions bounced around in my head. Frustrated

over my lack of concentration, I set the book aside and brought my empty dinner bowl to the kitchen sink.

Maybe if I have a few answers about exactly who this mysterious man is, then I'll be able to stop thinking about him.

I retrieved my laptop from my bedroom and went back to the couch. Once the computer was fired up, I started to type "Blue Eyes" into the search engine, but then I caught myself.

Seriously? What's wrong with me?

I erased the letters and typed "Stone NYC" instead. I scrolled through the list of articles. Information on gemstones, imported stones, and commercial stones populated my screen. I frowned at the findings. It was obviously not what I had been looking for.

I narrowed the search and tried "Stone NYC Investor Wallys." That turned up better results. Right away, I saw an article related to Wally's, and I clicked on it.

> "Despite the many problems, there may still be hope on the horizon for Wally's Grocery Store. The New York City real estate tycoon, Alexander Stone, is looking to step in and possibly save the struggling grocer."

Alexander Stone? I've never heard of him.

I was pretty sure it was the same Mr. Stone I was introduced to. I clicked on the internet images to see if there were any pictures of him.

I sucked in a breath, my stomach instantly clenching into a knot. There he was, gazing at me through the screen. Even on a computer screen, those smoldering blue eyes could sear right through me, causing desire to burn hot in my belly.

Easy, girl. It's just a computer image.

Reining in my wild thoughts, I changed the search to "Alexander Stone NYC." The number of articles that came up was staggering. I clicked on the first one.

"This afternoon, New York City's beloved opera house announced they would begin their long-awaited renovation, a project made possible by the $4 million-dollar donation from The Stoneworks Foundation. The opera had been experiencing extraordinary difficulties over the recent years and is extremely thankful to Alexander Stone for his support."

The article went on to talk about the financial difficulties the opera had been struggling with, but I didn't finish reading it. I clicked the back button to see what else I could find.

"The groundbreaking ceremony for a new women's shelter in Queens took place on Monday, with Alexander Stone present to cut the ribbon. Mr. Stone, the founder of The Stoneworks Foundation, has donated $1.2 million to build a shelter for battered women. The shelter should be near completion early next year."

Interesting. So, what's wrong with him?

He was good-looking, rich, and involved in charitable causes. I found it hard to believe any guy was that picture-perfect. I clicked on the next article.

"Stone Enterprise strikes a $280 million-dollar deal with the near-bankrupt Rushmore Industries to purchase one of the tallest residential buildings in New York. Soaring over 1,000 feet high, Stone Enterprise plans to remodel the neglected Rushmore building. It will eventually hold 92 luxury apartments and two penthouses. Wall Street says the purchase was a steal and predicts it will pay for itself in less than two years, as the penthouses alone will contract for at least $84 million each once they are completed. CEO

> Alexander Stone did not comment when asked if he was going to rename the building."

Two hundred eighty million! Wow—this guy isn't just rich—he's that *rich!*

I may have been fortunate enough to grow up comfortably, but even Frank didn't bring in that kind of dough. Not even close. I moved the mouse to click on the next article. This one was a gossip column from the local entertainment magazine, dated two months earlier.

> "Alexander Stone, one of New York's most eligible bachelors, arrived at the Chamber of Commerce Ball with yet another red-headed bombshell on his arm. Who knew there were so many stunning redheads in New York City?"

Hmmm...yes. Who knew?

The article contained a picture of a drop-dead gorgeous woman with flowing red locks, holding the arm of Alexander Stone. She looked like she just stepped off the stage of America's Top Model.

Enough of that.

I hit the back button again and came across another sleaze article. This one was a little more recent, dated only three weeks ago.

> "Alexander Stone, the 32-year-old real estate mogul, refused to answer questions regarding his relationship with Miss Suzanne Jacobs. The couple has been seen together at three separate charity engagements, causing the rumor mills to fly. Anyone who follows our column knows Mr. Stone is never seen with the same woman twice. Could she be the one to

finally capture his heart of stone? Miss Jacobs was unavailable to answer our questions."

Never the same woman twice? Bingo—that's what's wrong with him.

All men were exactly the same. Alexander Stone was just another stereotypical millionaire playboy.

Good luck with that one, Miss Jacobs.

I gave in to a big yawn and stretched my back. The hour was nearing midnight, and I had to work the next day. It was my turn to work the mid-shift, so at least I got to sleep in a bit. I closed the laptop and headed back to my room.

I wearily climbed into bed, pulled the blankets up, and tucked them beneath my chin. Within five minutes of my head hitting the pillow, I fell asleep, putting all thoughts of those powerful blue eyes to rest.

3

Krystina

When I arrived at Wally's for my shift the following day, Jim was waiting for me by my locker in the break room. He didn't say anything to me at first, but he looked like he was steaming over something. He stepped aside so I could open my locker and deposit my things inside. Pretending to be preoccupied, I ignored the indignant look he threw at me and glanced down at the broken screen of my cellphone. I made a mental note to stop by the cellphone store tomorrow morning to see about getting it replaced.

"Are you even going to say hello?" Jim eventually spat out.

Yep, he is definitely pissed off.

"Um...hi, Jim."

I didn't know what else I could say. I wanted to avoid engaging in a conversation that would inevitably lead to one thing, and I didn't have the energy to deal with Jim's advances today. I was tired and irritable from a restless night. Dreams of Alexander Stone's blue eyes haunted me all night, making it impossible for me to concentrate on much else this morning.

"Your bruise looks pretty nasty," Jim informed me in a cynical voice.

Gee, how nice of you to say. Like I don't already know. What bug crawled up your ass today?

I silently counted to ten in an attempt to reign in my temper.

Be nice.

"Jim, is there something wrong?" I asked, my voice coming out clipped, despite my efforts to remain patient.

"Oh, no. Nothing is wrong. Besides the fact I had to clean your coffee spill *and* your drool off of the floor in aisle nine yesterday."

"My drool?" I eyed him quizzically.

"Oh, come on, Krys. You could barely even speak when that guy Stone was looking at you. I've never seen any woman act so gaga over a guy, especially you!"

"I don't know what the hell you're talking about," I said curtly.

Was I that obvious?

I made a move toward the door, but he blocked my way.

"Is it because he's loaded?" Jim asked accusingly.

The fact he thought so little of me stung. I couldn't explain to *myself* why I lost my head yesterday. I couldn't possibly explain it to Jim. Yesterday I didn't even know who the man was, let alone that he was filthy rich. Jim was so far off the mark.

"Move out of the way, Jim. I didn't sleep well last night, and I have zero energy for an argument today."

"No, seriously—I want to know. I can't figure you out. You're always so disinterested, like you hate men or something," he said in exasperation. "What makes this guy so different?"

"I'm not having this discussion with you."

"You never want to have any sort of discussion with me! I've been asking you out for as long as I can remember, only to have you turn me down every time!"

His voice was getting louder by the minute. I looked around and was thankful to find we were the only ones in the break room at that moment.

"I don't always turn you down," I weakly replied.

"No, you're right. You always put me off instead."

Ouch.

He was right about that one, but it hurt all the same. I took a deep breath to calm my own rising temper and resigned myself to the inevitable. I should have been more truthful a long time ago.

"Look, Jim—I could apologize, but I really have nothing to apologize for. I just have no interest in dating."

"Why not? Are you a lesbian or something?" he asked, reaching up to scratch his head in confusion.

"No, I'm not a lesbian," I said with a light laugh, momentarily amused.

"This isn't funny to me, Krys."

He was right. Making light of this wouldn't help the situation, and I sobered almost immediately. I had to make sure he understood my position once and for all.

"I'm going to be honest here. You're a great guy, and I don't want to hurt your feelings, but you don't want to be with someone like me. Besides, you and I both know there's nothing there. No spark," I finished frankly, waving my hand back and forth between the two of us. "At least not for me anyway."

I tried to be gentle, conscious of his feeling toward me, but I was sure I came off as a crotchety bitch. I sucked in situations like this.

He stared at me for a long moment, taking in what I had said. I watched his face fall, and his shoulders slump, all of his anger slipping away to a look of defeat. He looked down at his feet and shifted his weight from side to side. He looked so deflated.

Maybe I'm being too harsh.

When he looked up, his eyes were pained with rejection.

"Well, at least you're giving it to me straight for once, even though I sort of knew all along. It just sucks hearing you say it out loud."

"Jim, I'm sorry. Really, I am. I don't mean to hurt you."

That was the truth, and it killed me to see his desolate expression. Although I found Jim to be somewhat annoying, he was still a decent guy. It would have been so much easier if I had just lied and told him I *was* a lesbian.

I'm such a jerk.

I moved toward the door again, unable to look at him any longer. This time, he didn't block my way.

"Krys?" he called after me. I paused in the doorway, afraid of what else he might say.

"Yes," I answered hesitantly.

"Your spark is in aisle nine."

"Excuse me?"

"Stone. He was asking for you a little while ago."

Oh, shit! Alexander Stone is here?

My heart began to race at the thought of seeing him again. For the life of me, I couldn't figure out why that beautiful man would want to see *me* of all people. But more importantly, I didn't understand why I became instantly excited by the mere idea of laying eyes on him again. That was a confusing concept I'd have to delve into later.

I tried to keep control of my composure, not wanting to look too eager and risk hurting Jim even more. I made a conscious effort to steady my voice and sound indifferent.

"Mr. Stone is looking for me. Are you sure?" I asked evenly.

"Yeah, he's here. You'd better get a move on," Jim said with a lazy shooing motion of his hands. "I get the impression he's not the kind of man that likes to be kept waiting."

Say no more.

"Thanks, Jim."

I turned to go, struggling to walk at a reasonable pace. It was hard to keep myself from running all the way to aisle nine.

As I rounded the corner of aisle nine, I noticed the end cap had been changed. The racking no longer stuck out. I moved to look at the new display but stopped short when I saw Alexander Stone standing just a few feet away. He was facing away from me and didn't see I had come up behind him. I couldn't help but pause to take in the view.

He was wearing a suit again today, although this time it was navy blue. He had removed his suitcoat and had it draped casually over one arm. Without the coat, I could faintly see the outline of his well-muscled back and shoulders through his pricy white collared shirt.

My gaze moved down past his tapered waist to his perfectly tailored pants. They looked as if they were made specifically to fit the magnificent contoured ass beneath them.

Boxers or briefs? Or maybe he just goes commando.

My cheeks flushed pink at the thought, and my hands clenched tight, fighting against the urge to reach out and touch him.

Down, girl!

He had a shopping basket of groceries in front of him, which I found somewhat strange. I didn't think millionaires shopped for their own groceries. I had always thought they had a hired minion to do it for them. Out of pure curiosity, I chanced a quick glance into his shopping basket. I could see a few boxes of pasta, almonds, bananas, chocolate, eggs, olives, honey, and pomegranate juice. It was certainly a peculiar combination of food items, to say the least.

As if he finally sensed my presence, his shoulders squared, and he slowly turned to face me. And there it was—the spark.

My heart began a steady pitter-patter that quickly evolved into a strong thumping in my chest. He was even better looking than I remembered—the definition of pure male beauty. He skipped wearing a tie today, and I had to try very hard not to look at the small area of skin revealed near his collar. I had no trouble imagining myself unbuttoning the neatly pressed shirt and running my hands over his chest, down his abdomen...

Get ahold of yourself—you're thinking like some hormone-crazed teenager!

"Miss Cole," he said with a short nod, the two words sliding over me like warm whiskey.

"Hello, Mr. Stone. I heard you were looking for me," I said evenly, proud that I was able to sound controlled despite the man's ability to turn my knees to liquid.

"Indeed, I was," he said. He was chewing gum. Alexander

Stone chewing a piece of gum was probably the sexiest thing I had ever seen in my life.

"Was there something you needed?" I courteously asked while watching his jaw move up and down over the piece of gum.

A slow leisurely smile began to form on his face, and he waited a moment before responding.

"I just wanted to see how you were doing after your fall yesterday."

Of course, that's what he wanted.

A potential investor in Wally's would naturally be concerned about the accident.

The word 'lawsuit' is probably a flashing neon sign over my head right now.

"Oh...my fall." I tried to hide my disappointment. I felt self-conscious about my black and blue eye and hoped my makeup did a better job of covering it than Jim led me to believe. "I'm fine—really. It's just a bump on the head. I owe you an apology for my clumsiness. Thank you for your assistance in helping me up."

I was talking way too fast, my words coming out in a rush, but his mere presence was unsettling. He made me feel like a scatterbrain, and I found it difficult to stay composed. However, if he noticed my hurried ramblings, he didn't let on.

"It was no trouble at all, Miss Cole," he assured me.

"Well, it's like Jim said. I could have gotten up on my own, but I was a little stunned from..." *From you. Stunned from you.* "From smacking my head on the end cap."

His eyes narrowed at the mention of Jim, and I wanted to slap myself for bringing him up. After all, they hadn't exactly hit it off the day before.

"Yes, Jim. I spoke with him a few moments ago," he paused and seemed to consider his words. "Is he your boyfriend by chance?"

"Oh, no!" I almost laughed but then stopped myself when I realized Stone was dead serious. I frowned, curious as to why whether or not Jim was my boyfriend should matter. "What made you think he might be?"

"He just seems rather protective of you, that's all."

Just great. Not.

"We're only friends. We've known each other for a long time."

"I see," was all he said, although he seemed to relax after hearing my explanation. Either way, the atmosphere had become awkward, and I felt the need to explain more.

Maybe I should have said coworker and not a friend. I sort of made it seem like Jim and I were close.

"Well, thanks again for helping me out," I said, resorting to politeness rather than tack on more unnecessary babble.

"I can assure you it was my pleasure," he said, emphasizing his last word. A hint of humor glinted in his eyes, causing a blush to creep up my neck and into my cheeks. It was suddenly very, very warm in Wally's Grocery Store.

Did he really need to say the word 'pleasure' like that?

The word rolled off of his tongue like ice cream melting from a cone. A vision of Alexander Stone's tongue, working its way around an ice cream cone, unexpectedly came to mind. Between my overactive imagination and his ridiculously hot gum chewing, I couldn't stop the wicked ideas from running through my head. The angel on my shoulder appeared with folded arms and shook her head in disapproval at me. I fought the urge to flick her away.

A ghost of a smile turned up the corners of Stone's mouth, almost as if he knew what I was thinking. I fought to ignore my awareness of him by focusing my energies on our conversation.

Just don't look at him chewing the gum.

"Your boss told me you've worked here for a while," he casually stated.

Small talk. Good. I can handle that.

"Yes. I started here after I moved to New York, so..." I did a quick calculation. "It's been about four years. I'm a student, and the flexible retail schedule is convenient."

I didn't want to tell him I had received my diploma months ago. It was too long of an explanation, and I was embarrassed to admit I hadn't found a job yet.

"You're a student? I didn't realize," he said.

I could swear I saw a shadow of disappointment come across

his face, but his expression was so impassive, and I couldn't be sure. He folded his arms and considered me carefully.

"Well, I *was* a student, I should say. I just recently graduated," I clarified reluctantly. "Most of my fellow classmates were able to land jobs at the places where they interned. My place of internship closed up shop, leaving me back to square one. Unfortunately, I learned a hard lesson about not putting all of my eggs in one basket, if you know what I mean."

I was talking too fast again, but at least I wasn't a mute like yesterday.

"Yes, I do," he murmured contemplatively. "Do you like your job here, Miss Cole?"

"I, um..." Another question. "Yes, very much so. Mr. Roberts is really good to work for," I answered evenly. I wished he would just spit out the gum. It was distracting.

"I'm glad to hear that."

He shifted in place and glanced down at his watch. He looked like he was getting ready to leave. As lovely as the view would surely be, I wasn't quite ready to see him go. I racked my brain, trying to think of a way to stall him.

"What about you, Mr. Stone? Do you like your job?" I blurted out.

One of his eyebrows tweaked up in surprise at my abruptness. Whether or not he liked his job was none of my business. But if he was insulted by my forwardness, he didn't show it.

"Of course, I do. I would never indulge in anything I didn't like," he replied in a measured tone, mouth moving slowly and deliberately around the piece of gum. A slight smile tugged at the corners of his lips as if he were enjoying his own private joke. "My job allows me to be in control of my own destiny. And I like to be in control, Miss Cole."

Just don't watch him chew. Don't watch him chew.

I repeated the chant over and over in my head.

"Control?" I practically squeaked.

"I am fascinated with the human mind. Understanding how a person thinks allows me to control a situation. And in my line of work, the only way to be successful is to have the ability to control the will of others. It gives me a certain measure of power, or the upper hand, as some might choose to call it. This can be quite useful when buying and selling real estate. But power comes with responsibility, and balancing the two takes a considerable amount of control."

Wow! That's a bit deep. This guy's a total control nut.

It was definitely not a simple answer for what I thought was an innocent question. But as I processed his words, I thought they reminded me of something you'd hear Bruce Wayne say in a Batman movie. An image of Alexander Stone wearing a black cape popped into my head, and I had to stifle the giggle trying to escape. It came out as a half snort instead.

"I'm sorry, but did I say something funny?" he asked curiously, cocking his head to one side.

"Um, no. Not at all," I said, attempting to cover up the sudden wave of silliness I was feeling. "I was just thinking your philosophy about power and control is a little extreme. Cocky...sort of."

"That may be your perception. However, I'm not an egomaniacal tyrant like you might think. I just happen to like all of my ducks in a row." He paused and glanced down at his watch again. "Now, as intriguing as this conversation has been, I have to get going. I'm glad your head is feeling better." He flashed one last delicious smile at me and turned to leave. "It was good to see you again, Miss Cole."

"Enjoy your day, Mr. Stone," I murmured pensively.

Ducks in a row, huh?

I couldn't help but wonder what it would be like to ruffle his feathers as I watched him proceed to the checkout line.

Boy, does that man have swagger.

On impulse, I strode nonchalantly over to where he stood and grabbed a pack of cinnamon-flavored gum off of the shelf in the checkout line.

"You forgot something, Mr. Stone," I said and casually dropped the pack into his shopping cart. My boldness surprised me. He stared at me in confusion for a minute, looking like he wanted to say something, but stopped himself.

I didn't give him the opportunity to respond. Instead, I threw a coy smile at him and sashayed away, not really sure what to think about my own abrupt and uncharacteristic spontaneity.

Alexander

SHE LEFT ME FEELING RELATIVELY STUNNED. CATCHING ME UNAWARES was not an easy feat, yet I had been almost knocked flat by a woman who appeared to be so completely harmless.

You surprised me, Krystina Cole. Maybe you're not as innocent as I had initially thought.

I glanced down into the shopping basket at the cinnamon-flavored gum, my curiosity piqued. She had initially seemed nervous but appeared to relax after a bit, revealing a certain degree of audaciousness by ending on a flirtier note. However, any further insight as to what might have been going on in her mind ended there. As hard as I tried, I couldn't read her. And it was goddamned irritating.

I proceeded through the checkout line, trying to decide what to do about the unreadable woman. Understanding the interworking of one's brain is what I did best. Pulling apart the many layers of an individual to get to the root of what drove them was a skill. Many took years to master the art, but I had a natural knack for it.

Until I met Krystina Cole.

Even a master's degree in psych wasn't going to help me to figure her out easily. She would be a challenge. She was like a puzzle I had to solve, the compelling reason behind the return trip to Wally's. Unfortunately, I'd failed at unraveling any clues and only exacerbated the mystery.

She said Jim was not her boyfriend, but she didn't exactly say she was single either. So, is she?

The lock of hair that falls over her brow. Did she style it like that, or is it mere happenstance?

The way she twists her hands. Is it a nervous tic, or does she simply have cold hands she's trying to warm?

And that delicate blush of hers...

I couldn't help but picture that blush spreading to every part of her. An image of her wide, unknowing stare came to mind again, and I shook my head to clear it.

Just forget her. She's too young anyway.

"Your total is thirty-seven dollars and four cents. Will that be cash or credit, sir?" asked the skinny blond working the register.

I focused my attention on the cashier. Her nametag read CASSIE in bold print.

Mid-twenties, been around the block, on the prowl for Mr. Right.

One look at her, and it was easy to assess she was the latch-on kind of girl. She was trying to look sexy and coy, peering at me through eyelashes that had too much mascara on them. I ignored her. She was cute, but she wasn't my type.

If only Krystina could be as transparent as this one.

I pulled out my credit card and absently handed it over to the coquettish Cassie, careful not to give her any encouragement.

Once my transaction was complete, I collected my purchases and left the grocery store. When I stepped outside, I blinked from the bright sunlight and reached into my suit jacket pocket for a pair of sunglasses. After my vision adjusted, I saw Hale waiting for me, double-parked at the end of the block. I headed in that direction.

Hale moved to get out of the car when he saw me, but I waved him off.

"I've got it," I called out to him. I deposited the groceries into the trunk, then climbed into the backseat. "One of these days, you're going to get a parking ticket."

"Don't worry. I have a few connections," he told me easily. "Where to now, boss?"

"Back to the office. I have more work to do on the Canterwell deal. Just drop me there, then run this food back to the house. Oh, and I need you to get with Stephen and gather some information."

"Yes, sir. I'll call Stephen now and have him get started on it. Is Canterwell looking to unload another property?"

"No, this isn't about Canterwell. It's about a person. I want all the information you can find on Krystina Cole."

4

Krystina

I stepped into the elevator of my apartment building, punched the number for my floor, and watched the doors slowly close. I leaned against the back wall and closed my eyes. It had been hours since my conversation with Alexander Stone, yet my head was still reeling from our encounter. I didn't know what had come over me. I really needed to talk to Allyson.

I was just about to insert my key into my apartment door when I heard my cellphone ring. I reached into my purse for my phone and gingerly answered the call, being extra careful not to slice my finger open on the cracked screen.

"Hello?"

"Hello, may I speak with Miss Krystina Cole, please?" asked a pleasant female voice.

"This is Miss Cole."

"Miss Cole, this is Laura Kaufman calling from Turning Stone Advertising. We received your résumé, and we're interested in setting up an interview with you for a position in our marketing department."

That's strange.

I had never heard of Turning Stone Advertising. I wondered how they got a hold of my résumé. Either way, beggars can't be choosers, as job interviews had been few and far between.

"I would like that very much. When would you like to meet?" I asked her, stepping into my apartment and quietly closing the door behind me.

"Does tomorrow morning at nine o'clock work for you?" Laura politely asked. I mentally ran through my schedule at Wally's. I was scheduled off for the next two days.

"That's perfect. Can you please tell me where you're located?" I figured that was an important place to start, considering I knew nothing at all about the company. I quickly went to the kitchen and pulled a pad of paper and a pen from one of the drawers.

Laura rattled off an address in the financial district then said, "Just go to the security desk in the lobby and ask for me. The guard will tell you where to go from there."

"Great! Thank you, and I'll see you in the morning."

I thought about the upcoming interview as I finished scribbling down the address Laura had given me.

Finally—an interview!

I put the pen down and did a little happy dance around the kitchen. This could be my opportunity to move on, a chance to step up to bigger and better things. The timing of this couldn't be more perfect, as I had recently begun to feel discouraged over the lack of employment opportunities available in New York.

I wondered about the size of the firm and the starting pay. Anything was bound to be better paying than Wally's. If I got the job and found out I didn't like it or the income wasn't what I had hoped, it was okay. All of it was inconsequential in the grand scheme of things. I would be working in my field and gaining experience to add to my résumé, something it was seriously lacking.

I knew I should probably get out my laptop and start researching Turning Stone Advertising. They had most likely gotten my résumé from one of those online job sites. But either way, it wouldn't look very good if I showed up to the interview unprepared. I glanced over at the clock in the kitchen and frowned when I saw the time. I needed to get ready for my dinner with Allyson. Interview prep would just have to wait.

I ARRIVED AT MURPHY'S IRISH PUB JUST A FEW MINUTES AFTER seven. I scanned the crowd for Allyson. The tavern was packed tonight. The jukebox blared "The Rocky Road to Dublin," and I tapped my foot in time to the music. I spotted William Murphy, the owner of the pub, tending the bar. He saw me come in and waved me over. I smiled and headed to him.

Peanut shells crunched under my feet as I navigated through the crush of people. William had once told me he never cleaned up the shells, or he would risk revealing a sticky beer-stained floor to his customers. Personally, I thought the tale was a big fat lie. He was so meticulous about his place, not a detail was forgotten. From the antique wooden barrels of Jameson to the vintage Michael Collins posters, I was sure the floors were mopped to a sparkling gleam at the end of every night.

"A pint of Guinness for the lady?" William asked when I reached him.

"Sorry, Will. Wine only for this girl—you know that," I chided.

"Aye, lassie!" he said with a feigned Irish brogue. "One day, I'll get you to come over to the dark side."

I grimaced and stuck my tongue out. I hated the taste of beer.

William let out a loud, boisterous laugh. "Okay, not today then. Since you won't go for a nice stout, what else can I get for you, my dear?"

"Actually, nothing at the moment. I'm meeting Allyson tonight for dinner."

"She's already here," he said as he pointed to the back of the pub. I looked over and saw her seated at a corner table.

"Thanks, Will. I'll catch you later."

I made my way over to where Allyson was sitting. She waved when she saw me approaching.

"I ordered you a glass of white already," she said after I sat down.

"That's my girl," I said with a wink.

Allyson gave me a smile in return, showing off her pearly whites. She was a natural beauty; so pretty she turned the heads of men everywhere we went. She had sparkling emerald green eyes that lit up whenever she laughed. She wore her blond hair long, never trimming more than an inch off at a time. Her hair was effortlessly straight, and I was often envious of her shower-and-go abilities.

"So, did you find your phone charger?" I asked her.

"How did you know I lost my charger?" she questioned back, narrowing her eyes and sounding slightly defensive.

"You left me a note. You only do that when your charger is missing, and your phone is dead," I teased.

"I just forgot it was in my gym bag," she mumbled with a scowl. I busted out laughing.

"You've already used that excuse, Ally," I goaded, my eyes threatening to spill tears of laughter. The truth was, Allyson lost just about everything, and I loved to pick on her about it.

"It's not funny, Krys! You try going almost twenty-four hours without a phone. It sucks!" she exclaimed earnestly, but I could see she was fighting back a smile.

The waitress came over to take our food order, breaking up our playful banter. As appealing as the chicken finger basket sounded, I stuck with the grilled chicken salad. Allyson, not one to have to worry about counting calories, ordered a burger and fries. I didn't know how she could eat that stuff and not add a single ounce to her petite frame. I'd be on the treadmill for a week if I ordered that.

"So, tell me—what's your good news?" I curiously asked after we placed our orders. I loved hearing about Allyson's latest and greatest.

"Well," she drawled out. "I landed the photography job with Ethan DeJames."

"That's great, Ally! I'm so happy for you!" I reached over and gave her a one-armed hug. Ethan DeJames was one of the fastest-growing fashion designers in New York, with brand new offices in Paris and Milan. This was great news, as well as a big step in the right direction for my friend.

"It's great to know I'll have a good steady income coming in now. I loved freelancing, but it was too tough waiting for the next job to come in." She held up her glass to me. "Drinks on me tonight, babe!" We clinked our glasses, and I took a sip of wine. There was an impish glint in her eyes that led me to believe there was more to her news than just a job.

"So what else do you have to tell me?"

She threw me a sly smile, and her eyes sparkled with mischief. Her look confirmed my suspicions—there was more.

"Guess."

"You have a new guy?" I predicted. Her grin widened. "Ha! I knew it! So, who is he? Tall, dark, and handsome like the last one?"

Her grin instantly faded into a scowl.

"Sorry—I didn't mean to bring up ancient news," I apologized with a wince. Allyson's last boyfriend was a wannabe model and a total jerk that was always putting her down. I swear it was because he was jealous of her apparent good looks. I don't think he could stand she was prettier than he was, or she should have been the one in front of the camera—not him. The relationship had been short-lived, and I was glad when they split up.

"It's okay. Mark was a loser anyways. Now, Jeremy, on the other hand..." She took on a faraway, dreamy look, and I started laughing.

"So, tell me about him. Hopefully, he's better in the sack than Mark was," I joked. That was another reason why Alyson didn't keep the last one around very long.

"I don't know. Yet," she added, the familiar gleam back in her eyes. "Jeremy is a photographer, like me. I was at Ethan DeJames' completing my new hire paperwork when I met him. It was his first day too. He told me he normally shot landscape, but when Ethan's recruited him to shoot their models, he decided to ..."

Allyson began talking rapidly, telling me every little detail of their first meeting.

But after a few minutes, her words began to fade in and out. I tried to listen, but I couldn't seem to stay focused on what she was saying. I couldn't stop thinking about Alexander Stone. The way he consumed my every thought was extremely annoying.

It's not like I want to go out with him or anything. Just because he looks like a Greek God with his dark waves and flashing blue eyes doesn't mean I wanted to sleep with him. Guys who look like him are nothing but trouble.

"Um, hello? Are you even listening to what I'm saying?" Allyson asked, interrupting my thoughts by waving a hand in front of my face.

"I'm sorry, Ally. I was listening...sort of. I'm just a little distracted today," I explained, feeling bad about my rudeness.

"What's wrong?" Lines of concern marred her pretty face.

"Nothing major, really." And that was the truth—nothing was seriously wrong.

I'm just a total head case over a man I barely know.

The waitress came back to the table with our food, and I was grateful for the interruption. I needed to figure out how to explain this without sounding like a complete nut job. As soon as the waitress walked away, Allyson pounced.

"Spill it," she demanded.

"I have a job interview tomorrow. I got the call just before I left to meet you." I paused and took a few bites of my salad. "Oh, and I think I met the hottest guy on the planet yesterday," I blurted out.

Shock briefly flashed across her face at my announcement, but she recovered quickly.

"I didn't see that one coming! Do tell!" she said, rubbing her hands together and wiggling her eyebrows. Allyson was always so animated when she spoke, and her vivacity made me smile.

"It's nothing like you're probably thinking, Ally. I only saw him twice, and it was fairly brief both times."

"Well, what does he look like?" she pressed.

"He's tall. Well-built, from what I can tell. Dark hair and blue eyes—really intense blue eyes. Definitely sexy, and I think he knows it too. He has sort of an arrogant gait when he walks." I felt my stomach do a little flip as I thought back to the sight of Alexander walking to the checkout line at Wally's.

"What's his name?"

"Alexander Stone," I said and waited to see if she recognized the name. Apparently, she didn't because she just threw another question at me, eagerly looking for more information.

"How did you meet him?"

I went on to describe my first encounter, and I didn't leave out any details—my fall, his arm around my waist, his promise to see me soon. She didn't laugh like I thought she would. Instead, she stared at me with wide eyes and signaled our waitress for another round of drinks.

"I can't believe you fell," she said incredulously, her eyes wide in shock.

"Yeah, I did. It was absolutely mortifying too!" I dropped my head into my hands and moaned.

"You said you saw him twice. *Please* tell me you didn't embarrass yourself a second time." I picked my head back up to look at her and started laughing at her expression. She looked thoroughly appalled at the thought of me humiliating myself again.

"No, I wasn't a total klutz the second time. But I wasn't exactly smooth either." I told her about what happened in aisle nine and made sure to include the tantalizing way Alexander had chewed a piece of gum.

"I love it!" she exclaimed, dissolving into a fit of laughter when I told her how I had tossed a pack of Big Red into his cart.

"Yeah, well...I wanted to throw him off his game, and I couldn't think of anything better to do. I'm not too sure my brilliant idea worked, though," I said with a frown. I thought back to his stunned look and felt slightly stupid over what I had done. "When I think about it, I can't even begin to figure out why I found his gum-chewing such a turn-on. I mean, it's gum. Gross, right? But it wasn't. It was all kinds of crazy sexy."

"He wants you," she concluded, popping a french-fry into her mouth.

"Are you out of your mind? I made a complete fool of myself!"

"I don't think so, Krys," she replied knowingly. "I mean, really—the guy came back to see you the very next day. He was concerned about how you were doing, asks you a bunch of personal questions, makes a crapload of sexual innuendos, and has a philosophical discussion on the fundamentals of control. If that doesn't scream 'I wanna screw,' then I don't know what does. Hell, the fact you are even talking about him tells me you want him, too."

"You're wrong, Ally," I said and felt my face redden. Her ability to read me was scary.

"Oh my God! You're blushing. You really do like him, don't you?" she said, obviously stunned. It was time to rein her in before this conversation got out of hand.

"You are making way too much out of this. First of all, he didn't make sexual innuendos. Well, maybe one," I conceded. "I think the rest was mostly made up in my head. And secondly, his questions weren't personal. They were completely platonic and work-related. Sure, maybe I wanted to strip him down right there in the middle of Wally's, but it wasn't like that for him. I'm certain his only concern was a potential lawsuit."

She frowned at me.

"You don't give yourself enough credit. You're beautiful, Krys. I don't know why you can't see that. Is it so hard to believe that maybe, just maybe, he was interested in more than just the bump on your head?"

"I think the guy has the potential to be a total control freak, Ally. Been there, done that—remember? I won't make that mistake again."

I remained quiet then and looked down at my plate. I was sure Allyson knew where my thoughts were heading, but she didn't say anything. Instead, we ate our food in quiet, and I silently prayed she wouldn't bring up the forbidden subject of my past, the painful topic I avoided at all costs. I didn't want to go *there*.

After several minutes had passed, she finally spoke.

"I know you don't want to talk about this," she began softly. "You have scars I can't even begin to comprehend. But—"

"You're right. I don't want to talk about it," I stated flatly.

"Honey, every guy isn't like Trevor."

"Don't you think I know that? I just haven't found the right guy yet," I snapped irritably. I didn't add I hadn't really been looking for Mr. Right either. Two years past and more shrinks than I can count, and my wounds were still raw. A part of me worried I'd never be whole again. "Maybe I *should* just become a lesbian."

"What?" Allyson frowned, obviously thrown.

"Nothing—just something Jim said earlier at work," I muttered. Allyson looked at me quizzically but dismissed my comment with a shake of her head.

"Look, Krys. Acknowledging the fact Stone even exists should be a sign for you. It's a sign you're ready to move on. It's time to get out there again. You haven't dated anyone since you and Trevor broke up," she reminded me.

"I've gone on dates!"

A few.

Allyson leaned back in her chair, folded her arms, and smirked.

"Name one guy that you've gone on more than two dates with since you and Trevor broke up."

There were none. I knew she was right, but I still couldn't help jumping on the defense. It certainly wasn't my fault every guy I met wanted to get jiggy with it after only five minutes of conversation.

"Alexander Stone is probably one of the wealthiest men in New York. He's way out of my league. He can choose any woman he wants—why in the world would he want me?"

"Don't be ridiculous. The fact that he's loaded means nothing. Right now, you have two years of celibacy talking for you."

"I haven't been celibate for two years! You forget about Bryce, the music guy. Remember him?"

"You can't possibly be serious!" she said in exasperation.

I frowned at her, knowing she was right again. I couldn't count the musician I went out with only once. Bryce was a futile attempt at fixing my shattered heart. He was my rebound after Trevor, the drunken one-night stand who never called me again. I wasn't even entirely sure if Bryce was his real name, and I regretted that night still to this day.

"I don't want to talk about Trevor or Bryce, Ally. And your outrageous imagination about Stone will just end up planting too many crazy ideas in my head. Trust me when I say I don't need your help with that."

I thought about the little devil that had been making quite a regular appearance on my shoulder as of late, putting all sorts of enticing images in my head.

Angels and devils? You're really cracking up, Cole.

"Yeah, right. You need to have more crazy ideas as far as I'm concerned," she quipped.

"Don't start with me. I'm perfectly fine being alone. I don't need a relationship or sex to be happy. Besides, I'll probably never see Alexander Stone again anyways. And even if I do, he prefers tall and curvy redheads."

In an attempt to change the subject, I told her about my internet findings on the wealthy Alexander Stone and his history with gingers.

"So, what? If anyone can persuade him to change his mind about redheads, it would be you."

"No, Ally," I said, a warning tone evident in my voice.

"I can just see the headlines now, 'Ridiculously Rich Alexander Stone Chooses Chestnut Brown Over Dull Red Head.' It could happen," she stated matter-of-factly with a devilish smile.

"Ugh—you're relentless!"

Through the loud noise of the pub, I heard the familiar clanking of metal on metal. I looked over my shoulder and saw William standing next to the bar tapping two spoons against his knee in time with the music, a favorite pastime for the regulars at Murphy's. A distraction was definitely needed if I wanted Allyson to drop the subject.

"Come on—Will is playing the spoons." I stood up, threw my napkin on the table, and grabbed her hand.

The subject was bound to come up again, but I was finished with it for now. The past was the past. Rehashing it never ended in a positive outcome. Tonight, I just wanted to have fun.

5

Krystina

I awoke to the sound of an alarm going off, shrill and piercing in my ears. I groaned as I reached over to shut it off, wishing I could hit the snooze button again. I had stayed out entirely too late, and I regretted giving in to Allyson's 'just one more drink' plead.

I was exhausted.

When I had gone to bed the night before, I was sure sleep would come quickly, the effects of dancing and a little too much alcohol helping me along. Unfortunately, I had no such luck. Instead, I had tossed and turned most of the night, the sandman evading me for hours until I eventually drifted off sometime after three in the morning.

I forced myself to roll out of bed and get ready for the interview. Groggy and fuzzy with exhaustion, I shuffled into the bathroom and started the shower – full force and blistering hot.

I chanced a look in the mirror and saw my eyes showed little signs of rest. The dark smudges under them would be difficult to disguise with makeup, on top of trying to cover the yellowing remnants of my bruise.

I climbed into the scalding shower and leaned my head against the tiled wall. I allowed the steam to envelop me and thought about the whirlwind of emotions that had consumed me during the night.

My history with Trevor had come back to the forefront of my mind, and I cursed Allyson for bringing him up. I had tried to force the depressing memories of Trevor from my head, only to find my thoughts slowly evolve into visions of Alexander Stone and the feelings he stirred deep inside me—feelings I didn't want to feel and had kept buried for so long. For the first time in years, I was physically attracted to a man. It pained me to admit it, even to myself.

I got out of the shower and towel-dried my hair. I knew I had to stop thinking about all this nonsense, especially since the probability of seeing Alexander again was slim to none.

I'm acting ridiculous. It's time to screw my head back on and focus my energies on the interview.

Moving to my bedroom, I turned on the stereo. Music was my personal therapy. I couldn't play an instrument, and I could barely carry a tune—but I could *feel* music. The right melody had the power to change my mood in an instant, and that's exactly what I needed right now to help rein in the desolate memories and unwelcomed thoughts.

I perused my iPod for the right thing and finally settled on "Stompa." The catchy toe-tapping tune was the perfect solution to get my body moving. I pressed play, closed my eyes, and allowed the singer's deep melodious voice to wash over me. As the song's beat began to pick up, a gradual smile formed on my lips, and my head started bopping in time to the ascending bass line. Already feeling an upshift in mood, I made my way to the closet and looked for something to wear.

When I finished dressing, I spun slowly in the full-length mirror, taking in all of my five feet six inches. I had chosen a simple knee-length navy blue skirt and a matching suit jacket over a cream-colored blouse. Low pumps on my feet and pearl teardrop earrings for my ears completed the classic look. I had styled my hair up in a loose twist, praying it would stay put until my interview was over. My makeup was subtle, with just a hint of coal on my eyes and a touch of pink gloss. I thought my overall appearance looked smart without seeming presumptuous.

I checked the time on my nightstand clock.

Crap!

I took too long to get ready, and I couldn't be late. I needed to land this job. As it was, I slept in later than I had intended and didn't leave myself any time to research Turning Stone Advertising. I was going into the interview blind.

I turned off the stereo, sent a silent thanks to Serena Ryder for fixing my mental state, and dashed out the door.

When I had reached the main lobby of my building, Philip, the doorman, greeted me.

"Good morning, Miss Cole," he said, his jolly face crinkling with a smile.

"Morning, Phil," I answered distractedly. "I need a cab today. Could you call for one, please? I'm short on time, or else I'd enjoy the good weather and go on foot."

Normally I would have talked with the retired cop for a minute or two, but I wasn't feeling very chatty at that moment. Anxiety over the interview was starting to set in, and I was eager to just get it over with.

"I shouldn't have to call for the cab. There have been quite a few on the street today, and waving one down shouldn't be a problem. Come with me."

I followed Philip outside through the lobby doors, blinking at the sudden wash of sun, and waited for him to hail me a cab. My foot tapped impatiently on the curb. It had been over a month since my last interview, and I was a bundle of nerves.

"Big day, Miss?" Philip asked, looking down at my foot that was attempting to beat a hole into the sidewalk.

"Yes, a job interview," I answered with a worried smile. The cab pulled up, and Philip opened the door for me. "Wish me luck!"

He nodded and gave me a small salute as he closed the yellow car door behind me. I gave the address to the driver, and the taxi sped away.

TRAFFIC WAS TERRIBLE UPON ENTERING THE FINANCIAL DISTRICT, BUT we still made good time. For once, I was thankful for the fearless and reckless driving of a New York City cabbie, despite the fact my knuckles were white from hanging on to the seat so tightly.

When the cab reached our destination, it screeched to a halt. I paid the driver and stepped out onto the pavement. I looked up apprehensively at the impressive structure towering before me. There was a large sign above the main entrance that read Cornerstone Tower in silver lettering. A sleek ornamental spire soared high above the building, piercing a stray passing cloud.

The sheer size of the place was intimidating, and I found my steps toward the revolving glass doors to be somewhat hesitant. I tilted my head from side to side, stretching my neck like a boxer headed into the ring.

I need to relax. I've got this.

However, as much as I tried to talk myself down, I was still a nervous wreck when I walked through the main doors. I knew my career opportunities in New York were starting to run out. If I wanted to stay in the city, it was vital for me to ace this interview.

The vestibule was large, and it took me a moment to locate the security desk. A man wearing an official-looking uniform sat behind a polished mahogany wood counter. He was looking at the security monitors and didn't notice my arrival.

I cleared my throat and said, "Excuse me, sir. My name is Krystina Cole. I have an appointment with Laura Kaufman today at nine o'clock."

The security guard glanced up at me before looking down at a logbook on the desk. He ran his finger over the page until he located my name.

"Yes, Miss Cole. Just take the elevator to the fiftieth floor. Ms.

Kaufman is expecting you," he said with a kind smile. He pointed down a corridor to his left. "The elevators are just down that hall."

"Thank you."

I made my way across the blue-veined marble floors to the bank of elevators. When I reached them, I typed the floor number into the keypad.

Here goes nothing.

The doors slid open, and I stepped inside. My ears popped as the elevator climbed higher and higher. When the lift finally reached its destination, a lavish waiting area came into view.

The room was furnished with several slate gray leather sofas. They were contemporary in style and positioned in a U shape off to my right. A low glass table sat in the middle of the sofas, displaying some sort of small stone sculpture. Eclectic artwork in varying shades of grays and blues adorned the stark white walls.

When I looked to my left, an attractive woman in a killer designer suit stood up from behind a desk. Her suit was vibrant emerald green, and it hugged every one of her flawless curves. Her makeup was impeccable, and not a single strand of her angled bob was out of place. She looked professional yet exceedingly sexy at the same time. When she walked around the desk to where I was standing, matching six-inch green stilettos came into view.

I would kill myself if I ever tried to walk in shoes like that.

I was suddenly very self-conscious of my modest navy-blue jacket and skirt.

"You must be Krystina Cole. I'm Laura Kaufman." She smiled and extended a perfectly manicured hand to me.

"It's nice to meet you, Ms. Kaufman," I replied as I shook her hand. She appeared to be in her early thirties, younger than I had anticipated based on our brief phone conversation. Her voice was so gentle and sweet, and I had pictured her to be the grandmotherly type. I couldn't have been more wrong.

"Please, call me Laura. Just one moment, please." She walked back behind her desk and pressed a button on the desktop phone. "Excuse me, sir. Miss Cole has arrived for her interview. Shall I bring her to your office? Or would you prefer the conference room?"

"Come to the conference room, Laura. I'm just finishing up with something," said a male voice from the speaker.

Laura turned back to me, "If you follow me this way, I'll bring you to Mr. Stone now."

Mr. Stone?

My eyes widened in surprise upon hearing the name.

No way. It can't be the same guy. Mr. Blue Eyes. Mr. Keep-me-up-all-night-dreaming-of-sapphire. Impossible.

Then the light bulb went on, a blinding glare that almost knocked me flat on my ass, as I remembered all of the things I knew about Alexander Stone.

Stone Enterprise. Stoneworks Foundation.

My stomach dropped as panic began to set in. The building I stood in was called Cornerstone Tower. And I was about to interview for a position at Turning Stone Advertising.

It has to be the same Mr. Stone. How can I be so ridiculously obtuse?

I cursed quietly under my breath, knowing the intelligent thing to do would be to leave immediately.

If I can't figure out what one plus one is, I'm obviously unfit for the job.

"Forgive me, Ms. Kaufman, but I assumed I would be interviewing with you," I said with a wobbly smile, scrambling to think of a way out of the situation.

"I'm sorry?" She looked confused by my statement.

"I, um..." I stuttered as I tried to think of something—*anything* that might prevent me from coming face to face with Alexander Stone again. "I didn't realize I'd be interviewing with Mr. Stone. I assumed since you were a large company, you would have an HR department to handle your hiring," I explained, not able to come up with anything better. I could only hope this actually *was* a large company.

Realization dawned on Laura's face.

"Mr. Stone must be considering you for an important position, or else that would normally be the case. Our human resources department usually handles the initial applicant screening. However, Mr. Stone personally conducts all of the interviews for high potential candidates," she clarified with a smile.

High potential?

My palms began to sweat as I silently followed the strawberry blond Laura to the conference room. Her subtle red hair was a reminder of all the articles I had read online about Alexander Stone's preference for redheads.

But surely that can't be a prerequisite for working for him? Or can it?

My stomach constricted into a nervous knot. Everything about the situation was terribly wrong. Not only was I a fool for not connecting the dots, but I also had the wrong hair color for the job.

Someone like Alexander Stone would want to hire someone competent and witty—not someone whose tongue got stuck to the roof of her mouth every time he was near. This was a disaster in the making. He was too *distracting*, nothing but sex and sin and every girl's spiciest fantasy. I couldn't imagine the thought of going through an entire job interview with him.

I felt like I was walking through a tunnel, my nerves gradually taking over every rational part of me. Apprehension caused my steps to lag slowly behind Laura as she walked to the door at the end of the corridor.

I toyed with the idea of bolting right then and there, but my window of time for a quick exit had ended. We had reached the conference room. I took a deep breath and made a conscious effort to still my fidgeting hands.

Keep it together—it's a job interview. I'm overreacting.

Feeling only slightly more composed, I stepped through the door Laura held open for me.

Maybe it's not even the same Mr. Stone.

But it was.

6

Krystina

Alexander Stone stood facing away from me at the far end of the room. Even though I couldn't see his face, there was no mistaking his powerfully built physique. He was on the phone, with one hand in his pocket, looking out through floor-to-ceiling windows at the Manhattan Skyline.

He turned to see Laura and me standing there and motioned to me to sit down. I looked at Laura for direction. She smiled and pointed to a chair near the end of a large etched glass conference table. I sat down, taking a minute to calm my nerves further, and took stock of my surroundings.

The furniture was sleek and modern. The table at which I sat was large enough to seat at least thirty people. The center of the table displayed a long, boat-shaped glass bowl filled with blue, white, and black stones. There were several high-tech-looking videoconference phones on the table as well.

The walls were all painted the same bright white as the waiting area. Two enormous flat-screen television panels adorned the wall to my right, one of them tuned in to Bloomberg TV with the volume muted. On my left, recessed shelves held a collection of blue vases, all varying in shade, size, and shape. The far wall was nothing but glass, revealing an impressive view of New York. The room undoubtedly exhibited power and wealth, but it was nothing compared to the man who stood in it.

I studied Alexander Stone as he paced the back of the conference room. He wore black suit pants and a white shirt. He wore no jacket again today, but I saw he had one draped over the back of one of the conference room chairs. His silver tie was loosened at the neck, and his top button was undone. He looked comfortable and self-assured, carrying himself with an air of sophistication and poise. He appeared larger than life, as if he were holding the world in the palm of his hand.

"Would you like something to drink? Coffee, tea, water? Mr. Stone is just finishing up his call," Laura offered, her voice low so as not to disrupt her boss. I looked up at her mannerly smile. I had almost forgotten she was there.

"Yes, please. Water would be great," I accepted, mirroring her hushed tone. Holding a glass of water would give me something to do with my hands, which fidgeted once again in my lap. Any sort of caffeine would just wreak havoc on my already tremulous nerves.

As Laura placed the glass of water on a coaster in front of me, Alexander ended his call and turned around to face us.

"Thank you, Laura. That will be all for now."

"Yes, Mr. Stone."

Laura quietly exited the room with a slight nod, leaving me alone with the formidable Alexander Stone.

He turned his attention to me and flashed a dazzling smile, revealing perfect white teeth.

God, this man is undeniably gorgeous.

"Good morning, Miss Cole. I apologize for the wait. I hadn't anticipated my call to run so long."

That's okay—I was enjoying the view of your scrumptious behind.

"It was no trouble at all," I murmured, rather than voice my actual thoughts.

He made his way toward me, his swagger ever so prominent,

and sat in a chair next to mine. He leaned back, crossed an ankle over one knee, and casually folded his hands together. For some insane reason, I felt myself blushing. I had to remind myself to breathe.

"Miss Cole, are you okay? You look flushed."

My hands immediately went to my face as I scrambled to find my voice.

"I'm fine. It's the high elevation. Sometimes it makes me lightheaded," I lied as I reached for my glass of water. I swallowed a huge gulp.

"High elevation?" he questioned skeptically.

I took another drink of water.

"Yes, this happens to me whenever I'm in tall buildings," I said, continuing the fib in a rush.

Tall building is an understatement. Stone owns a skyscraper.

"I see," was his only response.

If I wasn't mistaken, I thought he looked amused.

He probably is. Women must fall all over him every day.

However, I didn't have the luxury to be amongst those women. I had to put the brakes on and get my wits about me. This was a professional interview for a *real* job. I could not allow myself to blow this because my stalled-out libido decided to kick into overdrive suddenly.

"Did you know I was the one you were interviewing? Because I don't believe in coincidences," I blurted out.

Smooth, real smooth.

"Of course," he answered without prevarication.

"I figured as much. But I have to ask, how did you get my résumé?" I asked with honest curiosity, finding myself relaxing a bit.

I can do this.

"It was only a matter of making the correct inquiries, Miss Cole. I was intrigued after our meeting at Wally's and wanted to find out more about you. I asked a few simple questions, and I learned you were a marketing major. An informal background inquiry filled in the blanks. Since I happen to have a position available in marketing, I arranged an interview with you."

"You ordered a background check on me?" I asked, instinctively feeling violated.

Didn't he need to obtain my consent for that?

I wasn't sure what to think about the infringement of privacy.

"It was nothing that technical, I assure you. Everyone I consider for employment receives a basic check before an interview is even scheduled. It makes things easier."

"Easier in what way?" I asked.

"Easier for all parties involved. You'd be amazed at what social media can reveal about a person," he replied nonchalantly, a smile forming ever so subtly on his lips. We sat there in a silence that seemed to stretch on for hours, yet I knew it was only a few seconds, a minute at most. I'm sure he sensed my unease, but he continued to watch me with one eyebrow tilted up, his eyes alight with humor, before finally speaking again. "Tell me what you're thinking."

"That I'm amusing you somehow," I admitted frankly.

"Nothing is amusing at all, Miss Cole," he said, the corners of his mouth twitching. I knew he was fighting a smile, and it was irritating.

What the hell was so damn comical?

"Really? Then why does it seem like you're trying not to laugh?" I retorted, a little bit too harshly.

"Your behavior tells me you didn't know *I* would be conducting your interview today. Is my assumption correct?" he asked, humor still evident in his features.

I'm such an idiot! I should have prepared for this!

"Um…sort of. Yes."

My statement earned a small chuckle from him, and it was maddening. I couldn't help but jump on the defense.

"Do you always laugh at your prospective employees?" I challenged.

"I'm not laughing at you. I'm laughing more at the quandary I find myself in. I've never met a woman quite like you. I find your innocence refreshing. Most women I meet are very calculating and extremely predictable. You're different somehow." He paused for a moment, his brow furrowing. "It's a nuisance, actually."

His arrogance astounded me, and I found his generalization of women insulting.

"I'm sorry I don't fit into a preselected mold, Mr. Stone. Would you rather I played into your defined notion that all women are the same?" I asked him, my voice loaded with contempt.

"You're asking an awful lot of questions, Miss Cole."

He had stopped smiling now, and his eyes turned icy.

Oh, shit. He's right.

The entire situation was beginning to spiral out of control. I was asking too many questions I had no right to ask. I was probably fired before I was even offered a position, and it was one I gravely needed.

My kneejerk reaction was to lash out. But I was too outspoken for my own good, and it could cost me this job. Temper aside, I knew I was being a hypocrite. After all, I was the one who thought all *men* were the same. So, I silenced my tongue, feeling ashamed at my boldness, and looked down at my hands.

He is Alexander Stone, a mega-rich millionaire, and I'm being rude.

"Can we proceed with your interview now?"

"Yes," I answered meekly.

"Yes, *Mr. Stone*," he added with an air of quiet authority.

My head snapped up.

Yes, Mr. Stone?

He hadn't yelled. Yet, there was no need to. His subtle command was enough to detonate through my system, causing a knot to form in my gut. He was a man well accustomed to getting what he wanted.

Warning bells went off as I recalled my conversation with Alexander from the day prior. My initial impression of him was correct—he really was a control freak. Every instinct I possessed was telling me to leave the room immediately, and this was bad. Really bad. Yet, for some totally insane reason, I found myself mildly aroused by his assumed authority and the power emanating from him. It compelled me to stay rooted to the chair.

"Yes, Mr. Stone," I repeated like a parrot.

I was like an errant child who'd just been scolded, my voice small and pathetic to my ears. I couldn't believe I was actually listening to him.

The mood swings I had experienced since entering this room were making my head spin. Anxiety, anger, embarrassment, and lust—I had felt them all, and I struggled to find stability within the hurricane.

I saw him looking down at my fidgeting hands. I stilled them immediately and took hold of my glass of water.

I need to remember why I'm here—I need this job.

"That's better," he murmured. He sounded satisfied, his face revealing a tiny smile. I couldn't be sure whether it was because I stopped fidgeting or because I followed his order. The one thing I did know was that the balance in the room had rapidly shifted. I remained quiet and waited for his lead.

"There is a position at Turning Stone Advertising that needs filling. While the company is merely a subsidiary of Stone Enterprise, I occasionally get involved in their day-to-day business requirements." He got up from his chair and walked to the window. With confident grace, he clasped his hands behind his back and continued, "I am always on the lookout for qualified and experienced applicants. In my world, incompetence is not something that can be tolerated. I like my people to be driven, reliable, and efficient. When I give a direction, I expect it to be followed to the letter, without question. When I find an individual who fits this persona, I hire them and pay them well, so they continue their employment with me. You, Miss Cole, have displayed that potential."

"I appreciate that you see the potential in me, Mr. Stone," I responded respectfully, making sure to say his name correctly.

"Exactly how much remains to be seen," he said thoughtfully, almost as if he were speaking to himself.

He turned to study me for a moment, and his careful scrutiny was intimidating. He reminded me of a lion stalking his prey. If I gave him the opportunity, I knew this man was capable of stripping my soul bare. No man has ever affected me in this way. He was irritating, arrogant, and alluring all at once. My stomach began doing that annoying flippy thing, and I shifted uncomfortably under his penetrating gaze.

"Tell me about your job duties at Wally's."

"Well, um, sir—Mr. Stone," I stumbled over my words, trying to remember whatever the hell it was I did at my current job. "I mainly stock shelves and build displays. Occasionally, Mr. Roberts will have me bring groceries as a courtesy to the homes of our elderly clientele."

"That's a very noble thing to do. It makes me feel good about my investment decision."

"So, you've decided to invest in Wally's?" I excitedly asked, momentarily forgetting I was supposed to maintain a professional demeanor. As much as I wanted out of my current place of employment, I enjoyed my time there. I didn't want to see Wally's close and was happy to learn the grocer might be saved.

"I am not going to invest in them per se. My business is in real estate, not retail food chains. I'm just going to buy their buildings, which will help relieve some of their overhead expenses. There are a few wrinkles that still need to be ironed out, but I'm confident an agreement will be reached sometime within the next month." He seemed annoyed at my interruption and didn't elaborate any further about the deal. Instead, he continued with his interview questioning. "You have a bachelor's degree from NYU in marketing. What made you choose that as your major?"

That question had me stumped. Nobody had ever asked me that, and I never seriously considered the reason why I had chosen marketing. I just liked it.

I mused over his question for a moment before coming to the conclusion my fascination was in sales. I thought the answer might sound lame, but I had nothing better, so I went with it.

"I understand and appreciate the power of persuasion.

Marketing, in a sense, is sales. If marketed correctly, you can sell anything. You just need to target the buyer accurately."

"The power of persuasion?" he seemed surprised at my answer and tapped his finger thoughtfully on his chin.

"Yes. I believe persuasion through advertising can be viewed as a form of art. For example, a television commercial may convince individuals to buy a product they don't need if marketed correctly. Images, music, presentation—it is all one big package, crafted and bundled up to influence the consumer."

"Very true," he said with an appreciative nod. "Now tell me, what persuades you, Miss Cole?"

He cast me an unsettling look, one that made me feel another little twist in my belly.

"Persuades me? I'm not sure I follow you."

"What influences you, or sways you, to do something you normally wouldn't?"

"Music," I stated simply, fighting to keep my faculties together. He cocked one sexy eyebrow at me, waiting for me to say more.

Focus on the question—not his eyebrow!

"Care to explain?" he pushed.

"Music can be a powerful source in marketing. For me, the right tune has the power to influence me one way or another in just about anything."

"That's a very interesting insight," he said with a catlike smile, making me think he had a secret only he was privy to. He leisurely walked back to the table to reclaim his seat next to me. "I'm curious. What sort of music would influence you?"

"Um…" I squirmed uncomfortably in my chair. "Well, I guess it would depend on what you were trying to sell me."

"Ah, but maybe the bigger question would be—are you looking to buy?" he asked suggestively.

Heat flooded my face for what seemed like the five hundredth time in the past three days. I hated that I blushed so easily, and I automatically brought my hands to my face to hide my cheeks. A strange and unfamiliar ache began between my legs, only adding to my mortification.

"High elevation getting to you again?"

"Something like that," I mumbled, and I would swear my face turned ten shades redder.

Turned on by interview questions. Great. I'm out of my tree.

"Tell me about your experience," he said suddenly, changing directions.

"My experience with what exactly, Mr. Stone?"

His cryptic line of questioning was confusing. I couldn't keep up. Perhaps I really was going crazy. Either that or his mere presence was turning my brain to marshmallow. I couldn't be sure.

"Your experience in marketing and advertising, of course."

He watched me, eyes full of wicked humor, waiting for my response.

This has to be the strangest interview ever. He read my résumé. He knows the answer. Why would he ask me that?

"Everything is on my résumé, Mr. Stone. There's not much more I can elaborate on," I flatly responded.

It was probably the worst answer I ever gave in an interview, but I had a nagging suspicion he didn't give a rat's ass about my experience in marketing. The twisting in my belly intensified, the conversation making me uneasy. It was full of double meanings and suggestive implications.

"I see." He seemed frustrated I didn't give him a better answer.

The intercom buzzed, making me jump, and Laura's voice came through the speakerphone on the table.

"I apologize for the interruption Mr. Stone, but your ten o'clock appointment is here."

Ten o'clock appointment? Have I really been here for an hour?

"Thank you, Laura. I will be finished momentarily," Alexander responded through the speaker, sounding mildly annoyed.

My interview, if you could call it that, had clearly come to an end. I stood up and straightened my skirt. Alexander Stone stood as well, his intense gaze never wavering, as he watched my every move. I felt naked, despite my blouse and skirt, and my skin grew hot under his scrutiny. I tried to figure out what he was thinking, but his facial expression was unreadable, cool almost. Yet, I was able to detect a sense of uncertainty in his eyes. His stare made me self-conscious, and I immediately moved to smooth out my hair.

"Your hair is fine, Krystina."

Holy crap—he called me Krystina.

I wondered what made him drop the formalities.

"Uh, thanks," was the only response I could muster.

"It's a bit restricted for my taste, but fine all the same."

What's that supposed to mean?

I tried to fathom what he meant by that when he reached over to one of the phones and pressed the intercom button.

"Laura, please reschedule my ten o'clock."

Holy hell—he wants to keep me here?

I didn't know if I could handle another minute in his presence. I wasn't myself when I was near him. My careful guard, the walls I tightly clung to whenever I was near another man, seemed to crumble to the wayside with just one look from him. I could feel my heart begin to race as I watched him move at a slow pace toward me, a predatory gleam shining in his eyes.

He took a step closer and reached for my hands. I would swear my fluttering heart stilled at the contact.

"Why do you twist your hands the way you do?" he asked, his sapphire eyes blazing into mine.

Was I fidgeting again?

I hadn't even realized I was doing it.

"A nervous habit," I explained. Incapable of withstanding his fiery gaze, I turned my head to the left and focused on the blue vases along the wall.

"Look at me, Krystina." He reached one hand up to turn my chin, so I was forced to face him. Something dark smoldered in the depths of those ruthless cobalt blues, and I wondered if he was going to kiss me. My legs trembled, and I cursed myself for wearing pumps rather than flats. "I make you nervous," he said, his voice becoming deep and throaty.

I couldn't talk. I was a wreck.

When I didn't respond, Alexander removed his hand from my chin and slowly ran a thumb over my brow. My breathing suddenly became shallow, as the air seemed to turn thick and suffocating.

"Your bruise is healing nicely."

"Yes, it is," I agreed, my voice barely above a whisper. He was way too close to me, clouding my senses so I couldn't think straight. I tried to step back, but he still held my hand firmly in his.

He leaned in closer, and I could feel his breath hot on my neck. I allowed the smell of him to envelop me—a mix of sandalwood and his natural male scent. The combination was deadly, like the sexy smell in the air tempting you to stay outdoors right before a wicked thunderstorm. And at that moment, I was more than willing to be struck by a bolt of lightning.

"This will never work, Krystina. I'm a bad match for someone like you. If you were wise, you would leave my building and never look back," he warned, his voice low and thick in my ear, causing a prickle at my nape.

The thought of why he might not be good for me had my toes curling in my shoes. I didn't care how bad he was. I could be the judge of that later. I dismissed the pesky voice in my head that said all men were evil. The devil was out, and he was doing a tap dance on my shoulder. The sudden need to taste Alexander's lips on mine was overwhelming.

He moved his hands and softly traced the pads of his thumbs over my collarbone, causing a tremor to course through me. He placed his palms on each side of my neck. His fingers rested at the base of my skull, making a circular motion at my hairline.

I was coming apart at the seams.

I closed my eyes at the intimate contact and allowed a small moan to escape my lips. His mouth hovered temptingly over mine. I could only hold my breath in anticipation of the kiss I knew was about to come.

The intercom buzzed again, and Laura's voice came through the speaker, loud and intrusive.

"I'm very sorry, sir, but Ms. Andrews is insisting on keeping her appointment. She's on her way up from the lobby now."

Alexander let go of me suddenly, as if I had shocked him,

causing me to stagger back a few steps. My knees wobbled, and I had to work to steady myself. My head was reeling.

Damn you, Ms. Andrews!

I didn't know who in the hell Ms. Andrews was, but I despised her at that moment.

I looked at him, now standing a good ten feet away from me. He closed his eyes and ran both hands through his hair. He gave his head a slight shake as if he were attempting to clear it.

When he finally looked at me again, his expression was blank. There was nothing in his appearance that would have revealed what had happened in the last few minutes.

"I would like to finish your interview, Krystina," he finally said, albeit rather abruptly.

"When would you like to reschedule, Mr. Stone?" I asked, my words sounding faint in my ears. I could barely get the words out, my body still swimming with unexplainable desire.

"I don't know...." His voice trailed off, uncertainty briefly clouding his features. However, he regained his composure instantly, once again adorning a poker face that showed no emotion. "It's probably best for both of us if you leave now, Miss Cole."

Formal. Back to business.

His tone was firm and detached. It was as if a switch had flipped, and he appeared completely unaffected by our encounter.

I was more than just a little bit stunned. I felt rejected. Speechless. I could only stand there, a shaky mess, gaping at him.

What game is he playing at? Is he going to reschedule or not?

And does he want me, *or doesn't he?*

In a daze, I bent to retrieve my purse from the chair where I had been sitting. When I turned, Alexander was waiting for me by the door.

"Laura will be at the reception desk waiting to see you out. Have a good day."

And with that, he spun on his heel and exited the conference room.

Well, that's just fine and great, Dr. Jekyll and Mr. Hyde. If you want to play head games with me, then you've met your match.

I was the master at wearing masks.

I quickly put on an expression of disinterest and exited the room, displaying an air of confidence I didn't genuinely feel. I certainly didn't need the lovely Laura to walk me out. I would show myself out.

I rounded the corner that would take me into the waiting area and made my way toward the leather sofas, walking at a measured pace. So preoccupied with keeping up my façade, I almost collided straight into a woman coming toward me.

She was strikingly beautiful with long, shiny black hair. She wore a deep purple-colored high-neck cotton dress that covered her slender frame from head to toe. The only show of skin was from the slit running up the side of her leg. The dress wrapped her body so tightly that she might as well have worn nothing at all.

"Excuse me," she said impatiently as if she was in a hurry. I quickly moved aside to let her by and continued to the elevators.

I heard Laura call out to me, but I ignored her and kept on walking. I knew I was being petty, but I risked crumbling my control if I opened my mouth. The elevator doors were opened and waiting. I needed to get to them quickly before they closed.

I stepped into the elevator and hit the button for the lobby. I just wanted to go home to think. I needed to figure out *how* I let all of this happen.

Before the doors slid shut, I spotted Alexander stepping through the door of an office off the waiting room. The beautiful black-haired woman hurried toward him and embraced him in a hug. I sucked in my breath as if I'd been sucker-punched. There was no denying the affection that passed between them.

Alexander looked over the shoulder of the woman. His blue eyes locked on mine.

Why you son of a bitch...

That was all I could think as the elevator doors slowly slid shut.

7

Alexander

I paced back and forth in my office like a caged animal, trying to figure out what had come over me. Yes, I wanted Krystina Cole. I wanted her from the first moment I saw her. But that was no excuse. I wasn't some horny kid who couldn't keep his dick in his pants.

I raked my hands through my hair, disturbed by the fact I had lost my head. It had been so unlike me. I understood the value of finesse, the importance of patience and diligence to achieve the desired result. And I never failed. Yet, Krystina Cole's stamp was imprinted into my brain, causing me to carelessly push aside any sort of self-restraint and taking what I wanted without any regard for the consequence.

I brought a hand up to rub my temple, trying to will away the images of her, but my efforts were in vain. I could still smell the soft scent of her hair. It was like strawberries and cream. The feel of her pulse racing as I held her slight hand in mine. The way her breath hitched when I touched her neck. Her lips, parting ever so slightly, just waiting. Waiting for me to devour her.

And the look of confusion on her face when I so rudely dismissed her...

I'm an asshole.

I needed a do-over—a mulligan.

Intent on rectifying the situation, I quickly strode toward the office door, hoping to catch her before she left. However, when I stepped through the doorway, a very angry Justine Andrews was blocking my path.

"Alexander! I've been trying to reach you for days!" Justine snapped. Her eyes flashed angrily as she quickly closed the distance between us. My back went ramrod straight, ready to jump on the defense. I braced for the worst, knowing she had a valid reason for being so irate.

Here it comes—the wrath of Justine. Apparently, I've pissed off more than just one woman this morning.

But before I could even think to utter an explanation as to why I hadn't returned her calls, she threw her arms around my neck, softening my defenses.

That's when I saw Krystina.

At first, she looked shocked, but then her expression changed to one of angry betrayal. I felt like I had just taken a solid blow to the head. I couldn't react if I tried. It was as if time was literally standing still.

It wasn't until the elevator doors closed, I realized what the scene must have looked like to her. I disentangled myself from Justine's hold.

"Christ, what has gotten into you? You have no patience! And your timing sucks," I bit out irritably, turning to go back into my office. Justine followed me, and I closed the door behind her, sparing the office staff from a screaming match. I could tell she was itching for a fight.

"Come on, Alex! You wanted your secretary to reschedule me —me of all people! And I think it's terrible I had to make an appointment to see you in the first place," she whined.

"Sorry. It's been a busy week," I muttered, taking a seat behind my desk. Justine gracefully sat down in the chair across from me and folded her arms in a pout.

I fired up my computer and opened my inbox. I started sifting through emails, deleting what wasn't needed, and sending off quick responses. I wasn't going to put much consideration into Justine's petulant attitude. She would get to her point eventually, and I didn't want to have some long, drawn-out brawl in the meantime. It was a waste of time—time that should be spent chasing down Krystina.

I came across the email from Stephen that had Krystina's information in it. I opened the file to reread it for the fourth time that day, hoping to find some piece of information that might help me to defuse the time bomb I had unintentionally set.

"So, what have you been so busy with? That pretty little thing who just ran out of here?" Justine taunted.

"That's enough," I said impatiently, silencing her with my hand. I closed my eyes and took a deep breath. When I opened them, I looked pointedly at her, warning her not to challenge me. "That woman was an interview—a very important interview that you interrupted. Believe it or not, I do have a company to run."

I didn't elaborate on what else she interrupted. Justine would go ape shit if she knew I had practically sexually assaulted a potential employee. Her interruption was most likely the best thing that could have happened, as much as I begrudged her for it.

"I know you're busy, and I'm so sorry to come barging in like this. It's just that...this is important, and I didn't know what else to do!"

The anguish in her voice caught my attention, forcing me to take a closer look at her. As always, she looked impeccable, which I've come to expect nothing less of her. The allowance I gave her every month was more than enough to purchase her designer clothes, high-end cosmetics, and perfectly manicured nails. However, I was among the few people in her life who could see through the smokescreen. And her makeup.

Although she did a good job of covering it, I could still see the subtle puffiness under her eyes and the faint redness around their rims. She had been crying before coming to see me.

"What is it, Justine?" I asked, adopting a gentler tone, even though I already had suspicions about what might really be upsetting her. This wasn't about a few unreturned phone calls.

It's probably her scumbag ex-husband again.

"It's Charlie," she told me, her eyes welling up with tears. She tried to blink them back.

I called that one right...

"What's the bottom feeder up to?" I asked irritably. I had zero tolerance for the gambling addict who used to be Justine's husband. He was a despicable waste of a human being.

"It's bad, Alex. He's been making threats."

"What do you mean? What threats?" I hissed through my teeth, instantly fueled with rage at the thought of him hurting her again. She had already been through enough. "I'll kill the fucking bastard if he touched you again!"

Justine winced. My tone was menacing, which I knew she hated, but I couldn't help it. She brought out every protective instinct I possessed.

"No, he didn't hurt me—at least not in the physical sense. He's been calling... a lot. I thought about just having his number blocked, but I was afraid because of what he's been threatening. It affects both you and me," she told me.

Fear shone through her tears, and she started to shake, the tremble causing her legs to bounce visibly. I hurried over to her side and pulled her up into my arms. I held her tight and stroked her long hair.

"It's alright. It doesn't matter what his threats are. He can't do anything to me. And I already told you—I won't let him hurt you anymore," I tried to assure her.

"No, no! You have to listen to me, Alex!" she shouted, shoving me away. She inhaled deeply, attempting to regain some of her composure. "Damn it! This is why I've been blowing up your phone. He's threatening to expose us – our past!"

I felt all the blood drain from my face, a pit settling in the depths of my stomach.

"And how would he know about our past, Justine?" I asked, my voice low.

"Because...because I told him!" she hiccupped, a fresh wave of sobs making her lose it all over again. "I had to tell him. It was part of my therapy a long time ago. And now, all these years later, I've barely made peace with everything myself. The last thing I want is a media circus. I couldn't handle it, Alex. I just couldn't."

My hands tightened into fists. It took every ounce of willpower I had not to smash something in the room.

"Fucking shrinks," I cursed under my breath. I never could understand why she put so much faith in those head nutters. I moved around to the backside of my desk to get her a linen handkerchief from my desk drawer. "Is it safe to assume Charlie wants you to buy his silence?"

She took the handkerchief and hesitated for a second or two before answering me. Guilt briefly clouded her features.

"Of course, what else would he want? He probably just came off of a bad run on the craps table. But you know how it is...just a little extra cash will put him on top again. I'm sure he has one of his hunches again," she sarcastically remarked.

Justine was bitter, and I didn't blame her for being that way. However, I did blame her for the handouts she'd been giving him, despite their recent divorce. Justine didn't spend every penny I gave her on herself but saved a part of it to keep the leech off her back. I never told her I knew about it but often wondered why she did it. He must have been reaching deeper into her pockets than I had assumed.

It needs to end. Now.

"I'll handle it."

"But how? You know him, Alex. He won't stop. He'll just come back again when he's down."

"I don't know what I'm going to do just yet. Let me make some calls, talk to my lawyer. Stephen will know what we can do about this legally. In the meantime, I don't want you to be upset about it.

And if he calls again, direct him to me. That should stall him for a bit. He's always been a chicken-shit when it comes to me."

"I'm sorry, Alex. I never thought he'd stoop this low."

"You didn't? Seriously," I said, disgusted with her naivety even after all this time. "The man has no conscience. You should have learned the first time he slammed your head into the kitchen wall."

"Yeah, well...I never was one to learn from my mistakes," she emitted spitefully. Her voice cracked, and fresh tears filled her eyes. I was instantly overcome with shame.

What the fuck is wrong with me today?

"Look, I'm sorry. That was a low blow. I know you did what you thought was best at the time. As for all of this other bullshit, I told you I'd handle it, and I will."

"I hope you can, Alex. He's asking for an awful lot of money," she said, voice full of disbelief, shaking her head back and forth.

I didn't bother to ask how much. It didn't matter. He wasn't getting another dime from her or me.

"I've got this. Go home, Justine. Call Suzanne. Plan a lunch date or a spa day. Something."

She readily agreed to the suggestion, and I hoped an afternoon of doing whatever it was girls did together would distract her. At the very least, she seemed calmer when she kissed me goodbye.

"Thanks. I owe you for this," she vowed.

I cast her a grim smile, knowing I'd never cash in on the favor.

As soon as I was able to shoo her out the door, I picked up the phone to get my lawyer on the line. When it came to someone like Charlie Andrews, it wouldn't matter how much wealth or power I possessed. He wasn't easily put off by intimidation. He was driven by his addiction, lacking all common sense. It was time to take a more drastic approach.

"Stephen, I want you and Hale in here ASAP. I have a problem that needs to be dealt with."

I slammed the receiver down without waiting for a response. Charlie was the last person I wanted to deal with at that moment. I had a full schedule ahead of me, with two crucial meetings later in the afternoon I needed to prepare for. Then there was the most pressing matter of all—finding a way to apologize to Krystina.

Her expression before she left my building was seared into my brain like I had been branded—her face so beautiful yet full of wounded indignation. I felt a stab of guilt.

Why do I feel guilty? She's just a girl.

A very pretty girl.

A girl whose alluring face appears in my mind without warning, disrupting all other rational thoughts. The fact rectifying the situation with Krystina had become first and foremost in my mind was unsettling.

This is ridiculous. I'll just find a way to offer an apology and move on.

But despite what I told myself, I knew erasing Krystina Cole from my mind wouldn't be that easy.

8

Krystina

I sat at the kitchen table stirring a spoon in a bowl of cereal. It had been three days since my interview with Alexander Stone. I wasn't naïve. I knew he wasn't going to call me to reschedule. It didn't really matter. I never wanted to hear from him again anyway. I was a fool for dropping my guard, even for a moment. I was smarter than that.

During the first few days after the interview, my jealousy had kicked into overdrive. Why I was jealous, I didn't know. I certainly had no right to stake claims on the man. Yet, I had come home that day in absolute rage and used Allyson as my sounding board. Being the best friend she was, she shared my anger and swore profusely over and over again, calling him every name in the book.

But then, as all great friends do, she listened while I cried. I cried over a lost job opportunity, and I cried over my stupidity. And the worst part of it all, I cried over *him*. I knew my tears were misguided. After all, I barely knew the guy. But the simple fact was, Alexander Stone stirred up emotions I managed to keep buried for so long. He had made me feel *alive* again and put a little crack in the walls I had so carefully built around myself.

And I hated him for it.

After my ordeal with Trevor, I had vowed to myself I would never again show that kind of weakness, and I had since mastered the ability to ignore the opposite sex as much as humanly possible.

How could I have been so dumb?

My thoughts drifted back to the time with my ex-boyfriend, and I couldn't stop the bitterness from creeping up inside me.

I had met Trevor Hamilton my freshman year of college. We were the stereotypical couple you read about in books. He was the wealthy, popular boy on campus, and I was the new girl, struggling to find my place in the vast city of New York. I had fallen for him practically overnight.

However, unlike the storybooks, we didn't have a fairytale ending. Trevor was a different man behind closed doors. He was controlling to the point of obsession. He told me what to wear, how to style my hair, and where to shop. He even went so far as to write down a schedule for me, planning my time and activities down to the minute. He took charge of every aspect of my life, slowly forcing me away from my friends and family. Sometimes it felt like I couldn't even breathe without his approval.

When I looked back, I knew I was partly to blame. I allowed Trevor to do it. I ignored the warnings from my friends. I assured my troubled conscience he was a perfectionist and the reason he was so controlling. I told myself he loved me and only wanted what was best for me. I became a victim to the adage—the one that talks about love making people lose their sight, oblivious to the realities surrounding them.

I had been as blind as a bat.

At least I was until that fateful spring day when he had called me to cancel our plans for the evening. He had said he was sick. I figured he must have felt pretty bad to cancel out on me, especially since Trevor never allowed any deviation of my schedule. I thought it would be nice to surprise him with homemade chicken soup.

As it turned out, Trevor wasn't really that sick at all. I ended up walking in on him doing the horizontal tango with some scrawny-assed blond.

In an instant, my whole world shattered. As hard as I tried to forget that day and the terrible weeks that followed, I could remember it like it was only yesterday. The yelling, the screaming, and the violence would forever be burned into the deep recesses of my brain. It had altered my opinion of the world and all the people in it, ultimately changing who I was.

It was the day that made my heart turn to stone.

Allyson, the only friend I had left, was there to pick up the pieces. She came home to find me a crumpled-up mess on the floor and worked tirelessly for months to make me see things for what they really were. It took me a while to come around, but eventually, I was able to see I didn't really love Trevor and what had happened wasn't my fault.

I knew now I was just in love with the idea society jams down everyone's throat—companionship wrapped in a white picket fence was the key to happiness. I couldn't think of a bigger lie.

All men are bastards. I don't need that headache.

I went to the sink to dump my now mushy cereal into the garbage disposal. I was dwelling too much on my disastrous history and had lost my appetite. I needed to remember my restraint and not give in to a small moment of weakness. I had given up on fairytales and pipedreams for a good reason. I'd be damned before I would let history repeat its self.

I just needed to get rid of one little problem—Alexander Stone. He was consuming my every waking thought. I fought to extinguish all thoughts of that extraordinary and complex man from my mind, but Allyson's words at Murphy's rang in my head.

Every guy isn't like Trevor.

But my hardened heart said Allyson was wrong. They were all like Trevor, every last one of them.

Assholes.

Alexander had only proved himself to be the same as the rest. I should never have let him get to me. It was time to toughen my resolve. I did it once before, and I could certainly do it again. I just needed to find a distraction.

I glanced over at the pile of bills on the kitchen counter, my first student loan payment sitting amongst them. A review of my finances and a job search would certainly be enough of a distraction, and it was long overdue.

I went over to the counter and began sorting through the overwhelming pile, trying to figure out how I would make ends meet with my salary at Wally's.

After an hour of crunching numbers, panic began to set in as I stared at the homemade spreadsheet in front of me.

I was severely in the red.

I reworked the math three more times to make sure my figures were correct, but the result was the same. I would have to make some major cutbacks if I didn't find a better-paying job soon, and I knew selling my car was inevitable.

It doesn't matter—I hardly use the beat-up old Ford anyway.

Parking in this city was so damned expensive and difficult to come by, and public transportation had just ended up being more accessible. However, a prickle of tears began to sting my eyes as a wave of nostalgia came over me at the thought of giving up my first car.

I'm being stupid—it's just a car. I'll sell it if I have to.

A knock on the door disrupted my thoughts. I went to the door, opened it, and found a FedEx package at my feet. I figured Allyson must have ordered something online, but then I saw it was addressed to me.

I brought the package into the kitchen and rummaged through one of the kitchen drawers for a pair of scissors. Placing the box on the kitchen counter, I cut through the packaging tape. A new smartphone was inside.

What the hell?

I never did end up making it to the cellphone store. When I picked up the phone, I noticed a note at the bottom of the box.

Waiting for you to reschedule. I thought this might help.

My contact info has already been programmed, along with some music to help persuade you. Listen to it.

The note wasn't signed, but it didn't take a rocket scientist to figure out who sent it. I powered on the phone and pulled up the contact list. Alexander Stone's name, email address, and three different contact numbers were already programmed into it, as well as *all* of my other contacts.

I fought the urge to smash the phone against the kitchen wall.

This has to be some sort of sick joke! Of all the nerve!

The cellphone rang loudly through the silent apartment, practically making me jump out of my skin. My mother's name showed on the caller ID.

Why are my calls going to this phone?

I warily slid my finger along the smooth touch screen to answer the call.

"Hello?"

"There you are!" my mother's voice exclaimed on the other end of the line. "I've been calling all morning, but your phone was sending me straight to voicemail."

I looked at my broken phone on the coffee table in the living room.

That's strange. The phone was turned on.

But the thought was fleeting, as an idea of a completely impossible scenario came to mind.

There's no way...he couldn't have.

I hurried to the table to inspect the old phone, and my jaw hit the floor.

Oh my God. That son of a bitch deactivated it.

I pulled the new phone away from my ear to look at it and felt my blood begin to simmer at his audacity.

I don't care if he's some mega ultra-powerful zillionaire! He has no right! This must be illegal somehow. Of all the sneaky, controlling, and underhanded things...

"Krys? Are you there?" asked my mother, her voice sounding faint as I continued to hold the expensive device out in front of me.

"Hi, mom. Yeah, I'm here," I said, bringing the phone back to my ear. I rubbed my forehead, feeling a headache coming on.

"How are you, love? I haven't talked to you in weeks."

"I'm good. Busy, but good."

"Busy finding a job, I hope. You insisted on spending all of that money going to college in New York, and you should have something to show for it by now."

I closed my eyes and let out a sigh.

Here we go.

"No, Mom. Not yet. In fact, I was just about to pull out my laptop and start another job hunt. You sort of caught me at a bad time."

"Honey, I don't know why you just don't move home. You know Frank could get you a job anywhere in Albany. I really wish you would stop being so stubborn about staying in New York."

"Mom, we've been through this a thousand times. I like living in New York."

"I know, but–"

"I have to go, mom. I really need to concentrate on finding a job."

I found sometimes it was better just to talk over her. She never listened otherwise, and I wasn't in the mood for a lecture.

"If you would only–"

"I'm hanging up now, Mom," I told her, my impatience coming out loud and clear.

"Okay, fine. I get it. You don't want to talk about it. I'll stop. That's not why I called anyhow. I called to tell you that Frank and I are coming to New York in a few weeks. I'm long overdue for a visit, and I want to get a jump start on my holiday shopping."

I groaned inwardly. As nice as it would be to see them, a visit from my mother and stepfather took a lot of energy—energy I wasn't really feeling at the moment.

"Sounds good. I'll look forward to it," I lied.

"Alright, honey. I'll let you know which weekend we are

coming after we finalize our plans. Good luck job hunting! Love you!"

"Love you too, Mom. Bye."

I hit the end button on the touchscreen. Rage returned with a vengeance as I stared down at Alexander Stone's gift—if one would even call it that.

It's more like a hostile takeover of my personal means of communication!

On impulse, I decided to send him a text, my fingers typing feverishly in anger.

TODAY 10:32 AM: ME

Who do you think you are?

The seconds ticked by, my fingernails clicking impatiently on the kitchen counter as I waited for his response. After a few minutes, I was ready to ditch the phone in the trash, but then it chimed with a notification of a new message.

10:38 AM: ALEXANDER

Good. You received the phone.

I could almost see his smug expression as I read his response. That fueled my fury even more. I responded in such a rush, and I misspelled everything.

If the prick could take the time to have all of my contacts reprogrammed, he should have at least turned on the auto spelling correct!

I started over, this time typing more slowly.

10:41 AM: ME

Yes, I received it—and you can take it right back too!

10:42 AM: ALEXANDER

It's yours. Keep it.

Ugh! Is he really that dense!

He was starting to push me over the edge. I wanted no ties to Alexander whatsoever, and I had no intention of keeping the stupid phone, as it would only be a constant reminder of him.

10:44 AM: ME

I don't want it.

10:45 AM: ALEXANDER

You could always go back to your broken one.

10:45 AM: ME

You deactivated it!

10:47 AM: ALEXANDER

And your point is?

10:48 AM: ME

Normal people don't DO things like that!

10:51 AM: ALEXANDER

I'm not normal people, Krystina.

You can say that again!

10:54 AM: ME

How did you do it?

10:56 AM: ALEXANDER

Do what?

10:57 AM: ME

Deactivate my phone???

10:59 AM: ALEXANDER

I know people.

11:00 AM: ME

Then tell your PEOPLE to change it back!

11:04 AM: ALEXANDER

No.

11:04 AM: ME

YES!

11:09 AM: ALEXANDER

I've rescheduled your interview for this afternoon.

11:10 AM: ME

Then you're going to be awfully bored this afternoon.

11:13 AM: ALEXANDER

Why is that?

11:14 AM: ME

Because I won't be there.

11:17 AM: ALEXANDER

Yes, you will. 2pm. My office.

11:18 AM: ME

I will NOT be there! And I want you to fix my phone!

No response.

Fine. I'll take care of it myself!

I hurried to my bedroom to get dressed. I hastily threw on a pair of jeans and a T-shirt, then rummaged around in my closet for a pair of sneakers. I located them quickly and tied the shoelaces with expert speed while thinking about the vicious things I would say to the clerk at the cellphone counter.

Someone is going to get his or her ass chewed off for this!

And HIM...rescheduling my interview...HA!

I headed back out to the kitchen but stopped short when I saw the FedEx box sitting on the counter. I forced myself to see reason. It wouldn't do me much good if I stormed into the wireless communications store and went off half-cocked on some poor defenseless sales clerk. I would probably end up getting myself arrested for acting like a crazed lunatic. It wasn't their fault Stone was an assuming jerk.

Knowing I had to get a handle on my emotions before I did anything rash, I took a deep breath to try and calm my mounting temper. Going to the store in my current frame of mind would only lead to a total catastrophe, and I tried to form a more sensible plan—one that didn't involve any jail time.

La Biga first. A caffeine fix would do me good. Plus, it would buy me some time to screw my head back on straight.

I eyed up my laptop, sitting on the coffee table.

Yes! I can look for a job online while I'm at the coffee shop, too.

After an hour or so of doing an employment search, I assumed a sufficient amount of time would have passed, and I'd be a bit calmer when I went to return the phone.

Satisfied with my plan of action, I grabbed everything I would need, including Alexander's asinine phone, and dashed out of the apartment to catch the Redline.

9

Alexander

My feet pounded through the last mile on the treadmill. Sweat dripped down the side of my face, and I wiped it away with my hand. A solid cardio workout was what I needed to clear my head, as work just didn't seem to be cutting it lately. My life, and all that was in it, had suddenly become uninteresting—all except for one thing.

Krystina Cole.

I had gone into the office that morning to find I was completely bored with the tasks awaiting me. There was no excitement, no challenge. The only highpoint from the morning had been reading Krystina's snappy text messages.

Disgusted with myself for lack of focus, I ended up canceling my appointments for the rest of the day and headed down to the gym in Cornerstone Tower. I had looked for my trainer, but he was with another appointment. I could have pushed for a session but decided it would be better to go at it alone. My sullen mood dictated the necessity for solitude.

Up until recently, I had been satisfied. I had money. I had status. And I've never once had to pursue a woman. Yet here I was, chasing after some chic I barely knew, playing a game I've never before had to play. I tried to shut it down, but Krystina's brown eyes haunted me even in my sleep. Images of her naked and kneeling consumed me, so much so I could barely think about much else.

And it was seriously pissing me off.

I finished the final mile and slowed the treadmill to a cool-down speed. I could have easily gone another five miles at a run, but I was done. Even the workout was boring me.

I've been too long without a Sub. That's my problem.

Grabbing a towel, I hit the showers.

Bracing myself against the shower wall, I let the water stream over me as I thought about the last time I had a good fuck. Nobody really stuck out in my mind, at least not one I'd care to hook up with again. I could only think of one person I wanted, despite my efforts to forget about her, and I wasn't even sure if she would even be open to my sort of lifestyle.

But I could show her the ropes...

Ropes.

The metaphor put another image in my head, and I slammed my fist against the tiled wall.

How old am I? I seriously need to get a grip!

I had to think about this rationally. Too many things had gone wrong since meeting Krystina. Despite what she thought, I really did have every intention of giving her a formal interview that day in my conference room. But at some point, my intentions had changed. I didn't mean to seduce her.

Or did I? Who am I kidding?

I've wanted her under me, hot and submissive, since day one.

Be that as it may, I had handled the situation with her without thinking and had been forced to wait it out. Krystina needed space after the interview gone wrong. There was truth behind the expression about patience being a virtue, so I had deliberately given her a few days to cool off, maintaining silent neutrality between us while I put together a plan. The cellphone swap was just the beginning of what I had in mind, even if she was ticked off about it. I had known before sending it she wouldn't be the most receptive. For once, I was able to predict her reaction accurately. But Krystina's anger had been a risk I was willing to take if it meant I got to see her again.

Stepping from the showers, I quickly towel-dried and threw on jeans and a T-shirt. I collected my duffle bag and the garment bag containing my suit from earlier in the day and headed out of the locker rooms.

As I approached the front desk of the gym, I saw Gretchen was working the counter. Gretchen was attractive, a pretty face with a tall and lean physique, and was currently sporting yoga pants and a pink crop top. She had been skirting around me for months, dropping elusive hints to show her interest in me every time we spoke.

She gave me a coy smile and averted her eyes down when she saw me approaching.

Definitely the submissive type. Maybe I should just scratch my plans for Krystina and satisfy my bug with this one.

I closed the distance between us in just a few short strides and stepped up to the counter. Gretchen's eyes remained downcast, even though she knew I was right in front of her.

"Hey, Gretchen," I drawled out, deliberately turning up the charm for the gym employee. However, even to my own ears, the greeting sounded false. Fake. I flashed her a toothy grin and a wink in an attempt to be more convincing.

"Good afternoon, Mr. Stone. What can I do for you today?" Gretchen asked. Her words were professional, but her tone was suggestive and could easily be picked up on by anyone with a sharp ear.

You can do a lot of things for me, baby. Particularly anything that will make me forget about a brunette's curls and big brown eyes.

"Actually, I need a couple of things. First, I need you to send this suit up to Laura. I want it sent out for dry cleaning," I told her, handing over the garment bag. "Secondly, I need to use an office for about fifteen minutes or so."

She took the suit from me and allowed her fingers to hesitate slightly on mine. Her gaze traveled from our hands to my face, her eyes narrowing provocatively. After a few seconds, she turned to place the bag on the counter behind her. When she spun to face me again, her cheeks were flushed a rosy pink.

Hmm. She's almost making this too easy.

"The manager's office is available for you to use if you will require a computer. Or you can use the meeting room if you want a locked door with a little more privacy," she offered.

It was hard not to notice the way she emphasized the last word. Or the obvious mention of a locked door. She shifted her eyes to the side, bit her lip, and nervously tugged on the ends of her blond ponytail.

She couldn't have been more conspicuous.

In the past, I've always brushed off her flirtations. She went against my rules. I never take on the unknown, or I'd risk jeopardizing too much. It was much safer to stick to women I knew had interests reflecting my own, as they understood the value of discretion. Privacy was hard to maintain for someone of my stature. Gretchen worked in my building, and people talk. People talk a lot.

Fuck the rules for one day. I should just go for this one.

But as soon as I thought it, I dismissed the notion and resigned myself to the inevitable.

Rules or no rules. It isn't going to work.

"I only need to make a couple of calls. Joe's office will be fine," I stated indifferently. My tone was clipped rather than polite, as I was irritated with myself for giving her even a moment of consideration.

"Whatever is easier for you, sir," she accommodated with a slight nod. The light in her eyes extinguished, her poise returning to all business. "I'll just phone ahead and make sure Joe clears the space for you."

"Thank you, Gretchen."

Any decent man would have felt a slight twinge of guilt about leading her on, only to shut her down seconds later. But I wasn't one of those men. For me, the rationale was simple. Gretchen wasn't what I wanted. She was easy. Simple. Lacking any sort of challenge. A one-time roll in the hay with her would never dispel the restless energy I had been dealing with for days. There was only one woman who held that power.

Krystina.

I walked away from the obviously disappointed Gretchen and headed down the corridor that would take me to Joe's office. When I came around the corner, I spotted the gym manager closing his office door behind him.

"Mr. Stone," Joe greeted when he saw me coming toward him. When I reached him, he extended his hand to me.

"Joe," I returned, accepting his handshake. It was loose, like a limp noodle, and cold and clammy against my palm. It was not the sort of handshake one would expect from someone with shoulders like a linebacker. "Thank you for the space. You saved me a trip back upstairs to my office. I'll only be a few minutes."

"Take all the time you need, sir. If you need the computer, I left the guest login password on the desk for you. I'll just be in the training room reviewing schedules. Please don't hesitate to call me there if you need anything else."

"Will do."

Once he walked away, I wiped my hand on the leg of my jeans, attempting to dry the dampness left there by the handshake. Joe was always nervous around me, although I could never understand why. In fact, everyone seemed to be nervous in my presence lately.

Has it always been like that? Or is it I'm just noticing it for the first time?

Even Krystina was tense around me. The way she twisted her hands together or fiddled with the hem of her shirt—I intimidated her. She practically told me as much in her interview.

I'm not that much of an asshole, am I?

I stepped into the small office and closed the door behind me, my thoughts once again returning to Krystina. Phase one in my plan had already been set in motion. It was time to forge ahead with the next step.

I knew she would not be showing up for her "rescheduled" interview. I never had the notion she actually would. But that was okay, as long as everything else fell into place.

I took a seat behind Joe's gray metal-framed desk and dialed Matteo Donati's cell number. Matteo and I had been friends since high school, and I knew I could count on him to be discreet.

"Matt, I need a favor," I said when he picked up.

"Whatever you need," he obliged, his Italian accent still prevalent even after the twenty years he had spent in the States. "What's up?"

"I need to arrange a private meeting with someone. It's got to be tonight. Is the restaurant ready to entertain a guest and me?"

"If you don't mind a nameless place with limited selections," he joked, despite the fact I knew he was frustrated. Matteo had mapped out every tiny detail for the restaurant, from the font printed on the menus to the wattage of the light bulbs. He had a true vision, but he was stumped when it came down to naming his lifelong dream.

"You're overthinking it. I'll help you figure out a name, don't worry," I assured him. "I know the place isn't finished, but I'm just looking for somewhere free of outside influences and interruptions. Can you make it work?"

"Enough is done that I could pull it off. Who's the guest?"

"She's a prospect for Turning Stone Advertising."

"She?"

"Yes, she," I confirmed. I knew the request was probably more than a little odd, especially for me. I made a habit of conducting as much business as possible at Cornerstone Tower. I pursed my lips, waiting for the questions to flood. To my relief, they didn't.

"I'll go out this afternoon and get the things I'll need to put a dinner together. I should have the place ready for you by six o'clock."

"That's perfect. Thanks. See you soon."

"*Ciao!*"

Confident Matteo wouldn't disappoint, I hit the end button

and made my next call. This request would be even stranger than the first.

"Hale. Get in touch with Gavin from Tech. Have him pull up the GPS tracker for the company phones. I need to know where Krystina Cole is right now."

There was a pause on the other end of the line before Hale spoke again.

"You're serious?"

"Yes, I'm fucking serious," I snapped, thoroughly irritated I had to tell him twice. "Just do it. She had an interview today that she didn't show up for."

Of course, it was an absolute lie, but there was no need for Hale to know I was completely bordering on stalking.

"Right, boss. Give me a minute, and I'll text you the location."

I have to be out of my goddamned mind.

10

Krystina

I sat at a little table in La Biga, staring at the heart-shaped pattern on the foam of my cappuccino. This was espresso number two, and my already frazzled nerves were jittery. I forced myself to look back at my computer screen and scroll through the job listings, attempting to keep thoughts of Alexander Stone at bay.

It was practically impossible.

Maria came over to my table to check on me, a worried expression on her face. "You look lost. Where is your beautiful smile today?" she asked, wiping her hands on her apron.

"I'm okay. I just have a lot on my mind," I said, forcing a smile.

"Tell Maria. Maybe you will feel a little better."

"Don't worry. It's nothing I can't handle. I just need to get rid of an annoying little problem, that's all."

"Difficulties with a man?" she assumedly asked. Her eyes were kind as she sat down in the chair across from me.

"Oh, you could say that," I admitted.

"Ah! Say no more. I understand. Men! Impossible to live with, but we need them all the same," she said with a knowing smile.

"No, we don't need them," I said firmly. "Men are nothing but trouble—the whole lot of them."

I heard the bells jingle on the café doors, signaling the arrival of a customer. Maria looked over my shoulder to see who had come in.

Oh, thank goodness!

That sound meant Maria would have to busy herself with another customer. I appreciated her concern for me, and I felt a twinge of guilt for wanting her gone. I just wasn't up for conversation at the moment, even if it was with the kindhearted woman.

"Maybe you'll change your mind when you see the handsome man coming our way," she said as she stood up, pointing her finger at someone behind me.

I turned to see whom she was pointing at and felt my stomach plummet to my feet. Alexander Stone, wearing blue jeans and a black T-shirt, casually strolled toward my table.

As much as I didn't want to look, I couldn't help but take in his godlike appearance. His denim fit loosely around his hips, while his fitted shirt stretched tight across his pectorals and around his bronzed biceps. He looked irresistible and self-assured, his blue eyes piercing through me like knives. If I had once thought he was mouthwatering in a suit, the man was undeniably deadly in a pair of jeans.

"Hello, Krystina," he greeted smoothly in that ever so cultured voice. A sexy grin spread across his features.

Oh. My. God.

A thousand emotions ran through me at the sight of him. It didn't matter that I hated him. It didn't matter that I never wanted to see this infuriating, arrogant man again. Just the sight of him flickered a spark, and I felt my heart skip a beat. I was practically swooning in only a few short seconds. His smile alone made my insides quiver. I had to remind myself I had been furious with him just moments before.

I'm supposed to be pissed off—not drooling like a dog after a bone!

But the reality was that I was more irritated because I was being so pathetic and allowing his pure male hotness to get to me.

So rather than reveal how utterly captivated I was by his presence, I threw him an icy glare, allowing my fury at him and myself to come out in full force.

"You have some nerve! Why are you here?" I demanded, my tone menacing. People glanced in our direction, and I realized I was shouting. Maria raised an eyebrow at me and quickly retreated behind the counter to busy herself with the pastry case. Angelo was there as well, concern showing plainly on his face. I knew they were alarmed by my sudden outburst and were probably straining their ears to catch my every word. I forced myself to lower my voice. "I don't want to see you!" I quietly hissed.

"I'm here to finish your interview," he casually stated as he sat down in the chair Maria had vacated. He appeared completely unperturbed by my wrath.

Is this guy for real?

His hair was slightly damp like he just took a shower. He smelled of soap and sweat with a mild hint of musky cologne. The very masculine combination wreaked havoc on my senses.

"Please, Mr. Stone. Take a seat," I sarcastically replied.

"Sarcasm is not becoming on you, Krystina."

"Don't call me Krystina," I snapped.

"Would you prefer to be addressed as Miss Cole?" he asked calmly, a curious expression on his beautiful face.

"Everyone calls me Krys, and that's what I prefer."

"*Krys* is a boy's name," he retorted.

"Well, it's my name all the same. And once again, it's the name I would like to be called," I said, my irritation reaching an all-time high.

"I'm not going to have this debate with you. Your name is Krystina, and that's what I'm going to call you."

He waited a second or two as if gauging my reaction.

When I didn't respond, a satisfied smile slowly formed on his face. I refused to waste my breath on an argument with him, so I bit my tongue instead of lashing out the many profanities I was thinking.

I turned back to my laptop and pretended to be searching for a job. It was either that or continue to stare like some nitwit at Alexander Stone. If I did the latter, then I'd have to acknowledge how incredible he looked or that he still made my insides turn to mush every time he flashed one of those to-die-for smiles.

I could feel his scrutiny, and I tried not to acknowledge him. But after several minutes, his careful watch won out, and I looked up.

His face was amused like he had been assessing how long I would be able to ignore him.

Oh, no. I'm not playing your silly mind games today.

"What do you want from me, Mr. Stone?" I asked impatiently.

"I already told you. I'd like to continue your interview. Since you didn't show up today, I thought I would bring the interview to you."

I glanced at the clock on my computer screen. It was half-past two o'clock.

"Are you really arrogant enough to believe I'd show up for the two o'clock appointment?"

"It's not arrogance. It's simply finalizing business," he said with a shrug, acting as if nothing was amiss. "As I recall, we left a few things unfinished."

The anger that had been simmering beneath the surface bubbled over, and I let him have it.

"That's certainly not how I would describe the turn of events. As *I recall,* you discarded me for your ten o'clock, and then you hijacked my cellphone!" He looked confused for a moment, but I didn't pause in my quiet rant. "What's the matter? The tall girl with black hair didn't fulfill the needs at Turning Stone Advertising? Oh, wait—I forgot. You prefer redheads, right? That must be why you're here. The black-haired bimbo didn't work out. For that matter, I can't begin to figure out why you would even interview *me*! I didn't think mousy brown hair did it for you. I'm not stupid, Stone. That was no job interview."

He didn't say anything, and the silence stretched on for what seemed like eons. I just continued to glare at him. He, on the other hand, wore a look of mild disinterest, exacerbating my anger even more.

"Are you finished now, Krystina?" he asked, still ever so reserved and calm. I was taken aback.

Yeah—I'm finished, all right.

I closed my laptop and stood up to leave.

"Sit down," he barked with command. I scowled at him. But then, to my surprise, his expression changed. He seemed frustrated almost and looked as though he was having some sort of internal battle with himself. He ran a hand through his hair, all of his careful control seeming to evaporate. Finally, he took a deep breath and, in a resigned voice, said, "Please, Krystina. Sit down."

Could it be? Alexander Stone, the man who defines the meaning of measured confidence, seems unsure of himself.

He reached out and placed a gentle hand on my arm. Curiosity got the best of me, and I sat.

"Let's clear the air and get a few things straight," he said. "First of all, the 'black-haired bimbo' you saw? That was my younger sister, Justine. She was rather upset with me that day because I hadn't made much time for her lately." His face softened, and he looked thoughtful. A small lopsided grin formed on his perfect lips. "The little snot actually scheduled an appointment to see me."

His sister. Sure, that's what they all say.

However, deep down, I knew he was most likely telling the truth. That woman was breathtakingly gorgeous, and her long, flowing, ebony hair had matched his color so perfectly. I studied Alexander's face, trying to see other similarities to the woman, only to find myself stunned once again by his extraordinary beauty. Two people that beautiful had to be related in some way. Maybe I misunderstood the affection I saw pass between them. Even now, as he spoke of her, the expression on his face was one of tenderness, not one of a liar. Airing on the side of caution, I decided to bite my tongue and just listen.

"Secondly," he continued. "There is a position available in the marketing division of Stone Enterprise. I would like to discuss the details of that once we get past this roadblock we seem to be experiencing."

"Is that what this is, Stone? A roadblock?" I snapped.

He hesitated before answering as if choosing his words carefully.

"I'll admit your interview took an unexpected turn. I'm usually very good at reading women, but... you're different for some reason." A sardonic smile tugged at the corners of his mouth.

"Yeah, well, nothing surprises me about you, Stone. I've got your type all figured out," I said cynically.

"I wouldn't be so assuming, Krystina. I'm probably nothing like you would expect. Isn't there an expression about not judging a book by its cover? You may find my pages are full of surprises," he stated, casting me a roguish look.

"I doubt that," I said with a false air of confidence. There was something about the gleam in his eye that was unsettling, but I couldn't put my finger on what it was.

"Then we can continue this cat and mouse game you seem to be so apt at playing," he said, his lips pursed with annoyance. "However, I would rather we discuss the reasons why I've sought you out."

"Fine. Have it your way, Stone. Talk. I'm all ears," I said, keeping up with my confident façade. I sat back and folded my arms, giving the appearance of total aloofness in an attempt to hide how shaken up I was by his mere presence.

"Finishing your interview would be an unnecessary formality. I already know I want you, Krystina." He paused, allowing me to digest what he had said. His eyes burned into me, and I struggled not to read too much into his words. "Despite what you think, I really would like to offer you a job. Very few firms are hiring, and your job searches have probably returned minimal results."

"You're right. Nobody is hiring," I admitted bitterly.

"Except me."

"Okay, I'll bite. What would this job entail?"

"Originally, the company was established for the sole purpose of providing affordable advertising to the business owners who have lease agreements with me. However, things have changed, and I am looking to push Turning Stone Advertising to the next level. As of right now, the company is small, and my personal knowledge of advertising is limited. If you came to work for me, I would have you manage the employees at Turning Stone and oversee all new incoming ad campaigns from start to finish."

I was intrigued, and I found myself straightening up a little in my chair. The thought of being in charge of an entire campaign was enticing and more than just a little intimidating. I leaned forward and put my elbows on the table, itching to find out more.

"How many employees do you have at Turning Stone?"

"Currently, only three. They are mediocre on their best day, but they get the job done. For now."

"Marketing can be very complex. Why would you start an advertising company if you didn't know how to run it?"

"I know enough of the basics. I could give direction to the few employees I have and turn a small profit. The end goal was to help my tenants, not to make a fortune from it. Advertising in New York is costly. I want the businesses that pay me rent to be successful. A profitable business continues to provide me with a monthly income. Whereas, empty buildings are costly," he finished, shrugging his shoulders indifferently.

"That makes sense," I said thoughtfully. "But it seems like you have it all worked out. Why do you need me?"

"Surprisingly, the small firm has exceeded my expectations, and other businesses have inquired about advertising with me. Because of my limited knowledge, I have refused to take on any outside clients. However, I've seen the potential money that can be made, and it would be foolish to hold Turning Stone back. That's why I am looking to recruit you. I want you to build Turning Stone Advertising into a lucrative business venture for me." He paused and rubbed his finger over his chin contemplatively. "If you can do that successfully, there may be the opportunity for a partnership down the road."

"Having a partner doesn't really fit your motif. You don't strike me as the type of person who likes to answer to people. A partner means you don't get to call all the shots," I told him skeptically.

He simply nodded his agreement and took my pessimism in stride.

"I'll admit I've never even considered the possibility of a partnership until now. But you have me at a slight disadvantage. Advertising is an unexplored territory for me. I may have the money to back the endeavor, but you have the knowledge I don't possess. I want your expertise, and in the meantime, I will pay you a substantial salary while you work on growing the business portfolio. You will be, in a sense, an investment for me."

All of this seems too good to be true.

"I don't know," I said, giving voice to my doubts.

"I don't know what you're so unsure about, Krystina. I am offering you the chance of a lifetime. You can build a company almost from the ground up, with no cost to you."

"Mr. Stone, I'm a recent college graduate with little to no experience in the field, other than a few brief internships in college. While I'm somewhat flattered you think I can do this, I'm sure you could find someone with better qualifications."

"Maybe. But I've done my research, and I think you are more than capable of doing what needs to be done. You're smart, determined, and driven. Those are three very admirable qualities in my book. And more importantly, I'm looking for someone fresh."

"Yeah, I'll bet you are," I responded with a snort. "Fresh meat is what you're most likely after."

The corners of his mouth tilted up slightly in a knowing smile, but he didn't take the bait.

"I want fresh *ideas*—someone who's willing to go outside the box and do what needs to be done. I often find experienced individuals are attached to narrow-minded ideas," he clarified.

"I'm still not buying it. What's the catch?" I asked suspiciously.

"You're very perceptive too, Krystina. Another admirable

quality," he said. His blue eyes flickered with mischief. "I may have a few other ideas for you as well."

"Such as?"

"You're an intelligent woman. Why don't you tell me?"

"Honestly, Stone. You're so damned cryptic all the time. I constantly feel like you're skirting around what you really want to say. Please, enlighten me," I said testily. I pursed my lips in annoyance. Any tolerance I might have momentarily had for playing his guessing games had reached its limit.

"You can consider it a proposition of sorts, but it's not something I wish to discuss here." He waved his hand in the air to reference the coffee shop. "We can talk about it more over dinner tonight."

Holy crap! Is megabucks asking me out?

Not that it should have mattered. I had promised myself I would not allow him to get under my skin again, no matter what. Even if this job were a golden opportunity, I was barely hanging on to my wavering conviction as it was. Going out to dinner with him would be my undoing. I was sure of it.

"You still didn't answer my question. But either way, I have plans tonight," I responded nonchalantly, lifting my chin in the air.

It wasn't a lie exactly. I had planned a date with a treadmill.

His eyes flashed again, but this time with a dark glimmer of words unspoken, searing into me and throwing me off balance. My confidence faltered, teetering as if on the edge of a precipice, and suddenly I wasn't so sure if I would be able to fight this battle of wills much longer.

"Fine. If you insist on me spelling out my intentions, then I will," he said and took an impatient breath. Placing his palms on the table, he leaned forward. "I've tried to get you out of my head, but my efforts don't seem to be working. So rather than fight the inevitable, I've decided to just go with it. I want you, Krystina. Any way I can have you. Preferably naked."

WHAT? He wants me naked!

My eyes felt like they were about to pop out of their sockets.

He said it so flippantly, his tone not even acknowledging the bomb he just dropped. And it was nuclear. The thought of being naked under Alexander caused goosebumps to trickle down my spine. His blatant honesty was ridiculously hot.

Too hot. This can't be happening.

I had to get control of this situation quickly before I succumbed to the fight.

"Um...I-I'm not sure I heard you correctly," I stammered, trying to recover from the apparent shock.

"You heard me. Be ready at six o'clock. My driver will be by your apartment to pick you up," he informed me as he stood up.

He has a driver? Of course, he has a driver. How silly of me.

Alexander pushed his chair under the table and turned to leave.

"Whoa, wait just a minute here! I said I have plans."

"Cancel them."

"What if I don't want to cancel? You can't just order me about, Stone." I tried to sound firm, but my voice sounded small to my ears.

"Do I strike you as the type of man who is easily put off? This is not a request, Krystina. We can finalize the details of your employment tonight, then move on to discussing more *interesting* things. Six o'clock," he reminded. "Oh, and one more thing. Don't return the phone I gave you. You'll need it when you come to work for me."

The phone.

I had completely forgotten about it. I sat there, still wide-eyed, not sure what to make of the turn of events that had just unfolded. His assumption that I was going to accept the job offer was irritating. Ordering me to join him for dinner just plain ticked me off. But the fact he came right out and said he wanted me *naked*... well, that had the devil on my shoulder rubbing his hands together in anticipation.

I was so flustered, and I didn't register he had walked away from the table.

Wait—what just happened here?

I turned around in my chair and almost called out to him, to remind him he didn't know where I lived, but then I stopped myself. Alexander Stone knew exactly where I lived. I had a new cellphone as proof.

I watched him saunter to the exit. The man had the sexiest ass I had ever seen. Just the sight of him had me throwing all reservations to the wayside. I wanted him. Desperately. No matter how hard I tried to fight it, I couldn't resist him. I knew, with absolute certainty, I would be ready tonight when his driver came to pick me up.

11

Alexander

I climbed into the black leather driver's seat of my Tesla Model S with a satisfied grin on my face. I had finally made some headway with Krystina.

Regardless of whether or not she took the job I was readily willing to give her, there would be no changing what happened that day in my conference room. And there would be no going back after our conversation in the coffee shop.

She would be difficult for me, of that I was sure. Her quick wit and firecracker temper made me want to put her over my knee.

But I have her attention now.

I was able to see she'd been intrigued by the job proposition, especially after I impulsively sweetened the pot with a potential partnership. And my cock instantly went hard when I saw the flash of desire in her eyes after I told her I wanted her naked. I knew I had gotten to her.

However, she had a suspicious nature about her, and she was extremely distrusting. That alone could pose a serious problem. I knew I would have to be careful, and I wasn't naïve to the risks I was taking with her. Krystina was a wild card. One wrong move and this could all blow up in my face. She was the antithesis to every rule I had in the book. But I found her to be irresistible nonetheless, and I would do whatever I had to do to possess her. If that meant a little extra effort on my part in order to tame her, then so be it.

Having cleared my schedule for the remainder of the day, I shifted lanes in the city traffic and headed toward the interstate. Using the touchscreen of the car, I activated the phone system to get Hale on the line. He picked up after the first ring.

"Hale, I'm leaving the city for a few hours. There's a parcel of land in Westchester I'm going to look at."

"Do you want me to meet you there?"

"No, that's not necessary. Did you get those papers to Charlie?" I asked.

"All set, boss."

"And he signed them?"

"Of course, he did. He would have been stupid not to. You had him. It was either he takes the lump sum once and for all, or you'd hit him with an extortion charge. Stephen was brilliant with the wording of the contract. Your sister can rest easy now."

"It fucking killed me to give that worm another cent. I just hope you're right," I said warily. "Charlie Andrews isn't the brightest bulb, but we shouldn't underestimate him."

"I don't think he'd risk doing any time in jail," Hale predicted.

"You don't know him as I do. The only reason he wouldn't want to end up behind bars is that it would mean time away from his dice. Keep an eye on him for a while, will you?"

"Sure thing. I'm headed to Stephen's office now to drop off the signed document."

"Good. After you have that all squared away, I'll need you to pick up Krystina Cole at her place at six. I have a meeting with her."

"A meeting," he repeated. I could hear the humor in his voice, and I frowned.

I had seen the knowing look on Hale's face in the rearview mirror when I told him to research Krystina the other day, and I could only imagine what he thought when I had asked him to track her location. I hated that I felt like I had to explain myself —which of course, I didn't. His contracted salary and job description did not include keen observations of my personal life.

"Don't start with me, Hale. I don't pay you to speculate. Just be there. I'll text you the address of where I want you to take her."

"Aye-aye, Captain."

Smart-ass.

I ended the call and turned onto the ramp for the I-495. After opening the car's glass panoramic roof, I hit the accelerator. Gripping the wheel, I embraced the blistering force of the vehicle and left the city madness behind.

Krystina

On the subway ride home from La Biga, I struggled to wrap my head around Alexander's job offer. The opportunity was incredible, to say the least. Different advertising schemes turned in my mind. The idea of finally putting my degree to use was exciting, and I had found myself wondering about the sort of businesses and products he would want me to market.

And a possible partnership? This is the chance I've been waiting for. I'd be a fool to turn it down.

But then again, there were some major strings attached to his offer, and I wasn't sure how I felt about them.

The feminist side of me wanted to scream. He offered me a job, only to follow it up with a not-so-appropriate proposition.

Who does he think he is? This is one stained blue dress short of a sexual harassment suit. If I had half a brain, I'd be Googling Kenneth Starr's case notes right now!

Yet, another part of me wanted him badly, totally negating the whole women's rights issue. I *wanted* to be harassed by Alexander Stone, despite all of his irritating qualities. I was flattered this mega-rich, ultra-sexy, walking God wanted *me*. It was a thrilling, heady feeling I just wanted to savor.

But I was very afraid of him, too.

I was terrified of getting sucked back into a world I had shunned for so long. I was still haunted by my past with Trevor. And although I had worked tirelessly to rebuild my independence and self-respect, I knew I allowed a man to break me once before. I could not let it happen to me again, or I'd risk jeopardizing everything I worked so hard to overcome.

However, I felt there was something different about Alexander Stone. Somehow, I knew he would not be like Trevor. It was a feeling deep inside me, a yearning I didn't completely understand.

Alexander may be rich and powerful, but that wasn't why I was drawn to him. He sparked an unfamiliar level of awareness in me, and I wanted to give myself up to him from the moment I first laid eyes on him. These newfound feelings were very uncharacteristic for me, and I didn't know what to do about it.

I think for tonight, the only thing I can do is be careful, play it cool, and let him take the lead.

When I finally reached my apartment, I was grateful to find Allyson wasn't home. It wasn't that I didn't want to talk to my friend; I just needed to sort out a few things for myself before facing her. I wanted a little time alone to mentally prepare myself for anything Alexander threw my way.

The man is full of surprises, but at least I know his true intentions now.

I went into my bedroom, turned on the radio, and looked for something to wear to dinner tonight. I wasn't sure where we were going, and I didn't know how to dress.

Casual? Semi-casual?

I wished Alexander had been a little more specific when he issued his commands.

I eyed up a red faux leather-trimmed skirt. The skirt was flattering on me with its subtle flirty pleats. If I wore it with my white cashmere sweater and some strappy heels, I could make the outfit look casual or dressy depending on the environment. I pulled the sweater and skirt out of the closet and laid them flat on the bed to see how they would look together.

Yep, this will work perfectly.

Singing along with Lana Del Ray, I turned up the volume on the radio before heading to the bathroom to take a shower.

I contemplated whether or not I should shave my legs. I knew what Allyson would say.

If I shave, I'm planning on sex.

I considered the little skirt I was planning to wear.

I will have to shave if I am going to wear that.

With that rationale in mind, I began to work a foamy lather over my legs. But as I ran the razor over my knee, Alexander's words played over again in my head.

Preferably naked.

I felt a little twist in my gut. He definitely wanted me—it was no longer just something my imagination had drummed up. I wasn't just shaving because I was going to wear a skirt. My legs were fine for appearance purposes, but they certainly weren't baby smooth.

Who am I kidding? I'm shaving just in case.

My heart skipped a beat as trepidation enveloped me. If confronted with sex, I wasn't sure if I could physically go through with it. Knowing full well the decision to have sex was ultimately up to me, I stopped mid-shave and tried not to worry about what was to come.

I'm putting the cart before the horse. I just need to relax.

I quickly finished in the shower and got dressed. Then I began the laboring process of taming my hair. I thought about just throwing it up in a clip, but then I remembered Alexander saying my hair was too restricted on the day of my interview. Little alarm bells went off, heightening my already skittish nerves.

Trevor told me how to wear my hair.

"Stop it, Cole!" I exclaimed out loud to my reflection in the mirror. Comparing the two men would get me nowhere, and I fought to shake off my unease.

Alexander didn't tell me how to style my hair. He only expressed his preference.

I left my hair down and ignored the badgering warnings running rampant through my mind.

As I was applying the finishing touches to my makeup, I heard a commotion in the kitchen. Tossing my lipstick in my purse, I went out to see what it was. I walked into the kitchen and saw grocery bags piled high on the island. Allyson was pulling a bunch of pots and pans from the cabinet. She had a guy with her, too. They were laughing over something, and Allyson lightly swatted her guest on the shoulder.

Perfect—she'll be too distracted to ask me a lot of questions.

"Hey, you!" she said when she saw me. "I hope you're hungry. Jeremy is making Chinese."

This must be Allyson's infamous photographer...

I gave him a quick once over. He appeared to be just shy of six feet and had an athletic build. His copper hair was streaked from the sun, and his face was tan. He looked like he spent a lot of time outdoors.

"I don't want to intrude on the two of you, but thanks anyway. Besides, I already have dinner plans for tonight. So, you're Jeremy," I greeted in a rush and reached across the island to shake his hand. "It's nice to meet you finally. I'm Krys."

"Hi, Krys. I've heard—" Jeremy started.

"You have dinner plans?" Allyson questioned in surprise, interrupting our introductions.

Damn!

Nothing slid by her.

"Yeah. Is that okay with you?"

"Of course, it's okay, but who are you going out with?" she pressed suspiciously, eying up my attire for the first time.

Pushy, pushy.

"I ran into Alexander Stone this afternoon at Café La Biga. He asked me to join him for dinner tonight. It's no big deal, really. We are just going to discuss the job thing again."

I deliberately left out the part about his *other* proposition.

"You're joking, right?" Her face creased into a frown. "I thought you said Stone was an asshole."

"He is, but I'm not doing myself any good by staying angry. I need a job, so I'm willing to hear him out," I replied awkwardly. I tried to act like the dinner was no big deal, but I was failing miserably. I could feel the heat creeping into my cheeks. There was no fooling Allyson.

"What about that chic? You know, the one with the black hair," she reminded me subtly, attempting to disguise her obvious concern by needlessly rearranging the groceries on the counter.

"Oh, that was just his sister," I said with a dismissive wave. Allyson stopped her pointless organization and narrowed her eyes doubtfully at me.

Oh, Ally! Don't make me explain it in front of your boyfriend!

I threw her a warning look, slightly shaking my head back and forth, just hoping she'd leave it alone for now. Before she could remark, Jeremy chimed into the conversation, effectively saving me from one hell of a complicated explanation.

"Wait a minute—you're going out with *the* Alexander Stone? As in 'Stone Arena' Alexander Stone?" He was looking back and forth between Allyson and me with a look of total disbelief on his face.

"What's Stone Arena?" Allyson asked, looking at me. I shrugged and looked to Jeremy, waiting for him to elaborate.

Jeremy threw his hands up in exasperation.

"Stone Arena is only the first Major League Soccer complex to hit New York!" He muttered something about women and sports, but I didn't quite catch it. "Stone's been pushing for this for years. It was finally just approved, and he earned the naming rights."

Was everything in this city named after him?

"Yep, sounds like the same Alexander," I said. Thankful Jeremy had distracted Allyson from her questioning, I walked to the front door, hoping I could just slip out. "I don't really know much about soccer. However, I do know my ride is probably here."

"Wait! Where are you going to eat? And are you taking a cab?" Allyson asked, quickly remembering her interrogation.

"I don't know where we're going, *mom*. He didn't tell me," I said sarcastically, pausing by the door. "And, no—I'm not taking a cab. Alexander sent a car for me."

"A car? Now that's impressive," she said, her voice awestricken, completely ignoring the derisive comment I threw at her. "Promise me we'll talk later? I want a full report."

"Yeah, yeah. Don't worry. You'll get the specifics. Oh, and I shouldn't be out too late," I added and raised an eyebrow at Allyson to make sure she caught the silent meaning behind my words. Telling her that I would be home early was code from our college days—signaling that I didn't want to come home to find her bare-assed on the couch with Jeremy.

"Gotcha," she said with a knowing wink. "We're probably going to catch a movie later, so I might not be here when you get back."

"No problem. You guys have a good night."

"You too. Have fun and be careful," she warned as worry lines spread over her face.

"I always am. Bye!" I yelled over my shoulder and closed the door behind me.

12

Krystina

When I exited my apartment complex, Alexander's driver stood waiting for me outside of a black Porsche Cayenne. I approached him, and I attempted to introduce myself, but he just gave me a curt nod as a way of greeting and motioned for me to get inside the awaiting car.

He was intimidating in an ex-military kind of way and didn't strike me as much of a talker. He wore a fancy earpiece on his ear, reminding me of the Secret Service, and I was afraid even to talk, much less ask him where we were going.

So instead, I sat in silence while we weaved in and out of the New York City traffic, having no idea where he was taking me.

When we arrived at our destination, the driver still didn't speak but merely opened the car's door for me. I stepped out onto the pavement, and he walked me to the entrance of a no-named building. I might have been worried about the nondescript place, but I saw lights on in the windows and a polished bar gleaming under muted lighting. For some reason, I found these little signs of life comforting.

The building's front door opened suddenly, and a stocky man with curly dark hair stepped out.

"Ah, finally! You are here! Come in, come in, please!" the man said with a slight Italian accent. His hands were waving in the air, motioning for me to get inside. His gestures seemed panicked almost, yet he wore a friendly smile on his handsome face. I could only raise my eyebrows in surprise at his overexcited presence. I wasn't quite sure what to make of him.

I looked behind me, but the silent driver had disappeared back inside the SUV, leaving me little choice but to follow the animated Italian through the front doors.

"My name is Matteo Donati. I will be serving you tonight," he called over his shoulder, walking briskly ahead of me. He was moving quickly, and I struggled to keep up with him, barely managing to stay vertical in my strappy little four-inch heels. I was already beginning to regret the risk I took by wearing them.

"Hi, Matteo. I'm Krys–"

"Hurry along. Mr. Stone is waiting," he said, completely cutting me off.

Heaven forbid we keep Stone waiting.

I followed the practically running Matteo through the vacant restaurant as if I was late for some monumental event. I truly felt like Alice must have on her adventure into Wonderland, except I was chasing an Italian rather than a white rabbit into an unfamiliar place.

The restaurant was eerily quiet and obviously not open for business. I found myself wishing Alexander's driver were still here. Ironically, I began to feel nervous over the absence of the brooding man. It was almost like he was my protection in this deserted place. Chairs were flipped up on the tables, and there wasn't a soul in sight. The lighting from the pendant fixtures was dim, revealing half-finished decorations and empty curtain rods. The shelves behind the bar looked like they had only been partially stocked. The only clue I would be eating dinner here came from the delicious smell wafting out of the kitchen, a mouth-watering aroma of garlic and sage.

Matteo paused in an open doorway off of the main dining area, giving me a moment to catch up to him. When I reached his side, he took hold of my elbow and escorted me into an intimately furnished room with soft guitar music playing overhead. At first glance, the room appeared to be set up for small banquets. But upon closer inspection, I realized this wasn't your typical run-of-the-mill banquet room. The furnishings reeked exclusiveness, the setting more appropriate for high-ticketed private gatherings.

Alexander Stone sat alone at a candlelit table set for two. As I made my way to him, I was suddenly overcome with anxious jitters, and my palms began to sweat. I couldn't fathom why I was suddenly so nervous.

He's just a man sitting at a table.

But then again, Alexander wasn't *just* anything.

He stood and pulled a chair out for me. I gave him a quick once over. He was killer as usual, in khaki pants and a charcoal gray poplin button-down.

"Good evening, Krystina."

"Mr. Stone," I greeted politely, discreetly wiping my damp palms on my skirt.

I tried to sit down gracefully and make myself comfortable in the offered chair, but it was hard to feel relaxed under his watchful eyes.

"I take it you've met Matteo already," Alexander assumed, reclaiming his seat across from me.

"Yes. He was at the door when I arrived," I said and gave Matteo a nod of thanks.

"Krystina," Matteo said and bowed before me, taking me by surprise. He took hold of my hand, placed a feathery kiss on the backside of it, and murmured something in what I recognized as Italian. Then he looked back up at Alexander, his expression coy, and said, "I think we have finally found a name for my place!"

Alexander smirked at him and shook his head back and forth.

"It appears you have yourself a fan club, Krystina," Alexander said dryly.

Matteo let out a boisterous laugh and released my hand.

"No worries, no worries! It was only an observation," he assured. "Now, *mi scusi.* I must go see to your *antipasti,*" Matteo declared with a loud clap of his hands and hurried from the room.

I couldn't help but laugh at his overly flamboyant performance, despite the fact I was totally confused by their interaction.

"What did he say?" I asked Alexander, curious about what Matteo had said in his native tongue that had Alexander looking so thoroughly annoyed.

"That you are a beautiful lady," he answered, his eyes softening as he regarded me. "You really are lovely, Krystina."

His voice was tender, all of the irritation with Matteo diminished.

I wasn't so sure 'beautiful' was a word I would use to describe myself, and I felt a red glow begin to blossom on my cheeks.

"I love that you blush so easily. It's refreshing."

I'm glad you're into the whole red in the face thing—I despise it!

Rather than give a voice to my embarrassment, I chose to cast my gaze down toward my lap and focus my attention on the soft melody playing overhead. I used the guitar's wide acoustical range as a distraction from my reddened face. I found the music to be calming yet seductive at the same time.

I peered at Alexander through lowered lashes only to find he was still watching me. His stare was doing nothing to cool the mortifying flames refusing to leave my cheeks.

"This music is lovely," I finally said, attempting to break his unnerving observation.

"I thought it might appeal to you. It's a guitar compilation by Tadeusz Machalski."

"I never heard of him."

"No, I don't imagine you would have. I stumbled upon him playing in the streets of Venice a few years back. I listened to him play for hours before I finally bought one of his CDs."

"Venice, Italy?"

"The one and only," he confirmed with a smile.

"Wow, I'm jealous. I've always wanted to go to Italy," I said enviously.

"Maybe I'll take you one day."

He said it casually while assessing me with those irresistible sapphire blues. His ability to constantly take me by surprise was astounding, and I struggled not to look like a gaping fish while I digested his words.

Vacationing in Italy with Alexander Stone?

I hated to admit it, but the idea sounded appealing.

Don't even go there—bad idea.

"What is this restaurant?" I asked, choosing not to explore *that* avenue of conversation. "I didn't see a name outside."

"That's because it doesn't have one yet. Although, it seems like Matteo might have an idea now," he said dryly, a frown returning to his face.

"This is Matteo's restaurant? I thought this might be your place," I mused.

"Hell, no!" he exclaimed and let out a loud genuine laugh.

It was a full, throaty sound that was pleasant to my ears. It made him seem more human and not so much like the heavenly Adonis he normally portrayed. His laughter was contagious, and I found myself smiling.

And for the first time since my arrival, I relaxed a bit.

"Why do you say it like that? Why not own a restaurant?"

You seem to have a hand in just about everything else in this city.

"Restaurants aren't my thing. Way too much stress. Like I said before, real estate is what I do. I just own this building. Matteo is the crazy one. If he wants to tackle the food business, more power to him. He's been after me to come down to try some of his dishes before the grand opening," he told me, reaching for a bottle of cabernet sauvignon. "I thought this would be the perfect time to take him up on his offer. Plus, I wanted a bit of privacy tonight so that we could talk freely during our meeting."

A meeting, huh? Okay. I'll play along.

I studied him carefully as he poured the deep red into two Bordeaux glasses. I tried to read what he was thinking, but as usual, his expression was guarded, and I got nothing. I accepted the glass he held out for me.

"We couldn't talk freely in a restaurant full of people?" I asked, taking a slow sip of the wine. I typically preferred white wine, but the red was surprisingly good, and I savored the bite of the bold flavor on my tongue.

"Unfortunately, no—at least not without any interruption. I try to keep a low profile, but restaurants are tough. I have expensive tastes, and influential people tend to frequent the restaurants I like." He paused and frowned, his brow furrowing in aggravation. "Lately, it's been a bombardment of parasites from Wall Street trying to convince me to go public. The lack of privacy is rather annoying."

While his words may have seemed slightly arrogant, his tone was bitter and resentful. I was intrigued and wanted to question him further, but Matteo arrived with our appetizers, interrupting the conversation.

"Ah, here we are!" Matteo said as he placed two plates in the center of the table. "*Insalata Caprese* and *Antipasto Italiano.*" Using a serving fork, he began to place portions of the appetizers onto side dishes for both Alexander and me.

"This looks great. Thanks, Matt," Alexander said, taking a bite of smoked prosciutto. "Mmm. It tastes great, too."

I went for the *Caprese* salad first since fresh mozzarella was a weakness of mine. The cheese practically melted in my mouth, and the tomato was bursting with flavor. I nodded my head in approval.

"Very good!" Matteo exclaimed, obviously pleased his guests of honor were enjoying the first course. "*Buon appetito,*" he said with a slight bow and left us to enjoy the array of cold cuts and cheeses.

"I don't know much about the stock market, but wouldn't you make more money if you went public with your company?" I asked curiously, continuing the conversation where we left off as I enjoyed a second bite of the seasoned cheese.

"Money doesn't matter. I'd rather be my own boss. If I offered stock to the general public, I would have too many people to answer to. And as you pointed out earlier this afternoon, answering to others is not something I would do well. I prefer to be my own boss."

"It must really suck to be a millionaire," I sarcastically commented.

"Billionaire, Krystina," he corrected matter-of-factly. I raised my eyebrows, slightly aghast by his pompous statement.

"If you're trying to impress me, it's not working. Millions, billions—it makes no difference to me once you hit six zeros," I said sardonically.

"I'm not trying to impress you with money. I'm just stating a fact," he said without a hint of conceit. "Those additional zeros, as you put it, make a big difference in the social circles of New York. It means keeping my personal affairs private is a little more difficult, and that's something I'm not sure you're ready to handle."

Maybe I was intimidated over his billions. Or perhaps it was the way he spoke so matter-of-factly. Whatever the reason, I found myself feeling extremely bothered by this conversation all of a sudden, and I pursed my lips in annoyance.

"Why would I need to concern myself with your privacy?"

"We'll talk about that later," he said, dismissing my question with a wave of his hand. "I want you to tell me about yourself first."

"I'm sure my background check told you everything you need to know already," I said fractiously.

"Krystina, the background check I had done on you was very limited. It doesn't tell me personal aspects of your life."

The seconds ticked by as I scrutinized him, trying to find any sign of a hidden agenda. His face revealed nothing but patience and genuine interest. He didn't push me but instead just ate his *antipasti* quietly while he waited for me to speak.

I had to admit to myself, I was actually enjoying this very normal back and forth chit-chat we had going on. It was a nice change from all of our previous conversations. I supposed it wouldn't hurt to let go of a few minor irritations and indulge his curiosities a little bit.

"Alright. What do you want to know?" I finally gave in.

"Why don't you start with where you grew up?"

Interesting question.

I wasn't sure what I expected him to ask, but it certainly wasn't that.

"I was raised in Albany—the Clifton Park area to be exact, but nobody ever knows where that is. I lived there with my mother and stepfather until moving to New York with Allyson to attend college."

"Who's Allyson?"

"Allyson Ramsey, my roommate," I told him. "My mom didn't want me to move here, but I fought her tooth and nail. She wanted me to go to school someplace in Albany."

"What's wrong with New York?" he prodded.

"Oh, lots of things. Safety, the cost of tuition, New York is expensive—you name it, and she made it an argument. But I don't think any of those things were the real reasons behind her not wanting me to move here. To be honest, I don't think she wanted to cut the strings," I said with a shake of my head. "I'm an only child, and I was her whole world for a long time. But that was years ago, and what I think is irrelevant because she would never admit it. My mother has a way of blocking out things she doesn't want to remember."

"Mothers can certainly be that way," he agreed. I sensed a level of irony in his tone, and I wondered what his story was.

"What about your parents?" I asked, hoping to gain a bit of insight.

"They're dead," he responded flatly.

"Oh, I'm so sorry."

"Don't be. I'm not."

His lack of emotion was startling, and I was taken aback. My apology for his deceased parents was an automatic reaction—one anyone would have. But his expression was cold. Emotionless. For a brief moment, I thought I saw a flicker of regret in his eyes, but it was quickly masked, and I could only stare in wonder at his complete detachment.

Well, this is awkward. He's not sorry that his mother and father are dead! Who says things like that?

Matteo arrived with our dinner, breaking the uncomfortable silence that had settled in the room.

"Time for the main course. For you, my dear, Baked Eggplant *Parmigiana*, one of my specialties," Matteo bragged, setting a steaming plate before me and turning to Alexander. "And for you, my friend, Stuffed Red Pepper. *Delizioso*!"

"I'm sure both will be fantastic, Matt. Thanks," Alexander said somewhat coolly.

Matteo eyed him questioningly but didn't comment on Alexander's tone. Instead, he simply nodded and left us alone to enjoy our food. Once he was out of the room, the uneasiness between Alexander and I returned.

I was itching to know more about his dead parents, but I didn't know what I could say without sounding like I was prying. His blunt statement was perplexing. So rather than risk putting my foot in my mouth, I just ate my food and said nothing. I was probably better off not knowing the specifics anyway.

It's not my business. Curiosity killed the cat. More detail means an increased risk of attachment—time to change the subject.

I sat there pondering over what else we could talk about. The atmosphere had become so uncomfortable after his revelation, and I wasn't sure where to begin. In fact, the more I thought about it, the more I realized how little I actually knew Alexander. The only thing I had to go on were a few tidbits I read on the internet. He was a mystery, and I grappled with finding a safe topic of discussion.

I could bring up the reason I'm really here. We haven't talked about that yet.

My brow furrowed in concentration.

So why am I here?

He had said in the coffee shop he wanted me naked, yet he had been nothing but a polite gentleman since my arrival. There were no sexual insinuations, no coy remarks. Nothing. Surprisingly, I found myself disappointed and frustrated by his mannerly attitude. He wasn't playing his usual part.

"You've become very quiet, Krystina," Alexander commented after a long while. I glanced up at him to find he was watching me curiously. "I can tell you're thinking something. I can almost see the wheels spinning in your head."

It's time to cut to the chase.

I put my fork down next to my plate and leveled my eyes to his.

"Look, I'm fairly certain you don't want to talk about where I grew up or about your parents who–"

"The subject of my parents is off-limits. Never bring them up again," he said frostily, stopping me midsentence.

Personal details are private. Got it.

"Okay, I can respect that. Besides, it's probably better if we stopped playing show-and-tell. I want to get to the bottom of this supposed meeting, Alexander," I said, deliberately dropping the formalities for the first time.

"You can call me Alex."

"But that's not your name," I jokingly threw back in his face in an attempt to lighten the sudden somber mood. My efforts seemed to work because he afforded me a sexy lopsided grin.

"Touché," he said with a wink and reached over to pour us both more wine.

"Thank you," I accepted graciously. Making a mental note to slow down, I didn't take a sip of the refilled glass right away. A plan was starting to formulate in my head, and I needed my wits about me if I was going to play this right.

"I think I was pretty clear this afternoon at the café, Krystina," he said in response to my question.

It wasn't really an answer at all, and I began to understand his polite behavior. I had a nagging suspicion he was trying to feel me out.

Is he leaving it up to me to make the first move?

If that were indeed the case, then it was very atypical for Alexander. He had told me himself—he likes to be in control. Putting the ball in my court was obviously not what he was doing.

I eyed him warily, trying to decide if I was ready to push our so-called relationship to the next level. He had already laid out his employment expectations. That part was perfectly clear. It was his other proposal I needed to be careful of. Taking it slow was an absolute must, but I didn't know if I had the gumption to take the plunge back into the world of dating.

If I take charge from the beginning, then maybe I can control the pace. I can do that. How hard can it be?

Throwing all caution to the wind, I swallowed a huge gulp of wine, took a deep breath, and plunged ahead.

"Yes, you were very explicit, as I recall. I b-believe you said something about...um...wanting me naked," I faltered.

Epic fail. Could I have said it any more awkwardly? God, I suck at this.

"Is that going to be a problem for you?" he asked offhandedly.

Is it a problem?

His mouth quirked up in an impish smile, and he looked like he was enjoying some sort of wicked thought.

"Well, um..." I started, pursing my lips in a frown trying to will away the flush the crept up my neck and threatened to enflame my cheeks. "What happens if I say it is? Would I still get the job at Turning Stone?"

His eyes turned dark as I awaited his response. I held my breath in anticipation.

"Of course, you would. I believe you are more than qualified to handle the position. It would just be without the fringe benefits," he added shamelessly. "However, I'm warning you now—I always get what I want. I *will* fuck you eventually, Krystina."

He didn't bother to disguise the determined glitter of lust in his eyes. I let out my breath in a quiet hiss.

Now there's the Alexander I've grown accustomed to.

His direct approach was crude and alluring all at the same time, leaving me squirming in my seat—and not because I was offended, but because it was so *hot*. An ache began to form between my thighs, and the devil on my shoulder started doing fist pumps in the air.

Alexander allowed his gaze to drift lazily over me, causing excited butterflies to dance in my belly. I was thrilled he was back to his usual, salacious self. But even so, I knew I still had to be cautious. He was dangerous, and I was like a moth to a flame. I had to ease into this gradually or risk being burned.

"Mixing business with pleasure is risky. What happens if things don't work out with us personally?" I asked. "I don't want to end up jobless and back to square one."

"We're both adults, Krystina. And as long as we keep it casual, I don't think we'll have an issue with managing our business dealings."

"Well, I don't do casual sex if that's what you're after. I think two people should at least date a few times before jumping into bed," I replied evenly, proud I was able to keep the tremor out of my voice despite my racing heart.

"That's very unfortunate," he said, shaking his head back and forth.

"Why is that?"

"I don't date, Krystina. It tends to complicate things that are much better off kept simple."

Bullshit.

"Then explain the hundreds of redheads you're constantly photographed with," I spat out, just a little bit too harshly. It was a gut reaction, a defensive move based on instinct, and I fought the urge to slap a hand over my mouth. I heard the level of contempt in my voice and regretted it almost immediately.

This was not going the way I had planned, even if I was just winging it. I was the one to start this line of conversation, and being a bitch every time he said something I didn't like would get me nowhere.

"I must say, your own background check on *me* wasn't very accurate," he pointed out. His mouth twitched like he was trying to hold back a smile.

"I'm sorry, but I don't have a slew of connected people on my payroll. I had to make do with my trusty friend Google," I scoffed, although I was thoroughly embarrassed my slip up had inadvertently revealed I had researched him.

"You shouldn't believe all the filth that can be found online," he said, showing a hint of disgust beneath his calm demeanor. There was a cool gleam in his eyes, and his jaw tightened. "The things you've seen or heard about me are based on pure speculation. I'm a wealthy man, and I am expected to attend numerous functions, many of which require a date. I'm not sure if the *two* redheads you saw pictures of could classify as hundreds, but either way, they were mere acquaintances."

"So, you didn't sleep with either of them?" I questioned doubtfully, not that it should matter one little iota. After all, I had already committed myself to no personal details. But those curvy redheads were definitely more than tempting with their come-hither smiles, and I felt compelled to know the answer nonetheless.

"The answer to that is completely irrelevant, but I'll indulge in your curiosities. No, I did not fuck either woman," he openly admitted. His change of verbiage did little to help the trust factor. He must have sensed my disbelief because he let out a long sigh, then adapted a more placating tone. "You can think what you want, but I have very little in common with those women. Their needs are very different from mine. I'm a man with a variety of sexual interests, Krystina. Knowing that about myself, I deliberately stay away from women who don't share my desires and adhere to the rules I've set for myself. There are no false pretenses that way."

Rules?

I wasn't *that* far removed from the dating scene. He made his sexual exploitations sound like business arrangements.

"You know what? Forget I even asked. You make it all sound so damned complicated," I muttered, shaking my head.

"It's not complicated at all—at least until I met you. For some odd reason, I find myself breaking many of my rules when it comes to you."

"Such as?"

"Well, take tonight, for example. I just told you I don't do the dating thing, yet here we are. This is, in many ways, like a date—and well out of the norm for me."

"Is that why you keep referring to tonight as a meeting? Dating isn't in your rule book?" I asked tauntingly, rolling my eyes at him. "I mean, really. Even if you only go out with someone once, you have to have some sort of relevant conversation before jumping into bed. That's what defines a date. You can't just walk up to a girl and say, 'Hey baby, let's fuck.' It doesn't work like that."

"Don't be crude, Krystina."

"My, my. Aren't you the pot calling the kettle black?"

The right corner of his mouth twitched again, showing me he was fighting back a smile. However, I wasn't finding this conversation even remotely humorous. It was frustrating.

Scraping the last bit of food around on my plate, I processed everything he had told me over dinner. The plan that I had begun to construct in my head was turning into a complete flop. This was never going to work. He had made so many mysterious implications tonight—rules, privacy, undefined sexual preferences. Whenever I thought he was being forthright, he would say something that would throw me for a loop.

Am I really that naïve? What is he trying to tell me?

One thing was certain—if I wanted to explore this thing between us, whatever it might be, there would be no testing the waters first. But before I dived in head first, I needed some straight answers from him.

"Look, Alex. I'm not entirely sure why I decided to meet you tonight. The longer I sit here, the more I'm convinced this is all a bad idea. So please, give it to me straight. What exactly do you want? And no more guessing games, or else I walk," I impatiently asserted.

His head snapped back, and he sharply sucked in a breath. He almost looked as if I had offended him in some way. At that particular point, I didn't care.

"Krystina, I'm disappointed at the fact you think I'm playing games. I thought I was being honest. A little cautious maybe, but honest." He cocked his head to one side, waiting for me to respond.

"What do you expect me to think?" I lashed out, shaking my head in frustration. "You asked me here to discuss a job, but we have yet to do so. You want me naked, yet you don't date. You like to be in control, and you have rules. You have made reference to having a variety of sexual interests—whatever the hell *that* means. To be perfectly honest, you're leading me to believe you're some sort of freak in the sheets!"

His mouth pressed into a hard line, and he looked as if he were trying to decide on his choice of words. He leaned forward in his chair, and his sapphire blues narrowed. They held a fiendish glimmer, sharp with an animal-like hunger that made me suddenly afraid.

Goosebumps traveled up my spine as I waited for him to speak again. When he finally spoke, his tone was direct. No-nonsense. Upfront.

"I'm not a freak. I'm a Dominant."

13

Krystina

"You're a *what*?" I almost laughed out loud.

"A Dominant," he repeated, eyes piercing through me like knives, completely extinguishing any joke I may have wanted to make. "I like to be in control of every aspect of my life. That includes the woman I choose to take to bed. I demand complete and utter power over them. That's what I want from you, Krystina."

My eyebrows shot up to the ceiling. I should have been seriously disturbed by his words. Given my sordid past with the controlling Trevor, everything he was saying should have had me hightailing it out of here—and fast. Yet oddly, my skin tingled with delight at the mere thought of this man wielding total control over my body.

But the angel was jumping up and down in front of the cheering devil and screaming, *"DANGER, DANGER! Run, you stupid girl!"*

"Sorry, no can do. I already gave up two years of my life for a control freak. I won't do it again," I told him, but my words sounded weak in a pathetic attempt to protect myself. He looked at me curiously but didn't question what I was referring to.

"I'm not looking to control your whole life, just the sex part of it," he said nonchalantly with a shrug as he settled back into his chair. The lewd way he spoke threw me off balance once again, fanning the flames that had ignited in my gut.

"Really? Then what do you call the hijacking of my cellphone?" I said, trying to maintain some sense of balance by reminding him of our argument earlier that afternoon.

"The phone was a gift," he said impatiently. "Maybe I overstepped my bounds, but that was not my intention."

"No matter which way you spin it, it was a very controlling and assuming thing to do."

"Look, Krystina. I want you to remain who you are. I don't want some mindless puppet. I think that might be the reason why I'm so drawn to you," he paused, looking thoughtful for a moment. "If you agree to this, I will own you in the bedroom alone."

Alarms rang shrilly in my head, warning me off of this unpredictable man. But my body was still betraying me, and I had to fight the overwhelming need to hurdle across the table and start tearing at his clothes.

I wanted him to control me. To *own* me.

Perhaps it was the two glasses of wine thinking for me, but I had unconsciously made a decision somewhere along the line. Despite my many reservations, I no longer wanted to take this slow. I wanted to have sex with Alexander Stone. Here. Now.

Absolute panic set in, as the realization scared the hell out of me. I wasn't ready for that. For *this*.

"I think it's time I go," I announced and stood up abruptly.

"So soon? Why?" I had obviously shocked him by my sudden need to leave.

"Because..." I hesitated.

Because you confuse me, and I can't think when I'm around you.

But I couldn't say the words out loud. Instead, I grabbed my purse, slung it over my shoulder, and said, "Thank you for dinner, Alex."

Alexander stood and came over to my side of the table.

"Krystina...I..." he started. His voice sounded strained, and I looked up, almost unwillingly, into his painstakingly beautiful blues. I waited for him to finish what he was going to say, but he just stared at me, expression bleak with uncertainty.

What is he so unsure about?

It was baffling.

"What is it, Alex?" I asked, my tone coming out clipped with impatience.

"Have dinner with me again tomorrow," he said, suddenly taking hold of my hands and entwining his fingers through mine. I could see the pulse pumping at his neck, the firm set of determination in his jaw. There would be no denying this man, but I had to try at least.

"I don't think that's a good idea, Alex. I need to go home, and... I just need to *think*."

He took a step closer, the predatory look in his eyes returning. His nearness sent my heart racing, causing blood to thrum loudly in my ears. I could feel the heat coming off his body, his delicious scent taking over my senses, wafting tantalizingly in my nose and making my head spin. He was so close. I could feel his warm breath mingling with my own, lips only mere inches away from mine.

"Alright. If that's what you really want," he said huskily. "But when you get home, I want you to think about what it's going to take for me to get inside of you."

"Vulgarity is not going to help–"

He left me no time to react, cutting off my words as his mouth covered mine.

Holy hell. Alexander Stone is kissing me.

His mouth was tender, with just the right amount of pressure. It was soft. Delicious. And everything I had imagined it would be.

Without warning, the kiss deepened, his mouth demanding more. He kissed me with a passion I had never felt before. Nobody had ever kissed me this way. Heat exploded through my veins. My mouth surrendered beneath his as I returned his kiss with newfound passion—a passion that had been long dormant yet filled with an intensity I hadn't known was in me. I moaned into his mouth, and he pushed his tongue past my parted lips, tasting me with gentle flicks.

He pulled my hips sharply against him, forcing my back and neck into a slight arch so he could have better access to my mouth. I found myself reaching up to run my fingers through his soft waves, pulling him closer to me and deepening the kiss, encouraging him to take more. He groaned against my lips, the vibration causing my nipples to stiffen in response. He ravished me like he was a starving man who couldn't get enough.

His fingers tightened on my hips, then moved around to my backside, effectively crushing me against his hard torso. Forgotten were my reservations, my doubts, and my hesitations. All that existed was Alexander's kiss, all-consuming, chasing away the pains of my past. A heaviness began to build in my chest and welled in my throat. I felt as if an enormous weight had lifted from my shoulders, and I almost sobbed from the relief. It felt so good just to *feel* again.

Much to my regret, Alexander broke the kiss and pulled slightly away. I was left breathless. His kiss was beyond intense—it was electrifying and charged me to the very depths of my core.

"God help me, Krystina. I want you. I shouldn't, but I do," he murmured, his voice hoarse and ragged, sapphire blues a blazing inferno of desire. I took a deep breath and closed my eyes, inhaling his scent that was already becoming so familiar.

A noise from the kitchen startled me and caused me to take a step back, forcing away Alexander's fiery gaze and lifting the fog that seemed to settle over my brain.

I was disappointed when Matteo stepped into the room, yet almost grateful for the distraction. I desperately needed a moment to absorb what just happened, and being pressed up against a heated Alexander Stone certainly wouldn't help.

"Leaving so soon?" Matteo asked, glancing at my purse that was still slung over my shoulder. "What about dessert?"

"No, unless Krystina wants something, I think we're all set.

Krystina?" Alexander asked, looking at me. My legs were trembling so bad I thought I might collapse.

Speak, Cole! Speak!

"I'm good. Thank you for everything. It was wonderful," I said with a shaky smile.

"Good, I'm glad you enjoyed it!" Matteo appreciated, oblivious to the static current crackling in the air.

Alexander gave Matteo a light slap on the back. "Thanks, man. I knew you wouldn't disappoint. Everything was amazing! I can't wait until you get the place opened."

"No thanks needed. This restaurant would still be a dream if it were not for you. I owe you, my friend," Matteo said sincerely. Watching the easy interaction between the two men made me realize they were precisely that—friends. Their natural camaraderie showed they were more than just business associates.

"Don't sweat it, Matt. Now go home. I'll take care of locking up the place," Alexander offered.

"I'm just going to take care of the dishes, and then I'll go. Krystina," Matteo said, turning to me and taking my hand as he had earlier in the night. "It was a pleasure meeting you, my dear."

He placed a soft kiss on the backside of my hand. His lips lingered just a little too long. I was still so keyed up from Alexander's kiss that my cheeks instantly went pink at the intimacy of the gesture. Matteo looked up at Alexander and flashed him a look even Satan himself would be jealous of.

"Get lost, Matt!" Alexander said with a scowl. Matteo laughed and released my hand.

"You make it too easy!" Matteo chuckled. He made quick work of collecting our dinner dishes and exited the room. I could hear him laughing all the way to the kitchen.

"You still want to leave," Alexander said once Matteo was out of earshot. It was a statement, but his eyes were questioning.

I didn't want to leave, but in the end, I knew it would be safer than staying here and facing the blatant sexuality between us. Much safer.

"Yes. I really should go," I said, summoning up the will from the depths of who knows where.

Alexander acknowledged me with a nod and pulled his cellphone from his pocket.

"Hale, we'll be out in two," he said in a clipped voice to someone over the phone before pocketing it again.

"Who's Hale?" I asked curiously.

"My driver. The one who brought you here tonight. Come on, I'll walk you out," he said, taking hold of my hand.

We made our way through the empty restaurant to the front doors. When we stepped outside into the cool night air, I wrapped my arms around myself to ward off the evening chill. Alexander's car was waiting at the curb to take me home.

"Hale will be by your place to pick you up tomorrow, same time," Alexander said as he opened the door of the SUV.

"Alex..." I trailed off as he placed a finger over my lips to silence me. I shook my head in a forced attempt to deny him.

"Tomorrow," he repeated seriously. "My place. No frills this time. No fancy dinner. Just drinks and conversation. A lot was left unsaid tonight. We'll talk some more and see where it takes us."

"This is a bad idea, Alex. You don't know anything about me. I'll be too much trouble for someone like you," I said quietly, trying to dissuade him once more.

"Baby, I already know you'll be nothing *but* trouble for me," he said with a chuckle, leaning down to place a light kiss on my forehead. "But the taste of your lips has persuaded me to go for it anyways. Have a goodnight, Miss Cole."

"Good night, Mr. Stone," was the only thing I could muster before climbing into the SUV.

I looked up at him once I was seated. That devilish gleam was back in his eyes.

"Wear a skirt again tomorrow. When I look at those long legs of yours, I like to imagine them wrapped around me," he said with a wink before closing the door of the vehicle.

Alexander

I WATCHED THE CAR PULL AWAY, FRUSTRATED THAT THINGS ENDED SO suddenly. Just when I thought I was starting to close the gap between us, she made for the door.

I scared her. She thinks I'm a freak in the sheets.

A smile tugged at the edges of my mouth after recalling her terminology.

Oh, baby. You have no idea.

Krystina didn't know how close to the mark she had hit. My usual direct tactics weren't going to work. I would have to tread more carefully. One wrong move and I'd blow it. I needed to change the game if I wanted to find my way into Krystina.

"Well, well...Stone dining with a woman. I thought I'd never see the day," I heard Matteo say from behind me. I turned around to find him leaning against the doorjamb of the restaurant entrance, scratching his head in disbelief.

"Christ, not you too. I've already been getting sideways looks from Hale. It's not what you think, Matt," I weakly denied.

"I gotta admit, when you called to ask me to set this night up, I was a little surprised. I just didn't say anything because I wanted to see this girl for myself first," he harassed with a knowing smirk.

I glared at him.

"Weren't you supposed to be going home?" I snarled. However, Matteo knew my words carried no real heat.

"I was just on my way out. But I'll stay and have a drink with you if you want?"

"Make it a stiff one," I said and followed him back inside.

I pulled one of the stools down from the bar and took a seat. Matteo ducked down behind the counter, and I could hear the clinking of glass. When he stood, I saw he had managed to produce a couple of old-fashioned lowball glasses and a bottle of Knob Creek, despite his limited stock.

"The liquor license just came through, and I have yet to order the really good stuff. It's not the expensive reserve you normally drink, but it'll still do the job," he joked. After he poured us each three fingers, I took the glass and downed it in one shot without even flinching. Matteo's eyebrows went up. "Wow. Last I checked, bourbon was supposed to be sipped. This woman must have really gotten to you."

I narrowed my eyes at him, refusing to comment. He took the glass and refilled it, but I pushed it away.

"I don't want anymore."

I was annoyed. Aggravated. Frustrated for so many reasons, but I couldn't pinpoint what was bothering me the most. The last thing I needed was another drink.

"Alright. Then what do you want? Besides the *bella donna*," he added, reminding me of just how beautiful Krystina truly was.

I eyed him ruefully, trying to determine how much I wanted him to know. Matteo and I had a business arrangement, but first and foremost, he was a longtime friend. He was a keen observer, and he was smart. I knew I could count on him to cut out the bullshit and give it to me straight.

"She bugs me, Matt," I admitted bluntly. He started choking on the swallow of drink he had just taken.

"Come again?" he asked incredulously.

"I want her, but she fights me every step of the way. Normally I'd just say forget it and move on, but I can't with her. The more she pushes, the more I want her."

"I can see why you do. She's young and smokin' hot. What's your dilemma?"

"She's..." I struggled with putting my thoughts into words, which was another rare oddity for me. "She's work. She's stubborn and snappy. Strong, yet she seems fragile. I don't know..."

"So that's it. For once, you can't weasel your way into someone's head," Matteo said with an easy laugh.

"No, it's more than that. I just haven't figured it out yet. I get the impression she's got a story. A past. I just don't know what it is."

"Well, let me give you some advice then. She's not for you, man. She doesn't strike me as the type to be into your thing. She seems too innocent. *Candida*. You'd better be careful with that," he warned.

Matteo had hit the nail squarely on the head. Krystina was captivating, so much so I found myself paralyzed with lust, fantasizing about her almost to the point of obsession. However, the look of total disbelief that came over her face when I told her I was a Dominant said she wasn't worldly to my more unconventional ways.

"I'm not a fucking moron, Matt. But I don't think she's that innocent," I told him, trying to convince myself as much as him. "She just needs training, that's all."

"Why would you want the hassle when you can just hit one of your clubs? There are plenty of willing Subs there."

I frowned at that, as I had been asking myself the same question for days. If I had a bug to get out of my system, Club O was the simple solution. The exclusive BDSM nightclub would have a plethora of submissive women ready to play. And it was safe. The women there appreciated the need for discretion.

"That's just it. I don't want just another Sub."

"*Si, si.* But you must remember, Krystina may not be willing. Have you thought of that, my friend? Have you told her what you are?"

"I did. She wasn't the most receptive, but I could sway her easily enough," I said with a shrug.

"You are like an ape. Such arrogance you have," Matteo chuckled, shaking his head back and forth.

"An ape? Coming from a hairy Italian?"

"Ah, now you only wish you had this chest! I am a natural Dominant! All the ladies bow to me!" Matteo began beating his chest like a gorilla, ready to exert his power.

"Yeah, right! You—a Dominant! You don't have the balls for it. Not enough confidence," I goaded. However, another thought came to mind, interrupting our wisecracks and causing me to sober.

"What?" Matteo asked after seeing my change of face.

"If this were all about confidence, it would be easy. But the situation is more complicated than that."

"How so?"

"Krystina questions everything. And I mean *everything*. That alone will make her a terrible Sub. She won't be easy to train, that's for sure," I paused and eyed up the second bourbon Matteo had poured for me. Changing my mind, I reached for it and sipped it slowly for a minute before continuing. "The subject of my parents came up tonight. It was by pure happenstance, but I practically bit her head off to stop her questions. I'm sure I only succeeded in creating more."

"If you are going to see this woman regularly, your background is going to come up. You won't be able to keep it buried."

"It's not a regular thing. You know me. We're just talking," I tried to deny.

Matteo raised his eyebrows, showing his disbelief.

"If you say so," he said with a smirk.

"It doesn't matter how you want to classify us. Just knowing what I know about Krystina, she won't drop it. My parents will come into question again, of that I'm sure. It complicates things because of Justine. I literally just diffused one situation. The last thing I need is another. It's my job to protect her."

"You can't always be there to shield Justine from her monsters," Matteo advised sympathetically. He knew my sister and was one of the very few who knew about our past. But despite his knowledge, he would never fully get it because he hadn't lived it. I shook my head in frustration.

"They are *our* monsters, Matt. You know that almost as well as I do. I'm just better at facing them than Justine is."

Matteo nodded his understanding.

"It looks like you have some decisions to make, so let me offer you another piece of advice. I think Krystina may be more innocent than you want to admit, but she doesn't seem gullible. Secrets never stay hidden forever. If you want to make a go with her, you shouldn't tempt the Fates."

I smiled wryly at my friend, the irony of his words like a bitter pill I had been forced to swallow.

The Fates.

Those fickle bitches had never looked favorably on me. I had learned early on to control my destiny and use my gut to point me in the right direction. It had yet to fail me, which was why I was facing the current predicament.

My instinct told me I shouldn't want someone like Krystina Cole. I was not the right man for her. Yet, what I shouldn't want and what I wanted had become two very different things.

14

Krystina

When I arrived back at my apartment after dinner with Alexander, I found Allyson alone on the couch with a bowl of popcorn and a glass of wine. The television was off, and the only light came from the kitchen. This was not a good sign. I kicked my shoes off into the corner of the front entryway and moved into the living room.

"Hey, where's Jeremy?" I asked casually, trying to assess how bad the situation was.

"He left a little while ago."

"Oh. I thought you two were going to see a movie."

"We were. Until Jeremy turned into a chauvinistic pig," she spat out loathsomely.

"You guys seemed to be having a good time when I left. What did he do?"

"It's not what he did—it's what he said. We got talking about you being out with Stone tonight. Jeremy thinks it's a good thing you found a financially stable man. A man like him would be able to take good care of you properly. Apparently, he thinks women should stay home and take care of the house," she finished with a scowl.

Yikes.

Rule number one—don't ever insult women's rights in front of Allyson. Sometimes I would swear she was a direct decedent of Susan B. Anthony. Not that I agreed with what Jeremy had said, but I sort of felt bad for the guy. Allyson easily riled when it came to this sort of thing. I could only imagine what she had said once her temper unleashed.

"Did you let him have it?" I said with a cringe.

"I yelled something along the lines of not being the barefoot and pregnant type and asked him to leave. So, he did," she finished.

"And that's it?"

"I may have had a few other choice words for him."

"Oh, Ally. Are you okay?"

"I'll be fine. It's better his opinions came out sooner rather than later. For now, distract me. I want to hear about your date with Stone."

"It wasn't a date. It was a *meeting*," I told her, deliberately emphasizing the last word.

"Sure. Whatever. Tell me about your meeting," she corrected to appease me.

"It was nice," I alluded.

"Come on, Krys. You have to give me more than that. What did he say about the job?"

"Oh, he—" I started but came up short. "Actually, we never talked about job details."

"Because it was a date," she concluded.

"It wasn't a date, Ally. Alexander isn't the dating kind. He told me as much himself. But you were right about one thing," I admitted, plopping down in the overstuffed chair across from her. "He does want me. And not just as an employee."

"Told you so!" Allyson exclaimed with a smug look of satisfaction. However, her face turned serious almost immediately before she asked, "What are you going to do about it, Krys? Do *you* want *him*?"

"No...well yes, sort of. It's really complicated. I can't get a read on him. The guy talks in riddles. I let him kiss me, though."

"Well, that's progress at least," she said with a laugh. "But back it up. Tell me how everything happened from the beginning. Maybe I can help you solve some of the mysterious Stone's riddles."

I told her everything from the cellphone delivery, his surprise visit at the coffee shop, to our dinner conversations. Even after repeating it all, I was still confused.

"I don't know what to do with this, Ally."

"There's nothing to do. Just go with it. It's time, Krys. Accept the job. Go out with Stone. Let yourself be wined and dined for heaven's sake. Don't overthink it and just enjoy it."

"Maybe you're right, but I'm scared, you know? Sometimes I feel like Trevor was only yesterday. Other times, it feels like it was a lifetime ago. I don't know if I can put myself out there again. Every time I think I'm ready, I go into a panic."

"Come here, doll," she said, patting the couch cushion next to her. I moved to sit down beside her, and she pulled my head down to her shoulder, rubbing her hand over my hair. "I know you went through hell, but not everything has to have a nightmarish ending. So, what if your picket fence went up in flames? You'll build a new one someday. But until that day comes, let yourself have a little fun. You're never going to get over what happened with Trevor until you take the next step. At the very least, Stone is loaded. He's sure to show you a good time. Take advantage of the V.I.P. treatment. I mean, come on! The guy sent a *car* for you!"

"Hmm...Alexander would definitely be able to keep things interesting," I said contemplatively. I looked up at her and debated whether or not I should tell her exactly *how* interesting Alexander could keep things. "I need to get over how much he intimidates me."

"Why? He didn't do anything to hurt you, did he?" she asked, pulling away and sounding alarmed.

"Oh, no. It's nothing like that. In fact, it might not be him at all and more about my fear of the unknown. At the end of dinner, he said he was a Dominant—whatever that means. All I know is I got all panicky and made for a quick exit. That's when he kissed me, and now, I don't know what to think," I finished.

"Whoa! He said he's a what?"

"A Dominant."

"Oh, no. This isn't good, Krys," she warned, her eyes as wide as a deer in headlights. She shook her head rapidly back and forth. "I mean, I'm all for you getting out there and dating again. Hell, I wouldn't care if you made the rounds with the entire Yankees team. But you can't go jumping in headfirst with someone like—"

A knock at the door interrupted her.

"Hold that thought," I told her as I got up from the couch to answer the door.

I found a very distraught Jeremy on our doorstep.

"Is Allyson here? I really need to talk to her," he said pleadingly.

I looked at the man and immediately felt sympathy for him. He seemed genuinely upset. But Allyson had been extremely irritated when I had come home. Letting Jeremy in the house now would be disastrous.

"I'm not so sure that's a good—" I started.

"I don't think there's anything to talk about," I heard Allyson bark from behind me. When I turned to look at her, her face was awash with fury. "Besides, Krys and I were in the middle of something. You're interrupting."

"Allyson, I'm really sorry. Please talk to me."

"I think we did enough talking earlier, Jeremy."

"You misunderstood me. You cut me off before I could explain. Please, just give me five minutes," he begged.

I was getting whiplash from the back and forth. The poor guy was practically begging. They needed to be alone to talk this out. After the night I just had, I was in no state of mind to play referee if it came down to it.

"Ally, we can finish this later. You and Jeremy go ahead."

"No. I want to finish our conversation," Allyson said fervently.

"And we will tomorrow. You two have stuff to work out. I'm tired anyway, and I have to work in the morning."

Allyson looked torn, eyes shifting between Jeremy and me. I placed my hand on her arm for reassurance.

"Alright, Krys. We'll catch up tomorrow," she finally conceded. She leaned over to give me a quick peck on the cheek. "Go get some sleep."

"Night," I said to her, then nodded to Jeremy, who returned it in kind.

As I headed to my bedroom, I gave in to a big yawn. It wasn't just a line I fed Allyson and Jeremy as an excuse to give them time alone—I really was tired. Since meeting Alexander Stone, my nights had been full of nothing but restless sleep.

I climbed into bed, meandering over what I should do about tomorrow night. Typically, I would have run screaming in the opposite direction from a man like Alexander and wouldn't even consider exploring that avenue of danger.

Yet, he had laid the world at my feet—a job offer I had been desperately waiting for and an ending to this burning need to be with him. And when his lips touched mine, my insides seemed to turn into melting wax, taking any thought or reasoning away from me. He didn't know it, but he held some sort of power over me, and that terrified me.

I thought about Allyson's outlook on life. Sometimes I wished I could be more like her. She was so carefree, jumping from one guy to the next, living in the moment. I could have resented her insouciant way of life, but I didn't. I loved her too much. Her unattached lifestyle suited her, and she was happy.

Her way of looking at things was probably right. I should just go for it and have a little fun. I had been alone for a long time. Maybe a quick romp in the sack would be good for me. I would have to remember to remain detached, of course. I wasn't looking to be struck by one of Cupid's arrows. It was just sex, not some lifelong commitment. As long as I remembered that, it shouldn't be too difficult.

I didn't need or want anything more, and neither did he.

THE FOLLOWING DAY BEGAN WITH THE USUAL BORING ROUTINE. I went to work, fulfilled the duties at my oh-so-monotonous job, and hit the gym.

However, throughout my unexciting afternoon, I contemplated the events of the previous evening. For the first time, I was actually thankful for the mindless tasks my current job offered. That, combined with the willingness of a red punching bag to accept the brunt of my frustrations, I was allowed time to think.

Stripped down to nothing but a pair of yoga shorts and a sports bra, I went to town on the bag, seeking its cathartic release with every blow.

Allyson's words echoed in the back of my mind.

"Let yourself have a little fun...."

I spun around and struck the bag with a forceful back fist.

I recalled the conversation I had with Alexander over dinner.

"I will fuck you eventually, Krystina...."

I turned again and landed a powerful roundhouse kick.

I could still see the flash of desire in his eyes when I left him. I could still feel the heat of his fervently intense gaze.

I inflicted another punch onto the cylindrical leather bag.

My lips tingled every time I remembered the sensation of his mouth on mine, and my body ached for him. But most importantly, I remembered how good it was to simply feel *something* again.

Forty-five minutes later, I was covered in sweat. I delivered a final blow to the heavy bag and reached a monumental decision. I was going to listen to Allyson's advice and move forward with Alexander. Whether it was just sex, just the job, or both—it didn't matter. My mind was made up. It was time I stop being afraid of the future and allow it to simply happen.

I grabbed a towel to wipe the sweat off my face and neck, collected my belongings, and headed for home.

And that's when my day finally began to get more interesting.

15

Krystina

I was never one to primp and prune for a lavish amount of time, but I sanctioned a solid two hours to prepare for my night out with Alexander. I wanted to look perfect for whatever was to come.

I fretted over wearing a skirt that was just the tiniest bit too short and worried about how to tame my crazy hair. Then, at some point during a wild frenzy of ripping apart of my closet in search of the perfect shoes, it occurred to me I never officially gave Alexander an answer about going out with him tonight, and I hadn't heard from him all day. A part of me wondered if I was wasting my time getting ready for an evening that might not even take place.

However, the thought quickly passed, as I felt confident Alexander was a man of his word. He had said his driver would be here at six o'clock, and I was sure he wouldn't bail on me.

Prepared and ready to go, I took the stairs down rather than the elevator, anticipation filling me with a restless sort of energy. I was surprised by how much I was looking forward to the night out. A giddy smile curved my lips as I made my way across the lobby of my apartment complex. As usual, Philip was at the door to greet me with his friendly smile.

"Looking awfully sassy tonight, Miss Cole. That's the second time I've seen that fancy ride outside. Is it here for you again?" asked Philip, eyeing me up and down with one eyebrow raised.

"It sure is, Phil," I said, blushing under the older man's scrutiny. I tried to discreetly tug at the hem of my black miniskirt, feeling very aware of its short length. I got the impression Phil disapproved of my clothing choice, even though he didn't comment about it. He was so dad-like, always looking out for the women in the complex. I often wondered if his watchful personality was the reason why my mother and stepfather were so insistent on me living here.

"Have a good time. And be careful," he warned, placing a gentle hand on my shoulder.

Why is everyone always telling me to be careful?

"Don't worry, Phil. I'm a big girl. I can take care of myself."

After giving him a reassuring smile, I moved past him and stepped through the door he held open for me.

I felt a sense of déjà vu as I headed down the walkway. Alexander's driver was waiting for me outside of the sleek black Porsche, just as he had less than twenty-four hours earlier. However, this time, I was taken by surprise when Hale opened the SUV door. Alexander was seated inside the car.

He was looking down at his phone but looked up at my arrival. I briefly saw a look of relief flash across his face.

Was he worried I would stiff him?

"Good evening, Krystina," Alexander drawled out slowly.

A bad-boy smile curled the edges of his mouth, and his gaze traveled leisurely down the entire length of my body. The heat in his eyes caused butterflies to quiver in my stomach. I nervously tugged down the edges of my skirt. For the second time since putting the article of clothing on, I felt very self-conscience over my bare legs teetering on heels that were just a little too high.

"Alexander," I greeted, nerves causing my voice to sound slightly breathy.

"You look amazing, Krystina. Stop pulling at your skirt," Alexander scolded, climbing out of the vehicle. Then, turning to his driver, he said, "I'll call you when we're ready, Hale."

"Yes, Mr. Stone," Hale said, all official-like.

So, the silent driver was capable of speech after all.

That was the first time I had ever heard him speak, as my previous interaction with him had been so reserved and formal, with only a few short nods used for communication. The raspy voice he revealed suited the persona I envisioned him to have. In fact, I half expected him to salute Alexander before he turned back toward the car.

"Ready for what?" I questioned, looking back and forth between Alexander and the Porsche. "I thought we were going to your place."

"We will eventually. It's a nice night, and I thought we would walk for a bit. Although, you should go back up and change your shoes first," he advised, looking down at my feet and frowning.

"What's wrong with my shoes?"

"You won't be comfortable walking more than a short distance in heels that high."

"I'll be fine," I said, albeit stubbornly. But in all honesty, I secretly wished for a pair of sneakers. My stylish four-inchers were definitely not made for an evening stroll.

"If you think so." He looked skeptical but didn't push the issue any further. Instead, he set his hand on the small of my back, and we began to walk.

"That's quite an impressive ride you have there," I observed, pointing to the SUV as Hale pulled it away from the curb and merged into traffic. "Is that a Turbo or a Turbo S?"

"Cayenne Turbo S," he said proudly. But I noticed his slight hesitation before he continued. "Expensive cars are a weakness of mine."

I glanced up at him and was able to detect a cautious smile on his face through the dim lighting of the street lamps. I was surprised by his hesitancy. He was normally so sure of himself.

"No need to be shy about that guilty pleasure with me. I'm

used to the car obsession. Frank, my stepfather, is fascinated with anything that has four wheels."

"I'm not shy. I'm just careful—I don't want to be accused of flaunting my money," he teased, poking me lightly in the side and causing me to jump.

Hmm, this is interesting...the playful side of Alexander.

"I could probably tell you something about every make and model of car out there because of him. Everything I know is because of his non-stop chatter at the dinner table growing up."

"What do you know about the Turbo S?" he asked somewhat dubiously. If he was trying to test me, this was one test I'd be sure to ace.

"Well, where should I begin? I know the hefty price tag packs five hundred fifty horsepower and is powered by a four-point eight-liter twin-turbo V8 engine. It can go from zero to sixty miles per hour in only four point three seconds, maxing out at one hundred seventy-five miles per hour. It has—" I stopped short when I saw Alexander was staring open-mouthed at me.

"You sound like you're reading from a spec sheet. Even I don't know those specifics off the top of my head! You got all of that from dinner conversation?" he asked incredulously.

"Yeah, sort of. Plus, I've had a car crush on anything with a Porsche logo since I was thirteen years old," I confessed with a slight shrug.

"You continue to surprise me, Miss Cole," he murmured. "It makes me wonder about what else you may be hiding from me."

"Frank owns a bunch of car dealerships back home. Car stats were sort of ingrained into me. It's really no big secret."

"It seems like you're fond of your stepfather. Do you have a good relationship with him?" he asked, guiding me around the corner onto Fifth Avenue.

"Oh, yeah—I don't have any issues with Frank. He has always been very good to me, but my mother is who I'm always battling with. She can be rather difficult at times, and that's putting it mildly."

"How so?"

I took a deep breath and tried to think of the easiest way to describe my mom.

"She's just bitter all the time. Really negative, you know? It's almost like she has something to prove. It's hard to explain if you don't know her."

"Maybe I'll meet her one day," he said easily.

"Oh, no. You don't want to meet my mother. She's stubborn and overbearing, to say the least. A part of me would swear she hates men. Her past is somewhat...well, tainted. Do you know that expression about a woman who's been scorned? That's her. I almost feel bad for Frank sometimes. It's a small wonder he's put up with her for so long."

"Oh, I don't know. She sounds like someone I'd find interesting," he said with a wink.

I watched him for a moment before realizing the hidden meaning behind his teasing. I was, in a sense, describing myself.

I felt the blood drain from my face as the comprehension dawned. It was like taking a blow to the head. Alexander probably didn't realize how close to the mark he had hit. At some point in time, I had become like my mother—untrusting, bitter, and resentful toward the entire male species. And while I loved my mother dearly, I did not want to spend the rest of my life sharing her negativities.

How could I have not seen it before? I'm miserable—just like her.

"Krystina, are you okay?" I looked up to see Alexander searching my face imploringly.

"I'm fine. Why do you ask?" I questioned innocently, trying to shake off the unsettling emotions raining down me.

"You just got really quiet all of a sudden."

I didn't offer him a reply, as I could not formulate any sort of response at that moment. No words could describe what I was feeling. I could only shrug and act unconcerned, and I was glad when Alexander didn't press the issue. This was a whole subject I needed to evaluate for myself—alone, without his speculative gaze.

"I haven't been here in ages," he said as we passed under the Washington Square Arch.

"This park is one of my favorite places. It's one of the reasons why I fell in love with New York—it's so full of life. There's always something going on in Washington Square," I said wistfully, taking in the activity around us.

"Yep, the place sure has character all right. I'm pretty sure the guy sitting over there feeding the birds is in the exact same place he was when I was here last," Alexander said with an air of disdain, nodding his head to a man sitting on a bench with pigeons dancing all around him.

"Oh, come on! The pigeon man gives this place charm! Besides, he's better than the lady who feeds the squirrels out of her purse."

"A woman who feeds squirrels?" he asked, features pinched in disgust. I started laughing at his repulsed expression.

"You don't get out much, do you?" I joked, then laughed again when he scowled. I tugged at his hand and led him to a park bench. "Come over here. We can sit, and people watch."

"What's to watch?" he asked, taking a seat beside me.

"Have you always lived in New York City?" I answered back with my own question.

"Yeah, why do you ask?"

"Because people who have lived here their entire lives tend to be immune to the charm around them. See that kid over there?" I asked, pointing to a young boy strumming a guitar under a tree. "Or the man just down the way with the puppets? You never know what you're going to see here. That's why it's fun. You can just sit back and enjoy the show."

We sat quietly and watched people come and go, a distant harmonica and the splash of the water fountain adding sound to the quiet evening.

After a while, a damp chill settled in the air, as the sun had completely set for the night. I reached down to rub my hands up and down my legs.

"You're getting cold," he observed. "Let's get going."

I nodded my agreement. Walking hand in hand, we started making our way back through the park.

I glanced down at our entwined fingers.

This is strange. He's acting like we're a couple.

Keeping in mind we were very much *not* a couple, I removed my hand from his. I put my hands in my sweater pockets and made a show of feigning a chill. Alexander didn't seem to notice my withdrawal but rather wrapped his arm around my shoulder as if he were trying to warm me. My attempt at keeping a bit of distance between us had clearly failed.

When we reached the Arch, he pulled his phone from his pocket.

"Washington Square. Near the Arch," he barked into the mouthpiece before pocketing the phone again.

"You should probably be a little nicer to Hale. If I end up working for you, I certainly wouldn't want you to talk like that to me."

"Not *if*, Krystina. *When* would be more accurate," he corrected.

"Confident, are we?"

"You start on Monday."

"Monday? I can't start that soon! I have to give Wally's at least two weeks' notice and—"

"A week from Monday then. That's more than sufficient," he stated as if what he was saying was completely sensible. When we reached the Arch, I stopped walking and turned to face him.

"Alex, I haven't even accepted your offer yet!" I said, my exasperation clear. I all but stomped my foot like a two-year-old.

"There's no need to keep going around and around about this, Krystina. I've already spoken to Walter Roberts. It's a done deal. Now, are you going to ruin the night, or are you going to get into the car?"

Speechless, I could only stare in shock at him for a moment before realizing Hale had pulled up to the curb with our ride.

Rather than argue about it on the sidewalk, I conceded to Alexander's point and begrudgingly turned to climb into the SUV.

The ride to Alexander's was short, but the silent trip felt like forever. I could feel the waves of tension rolling off me. I didn't want to fight, yet I couldn't help but be more than just a little bit vexed over the situation. I had planned to accept the job at Turning Stone but would have preferred the opportunity to do so on my terms rather than have it assumed for me.

I need to get over it. There's no sense in letting a technicality spoil the evening. The end result is the same.

I focused my attention on my hurting feet instead, sore from walking too far in heels. Partially slipping off a shoe, I reached down to rub the ball of my foot. Comfort before fashion had always been my rule, and I was paying the price for my stupidity tonight.

"Dammit, Krystina. I knew I should have made you change your shoes," Alexander swore, lips pursed in annoyance.

"Sorry, Jimmy Choo's got the best of me today," I said wryly. "Normally, I know better, but I didn't think we'd walk so much. I'm fine, really."

"We're almost to my place. You can put your feet up once we get inside," he said irritably. He was evidently unhappy with my lack of practicality.

I only wore them for your benefit!

I rolled my eyes and almost said the words aloud, but the car came to a halt just then, signaling our arrival.

I glanced out the window to see a towering condominium complex. Hale came around to the side of the car and opened the door for Alexander and me. When we stepped out of the vehicle, a brisk wind slapped me in the face, and I shivered from the assault. I could smell rain in the air, and I knew it wouldn't be long before Mother Nature replaced her generously warm October temperatures with harsh winter winds. Alexander and I hurried into the building.

The lobby of the building was very swank-looking, with its marble floors and gold embellishments throughout. A young man, wearing what looked like a bellhop uniform, was changing the trash bag of a garbage can in a nearby corner. When he glanced up and saw us approaching, he immediately dropped the bag and scrambled over.

"Mr. Stone! I'm so sorry, sir! I didn't know you pulled up, or else I would have—" he began, but Alexader interrupted him.

"Don't worry, Jeffrey. Finish what you were doing," Alexander assured and waved him away. Jeffrey anxiously began fumbling in his pockets.

"At least let me get the elevator for you and your guest! I have your key card somewhere..." he trailed off, still frantically searching. Alexander watched him patiently for a moment or two before flashing his own keycard for Jeffrey to see. The frazzled young man paled. "Oh, no. If my boss finds out about this, he'll kill me!"

"Your boss is on my payroll. I assure you, your secret is safe with me."

"Thank you, Mr. Stone," Jeffrey said, seeming somewhat doubtful. He hesitantly nodded his appreciation, then returned to his task of taking out the trash.

Alexander led me over to a bank of elevators. I raised my eyebrows in surprise when he swiped his keycard through a slot labeled "Penthouse." Although, I shouldn't have been shocked in the least bit.

Like he would actually live in anything other than a penthouse.

"You're not going to tell his boss, are you?" I asked, glancing back at the very distraught Jeffrey. From the way he had panicked, it was quite apparent Alexander was a force to be reckoned with around here.

"Of course not. Jeffrey's a little overzealous sometimes, but he means well." Alexander paused then and gestured me into the elevator to his private residence. "After you."

When the doors closed quietly behind us, all thoughts of the eager Jeffrey left me, and I was immediately overcome with tension once again. However, this time, it was for an entirely different reason than in the car ride over. In the enclosed space with Alexander, I could almost see tiny molecules of sexual tension colliding and rupturing in the air between us.

I clasped my hands together to stop them from fidgeting, but the effort only seemed to increase my awareness. My breathing became irregular, coming out in short bursts. Vivid images of our kiss last night in the restaurant filled my head, causing my imagination to run rampant. To my mortification, my panties began to feel damp, clinging to the sensitive flesh between my legs, heightening the completely unexpected burst of arousal.

We're only two people in an elevator, for Christ's sake!

I wanted to reach out to him so badly, to run my hands up his torso, over his shoulders, and into his hair. All I had to do was step slightly to my left, and he would be within my reach.

Just do it.

The devil on my shoulder was taunting me, pushing me to take what I wanted without regard.

I looked up at Alexander. His heated gaze bore into me, causing my face to turn ten different shades of magenta. I could swear he knew what I was thinking.

He reached over and pressed a button on the panel in the elevator. The lift suddenly came to a halt.

"Alex, what are you—"

I was abruptly silenced as he pushed me roughly against the back wall. He pinned me there with his powerful arms, his hard body pressed against mine. There was a fierce look in his eyes, almost dangerous. I began to panic over the lack of mobility. I couldn't move if I tried.

And I was terrified.

Alexander

I CRUSHED MY MOUTH ONTO HERS. FUELED BY ABSOLUTE LUST, I devoured Krystina with the intent of kissing her senseless. I don't know what possessed me to do it. Maybe it was her cheeks that flushed scarlet when I looked at her. Perhaps it was those fidgeting hands. Or perhaps it was the way she rolled her eyes at me when I lectured her about the insensible fuck-me shoes—shoes I wanted to see her wearing without any other stitch of clothing.

She thought I didn't notice when she pulled her hand from mine in the park. But I knew what she was doing, and I wasn't going to let her push me away again. I shoved my tongue through the seam of her lips, my urgency to taste her completely unleashed. I didn't allow for a slow build-up like I had the night before. Instead, I refused her any sort of finesse and took her mouth fully. Like an assault. Hard. Powerful. Needy.

I allowed my teeth to graze over her lips, nipping at her pouty lower lip before moving down her jawline to her neck. I breathed in her scent.

Mother of God, she smells divine.

She was a sultry combination of red plums and jasmine, making her ripe for the picking. I tugged on her earlobe, and she let out a small gasp. I groaned from her sudden intake of breath, her response like a lightning bolt to my groin. Gathering her mass of curls in my hand, I kept her pinned against the wall and attacked her mouth again. I pressed the full force of my weight against her, holding her firmly in place, making her boneless in my grasp.

I knew I could probably take her right then and there. From the way she pushed her hips up against me, I could tell her need was hot. It was all I could do not to hike up that little excuse for a skirt and bury my cock in her heat. To be lost in her. In everything that was Krystina.

But it wasn't the right time. Not like this. I wanted her to feel the way that I did first, to have her endure some of the same hell I had experienced day in and day out since our first meeting. She drove me to the point of madness, and I wanted her to suffer right along with me.

Summoning all of the willpower I could attain, I tore my mouth away from hers.

"If the elevator stays immobile for too long, someone will call security, and I don't want the hassle," I excused. Even to my own ears, my voice sounded hoarse. Raspy. Like I was a dying man struggling for his last breath.

Who was supposed to be punishing whom here?

I stepped away from her and moved over to the elevator panel. I pressed a few buttons, and the elevator resumed its ascent. Krystina, on the other hand, remained unusually silent, cheeks flushed and eyes wide with shock. She had a slight tremble about her, and I had to suppress a satisfied smile. She was most definitely turned on.

When the double doors opened, I led her through the spacious main foyer of the penthouse and into the dining area.

"You have a great place," she finally spoke. I watched her as she took in the details of my residence. She was smiling, and her eyes were wide with fascination.

Personally, I had begun to get tired of the penthouse, although I didn't tell her that. She was too much of a joy to watch, eagerly absorbing every detail like a sponge, and I didn't want to ruin it. As she had in the park, she was able to see things I had stopped appreciating long ago.

"Have a seat," I told her and pulled out a chair at the dining room table for her to sit.

Once she settled in comfortably, I pulled another chair over to her. Then, bending to lift her right leg, I removed one of her shoes and placed her bare foot on the opposite chair.

"Alex—" she started in protest, but I cut her off.

"You need to elevate your feet, or else they'll swell, and you'll never get your shoes back on later."

"My feet are fine!" she said, seeming embarrassed. I ignored her quick tongue that could never stay silent for long and lifted her other leg to repeat the process. "No, really. I insist."

She leaned forward, attempting to stop my progress with the left foot, but I swatted her hands away and continued.

"Do you have to argue with everything I say? Just keep your feet up, Krystina," I ordered, placing her foot on the chair. "I'll be right back."

I left her gaping after me, her mouth opening and closing like a fish, and went into the kitchen.

I pressed my lips together in a tight line. I had thought a little evening stroll would soften her. But, evidently, I was wrong. I was quickly learning how much Krystina despised being told what to do.

Every time I thought of a new approach, she would pose questions. Or Argue. Or just be Krystina. It didn't matter what I did—she thwarted my every move. I knew she'd be a problem since day one. I knew she would be work. But her disobedience was a rather significant obstacle we'd have to overcome. And soon.

I grabbed the handle of the refrigerator and yanked it open, the force causing the bottles in the door to clank together dangerously.

Easy now...

I was too worked up. It was that sassy mouth of hers—so damn sexy—but it never shut up. I never knew if I wanted to gag her or kiss her. Knowing that, I should have held back in the elevator. I only succeeded in frustrating myself by kissing her, and I was still hard as a fucking rock because of it. I had to think sensibly and maintain control, which I found myself grappling with whenever I was with her. She made it too damned difficult.

I pulled a platter of cheese and fruit from the fridge and set it carefully on the counter. There was no point in slamming things around the kitchen. I'd most likely end up scaring Krystina if she wasn't already terrified after my revelation last night.

Candida.

Matteo's advice was still a warning in my head, a troublesome reminder she was innocent. How innocent remained to be seen, as she wasn't an easy one to read. Finding out the answer to that question was imperative before things went any further.

After unwrapping the cellophane from the platter, I moved over to the minibar to choose a bottle of white from the wine cooler. I perused the selections, trying to decide what would pair best with the cheeses.

Sauvignon Blanc or Chardonnay? Both will go nicely, but which would she prefer?

I glanced over at Krystina, intending to ask her if she had a particular wine preference. However, she had a look about her that made me pause, and I didn't want to interrupt the picture she painted before me.

She was running one delicate hand over the wooden top of my dining room table. She wore a soft smile on her lips, appreciating the craftsmanship of the design. She looked beautiful sitting there, feet up on the chair, seeming completely at ease. And at that moment, I realized she had never before looked quite like that in my presence. She had never appeared so completely relaxed.

So unguarded.

I stood there studying every beautiful line of her captivating face. Seeing her that way made it almost hard to believe she was capable of so many smart remarks and witty comebacks. Perhaps her sharp tongue and contentious behavior were defense mechanisms, which she relied on when uncomfortable. If that were truly the case, I would need to take corrective actions to remedy that problem. I had to calm her, or else I'd never get through the weeks ahead.

Weeks?

Since when do I think long-term about these things?

The idea was novel for me, and I was stunned to discover I liked the idea of her being here more regularly. In my space. With me. It was a distressing sort of feeling.

This can all go to shit at a moment's notice. Take it one step at a time.

A change of tactics was needed, for Krystina's sake as well as my own. My normal methods of operation would have to be thrown out the window. Attempting to take control by laying down the law would only backfire, so I began to construct a new plan—one that would make Krystina feel more at ease. Once she was relaxed, I would start to work on her trust by giving her what she's been asking for.

Full disclosure.

Krystina would have no doubts about what I wanted from her after tonight. She would know exactly who and what I was. She would either run, or she would stay. If she stayed, then that's when the true test would come into play—tonight, I would discover if Krystina could put away that independent mind of hers long enough to pass her first lesson in submission.

Finally feeling like I had somewhat of a solution to Krystina's argumentative nature, I turned my attention back to the wine selection. Smiling to myself, I settled on a bottle of *Joh. Jos. Prüm* Riesling.

Sweet. Like her.

I grabbed two crystal wine goblets and went back to the dining room, focused on the mission ahead. I could only hope Krystina would keep herself open to what I had in mind.

16

Krystina

My head was still reeling from our kiss in the elevator. Alexander, however, acted like nothing was amiss and went about his business in the kitchen. Even though the kiss had only lasted a few moments, it was long enough to cause an electric charge to shoot straight to my tightened nipples. I'd been left panting and yearning for more when he'd pulled away. Even at that moment, I suffered from a tremble of sexual desire, and my lips still felt swollen from his assault.

Now, finally having more than five feet of space between us, I was able to focus on settling my wild hormones. It was quite obvious two years without sex was working against me. I inhaled a few deep breaths, closed my eyes, and counted to ten.

When I opened them, I felt considerably calmer and much less like a horny teenager in anticipation of the after-prom party.

Having a clearer head, I took a moment to get a better look at the penthouse. The layout of the impressive space was wide open, and I was able to see most of the living areas from my seat at the table. The kitchen layout was catalog perfect, with its black marble counters and appliances any top chef would drool over. I was able to see Alexander as he gracefully moved around the resplendent kitchen, collecting items from the refrigerator and rummaging through the drawers of the sleek maple cabinetry.

From the kitchen, the living room flowed almost seamlessly, opening up to a vast space outfitted with black leather furniture, elegant cream-colored area rugs, and hammered bronze metal artwork for the walls. Each piece looked as if it were custom-made for the room. The whole place screamed luxury with its expansive wall-to-wall windows, revealing remarkable views of the Hudson.

The dining set where I sat was made of polished tigerwood with an intricately designed wrought iron pedestal. I ran my hand over the tabletop, appreciating its beauty.

This piece alone must have cost a small fortune.

To say the penthouse was grand would be a complete understatement. But despite its apparent luxuries, it seemed to lack something. It was cold almost, and just a little too perfect.

Alexander came back to the table, a large tray in one hand and a bottle of white wine in the other.

"What's all of this? I thought you said no frills, Alex."

"It's wine and a cheese platter I picked up earlier today. I'd hardly call this anything fancy," Alexander said dryly, placing the tray on the table.

"You bought it? Don't you have a maid or someone to do that for you?" I hoped the question didn't come off as rude or assuming, but I couldn't help it. I felt intimidated and small in the imposing surrounding.

"I do, but it's her day off. I'm not much of a cook, so if you want more than this, we'll have to order takeout. It's just you and me tonight, baby," he said with a wink.

My stomach tightened upon hearing we were completely and utterly alone. As absurd as it might sound, I had assumed someone as rich as Alexander would have had a twenty-four-hour staff at his fingertips.

"We're the only ones here?" I asked, unable to hide the nervousness in my voice.

"Don't be afraid, Krystina. I won't bite—at least not tonight," he joked.

I looked up at him in surprise. I wasn't so sure if he was just yanking my chain.

After pouring us each a drink, Alexander lifted my feet from the chair, sat down, then rested my ankles on his thighs. He began a slow circular massage on the ball of one foot. I practically sighed from the pleasure of it.

"You don't have to do that, you know," I told him halfheartedly. I *really* didn't want him to stop.

"I want to," he said casually and continued to rub.

I certainly wasn't about to argue with him and his magical hands, so I relaxed into the chair, sipped a bit of wine, and nibbled on some cheese.

Ahh, a girl could get used to this.

I watched Alexander, so careful and concentrated, fingers working mini-miracles over my aching feet. So far, the night had gone off without much of a hitch. And while things seemed to be going smoothly, it was somewhat bizarre at the same time. He said last night he didn't date, yet last night and tonight were exactly that—a date, at least in every sense of the word.

"I've put some thought into the conversation we had last night," I said. "I've decided I'm not looking to date anyone any more than you are. I don't know why you're putting on this false charade. The only things missing are a few candles for ambiance."

I was careful to keep my tone light as I gestured to the room around us.

"There's nothing false about this whatsoever. I mean, we could just fuck now and get it over with, but I don't think that would work for you. I can see the questions constantly circling in your head. You're curious about me. Because of that, I've been giving you space to think about what you want—at least for the time being. You shouldn't read too much into this, Krystina. I truly meant what I said. I'm not the dating kind," he reaffirmed. "To classify last night and this evening as a date would only result in certain obligations I cannot meet."

"No strings attached sounds good to me," I said, somewhat hesitant in these unchartered waters. "Although, I'll have to admit I'm not very good at this sort of thing. Let's just pretend I'm willing to agree to what you want. How do you want this to work?"

"It's simple. You work for Turning Stone during the day, and your evenings and weekends are reserved for me," he pragmatically stated as if he were proposing something so very normal.

He might as well have said he wants to control my entire life.

Trevor and his ridiculous schedules stood out front and center in my mind. The similarities between my past and the current situation were not lost on me for one minute. Sex was one thing but allowing him to control every minute of my day was a whole different beast. Reclaiming my independence was a hard-fought, uphill battle. I was proud of what I overcame. Agreeing to what he suggested would be a giant step backward and risked everything I tried so hard to protect.

"I have a life, Alexander. You can't possibly expect me to give it up to be at your beck and call."

"I know that, and I won't be unreasonable. I understand you have friends and family who need your attention as well. I didn't mean *every* night in the literal sense. But trust me, sweetheart. When I call, I'll make it worth your while," he said temptingly. He flashed me another one of those to-die-for smiles as his hands continued to massage the joints in my feet.

His sexy James Dean maneuvers were making my head spin.

Stay focused!

"So, let me get this straight. I work with you during the day, you sign my paycheck, and then I become your kinky concubine at night."

He grinned and cocked his head to one side. Eventually, that grin turned into an easy laugh.

"You could simplify it like that if you want."

"I never thought going to bed with someone could make me sound like a hooker," I laughed in return, forcing myself to dismiss the angel waving the scarlet letter in front of my face. She wasn't finding this conversation even remotely funny.

"Don't cheapen it that way. I'm asking you to submit yourself to me willingly," he said guilefully, sapphire eyes gleaming with mischief. "And you will agree to it because it will please me."

"I suppose next you're going to tell me women agree to this arrangement all the time?" I asked, still slightly guarded and somewhat skeptical.

"I typically don't have trouble working it out. Although some women make it more difficult than others."

"I can certainly see why some might have a problem with giving up every spare moment of their time for you," I said dryly.

"Oh, no. It's nothing like that. I meant some women prefer to secure non-disclosure agreements first, which I find completely pointless but will agree to when I have to," he explained.

"Non-disclosure agreements? Wait—forget it. I don't want to know. In fact, the whole idea of us working together, sleeping together—it's all crazy. I don't see how we can mix the two," I told him, feeling completely disconcerted over the situation I had landed myself in.

Maybe it's time I take heed of the angel's warnings.

"If you are worried about us being able to work together during the day, I assure you, our paths will seldom cross. I am a very busy man."

My head snapped up to look him in the face.

"Don't worry, Alexander. Facing you at work is the least of my concerns."

"It should be," he said, eyes burning into me with unspoken secrets. "The things I will do to you are not things civilized people talk about during the light of day."

Why couldn't I have chosen to take a crack at a normal guy?

There had been plenty of opportunities over the past couple of years. Yet, I'd chosen to get back in the game with a man who was anything but ordinary.

Only I would choose Mr. Danger-licious.

But, despite the many uncertainties I felt, the very idea of submitting myself to Alexander sparked a dark edge of desire I didn't know I possessed. It stirred in the depths of my belly, diffusing a warm tingle throughout my body whenever I was near him. There was no denying how much I desperately wanted him, and my little devil friend began to construct a red and white striped tent around the disapproving angel in preparation for a full-blown circus.

However, before I became a showgirl for Barnum and Bailey, I needed to find out exactly what he wanted me to submit to.

What things did he want to do to me? Why couldn't civilized people talk about them?

But I was afraid to voice my questions. Instead, I evaded.

"It's only sex, Alexander. People talk about it all the time," I said weakly.

He lowered my feet to the floor, shifted his chair closer to mine, and rested his hand on my knee. He looked down and shook his head as if he were frustrated with me for some reason.

"Look, I'm sorry. This is a lot to process," I said, feeling defensive. "I've never done anything like this before. Casual sex isn't something I normally do, and it makes me worry about what I'm getting myself into. My experiences are pretty limited."

"Exactly how limited, Krystina?" he asked, lifting his head to reveal troubled eyes.

I tried to decide how much to tell him. My only real partner had been Trevor. The sex was good, but nothing kinky. In fact, I wasn't even sure if I experienced a true orgasm with him. From the way I've heard Allyson talk, an orgasm was the most mind-blowing thing ever. I suddenly felt like a babe in the woods.

"Well, there was Trevor. I dated him for a couple of years. But then he cheated on me, and well...let's just say it ended bad. Really bad."

Alexander leaned forward in his chair, eyes dark and narrowed into slits.

Well, that's interesting. Does that bother him?

"Is that why you don't trust me?"

"I don't know you, Alex."

"Okay, fair enough. But tell me this, how was the sex between you and your...ex?" he asked, obviously choosing not to say Trevor's name. I felt color surge into my cheeks at his forwardness.

"It was okay," I answered shyly, with a little shrug of my shoulders.

"You say it so casually. Was the sex good, or wasn't it?" he pushed further.

"I don't know how you expect me to answer that. I don't know —it was sex. What else can I say about it?" I said meekly.

"Krystina, don't be daft. Did you orgasm with him or not?"

Again, his brusqueness threw me off guard. My cheeks flushed a deeper crimson, the heat spreading to the tips of my ears, and I was embarrassed to say I didn't know.

"These are really personal questions, and the answers are none of your business," I responded quietly.

"Last night, we agreed to no games, remember? I'm giving you brutal honesty, and I expect the same in return. Like you, I also need to know what I'm getting myself into. Talk to me, Krystina," he demanded.

"I don't know, okay! I don't know!" I exclaimed, my embarrassment reaching an unparalleled level.

"That's typical," he frowned and leaned back in his chair, folding his arms in a display of obvious disgust. "Most college boys don't know what to do with a woman. What about your other experiences?"

"There was this other guy, but that was nothing," I dismissed.

"What other guy?"

"Nobody, just a guy."

"Krystina..." he warned.

"Geez, you're pushy! It was a one-night stand, all right? Wham-bam-thank-you-ma'am. Not something I like to brag about. Are you happy?"

"That's it then? Two guys?" he asked in astonishment.

"Is there something wrong with that?" I shrunk under his confounded look. He was making me feel like some sort of prude.

"Well, it's just that...I knew you were probably inexperienced, but I didn't realize I misjudged you by so much. That day in the grocery store...the cinnamon gum..." His voice trailed off. He raked his hands through his hair in evident frustration.

Hmm...the gum thing did throw him for a loop after all.

I felt a little smug, but not enough to cover the embarrassment over my lack of sexual expertise. I automatically jumped on the defense.

"Well, excuse me, Mr. Let's-fuck-and-get-it-over-with! I'm sorry I don't have enough notches in my bedpost for you, but that's me. Take it or leave it."

"Damn it, Krystina! What am I supposed to think? Of all the flavors of gum on the shelf—peppermint, spearmint! You chose cinnamon."

"So, what?" I asked, confused by his outburst.

"Cinnamon is an aphrodisiac! I thought you were trying to imply something when you tossed it in my cart," he said as justification for his apparent bafflement.

"It is?" I asked in surprise.

That's an interesting little fact.

I almost laughed at the irony of our situation.

"Why else would you have done it?"

"I, um..." I trailed off.

Because the way you chew a piece of gum is hotter than hell.

"Forget it. I guess that's what I get for assuming and thinking with my dick. Fuck," he swore, shaking his head.

He stood up and began pacing the room.

I just sat there completely mystified by his behavior. He was usually so composed, only giving me the occasional glimmer as to what he might be thinking. Never had I seen him so conflicted.

And all because of a gum flavor?

"It's no big deal—just a misunderstanding, Alex," I reassured. He stopped pacing to look at me.

"You really have no idea what I am asking of you, do you?"

"Of course, I do. I'm not that naïve."

At least I didn't think I was.

"What do you know about BDSM?"

His question took me by surprise. I raised one eyebrow at him, racking my brain to try and recall any knowledge on the subject.

BDSM was that kinky shit, right? When a guy liked to dress a girl in a costume and give her a spanking? But what does that have to do with chewing gum?

I made a mental note to start reading sleazy romance novels instead of crime and mystery.

"I know enough," I said, raising my chin with false confidence. I was trying to hide how much of an amateur I really was, all while attempting to wrap my head around the fact he wanted me to play the starring role in some twisted sexual fantasy.

The simple fact was, I knew some stuff, but not a lot. And the more I thought about the subject, the more I realized how limited my knowledge was. Either way, if Alexander thought I would parade around looking like the English interpretation of a French housecleaner, he had another thing coming to him.

He eyed me up and down. His gaze was heated with desire, although I saw a flicker of uncertainty in the depths of his eyes as well.

"You think you know what I'm talking about?" he challenged. "We'll see about that."

17

Krystina

Alexander walked over to the corner of the living room to an elaborate entertainment center. After a moment, music filled my ears. It was a steady drumbeat mixed with guitar strings that were rough around the edges, the beginning notes sounding as if a first-year guitar student were playing them. Alexander turned to look at me, and his eyes were scorching.

"I don't expect you to make a decision right now. However, I would like to have tonight with you. I want to give you a taste of my world," he said, his voice hypnotic as he walked to me. "Will you let me, Krystina?"

My mouth suddenly went dry.

This is it. This is what I want, right? Then why am I fidgeting?

I stilled my hands immediately before he could see how nervous I truly was.

When he reached the table, he claimed a seat across the table from me, rather than sit next to me as he was before. I think he knew I needed that space between us to make a decision. The seconds ticked by as he waited for my answer.

I listened to the music as it evolved. Its harsh notes transitioned into something darker, and the singer's voice revealed a slightly raw edge that was potent to my system. If Alexander was trying to persuade me with music, it was working. My pulse beat at a frenzied pace, the blood a loud drumming in my ears. The angel began to unroll a white flag of surrender, and the devil had invited a few friends to the Big Top. I was a goner.

"Yes," I finally answered in a whisper.

"Come here, Krystina," he said quietly. It was an order, one I felt compelled to obey, regardless of how nervous I was. I stood up and cautiously walked around to his side of the table.

"Sit down," he said, patting his thighs with his hands.

"What is this song?" I asked as I hesitantly lowered myself down to his lap.

"Didn't you listen to the music I loaded onto your phone?"

"No," I breathed. Alexander ran his hand up my arm to cup the side of my neck, and my heart rate accelerated at his touch. I listened to the music, savoring the feel of his hands as they circled my neck. The song lyrics flowed through me, the words so apropos for my current situation.

"You're a naughty girl," he said and *tsked* at me. "You'll need to learn how to follow instructions better if you want to be with me."

"I've never been very good at following directions," I murmured under the heat of his fingertips as they caressed my collarbone and shoulders. I knew I was in so far over my head, I was practically drowning. But I couldn't shake my fierce desire. I wanted to learn more about his mysterious world. I was drawn to the unknown. I craved him like he was a drug, and I was the junkie who needed a fix.

"Such a beautiful mouth," he said huskily, running the pad of his thumb across my lower lip.

"It's, um...just a normal mouth," I could barely speak the words, my breathing coming out in rapid succession, as his thumb continued to trace the outline of my lips. He was making it difficult to concentrate. "I always...thought...my lips were a little too thin."

"You're talking too much, Krystina," he growled suddenly,

grabbing my head in between his hands and crushing his mouth to mine.

There was nothing easy about his kiss. His passion was demanding as he pushed his tongue past my oh-so-willing lips, taking what he needed. Our tongues danced to the titillating music playing, consuming me as his hands moved possessively up and down my back.

His grip progressed over my ribs and to my waist, grazing the sides of my breasts on the way down. I felt myself shiver at the contact, my desire building and causing a fervent ache between my legs.

Oh, God. What is happening to me?

I wanted this man like I'd never wanted anything else in my life.

I couldn't think as I felt his hand run down my thigh, then up under my skirt. His breath was hot on my neck, lips nipping their way over the line of my jaw. When I felt the sharp tug of his teeth on my earlobe, I may as well have turned to putty, malleable and complaisant in his arms.

His hand massaged my thigh, working around past my hips and around to my behind. Cupping me there, he held me firm to him. I couldn't move in his dominating hold. I could only feel the fire burning with need in my belly.

His magical lips worked their way back up my neck, and he began the ruthless attack on my mouth once again. Without warning, he parted my legs roughly and slipped a finger under my panties. I had a fleeting moment of panic over how quickly the evening had evolved, but it was quickly replaced by desire as his fingers made contact with my most private area.

Oh, yes. Just touch me, please.

Feeling more than willing, I easily pushed aside the thought we were moving too fast and allowed myself just to feel the pleasure of his touch. The throbbing between my spread thighs intensified, and I ached to be satisfied.

"So wet," he murmured, slipping one finger inside of me. I

wanted to cry out from sheer ecstasy but felt embarrassed by how turned on I was and held back.

He pulled his finger out and ran it through my wet slit, spreading the moisture around. His thumb circled my clit as his finger moved back to push rhythmically in and out of me. Gathering my hair together with his free hand, he forced my head back, allowing his mouth better access to my neck. I moaned in pleasure from the grazing of his lips and the torturous in and out motion of his hand.

"You like this," he said, voice rough, as his hand tugged harder at my hair. Fire coursed through me, the ache turning into something vicious, and I could only moan again in response. "You want to come."

"Yes, please!" I shamelessly begged. My body tried to writhe under the power of his circling thumb, but he held me still, not allowing me to move.

"I want to show you how you can come for me. Pain and pleasure, Krystina. Are you sure you want to know?"

My body strained against him. I didn't care what he did to me, just as long as he continued doing that with his hand.

"Yes, Alex. I want to know," I breathed. He pulled his hand away, leaving me empty and gasping for more.

"Stand up and bend over the table."

"Um, e-excuse me?" I stuttered over the question. My brain was in a fog, and I didn't think I had heard him correctly.

"I want you to bend over the dining room table," he repeated.

I slowly stood on shaky legs, my body trembling from the onslaught to my senses. I hesitated for a moment, the rational side of me rearing its ugly head.

Why does he want me bent over the table?

Alexander was able to read the uncertainty in my eyes, and he shook his head back and forth in a scolding manner. I suppressed the swirling questions and allowed him to turn me, so I was facing the table.

He pressed his hand to the small of my back and nudged me down, so I was bent at the waist, chest on the table. He pulled my arms, so they were stretched over my head, locking them in a viselike grip with one hand. His body pressed into my back, and I could feel his hardness straining through his jeans. His other hand moved down past my waist to raise my skirt over my hips.

"I've wanted to tie up these fidgeting hands from the first minute I saw you." His voice was hoarse in my ear. "But I don't feel like wasting time going to get what I need. So, for now, just leave them above your head and don't move. I want you to be still."

Oh, shit. He wants to physically tie me up!

I felt his weight shift as he moved to stand up behind me. He looped a finger under my panties and slowly slipped them down my legs. I felt a shiver run down my spine in anticipation as he worked his way back up my legs, leaving a trail of kisses along the back of my knees and thighs. His hands moved slowly over my behind, molding my cheeks in his palms.

"So beautiful," he whispered. "Now open your legs for me, Krystina."

I wavered, feeling exposed and vulnerable in this position. He must have sensed my reluctance because he coaxed my legs apart and inserted his finger back between the soft folds of my entrance. He began that torturous circular motion all over again while his other hand continued to caress my backside. The pleasure was unbearable, and I moved my hands down to my sides, searching for something to hang onto.

Alexander stopped suddenly, making me cry out in frustration.

"No, damn it—don't stop," I pleaded. I hated I was begging, but I couldn't help it if I tried. I was too far gone.

"Put your hands back above your head. I told you not to move them."

I hurriedly put them back, my desire a violent force I couldn't control. It felt so good I wanted to scream from the feverish hunger blazing inside me.

"That's a good girl," he murmured. With deliberate slowness, he began circling inside of me once again. "Have you ever heard of an erotic spanking?"

If he had asked me that question two days ago, I would have

laughed in his face. The term just sounded ridiculous. But today, I could only hum in pleasure at the mere suggestion of it.

I felt a second finger slip inside me, curving and stroking the sensitive tissues. I closed my eyes, enjoying the electrifying sensation of his flexing fingers. In a matter of seconds, I was almost to the breaking point, a roar beginning in my ears.

His fingers pushed deeper inside of me and stilled.

"Oh, no...please—" I began, but my words cut off abruptly when a hard smack landed on my ass. I cried out, but not from pain. It was because of the constant stop and go of his merciless hand. He rubbed the cheek he had slapped, then continued his assault with his fingers once again.

A second slap.

The sting was more apparent this time, but Alexander's fingers didn't stop their perpetual rhythm. If this was how he got his kicks, I didn't care. I could handle it. This was beyond any erotic fantasy I had ever had. I would do anything he asked of me, just so long as he didn't stop working his finger over my swollen nub.

"Do you want this?" he asked, his voice hoarse and raspy. He sounded as keyed up as I felt. I was surprised to find myself *wishing* for him to spank me again. It seemed wrong, yet so right at the same time.

"Oh, God yes..."

"Say it, Krystina. Tell me what you want."

What does he want me to say?

I was terrified of getting it wrong and risk jeopardizing the release I was so desperately searching for.

"This! I want this!"

"Not good enough." A third slap. "Tell me what you want. Now. Tell me now!" he demanded.

I just screamed out the first thing that came to mind.

"I want to come!"

"My name, Krystina. Always say my name."

"Alex! Make me come! Please, Alexander, don't stop," I begged, pure animal instinct kicking into overdrive.

The motion of his fingers intensified, pumping faster inside of me, sweeping in and out and over my clit. A fourth hard smack landed on my behind. Then another, until I eventually lost count.

Stars collided in an explosion that reached an unbelievable height as I felt myself go over the edge. My body tensed as my insides convulsed around his ruthless fingers. I involuntarily arched my back from the pleasure that rocked me, vibrating through to the very core of my being.

I gasped as Alexander slowly withdrew his fingers from me. He rubbed his hand up and down my back, allowing me a moment to just lay there, face down on the table, savoring in the aftermath of the most intense sexual experience I had ever had.

I knew now, without a shadow of a doubt, I never had an orgasm with Trevor. And now that I knew what that warm, liquefying sensation was like, there was no going back. I was all Alexander's to command.

Alexander guided me to a standing position and pulled down the skirt still hiked up around my hips. When I turned around to face him, his mouth met mine with the softest kiss. As sweet as his lips were, I didn't want gentle. He had shown me the meaning of true passion, hard and fierce, and I wanted more. I *needed* more. I intensified the kiss, pushing my tongue past his lips, pulling him closer to me. He moaned, giving in to my demand as his hands framed my face, pressing himself hard against me.

When he pulled his lips away, I felt winded, and my desire for him built up to a whole new level. I reached for him, my hands moving over his shoulders and down his chest, as I nipped my teeth along his neck. I tugged at his shirt, pulling it free from the waistband of his pants. I wanted to feel his bare flesh under my hands.

When my fingers made contact with the rock-hard muscles of his abdomen, I felt him still under my touch. But I didn't stop. I continued to work my hands up, over his contoured chest, then back down again to his belt buckle. I would have started to undo his pants, but he stopped me by capturing my hands with his.

"I want you, Krystina. Probably more than you know. God

knows I've waited long enough to have you. But not tonight—you need to decide if you really want this first."

"Oh, trust me. I want this," I said, reaching for him again.

"No, stop. I'm serious," he said, pulling out of my reach and tucking his shirt back inside his pants.

"You don't want to?" I asked, suddenly feeling confused.

"Fuck Krystina, I want you so bad I ache. I can assure you, it's not that," he said, raking a hand through his hair. His face looked pained, tormented. "Being with me is not a decision you should make rashly. Submission is a gift, one that is not given easily. It takes a considerable amount of trust to put your body in the hands of someone else."

"I wouldn't be here tonight if I didn't know what I was doing, Alex," I said, crossing my arms in frustration.

"The way your body reacted tonight...so responsive. Almost too responsive," he said pensively. "You need discipline. You're untrained, and I'll need to teach you a lot. This won't be easy for you. I'll demand things that you might not be able to give. I won't coddle you, and it won't be teddy bears and roses with me. If that's what you're expecting, you should walk now."

"You don't know anything about what I want," I said stubbornly. "And as for the roses—I learned a long time ago never to expect that. Ever. You don't have to be concerned about me."

"Good. For once, we can agree on something," he said with a small chuckle. "But in all seriousness, take at least twenty-four hours to think about this. I need you to make sure you know *exactly* what you're doing."

"I want to do this, Alex. Taking a day to mull things over isn't going to change that," I persisted. Now that I'd decided what I wanted, I was digging in my heels.

"Perhaps, but I'd prefer it if you had no regrets. If you decide tomorrow morning you still want to give this a go, then I promise to make it worth the wait," he said with a devilish grin.

Oh, no. That bad-boy charm isn't going to make me melt this time, buddy.

But as I studied his face, a different reality set in.

He doesn't want me. I'm being dismissed.

Rejection hit me in the chest like a tidal wave, effectively taking the breath out of me in a solid *whoosh.*

If he doesn't want me, then fine. I don't need him. Hell, I barely just decided to have sex again—I'm certainly not going to beg for it. Waiting another two years is no skin off my back.

"You know what? You're right. I think it's time for me to leave," I pronounced suddenly. I marched over to where my shoes lay next to the dining room chair. I sat down and hastily began putting them on. I was so angry over his rejection my hands shook, causing me to fumble with the buckle fastening.

"Let me help you," Alexander said, kneeling on the floor in front of me and taking hold of my foot.

"I don't need your help," I spat out. But I sat upright and let him put the shoe on anyway. It was either that, or I would continue to be a fumbling fool with the stupid shoe straps. Within seconds, he had both shoes securely fastened to my feet. His efficiency was infuriating.

"Krystina, look at me," he said gently, rubbing his hand up and down my calf.

"No," I hissed. Instead of doing as he asked, I deliberately looked the other way and crossed my arms. I knew I probably looked like a pouting three-year-old, but I didn't care. I've dealt with rejection before, but it was never quite like this. I had practically thrown myself at him a few minutes earlier. I didn't know how I was supposed to react now.

"Look at me," he repeated, his tone completely different this time. Gone was the soft cajoling, replaced by a deep gravely sound. This was a demand—one I knew would be in my best interest to obey. I slowly turned my head to look at him and his mouth tilted up in a sardonic smile. "There may be hope for you yet."

"What's that supposed to mean?" I asked, surprised by his expression.

"It means that up until ten seconds ago, I didn't think there was a submissive bone in your body. Apparently, I was wrong. The way you looked at me just now..." he trailed off as if searching for the right words. When he spoke again, his eyes were dark as midnight, his voice thick with desire. "It was more than just the turn of your head. Your body language changed. You have more strength than I originally gave you credit for. I underestimated you."

My anger fled, replaced by that all too familiar twisting in my belly. God help me, but I wanted to take him right then and there.

"Um...is that supposed to be a compliment?" I asked, looking at the area rug under his knees. I focused on the subtle swirls in the carpet embroidery, unable to look at his face, into those scorching blue eyes that made it difficult for me to breathe, let alone maintain any sort of self-control.

"Take it as you will, but at the very least, strength is an important attribute," he replied, moving to a standing position in front of me. "You'll need to be strong if you want to learn how to submit to me properly. I believe I can teach you, and I'm very much looking forward to it."

"I sense a 'but' in there," I said, trying to hide my disappointment.

"Tonight isn't the right time. You're too keyed up. I did that to you, knowing all too well how compliant you would be after I gave you a taste of what could be. It's killing me to send you home, but you'll thank me later."

"Maybe you're right," I finally conceded with a frown. He was making sense, but his practicality was enough to drive me insane.

"I know I'm right. Now, come on," he said, leaning down to plant a gentle kiss on my forehead. His lips lingered, a reassuring sign I wasn't being rejected. "Hale is downstairs waiting to take you home."

We walked hand in hand to the doors of the penthouse elevator. I no longer felt like I was being dismissed, but I couldn't shake the feeling of melancholy that settled over me. I felt like we were finally starting to make some headway, and I was sorry to see the evening come to a close.

When the elevator door opened, Alexander leaned down and pressed his lips softly to mine.

"Let me know as soon as you make a decision."

"I think I made myself pretty clear already, Alex," I quipped.

"You know what I mean. Think about it some more, and we'll get together again tomorrow night if that's what you want. As for me, I'm going to take a cold shower and try to get the images of you bound and naked out of my head."

"Bound and naked—" I faltered and stared at him with wide eyes, but he silenced me with another kiss. I reached up to run my hands through his soft waves, pulling him closer so I could take more. I *demanded* more. He groaned against my lips in response, revealing a frustration matching my own before he gradually pulled away from me.

The kiss was short, but for the third time that day, I was left without words and gasping for breath.

How did he do that to me in just a matter of seconds?

I would swear he did it on purpose just to shut me up, knowing one kiss would render me speechless. The look on his face told me I was dead on.

He smiled ruefully at me, cocking his head to the side.

Oh, yeah. He knows exactly what he's doing to me.

He took a step back, so he was no longer blocking the lift doors, leaving me alone and weak-kneed in the elevator.

"I'll look forward to seeing you tomorrow, Miss Cole. Good night," he said, and the doors slid quietly shut.

18

Krystina

I lay awake in bed that night, all thoughts of sleep far from my mind as I tried to process all that had happened. This past week felt surreal, and it was almost overwhelming. What had started as a clumsy bump on the head at Wally's had turned into so much more. I struggled to wrap my head around the turn of events.

How had so much changed so fast?

I wished I could talk to Allyson about this, but she wasn't home. A text from her earlier in the afternoon told me she and Jeremy had made peace and were going out for the evening. Unfortunately, it was well after midnight, and I didn't expect her back anytime soon.

I gave up on trying to sleep, got out of bed, and went to the kitchen. Maybe if I had a glass of wine, my nerves would settle down, and I could sleep.

When I returned to my room, I went over to the stereo and flipped it on. I began to fiddle with the station selections searching for a song I liked when I remembered the music Alexander had loaded onto my phone. I wasn't thinking clearly when he had asked me if I listened to it, my mind too focused on his hands working over my body. Now I wondered what sort of music was on it.

Why did he ask me if I had listened to it?

I picked up the phone and opened the music folder.

Wow! There has to be at least a thousand songs on here.

There were several artists I recognized, but most of them I hadn't heard before. He had separated the music into three different playlists. The first was titled "Persuasion," the second one was "Surrender," and the last was called "Control."

Curious, I selected the first playlist and plugged the phone into the speaker dock of the stereo. A soft guitar melody played through the speakers, and I immediately recognized it as the artist Alexander had stumbled upon in Venice.

As I allowed the gentle notes to flow through me, a barrage of memories from the past two days overcame me. Alexander was dangerous for me; I knew that almost from the beginning. My experience, or lack thereof, was definitely going to be an issue. I was a quick learner, but the learn-as-you-go method was not going to work in this situation. If I was going to do this, I needed to establish some ground rules first.

I sipped my wine and wondered about the non-disclosure agreements some of his *other* women asked him to sign. I was curious about what these agreements entailed.

Maybe I should draw up an unofficial contract of sorts, just to make sure we're on the same page.

Setting a few of my own stipulations might help me to protect myself, as well as get a clear understanding of exactly what he wanted me to submit to. It didn't have to be anything extravagant, but only informal guidelines on which we could both agree. I glanced over at the digital alarm clock on my nightstand.

"Well, there's no better time than the present," I said aloud to myself, opting to make a list while my thoughts were still fresh, despite the late hour.

I frowned when I looked down at my near-empty glass of wine and headed back to the kitchen to refill.

It's going to be a long night—I should just grab the bottle.

I returned to the bedroom, bottle and glass in hand, and switched the music to Alexander's next playlist. I recognized the rough guitar chords immediately.

Oh, shit. Not this song.

Goosebumps prickled down my spine, the song giving me flashbacks of Alexander's skillful fingers between my thighs. I immediately felt a little stirring deep in my belly.

Leaving the song playing, I pulled out my laptop, opened a blank document, and absently thought about what music could be on Alexander's "Control" playlist. I probably didn't want to know. At least not right now. If the first two had me feeling all hot and bothered, I could only imagine what the last one would do to me.

I tried to tune out the music and contemplated where I should begin my typing. A list of bullet points should be sufficient enough. It didn't have to be anything fancy, and the job at Turning Stone seemed like the most logical place to start. That was simple.

My fingers began moving over the keys, rushing to get the easy part out of the way first.

Work Requirements

- I will work for Turning Stone Advertising and follow the limited job description outlined at the coffee shop. Additional job expectations can be discussed and agreed upon at a later date.
- Retirement options and benefits are a prerequisite for me to accept employment.
- Salary to be determined but must exceed current pay at Wally's by a minimum of fifty percent.
- If my employment ends due to our personal dealings, a severance package must be determined.

I paused over the last two bullet points, not wanting to sound too presumptuous. I was really looking forward to working in my chosen field, but I also had bills to pay. So, after only a moment of hesitation, I decided to leave it as is. If it was going to be an issue, then Alexander and I could haggle over it when the time came.

I moved on to the next part of our agreement.

How should I title that?

This part of the list would definitely be more complicated. Settling on the first thing that came to mind, I began to type again.

Extracurricular Activities

- Exclusiveness: we will not be tied together like we are dating. However, I insist you do not sleep with other people while you are with me.
- I can come and go as I please. You are not allowed to control my life. You are my boss in the workplace only. This is merely a business arrangement with sex as an added bonus.

I frowned at the last bullet point.

When it's put like that, I really do sound like a prostitute.

I didn't dwell on the thought too long, or I'd risk scratching the whole idea of sleeping with Alexander. Of course, the fact I was even putting all of this on paper was ludicrous, but I continued to type nonetheless.

- I am not on any form of birth control but agree to take care of it as soon as possible.
- STD testing is mandatory. I will provide you with a doctor's report showing I'm clean. I expect you to do the same.
- Condoms: until I get on the pill and a clean bill of health comes for both of us, condoms must be worn.
- Clarification of my role as a 'submissive' can be outlined in the space below.

I made a bunch of blank lines under the title 'Alexander's Expectations,' then sat back and reread what I had typed. I tapped a finger on my chin and tried to think of anything else I should put on the list. I thought what I had come up with was pretty straightforward. It was responsible, to say the least, and should be a good enough start. After that, he just needed to outline his specific requirements.

Hopefully, he doesn't request I run around wearing a maid's costume. That would be weird.

Laughing to myself, I clicked the save button and closed the laptop.

Flopping onto the bed, I stared up at the ceiling. The music had changed, and another one of Alexander's sexy tunes started to play.

Oh, God—what WAS this music?

It was making me edgy. Restless. And I could barely wait to go over my list with Alexander, the anticipation killing me.

Why should I hold out until tomorrow?

Maybe it was the wine deciding for me. Or perhaps it was his music. Either way, it didn't matter. I knew I wanted him.

Now.

I went and grabbed my phone off of the speaker dock, silencing the music so that I could send him a text message.

TODAY 1:28 AM: ME

I've made my decision. You just need to agree to my terms.

My phone chimed almost immediately with his response. I looked at the clock. It was one-thirty in the morning. I was surprised he responded right away but happy he was still awake.

I couldn't have planned this more perfectly if I tried.

1:31 AM: ALEXANDER

What are your terms?

1:32 AM: ME

I want to meet.

1:34 AM: ALEXANDER

Tomorrow night at 7.

1:35 AM: ME

I don't want to wait. Come to my apartment now.

1:36 AM: ALEXANDER

No. It's late.

Well, didn't that just suck? I want a piece of Mr. Danger-licious now.

I went to type my response and found I was struggling to spell correctly. Even the spelling autocorrect wasn't recognizing my mistakes. I glanced over at the empty bottle of wine on my nightstand.

Geez, I'm really drunk.

I should have known better. I knew I was a lightweight, and two glasses of wine were typically my limit.

Who in the hell gets drunk alone?

I turned my attention back to the phone, now wishing I had waited until morning to text him. He was right. Meeting up tomorrow would be better. It was late, and I needed to get my drunken ass to bed. I threw the first plan out the window and focused on plan B instead.

1:43 AM: ME

Fine. Tomorrow then. Where should we meet?

1:45 AM: ALEXANDER

I'll have Hale pick you up. You can come to my place again.

1:46 AM: ME

Okay. See you then.

1:48 AM: ALEXANDER

Don't disappoint me.

1:50 AM: ME

Don't worry, Mr. Danger-licious. I won't.

1:50 AM: ALEXANDER

???

Oh, now you've done it, you stupid lush.

I wished there was a way to un-send the stupid, made-up word. I was trying to think of how to respond when the phone started vibrating in my hand. Alexander Stone's name popped up on the caller I.D.

Crap! He's calling. Now what?

Pure panic set in as I stared at the ringing phone, trying to decide whether or not I should answer it. Talking to Alexander wouldn't be very smart, especially considering my current state of mind. I had way too much wine in my system.

The phone continued to ring as I tried to make a decision. I didn't think I could handle him at that particular moment. But then I reconsidered. Maybe I could.

Okay, Stone. It's time to have a little fun with you.

A sly smile formed on my lips as I slid my finger along the touchscreen of the phone.

"Hey, sexy," I purred.

"Krystina?" he asked hesitantly.

"Yes."

"Where are you?"

"I'm home, all by my lonesome little self," I told him, trying to keep my words from slurring.

"Are you...ah, okay?"

"Oh, I could be better. But someone rejected me tonight," I said in my best pouty voice.

"Have you been drinking?"

"Oh, come on now! Who drinks alone, you silly boy?"

"Hmm. You sound...off."

Damn!

I thought I was doing a good job.

"It's not my fault. You make me crazy, Alexander Stone."

"I do, huh?" he asked.

"Oh, yes. You're so myst...myst-er-ious." I struggled to get the word out.

Note to self—use small words right now.

He was silent on the other end of the line. I could hear traffic in the background, and I absently wondered where he was at this time of night.

"Are you still there?" I asked him.

"I'm here, Krystina," he answered patiently. He was talking to me like I was a child, and it was annoying.

"Why do you make me so crazy?"

"Trust me, Miss Cole. Crazy doesn't even begin to describe the things you do to me."

"I like it when you call me 'Miss Cole.' It's so proper, yet so hot at the same time."

"I'm not sure how to respond to you right now. You're usually much more inhibited."

"You make me like this," I told him. I thought about my little angel and devil friends. The devil had the same mischievous smile Alexander did. "You...you're dangerous to me. Like the devil, constantly tempting me."

"Oh, really? And are you an angel?"

"Actually...um, yes. I am an angel," I said confidently, voicing my sudden revelation. "But you mister—you're that pesky little devil on my shoulder drowning out my angel's warnings."

"What in the world are you talking about, Krystina?"

"You know—a sub...a subconscious. Good versus evil. Like in the cartoons."

There was silence for a moment before the line suddenly went dead.

Aww, what a party pooper. I was just starting to have some fun, too. Oh, well.

I knew I would probably hate myself in the morning, but I didn't particularly care. At that moment, I envisioned Alexander as my own little devil, and my skin began to tingle from the memories of his hand spanking my behind.

I should have pushed him further tonight. I know he would have fucked me if I had any clue as to what I was doing. But no—I had to be the good little girl I was and left when he dismissed me.

I should have Allyson give me some pointers on how to be more aggressive with men.

I went back to my room and plugged the phone back into the dock. I laughed out loud when "Sweater Weather" started playing.

"I love this song!" I shouted to the empty bedroom.

And it was a sexy song too. I danced around my room, not caring that I probably looked like an idiot. It felt good. It made me wonder what it would be like with Alexander—to feel him inside me for the first time. A shiver of anticipation ran through me at the thought.

Lost in my own little what-if sexual fantasies, a loud knock at the door of my apartment had me leaping out of my skin, interrupting the solo dance routine I had been rocking.

"Krystina! Open up," came Alexander's voice loudly through the door.

Oh. My. God. He's here. At my apartment.

I quickly went to the door, as fast as my inebriated state would allow, bumping into half the furniture along the way. I opened the door, and there he stood. I hungrily drank in every glorious sexy inch of him.

"I've been knocking for five minutes. Why didn't you answer sooner?" he demanded.

"Well, hello to you too," I said, eyeing him up and down. I went to lean against the doorjamb, only to miss it entirely and almost fell over. Alexander grabbed my arm to steady me. He gave me a quick once over, a frown forming on his beautiful face.

"You're trashed," he said with obvious annoyance.

"Maybe a little. How'd ya get here so fast anyway?"

"If you had paid any attention earlier, you'd know I don't live far from here."

"Well, isn't that just handy? Wanna grab a quickie?" I asked suggestively.

"No," he said firmly, brushing past me to enter my apartment. He walked around the apartment, opening doors and peering into rooms. "Why the fuck are you drunk, Krystina?" he snapped over his shoulder.

"Did you just come here to yell at me, Stone?"

"I came to make sure you were okay and to put you to bed," he said.

His tone was so stern, and it was a total turn-on. I wanted to pounce on him and have my way with his body, just like he did to me in the penthouse.

He had changed his clothes from earlier and was no longer wearing jeans and a button-down. Now he was in running pants and a T-shirt. I looked at the elastic waistband around his hips and thought about how easy it would be to slide the pants right down past his knees.

"Oh, you can put me to bed, alright. But only if you're going to join me," I seductively offered when he came back over to where I was standing.

"Where's your roommate?" he asked, ignoring my insinuation.

"She's not home. She's probably off having some hot and steamy make-up sex with her boyfriend." I brought my hands to his hips and tried to slip them inside the stretchy material around his waist.

"Is that so?" He gently removed my hands and turned me around toward the hallway leading to the bedrooms.

I just want to touch him. Why is he being so difficult?

"Yeppers. But apparently, she's the only one," I said in frustration. "My vagina just collects cobwebs. Except for earlier tonight. You managed to remove some of them for me. Want to remove a few more?" I asked him, trying to flash the best come-hither look I could muster as he ushered me into my bedroom.

"I hear you're listening to the music I loaded onto your phone. That was probably not a very good idea tonight," he said, moving to the stereo to turn it off.

"Why not?"

"Apparently, my 'Persuasion' list worked. Along with a bottle of wine," he added, pointing to the empty bottle on my nightstand. His expression was amused as he turned down the blankets of my bed.

"You know...I think you're right. That's a dirty trick you pulled on me, Stone—using music to persuade me."

"Climb into bed, angel. You need to sleep."

"You didn't answer me before. Are you coming to bed with me?"

"No, Krystina. I'm not coming to bed with you."

"Why not? Don't you like drunk sex?" I pouted. The room was starting to tilt a little bit.

Maybe it would be better if I did go to bed.

I climbed into bed, not very gracefully, and waited for him to pull up the covers.

"I don't want to be with you like this. Not today anyway." He leaned down and brushed the gentlest of kisses on my forehead. "Don't worry. I'll have you tomorrow night. I promise."

He tucked the blankets around me and moved away to shut off the bedroom light. I didn't want him to go. He promised he would *have* me tomorrow, but oh how I wanted him right at that moment. I closed my eyes, wishing he would crawl into bed next to me.

Maybe when I open them, he'll be here with me.

That was my last thought as the darkness pulled me into a dreamless sleep.

19

Alexander

Within seconds, Krystina was passed out cold. I stood there for a while, just watching her sleep. Her breathing was already soft and regular, the lush mounds of her breasts rising and falling beneath the thin cotton T-shirt she wore. Moonlight flooded through the slats of the blinds on the window, casting a subtle halo around her head and giving her an angelic look.

Her picturesque appearance caused a restless sort of feeling to settle into my gut. It was unfamiliar and unwanted.

What the fuck is wrong with me lately?

I sharply exhaled and shook my head in aggravation. To say the entire evening was troubling me would be a complete understatement. Krystina's limited experience with sex was a concern, but her naivety was an issue that would easily resolve itself, given some time. It was more than just that. I was more bothered by the fact that I was in her apartment, unsure of what possessed me to come here in the first place.

I had immediately known something was wrong when I called her. It was the *not* knowing what it was that made me feel powerless, compelling me to go to her. I had been consumed with worry over her welfare, and I simply reacted.

Drunk text. That's all it was. How was I supposed to know she would demolish a bottle of wine all on her own?

But my effort to shake off the uneasiness was in vain. The apprehension crawling over my skin was not just because I had left the comforts of my bed out of concern for a drunken woman. I was troubled because every response Krystina emitted from me was foreign. I am always in control of the situation, no matter what the circumstance was. My wants and needs are always the endgame. Yet, throughout the evening, I had found myself reconsidering those needs more often than not.

When I eventually turned to leave, an extensive CD collection under the bedroom window caught my attention. Knowing Krystina was easily influenced by music, my interest piqued, and I went over to the long lines of shelving to get a closer look. I squatted down to see the selection better through the slant of light coming in through the bedroom door.

As I began to read the artists, I quickly saw the CDs were in alphabetical order. Her organization was unexpected, and I chuckled to myself. Justine used to say I was neurotic for doing similar sorts of things when we were growing up. I made a mental note to tell her I wasn't a minority.

I glanced over my shoulder at the rest of the room, looking to see if Krystina had anything else in order, like the CDs. There were a few books on the antique white wooden desk in the corner, but other than those, there wasn't anything that needed to be cataloged quite so precisely. However, everything about the room was neatly arranged.

The furnishings were older in style, giving the room a tastefully done vintage appeal. There were no clothes strewn about, showing Krystina had an appreciation for tidiness. Quotations written in black calligraphy were framed and hung cleverly around the room.

I stood and moved closer to the wall to read what some of the quotations said. Krystina appeared to have a fondness for Maya

Angelou. Every frame was filled with words by the poet, most of them being about strength, perseverance, and determination.

That's an interesting piece of info I'll have to remember for later.

Closing the door behind me with a quiet click, I left the bedroom and made my way into the kitchen. I knew Krystina would feel like garbage when she woke, so I began searching her kitchen cabinets with the hope of finding some ingredients to ease her morning pain.

I was pleased to find the kitchen fully stocked, showing me at least one of the women in the apartment liked to cook. The cupboards were well organized, with all the food labels facing front. I smiled to myself when I saw it and was curious about which roommate was so meticulous. But then I recalled Krystina's CD collection and immediately knew anyone who would go through the painstaking task of alphabetizing hundreds of CDs would surely strive for an efficient kitchen.

After collecting everything I needed, I filled the teakettle and set it on the stovetop. While I was waiting for the water to boil, I wandered around the apartment. I needed to learn more about the many layers that made up Krystina, and an individual's personal space told a story. Her bedroom had only been the prologue.

The apartment was big in comparison to New York standards. And like her room, it was stylishly done, in an eclectic sort of way. Overstuffed furniture filled the main living space, the kind a person could just sink into and fall asleep. There was no formal dining room but rather a spacious breakfast nook in the kitchen and a large island with four bar stools on one side. The windows throughout the apartment bore no curtains, but it wasn't necessary. The bamboo roman blinds would give all the privacy needed when they were fully closed.

Overall, the two women maintained a tidy space, with feminine touches throughout that gave the apartment a cheerful, lived-in look. The only things lying about were a few magazines, and a book stacked neatly on the coffee table. Curious, I went over to the table to retrieve the book.

Hmm...James Patterson.

Crime and mystery were a far cry from inspirational poems, and I wondered if the book belonged to Krystina or her roommate. I glanced down at the magazines underneath the novel. The top one looked like a woman's gossip rag, the cover advertising the hottest male celebrities of the year and an article on how to get your man to commit. I pinched my face in disgust.

If I were a betting man, I'd wager the magazines did *not* belong to Krystina.

I placed the book back down just as the kettle began to whistle. I hurried back into the kitchen before the noise could wake the sleeping beauty. I finished preparing the hangover remedy in no time, collected the remaining things she would need, and went back into her room to leave it where she would see it in the morning. The drink would be cold by the time she got to it, but it would still do the trick.

After placing the steaming mug on the nightstand, I glanced down at Krystina. She was still sleeping soundly under the lily-white comforter. I took a step closer and reached down to brush away a thin lock of hair that had fallen over her face. She hummed at my touch, and her dark lashes fluttered, but she didn't fully stir. I slowly pulled my hand away, not wanting to wake her, and took a step back.

"Goodnight, Krystina. My angel," I whispered.

I had driven the Tesla over to Krystina's place, but I decided to leave it on the street and retrieve it in the morning. I needed to walk, and I could only pray the crisp night air would help me clear my head.

The light at the corner of Thompson and Bleecker Street changed, signaling it wasn't safe to cross. There was little traffic on the road, and I crossed despite the flashing red hand. Following pedestrian rules just seemed moot at this time of night. Not to mention I was too tired to really give a damn.

As I crossed over to the street that would take me into

Manhattan, I thought about the past week. I analyzed every minute spent with Krystina, carefully going through it all like I was deciphering a playbook. There were too many uncertainties, and I had to put it all in order where it belonged.

Krystina had been throwing curveballs at me since day one. And while I may have struck out on a few, I was able to grasp my mistakes and change tactics accordingly.

At least until tonight.

It was no longer Krystina who was taking me by surprise but myself. The rules in my own game had become blurred lines.

It didn't seem possible that just a few hours earlier, I had Krystina's ass in the air, beautiful and rosy pink from my hand. She had been arching and gasping, ready to lose her mind at the slightest touch. But I didn't take her. Normally, my rationale would have been every sub has to start somewhere. I've been with new subs before. Some of them work out well, but some only like the idea of being dominated and fail miserably when trying to get their feet wet.

Tonight, Krystina had been willing. I saw it in her eyes. Definitely submissive, despite the way she held her guard and fought tooth and nail over every little thing. It had taken every ounce of willpower I possessed to push her away. My opportunity to teach her had been there, but it seemed wrong. Somewhere along the line, I realized I didn't want Krystina just to test the waters. I wanted her all in—completely and without any regrets. And not just for a one or two-night fling—I wanted it to be a regular thing.

However, after seeing the meticulous organization of her apartment tonight, my reservations about whether or not we could be a feasible match grew even more. It appeared Krystina liked order and control almost as much as I did. I may succeed in uncovering her submissive side, but I wasn't confident she could surrender complete control. This was a significant concern, and I wondered if she could trust me enough to let go.

She has to.

There could be no debate about it. For the longer I knew her, the more I found myself compromising my ideals to accommodate her, and there was very little left for me to give. I was capable of a compromise now and then, but I wasn't able to relinquish total control. Doing so could be disastrous.

Maintaining restraint was an absolute necessity, as I could not allow myself that sort of vulnerability. The blood running through my veins didn't leave me any other option.

Because, even in her drunken stupor, Krystina didn't know how right she was.

She truly is an angel, and I am the devil.

20

Krystina

There was a stabbing pain piercing through my right eye. I tried to blink to rid myself of it, only to find myself blinded by the bright sunlight coming through the blinds of my bedroom window. I brought my hands up to my head and squeezed my temples. I moved to sit up and felt my stomach pitch. I felt like a bus had run me over. I slowly opened my eyes and allowed them to adjust to the light.

When my vision finally came into focus, I remembered the amount of wine I had consumed the night before.

I'm such an idiot—why did I drink so much?

I glanced over at my nightstand clock to check the time and saw a bottle of aspirin and a note propped up by a mug. I groaned out loud as the rest of the memories from the previous night came flooding back.

Please, let it be just a dream.

A nightmare was probably more accurate. But I knew it was neither as I reached over for the note on the nightstand.

Take two aspirin and drink this. There is more in your

refrigerator if you need it. Dry toast will help you, too. No coffee. It will make you feel worse, and I want you better for later.

Looking forward to tonight.

Affectionately, The Devil on Your Shoulder

"Oh, no!" I said to myself and threw myself back onto the pillows. The action didn't exactly help the rolling in my stomach, but nothing could be more terrible than the mortification I felt at that moment. I could only imagine what he thought of me.

Did I have to tell him about that? The angel and the devil? The stupid, childlike subconscious that had been ruling me lately?

I couldn't think of a time when I've ever felt more foolish in my life.

I looked over at the ceramic mug on the nightstand and peered inside at its contents. It was an amber-colored liquid with a lemon floating in it. I picked up the mug and took a whiff of the concoction. It smelled like herbal tea. I slowly took a hesitant sip and had to force back a gag at the sickly-sweet taste.

What the hell is this stuff?

It certainly wasn't anything I kept in the house.

However, after a moment, my parched taste buds recognized it was, in fact, something from my kitchen. It was brewed chamomile tea with a ridiculous amount of honey. The lemon was probably to help me detox. Having finally realized what I was drinking, I greedily threw back the entire mug, my mouth and body desperately screaming to be hydrated.

Surprisingly, my rolling stomach settled after only a few moments, allowing me the strength to climb out of bed. I grabbed the bottle of aspirin and went to the kitchen to get more of Alexander's miracle elixir.

When I entered the kitchen, I found a loaf of bread waiting for me on the counter.

Dry toast.

Alexander must have left the bread out for me. And, as

promised, there was more tea waiting for me in the refrigerator. I smiled at his thoughtfulness, but his actions made me feel even more ridiculous.

I thought about how I should handle the events of last night as I put two pieces of bread in the toaster. My brain felt fuzzy, and putting my thoughts in order was a struggle.

I owe him an apology for sure, but I definitely don't want to call him.

There was no way I could have an actual conversation with Alexander after my irresponsible drunken behavior. After the way I had acted last night, I was sure he'd want to cancel our plans for this evening, however tentative they may have been. I had to come up with a way to give him an out, as he was probably just trying to be nice in his note.

I needed to be realistic.

Why would the sophisticated Alexander Stone want anything to do with a boozing twit like me?

I just wanted to send him a text, but that seemed too impersonal for some reason. Then I remembered he had programmed his email address into my phone. Maybe an email would be better. I could say a bit more in an email and perhaps even make a joke about my embarrassing angel and devil revelation. Then I could give him the opportunity to bow out gracefully.

The bread popped from the toaster, and the smell of it provoked a hungry growl from my stomach. Skipping the butter as Alexander had suggested, I placed the dry toast on a plate and went back to my room. Once there, I sat at my desk and fired up the laptop. On the screen was the agreement I had written up the night before.

Probably no need for that now.

But I saved the document just in case. Once it was saved, I archived the file into a folder and exited the screen to open my inbox.

TO: Alexander Stone

FROM: Krystina Cole
SUBJECT: My Apologies

To The Devil On My Shoulder,
Thank you for taking care of me last night, but I must apologize for being such a lush. I am not in the habit of losing self-control the way I did, and I hope you do not use last night as a reflection of my true character. But, either way, after my behavior, I would completely understand it if you wanted to cancel our plans for this evening.

Sincerely,
Krystina

I thought my words were apologetic and tactful all at the same time. I gave him the chance to withdraw his invitation without sounding too pathetic.

Perfect.

Pleased with my email, I hit the send button.

However, after I clicked the key to send my apology into the world of cyber communications, a wave of sadness came over me. I felt like I was saying goodbye in a strange way. Alexander had cracked open a door I had managed to keep closed for so long, and it pained me to think I would have to close it again.

What if he decides to take me up on my offer and cancel our plans for tonight?

For the first time in years, I had left myself vulnerable, and I was afraid of rejection.

Maybe I shouldn't have given him such an easy out.

After about ten minutes had passed, my computer pinged, signaling the arrival of a new email. It was from Alexander. I eagerly opened the incoming message.

TO: Krystina Cole
FROM: Alexander Stone
SUBJECT: No Apologies Needed

To My Angel,
No worries. It happens to the best of us. As for your behavior, I must admit I rather enjoyed your loose tongue. You gave me a small insight into what you are really thinking, something I find myself struggling with frequently.
I am looking forward to our evening together. Do not consider canceling. I'll be waiting in anticipation until I can see you again.
Until Later,
Your Anxious Devil

I smiled to myself after I read his response. It looked like I was about to have a very busy day.

I KNEW I COULDN'T GO TO ALEXANDER'S TONIGHT WITHOUT A LICK of knowledge about BDSM. He was insistent I knew what I was getting into. And if I was honest with myself, I knew practically nothing. Research was key to a better understanding. I had felt very naïve last night, more times than I cared to admit. I needed to broaden my horizons, expand on my awareness—if for no other reason than to protect myself. This was an unknown world to me, but one I wanted to explore. Walking into it blindly would be extremely foolish.

I made myself comfortable in sweats and a T-shirt before sprawling out on my bed with my laptop. It was time to get an education.

My initial search results of BDSM turned up descriptive online encyclopedia definitions and various shopping pages.

Boring.

I wasn't looking to shop for vibrators and leather outfits, and I certainly wasn't interested in clinical definitions.

Hard limits, soft limits, safewords, blah, blah, blah.

I wasn't even sure what all of it meant.

So, what is it I'm looking for?

I bit my lower lip, trying to decide on what exactly I wanted to find out. I thought perhaps something with pictures would give me more to go off of. I clicked on the images tab.

Holy fuck!

The extreme images that filled the screen were nothing like what had happened in Alexander's penthouse last night. Even his crazy insinuations would never have led me to envision the things I was viewing. Nothing could have prepared me for what I saw on the screen.

The pictures were borderline frightening, and some were outright disgusting. Women brutally tied up and caged, with weird contraptions hooked up to their female parts. It looked painful, and a lot of it looked dangerous.

Is this what Alexander wants?

I thought I had a mild understanding of what he wanted, but now I wasn't so sure. My eyes grew wide, and I felt my heart begin to pound inside my chest as I tried to decipher what the pictures were portraying.

A Nine Inch Nails song began to sound in my head, and I slammed the laptop closed. I couldn't imagine how any sane person would get off from being bruised, burned, or poked at with needles. To me, there was nothing sexual about the sadistic images I had just seen. They were beyond extreme for obvious reasons. I could not believe that was what Alexander wanted.

Wait...what was it I was reading about hard limits?

I hesitantly opened the lid for the laptop and went back to the link I had initially considered boring.

At least that page won't give me nightmares for the rest of my life.

I read the dry and very long explanations about the history and culture of the Dominant and the submissive.

There has to be something better than this!

It was impossible to believe there wasn't just a basic explanation available. After reading for more than an hour, I still felt like I knew nothing.

I finally found a page of S&M resources and began scrolling through the articles. The more I read, the more I found kinky play was actually very normal. But more importantly, I learned of the different levels of BDSM.

Most people's kinks were fairly mild, practicing only my initial ideas of BDSM. A few spanks and some role-playing. Yet, other people were more extreme—like the scary pictures I just saw. I just couldn't figure out what the middle ground was in it all.

This shit is way too complicated.

I could research all day and into the night and still not really understand it. There was only one thing I was sure of—Alexander had some serious explaining to do.

21

Alexander

I pressed the button for the intercom on my desk, ending the call with George Canterwell. Leaning back in my chair, I rubbed a hand over the back of my neck. It was shaping up to be a long week, and it had barely even started.

Stone Enterprise had been purchasing properties from Canterwell for a couple of years. Our transactions had been easy at first, as he was pulling up stakes, retiring, and traveling the world. He wanted to be done with it all, and scooping up his properties for a low price had been simple. But old age, and his new young wife, had made him a greedy bastard. While I could appreciate his ruthlessness, I wasn't willing to pay more than market value for what he had to offer. It was time to cut ties with the old man and move on.

The intercom buzzed, and I groaned.

Laura better not tell me it's Canterwell calling back.

"Yes," I clipped into the speaker.

"Mr. Stone, Kimberly Melbourne is here to see you," Laura informed me.

Good.

My appointment was twenty minutes early but would be a welcomed change of pace after a stressful morning.

"Tell her I'll be right out. Also, I'm going to send over some info regarding a property in Westchester. I need you to set a meeting time with the property agent. I'd like to negotiate a selling price."

"Yes, sir. I'll have the date and time uploaded to your calendar within the hour."

"Thank you, Laura." I quickly sent her the link containing the information about the listing. I wasn't sure what I was going to do with the land yet, but I liked what I saw. It would be an excellent investment if I could obtain it for the right price.

Once the computer gave the *swooshing* sound signaling the email was sent, I got up from my seat behind the desk, threw on a navy sport coat, and made my way out of the office. I found Kimberly Melbourne sitting on the sofa in the waiting area, picking invisible pieces of lint off of her pricy business suit. Her hair was pulled tight into a severe twist that matched her perfectionist personality.

"Kimberly," I greeted when I approached her. The design engineer looked up at the sound of my voice and stood to extend her hand for me to shake.

"Mr. Stone," she nodded in return. I took hold of her outstretched hand. Her grip was firm. No nonsense. It was why I appreciated her so much. She was confident, efficient, and she worked fast.

"Thank you for taking on this project at such short notice. I know how busy you are, but my new marketing director will begin her employment sooner than I had anticipated. I would like her space completed before she starts."

"Oh, don't even think twice about it," she brushed off with a wave of her manicured hand. "It's been a while since you've sought my expertise. When you called, I was more than happy to accommodate."

And I'm sure the sum I offered had you dropping your other clients to be here.

How she managed to juggle her schedule was no genuine

concern to me. What mattered was she was here, and Krystina's office would be complete before Monday.

"I appreciate that. Now, if you'll follow me this way, I have a large space I want you to take a look at. The thirty-seventh floor vacated about six months ago, and the old tenants left a bit of a mess. Rather than clean it up, I had the floor gutted until I could decide what to do with it. That said, you'll have a fairly clean slate to work with."

Together, we headed to the elevator and began the descent down to the floor that would soon house the marketing division of Stone Enterprise. When the doors opened, a dusty construction site was revealed. Plastic sheets hung from the ceiling, blocking off certain areas where work was already underway. The loud vibrations of machine sanders could be heard from various points of the floor.

"I didn't realize you had already begun work, Mr. Stone," Kimberly said, seeming somewhat surprised by the mess before us.

"Only the walls, Kimberly. I wasn't kidding when I said I had the floor gutted. I had my construction engineer get started on the basic drywall work since that takes some time. Rooms still need to be divided, flooring has to be decided on, paint, and the works."

"And that's where I come in," she finished with a smile. "You've given me a blank canvas, Mr. Stone. I'm looking forward to the design."

"Before you leave today, I'll get you in touch with all parties needed for the job. Very little will be brought over from the existing offices. I've already instructed Gavin, my computer technician, to purchase the needed workstations. And as for the blank canvas, you'll also have a blank check. My accountant will see to it that you have everything you need on this project."

She didn't even flinch at that, having worked for me in the past.

"Perfect. Any thoughts on what your Marketing Director might like?"

"Her name is Krystina Cole. And honestly, I don't know much about her décor preferences," I said with a frown. "She loves music. I think it's safe to assume she will use it often in her radio or television advertising strategies. Whatever you decide, her office needs to incorporate a high-end sound system at the very least."

"That will be easy enough. What about the other areas of the floor? Do you think Miss Cole would want the space divided up into separate office spaces? Or perhaps cubicles?"

"No cubicles. I detest them," I told her.

"I didn't think so, but I thought I'd ask just in case. Since this floor will be for marketing, separate offices will most likely work out better. They will allow people to think creatively, without any interruptions from the person at the next desk over."

"My thoughts exactly," I agreed. Kimberly placed a finger on her chin and looked around contemplatively.

"Any preference on room sizes?"

"Miss Cole's office should be spacious. You can't see them from here due to the hanging plastic, but there are large windows at the far end of the floor. Incorporate those in her personal space. She'll need a sizable conference room of sorts, a place for meetings and design planning. As for the other areas, I think eight to ten offices should be sufficient enough. You'll have to get with Josh Swanson on the space layout. He's here somewhere..." I trailed off, scanning the floor for the whereabouts of the construction engineer.

As if on cue, Josh came out from behind a hanging plastic sheet, his dark hair, shoulders, and arms completely covered with drywall dust. He removed a pair of safety glasses from his face, giving him a raccoon-like appearance. He looked surprised to see us standing there.

"Mr. Stone, I didn't realize you were here. You'll have to pardon my appearance," he joked casually, attempting to remove some of the dust covering him. "What can I do for you, sir?"

"Josh, I'd like you to meet Kimberly Melbourne. She will be the designer for the project. Kimberly, this is Josh Swanson, my construction engineer."

"It's nice to meet you, ma'am," Josh told her with a nod. "I'd shake your hand, but as you can see, I'm full of dust and drywall mud."

"That's okay! You can keep the mud to yourself," Kimberly said with an easy laugh.

"We just started work. So far, we've managed to get the drywall up and seamed. We're just finishing up with the sanding today."

"You've made great time, Josh. I'm happy with the progress," I appreciated. "From this point forward, you can take direction from Kimberly. I trust her judgment. Whatever she wants, build it."

"I have a tight time frame to work with. I promise not to come up with anything too extravagant," Kimberly assured him.

"Do you want to take a look around? I can show you what we've done so far?" Josh asked us.

"Absolutely. I want to get a good look at the space I have to work with, as well as take some measurements," Kimberly said. She reached into her oversized shoulder bag and pulled out a tape measure and a pad of paper.

"The two of you can go on ahead. I'll catch up with you momentarily," I told them.

Once they had stepped away, I pulled out my cell to call Krystina and ask her about any specifications she might have for the office. I dialed her number but paused before hitting the send button.

If I called her, she would know what I was doing. As of right now, she had no idea I was giving her an entire floor in my building. She didn't know she would have her own domain—her own world within mine—and full access to every convenience Cornerstone Tower had to offer. I wanted her to be surprised.

Deciding to keep her out of the loop for a bit longer, I pocketed the phone rather than calling her. I looked over to where Kimberly and Josh were standing. Kimberly was pointing to something on the ceiling.

What would Krystina want in a workspace?

I thought about Krystina's apartment as I made my way over to the engineers. Her home wasn't flashy, the colors more muted. Her bedroom was much of the same, only slightly more eclectic, with its Maya Angelou quotes, and lily printed bed comforter. Her space was soft. Feminine.

"Josh and I were talking, and we thought about opening up the ceiling. Exposing the ducts will give the floor a more industrial and modern feel," Kimberly explained when I reached them.

"No, nothing too trendy," I told her.

"Oh, um...okay," Kimberly said, glancing at Josh.

But neither of them knew Krystina like I did, even if my knowledge was limited. She had a conventional way about her. She would want her office to be warm and inviting, not looking like a busted open industrialized warehouse. It would be too cold for her tastes.

"Stick with traditional. Earth tones will be best," I advised.

"I can work with that. Once we figure out the floor plan, I'll collect some paint chips, then Josh and I will go through them together to decide what color is going where."

"And lily's," I added as an afterthought. "Miss Cole likes lilies."

They both took on a curious look, but neither of them asked how I knew that piece of information. They knew better than to question me.

"Music, earth tones, and lilies. I'm sure I can find a way to tie it all together," Kimberly said confidently.

Josh looked skeptical, but I paid him no mind. Kimberly was the best in her field. She had twenty years of experience, and five of them were spent working for me. I knew she would find a way to incorporate my wishes into a design that would flow seamlessly.

"I don't care how you do it, as long as it's done right."

I LEFT KIMBERLY AND JOSH TO TACKLE THEIR NEW PROJECT AND headed back to my office. Once I was there, I went through the last few remaining items in my calendar. I sent off an email to my accountant with an update on the construction, and I responded to a few others needing my attention.

I noticed Laura had scheduled an appointment with the

selling agent in Westchester, and I was pleased to see the notes she had included in the calendar. Laura was the best PA I've had in my employment to date. Not only was she efficient, but she also had a knack for obtaining useful information. Apparently, the seller was anxious to move on the property.

Back taxes.

That would make negotiations all that much easier. I made a mental note to give Laura a raise.

A call to Justine was the last order of business. I almost dreaded it, only because I knew she was probably waiting for an update on the Charlie situation. However, as much as I wished she'd let it go and let me handle things, a call to her was necessary today. We needed to discuss the charity dinner taking place in a few weeks.

Justine was the driving force behind the fundraising efforts for The Stoneworks Foundation, and I wanted to check on the progress of the largest annual fundraiser the foundation hosted. The success of this dinner would ensure Stone's Hope Woman's Shelter would open on time.

I dialed her cell number and waited for her to answer.

"Hey, Justine. It's me," I said once she picked up.

"I'm so glad you called. I don't know what you did, Alex, but Charlie hasn't called or texted in the past twenty-four hours," she launched in immediately, just as I knew she would.

"I told you I'd take care of it, and I did."

"Can I ask? What did you do?"

"We got him to sign off on a gag order, or else face an extortion charge. It was a piece of cake. Don't worry about it. The contract is air-tight, and the secret is safe."

"I know you're only doing this for me. I'm so sorry," she said regretfully. "I didn't want to have to involve you. You don't know how much it means to me."

I leaned back in my chair and sighed.

"Yeah, well...if it weren't for me, you wouldn't have to worry about the media. Besides, I don't want a media fiasco any more than you do. Have you talked with Suzanne?"

"Yes. She knows the gist of what's going on. I had hoped we could meet for lunch today, but she was tied up at work. We planned a spa day for later in the week. I'll fill her in more then."

"Glad to hear. How is the planning going for the Stone's Hope fundraiser?"

"Oh, that's another thing I've been worried about! Charlie knows about the amount of work that goes into this event. It would be just like him to ruin it," she said, voice full of scorn. "He gets off on causing a scene. I could just see him running his mouth the day of."

"So, what's the status on the dinner?" I asked her again, reeling her back in from her rant.

"Oh, sorry. Yes. Actually, things are going smoothly. The tickets are almost all sold. We have some big donors stepping up with large ticket items for the silent auction. Florist is all set, and the menu has been decided. I only need to meet with the band and discuss their fee."

"If you think they're good, pay them whatever they want. That will be my donation from Stone Enterprise."

"We'll see. I have yet to actually hear them play myself. If I don't like how they sound, I'm going with the band used at last year's Chamber of Commerce Ball. I already have them lined up anyway, but I thought I'd check out someone different than the usual. Once I decide who I'm going with, we can discuss who is paying."

I was happy to hear she had everything under control. I was right to appoint her as Head of Relations and Fundraising for the Stoneworks Foundation. Justine was better when she had a focus —a cause she could throw herself into. Stone's Hope was a perfect fit for her.

"It sounds like you have a good handle on things. I have to run now, Justine. But let me know about the band either way."

"Will do. And Alex...thanks again for Charlie."

"I got your back. Always," I said earnestly. Justine was like a fragile bird with a broken wing. It was my duty to be strong for her, to get her through whatever shit was thrown at her. I had to break the endless cycle that was her life—that was our lives. "I'll talk to you later, Justine."

I ended the call and eyed the clock. It was a good day—a productive one—but the time had gotten away from me, and I still had a few stops to make before seeing Krystina tonight.

Satisfied I was leaving everything in good order until tomorrow, I dialed Hale.

"Calling it quits for the day, boss?" he asked upon answering.

"You got it. Bring the car around. Krystina is coming by tonight, and I have a few errands to make before I send you to get her."

The silence on the other end of the line at the mention of Krystina ticked me off. I hung up rather than waiting to hear what Hale might have said.

I could admit a woman at my place two nights in a row was a rarity for me. But Hale didn't know how bored I had become as of late. I was tired of the predictable woman. They were mundane. Simple to figure out and easily influenced. Krystina was everything but those things.

I locked the desk drawers, then turned to power off the computer. Before I hit the shutdown key, I reread the emails between Krystina and myself from earlier in the day.

My Angel.

Krystina had understandably been embarrassed, but there was no need for her to try to push me away.

Again.

I wouldn't allow it to happen anymore. It was time to break through her defense mechanisms and tame the firecracker she was. However, the path ahead was going to get rough, for I knew Krystina wouldn't go down without a fight.

22

Krystina

True to his word, Alexander sent Hale to pick me up promptly at seven o'clock. I was somewhat disappointed Alexander wasn't in the car, but the drive to the penthouse ended up being a short one. Alexander lived closer to me than I had realized.

When we arrived, Hale walked me through the lobby of the building to the penthouse elevator and inserted his key card. While we were waiting for the lift to come, I glanced over at the security desk and saw Jeffrey, the young man who had been so eager to please Alexander. He nodded his head politely when I caught his eye, and I afforded him a small wave in return.

"Please step inside, Miss Cole. Mr. Stone is waiting for you. Enjoy your evening," Hale said to me.

I looked up at him in surprise. That was the first time Hale had ever spoken directly to me. Even more shocking was the ghost of a smile playing on his lips. He was usually so stern and severe, and I was caught off guard.

I looked at him, I mean *really* looked at him, for the first time. He was much older than me, probably around fifty if I had to take a guess, and not nearly as menacing as I had initially thought. He had kind eyes, the sort of eyes that would light up with laughter given the opportunity. My guess was Alexander didn't give him much time for laughing.

The fact Hale had suddenly found his voice had left me in a lurch, and an uncomfortable silence settled between us. I had never thought about conversing with Hale, as I had always been so focused on Alexander.

Does Hale know about his boss's alternative lifestyle? And if he knows, does he approve of it? What must he think about me?

As the new realization took root, I found it difficult to look Hale in the eyes. The confidence I had felt upon entering the building was suddenly gone, replaced by embarrassed insecurities. Words tumbled out of my mouth awkwardly.

"I, um...thanks, Hale," I timidly returned and quickly ducked into the waiting elevator.

The doors closed, and I waited while the lift climbed. Alone, in the confined space of the elevator, my apprehension grew. I knew I was acting ridiculous, but I couldn't control my wavering conviction. And it wasn't just because of the awkwardness I had just experienced with Hale. After the research I did earlier today, I couldn't shake the feeling I was walking blindly into a lion's den.

I swallowed a lump beginning to form in my throat as the elevator continued its ascent. The downward force of rising so quickly did nothing to help it, and the lump soon settled into a knot in the pit of my stomach.

What am I doing? I must be crazy.

The elevator came to a halt, and the doors slid open. Alexander was waiting for me. He was leaning against a wall, a diabolical expression on his handsome face.

"Good evening, Krystina," he drawled out.

Just one look at him, and I instantly paled. I struggled to control the tremble of nerves threatening to take over.

I didn't step into a lion's den. It's more like I casually strolled into the devil's lair.

Pictures from the internet, combined with childhood nightmares of monsters and vampires, flashed in my mind. I had no trouble picturing Alexander wielding a whip, with me shackled to some dirty dungeon wall while a strange masked man sucked my blood.

"Krystina, what's wrong? You look like you've seen a ghost." Alexander rushed to my side in alarm, his long legs closing the distance between us in a matter of seconds.

"It's nothing. I just...it's nothing," I said, shaking my head to rid my overactive imagination of the dark images.

This is real life, not some Stephen King flick.

"I hope you're still not worried about being drunk last night because I can assure you, it's no big deal. It happens to the best of us," he stated offhandedly.

Yeah, right.

I found it difficult to believe the sophisticated Alexander Stone allowed himself ever to get drunk. Not even once.

"No, no—it's not that," I assured him, still feeling uneasy. "We just need to talk about some things, that's all."

"Come into the living room. I already have drinks poured and a fire going," he said, gently taking hold of my elbow and guiding me over to one of the leather sofas.

The heat of the fire felt good, warming my suddenly cold and clammy hands. Once we were comfortably seated, Alexander handed me a glass of some sort of yellowish-brown liquid. Brandy, port, whiskey—it didn't matter what it was. I took a huge gulp, experiencing the pungent syrupy taste as it went down. I allowed myself a minute to gather my thoughts, letting the warmth of the alcohol wash over me.

Alexander's eyebrows rose in astonishment.

"Sorry," I apologized sheepishly and quickly set the drink on the coffee table.

"Krystina, just tell me what's on your mind," he demanded, but his concern was unmistakable. The way I half emptied my glass had understandably taken him by surprise. It even took me by surprise.

Drunk last night, pounding em' down again tonight. At this rate, I'll be in AA before the end of the week.

"I'm not sure where to start..." I trailed off.

"Take your time." He watched me, patiently waiting for me to continue.

It's okay. He needs to know, and you need to have your questions answered.

I took a deep breath.

"Look, I haven't been with anyone in two years...at least not sexually. And to be honest, I haven't wanted to. Being alone has suited me just fine. I had no interest in relationships or dating, and even sex. Until I met you."

"Krystina, if you want a relationship—"

"Please, Alex. Just listen. I have to get this out," I conveyed, holding up a hand to stop him from talking. "I'm not looking for some lifelong commitment—I'm good with just the sex. But you have to understand agreeing to be with you is a huge step for me. We must keep it simple—no strings attached. I'm not ready for any emotional attachments. I'm trusting you'll keep it that way."

"I thought that's what we already agreed on," he voiced cautiously. "I'm not entirely sure where you're going with this."

"Last night, things got a bit complicated. At least for me, they did. You were right—I am extremely uneducated, especially on the whole BDSM thing. Up until this afternoon, I thought you just wanted to spank me and, well... you know. Play doctor or something," I confessed.

My heart began to thud a rapid beat, quickened from nervous angst. My ignorance on the subject was beyond embarrassing, and I fought the flush threatening to overtake me.

"Role-playing can be a part of BDSM. It would depend on your preferences." He was still somewhat guarded, and he waited tenaciously to see where I was going with my admission.

"Yeah, well...about those preferences. I did a little bit of research online today."

Heat rose up my neck. As much as I tried, I couldn't stop it. And when I saw his eyes widen with curious speculation, it only heightened my humiliation further, deepening the crimson slowly covering my cheeks.

"And *what* exactly did you find, Krystina?"

"Lots of crazy shit. Toys, weird contraptions—you name it, I saw it. After seeing everything, I'm sort of confused now. I know there are levels of BDSM, S&M—whatever you want to call it," I rambled. "I just need to know exactly what level *you* are before I get involved any deeper. Because, I have to say, some of the crap I saw was pretty freaky."

"Oh, no..." he said, his handsome face revealing genuine alarm. He ran his hands through his hair and stood to pace back and forth in front of the coffee table. "Look, I can only imagine what you saw and what you're probably thinking. I'm not an extremist, so let's be clear on that much, at least."

I breathed a sigh of relief, and my rapidly drumming pulse seemed to slow a bit. I didn't honestly believe he was some twisted and demonic nympho who wanted to cause physical damage to me but hearing him say it aloud gave me a bit of consolation, at least.

"So, what level are you then?" I asked. I tried to keep the worry out of my voice, but it was hard feat to manage since I wasn't entirely sure what level I'd actually be comfortable with.

"I'm not really sure I would classify myself a particular level. This sort of thing isn't that clinical. It's about what we agree to do together and about what the submissive wants more than anything. Despite what you may have found online, BDSM is not abuse. At the end of the day, you are the one in control, Krystina. Not me."

"Now you're confusing me. How can I possibly be in control? I thought I was the one who was submitting to *you*."

"You are. But it's my job, as a Dom, to take care of you. I must be in tune with your needs to satisfy your every want and desire. If I'm not, and I make it all about me, then it is abuse." The baffled look on my face was unmistakable. He stopped pacing, stepped up to me, and rested his hands reassuringly on my shoulders. "Forget about the nonsense you saw online and think about it seriously for a minute. Yes, I enjoy the high I feel when I'm in control and knowing I have the power to push you to your breaking point. But at any given moment, you can call everything to a halt. I may be the one who wields the whip, but you control the limits just by using a safeword."

My stomach dropped at the thought of him using a whip, and I found myself wincing.

At least I know what a safeword is. Thank God for online research.

"I can't just say 'no'?" I asked, trying to keep the fear I felt out of my voice.

"The word 'no' can be misunderstood, especially in a role-playing scenario. Picking a safeword is better."

"But what if I'm tied up and helpless? You said you might push me to do things I don't want to do. How can I trust you'll stop even if I do use a safeword?"

"That's the reason why I told you submission is hard. It's not about making you do things you don't want to. It's about exploring together. I can show you the way, but you'll need to trust me," he said softly, leaning forward to brush a curly tendril of hair from my forehead. "I'm giving you my word. I would never push you further than you were willing to go, Krystina."

I looked up searchingly at his face and tried to find something, anything that would give me insight as to what he was thinking. There was nothing sinister and evil in his sapphire eyes, but only patience and understanding.

"I believe you," I told him. And that was the truth, as much as it astounded me. I was shocked at my ability to trust him so easily, a man I barely knew. But even so, we weren't finished just yet. "There's still more we need to talk about, Alex."

"What other questions do you have?"

"I don't have more questions, per se. Just a few things we need to sort out. You gave me an idea last night when you talked about women requiring non-disclosure agreements." I leaned down to retrieve a pen and the list I made from my purse on the floor by my feet.

"Is that what you want?"

He sounded surprised.

"Oh, no. It's nothing like that. It's more like a set of rules to follow if we are going to...um, do this." I was suddenly second-guessing my stupid idea. I thrust the computer printout at him before I could change my mind. "Here—I made a list. Just read it."

He took the list from my outstretched hand and reclaimed his seat next to me on the sofa. He silently read over the catalog of stipulations. When he finished, he looked at me, mild humor sparkling in his eyes.

"So, that's it?" he asked, placing the paper on the coffee table.

He was trying to suppress a smile, but I ignored him and continued.

"I think I covered the basics. You just need to write down any requirements you might have. See, I left you a blank space right here," I finished all business-like, pointing to the blank lines on the paper with my pen.

"You didn't include anything about your limitations, Krystina. That's sort of important," he said dryly. "My interests in the bedroom aren't exactly mainstream. Can you think of anything you might be opposed to?"

Blood. Pain.

I looked searchingly into his eyes, trying to find the right words to explain what I was feeling without exposing my underlying fears.

Stop it—he said he wouldn't hurt you. Trust him.

"Um...I don't know. Like what?" I asked, attempting to be open-minded.

"You did the research. How about restraints—"

"No—don't say it!" I burst out. I was suddenly seized with overwhelming panic at the idea of actually discussing this out loud. "Write it down, please. It will make it easier for me."

He instantly appeared amused, although he didn't actually laugh. He didn't have to—the look on his face alone spoke volumes and told me I was being ridiculous. I felt like a teenager trying to avoid the sex talk with a parent. It was absurd. My only rational defense was, if I *read* his not-so-normal preferences, I would be able to keep my composure if anything surprised me.

"Okay, I'll play this your way if it means I get to strip you out of those clothes," he said suggestively with a wink. However, his blue eyes were alight with laughter, the truth in them cutting through his rudimentary comment, as he picked up the list again.

I should have been upset he found the situation funny, but I wasn't. Even his salacious remark didn't register on my radar. I could only focus on one thing—the ball of nerves bouncing around in the pit of my stomach as I waited for him to write.

But he didn't write. Instead, he just sat there watching me. It was maddening.

Why isn't he writing?

"What are you waiting for?" I practically snapped. My nerves were shot.

"Can I have the pen, please?"

"Oh!" I exclaimed, feeling foolish. "Yes...here. Sorry."

I passed him the pen I had been clutching tight in my hand. Instead of taking it from me as any ordinary person would, he used two hands to remove it slowly from my fingers, letting his touch hesitate ever so subtly over my knuckles. My heart fluttered from the intensity of that one little action.

Who knew handing someone a pen could be so frigging erotic? I may never look at a pen the same way again.

"You're blushing," he said huskily, a crafty smile on his face. My hands immediately went to my face. He reached up to pull them away and ran a finger along my jawline. A shiver raced down the length of my spine.

After a moment, he dropped his hand. The hungry look that had flashed in his eyes was now gone, and his face turned serious. He looked down at the paper in front of him.

"BDSM is all about limits, Krystina," he said, getting back to business. "There are hard limits, and there are soft limits. It's important that we have an understanding. For example, I won't do anything with fire or electrical stimulation."

"You're joking, right?" I asked incredulously, his words immediately bringing me back down to earth.

Fire or electrical stimulation—what the fuck?

I thought my eyes might pop from their sockets. This was serious.

"No, Krystina. I'm not." He studied me for a minute before seeming to come to a decision. "How about I just write down the things I *would* do, and we can go from there. Do you want me to write down everything?"

"You might as well put it all out there, right?" I smiled meekly at him.

Soft limits, hard limits—what does it matter? It's all Greek to me.

Alexander got to work on the list while I sat there in anticipation, wondering about the words I would read. As I watched him write, I studied his face for any inclination to what he might be thinking. Occasionally his brow would furrow in concentration as if he was trying to remember something, but his mild expression revealed nothing.

Minutes went by, every one of them seeming like an hour. I tried not to peek at what he was writing but, after a while, my nervous energy was replaced by impatience.

How many kinky scenarios can there possibly be?

I was about to say something when he abruptly put the pen down and tossed the list onto my lap.

"Happy reading," he said, his expression wary.

I gingerly picked up the paper, terrified of the words he had written.

You told him to write it down—just read you chicken!

I looked down at the list and began reading his perfectly written letters.

Impact Play

- Spanking, Whipping, Caning, Flogging

Bondage

- Rope, tethers, cuffs, scarves, collaring, suspension

- Partial body restraint: hands in front or behind, feet bound, spreader bars

- Full body restraint: standing with wrists tied to ankles, hogtie, furniture binding)

- Gagging (gag balls, etcetera but nothing that will impact the ability to breathe. I will not participate in any sort of asphyxiation or edge play)

"Holy crap! I don't even know what some of this stuff is!"

"Did you finish reading?"

"Not yet. I'm still trying to absorb the fact you want to beat me black and blue!"

"Krystina, I would never, ever cause you physical harm. I already told you that if you didn't like what I was doing at any point, you'd only need to use a safeword, and I would stop. Now, please finish reading," he said impatiently.

Enhancements

- Toys: vibrators, nipple clamps, genital clamps, anal beads and plugs, ben wa balls, etc)

- Ice and stimulation lubes (hot, cold, numbing)

- Wax (I've used it before but would prefer not to. We can discuss)

We can discuss! We will be discussing more than wax!

Other

- Masturbation, oral sex, anal sex, threesomes, nudity and role-playing

I lifted my head to look at him, my eyes full of disbelief. I could never do this stuff.

He's out of his mind. Over the top, mad as a hatter, crazy.

I took another long swig of my drink, the contents stinging my throat.

"What is this stuff?" I asked, swirling the last remaining drops of the potent liquid around in my glass.

"It's a tawny port."

"It's gross," I said.

"I can get you something else if you'd like."

"Oh, no. This is working just fine," I told him, then tossed back the rest of the liquid encouragement.

"Talk to me, Krystina. I want to know what you're thinking."

"That you are certifiably insane."

23

Alexander

Krystina's eyes were impossibly large in her lovely face, and I could sense her frayed nerves. I knew she was nearing her breaking point before I even had the chance to really push her. I was so close, but her lack of knowledge kept getting in the way.

She thinks I'm a lunatic.

I was scaring her, and now a crossroad had presented itself. I had to ease her fears, or I'd risk her walking away from me forever.

The entire situation was not only new for her but new for me as well. I've never taken on a regular sub before. All of my exploits had only been a one or two-night fling, having never wanted anything more than that. But here Krystina was, sitting there wide-eyed and confused, her perfect skin begging for me to take all the time in the world to kiss and explore every inch of it.

The mere idea of her leaving caused a feeling of dread to descend upon me, although I wasn't sure why. I only knew I wanted her to stay.

"Do you want to leave?" I asked.

"No, of course not. I'm just trying to grasp...all of this," she said hesitantly.

I tried to mask the feeling of relief washing over me.

Good. She wants to stay. Keep the dialogue open.

"You know you can ask me anything you want," I offered. "I think we're beyond keeping barriers now, so I'll give it to you straight."

She cast her gaze down and began to fiddle with the hem of her snug cotton shirt. I knew she had a question balancing on the tip of her tongue, and I patiently waited for her to ask what was on her mind. I could only pray she kept her questioning to the subject at hand and avoided any prying into my past.

"Have you done this stuff with a lot of women?"

Shit.

The question was unexpected and potentially dangerous. Although it was a fair one, I was curious as to why it was a concern. I had to be careful with the answer because one question could always lead to another.

"There have been a few," I evaded.

"That's not exactly giving it to me straight, Alex," she said sarcastically. Normally I would be offended, but I found her ability to call me out refreshing, and I told her as much.

"Cutting through the BS to discover the truth. You really are a breath of fresh air. I'm not used to people being that way with me."

"So? Have you?" she pushed.

"Yes, Krystina. I have."

"How long have you...well, been into this sort of thing?"

Careful now...

"You make it sound like I have a disease, Krystina," I laughed, slightly uneasy with the possibility of where this conversation could lead. "In all honesty, I've had these interests for years. It's just who I am."

End it there. She doesn't need to know the why.

"Is it easy to find women who like to do this stuff?"

"It's not too hard. The club scene makes it pretty easy, actually," I admitted.

"Clubs?"

"Yes. There are clubs throughout the city, discreetly hidden, of course."

"What do you mean? Like a secret society of some sort?" she asked, pinching her nose up in confusion. She made me laugh, her innocence easing the tension that had settled in my shoulders.

"Krystina, this is real life. Not the DaVinci Code. I mean regular clubs. They're just not open to the general public, making it easy for me to maintain anonymity. Membership is required, and they don't advertise. Generally, the whereabouts of these sorts of clubs travel strictly by word of mouth."

"Oh, I see," was all she said. Her brow creased as if she were trying to put together the pieces of a puzzle.

I deliberately skirted around any further probing into my background. However, Krystina wasn't that naive. I was as honest as I could be, but she knew I wasn't giving her everything. I could only hope that what I did give her was enough, and she'd be accepting. Because from where I was standing, we were not moving ahead. She had yet to consent to take the next step.

She looked down at the list and began reading it over again, picking it apart line by line. Minutes stretched on, the silence maddening.

She's going to keep asking questions. I shouldn't have put it all down in black and white.

My patience was running thin. I was failing. I thought I could teach her, but I was proving to be inept. Either we would navigate through this together, or not at all. I had waited long enough.

"I should have known better," I snapped, irritated with myself for allowing this to go on for so long. "I wrote it all down because you asked me to because you're unsure, but this is obviously not working. So from now on, we do this my way. Come with me."

I stood up, grabbed her hand, and pulled her up from the couch.

"Where are we going?" she asked, obviously startled by my abruptness.

"To my bedroom. I want to show you something. And don't worry. I promise not to touch you—yet."

I led her down the hall toward the closed door of my bedroom. With each step we took, I could feel the pulse in her wrist drum faster and faster. Her palm broke out in a cold sweat. She seemed genuinely terrified. Her fear caused an ache to pull at my chest. I didn't want Krystina to be afraid of me, and the only thing I could do to erase her fears was to show her.

Reining in my impatience, I reminded myself to be gentle with her. The internet had planted too many false notions in her head, and it was my job to prove there were other ways to my world.

Just take it slow. Wait for her acceptance.

When we reached the door, I paused before opening it. I turned to her, released her hand, and brought my palms up to rest against each side of her face. I had initially planned to offer words of assurances, but as soon as I had freed her hands, they began twisting together near her waist. Instantly, my cock hardened, and I had to fight the instinctive need to drag her to my bed and tie her to the rails.

What is it about those damned fidgeting hands that makes me want to fuck her senseless?

I ignored the throbbing in my groin and focused on the task ahead. I couldn't afford to screw this up just because my dick had a mind of its own.

Patience. Restraint. Finesse.

"I need you to keep an open mind, Krystina. Can you do that for me?"

I saw a lump move down her throat as if she were attempting to swallow her nerves. Her eyes were indecisive, and I had a fleeting thought she might bolt on me. On impulse, I pulled her close. Folding my arms around her, I held her flush against my body and pressed my lips down to mold against hers.

When I pulled away, I knew my eyes were pleading.

Don't run—not after I worked so hard to get you here.

And at that moment, whether it was because of my kiss or the beseeching gaze I cast upon her, I saw her indecision change into something else. She suddenly looked determined.

"I can't make you any promises, Alex. But I'll try."

"That's all I'm asking for, angel."

Krystina

I WAS OVERWHELMED WITH ANXIETY AT THE MERE THOUGHT OF seeing Alexander's bedroom. I didn't know what to expect behind the closed door.

A dungeon, perhaps? Maybe a cell full of manacles and chains?

But when he opened up his bedroom door, it looked nothing like a dominator's pleasure lair. The room was actually very normal looking, with modern decorations placed tastefully about the room. Strategically positioned recessed lighting subtly illuminated the space, giving it a warm glow, despite the fact the walls were painted a dark stone gray. I began to breathe a little easier.

Like the rest of the penthouse, all of the furniture was sleek and contemporary in style. However, my gaze was drawn to the bed as it stood out from the rest of the room. It was a showcase piece and nothing like anything I had ever seen before. It was covered in a black satin bedspread and was similar to a four-poster bed, except it wasn't made of wood. Instead, the framework was black metal, molded into an intricate tubular design. Sheer black curtains hung down from metal rings, giving the bed a slightly sinister look yet maintaining an alluring appeal. A mirror took the place of a headboard. The entire effect reminded me of a plush concert stage set without the flashing lights.

Alexander watched me carefully, assessing my every reaction. I could almost see him trying to cut through the layers to get inside my head.

"What is it, Krystina?"

"Well...your room, the bed—it's very modern."

"Do you know what this bed is?"

"No. Should I? I mean, the mirror is a little kinky, but I suppose one would get used to it after a while."

"This is a bondage bed. Here, let me show you."

He walked to the bed and reached to the right of the top rail. He unhooked a latch of some sort and lowered a bar down to the opposite corner. Then, moving to the left side, he repeated the same thing until the bars formed a large "X" at the foot of the bed.

"This is a saltire cross, also known as a St. Andrew's Cross. It's probably one of the most commonly used pieces of bondage equipment."

I swallowed nervously. When he had moved the bars to form the cross, small metal loops were revealed. I didn't see them when the bar was fastened upright, as the intricate scrolls of the bed's framework had camouflaged them. They ran the entire length of both cross-sections. My imagination ran rampant.

"What are the little loops for?"

Instead of answering, he pulled me to the newly formed cross. Moving behind me, he gently pulled my arms up over my head, resting my wrists against the top portion of the X. His hands slid slowly down my arms and to my waist, causing a tremor to run through me. He leaned in closer, and I could feel his breath hot on my neck.

"One day, I'll have you tied to my cross, Krystina," he whispered in my ear. "And the metal loops are what I will use to secure your cuffs."

My breath caught in my throat, and my heart started beating double-time as I waited to see if he would do as he suggested. But instead, he stepped away from me and moved to the far-right corner of the room. I lowered my arms and backed away from the cross, thankful and disappointed all at the same time. While the thought of being bound to a cross had surprisingly aroused me, I wasn't sure if I was quite ready for that.

Alexander stood near a settee, his expression inscrutable.

"Are there more metal loops hidden in that chair?" I half-joked.

"This is a variation of spanking horse that is also custom made to blend in with the bedroom furnishings." He slid the settee away from the wall and turned it until I had a view of the backside. The back of the chaise revealed an angled plank with a narrow-padded bench along the bottom. It reminded me somewhat of a church pew. "Once you become more comfortable with submission, I will have you kneel on the bench and lean forward over the back. I can choose to either leave your arms free or restrain them to the legs of the furniture."

He pointed down toward the legs of the chair.

More clandestine loops.

He didn't wait for my response but moved to a door in the room's opposite corner. I thought it might have been a closet or a master bathroom, but then he pulled a key out from his pants pocket.

"Wait here," he told me before opening the door and disappearing inside. I tried to peer inside, but it was too dark, and I couldn't quite see. When he returned, he was holding a variety of objects. One of them, I knew for obvious reasons, was a whip.

"I'm not sure if I'll be too keen on the whip, Alex," I said with a nervous laugh.

"It's not a whip. It's a flogger. And don't be so quick to judge," he said, seeing my facial expression. "Feel it. This could only inflict pain on you if I allow it."

I took hold of the flogger he held out to me. He was right. The braided strands felt like silk against my fingers as I ran them across my hand. A quiver of excitement ran through me at the thought of Alexander running this softly over my body.

Okay, maybe this isn't so bad.

"What's that?" I asked him, feeling a little bolder as I handed back the flogger and pointed to the long metal bar he held in his other hand.

"This is a spreader bar."

I looked at the cuffs on each end of the bar.

Large enough to wrap around my ankles.

A tightness formed in my belly as I envisioned myself laying on Alexander's covert bondage bed, with cuffs around my ankles, and spread wide for him.

"Krystina, please stop your hands from fidgeting, or else I'll end up reneging on my promise not to touch you."

I slapped my hands to my sides, although a part of me wanted to keep fidgeting so he *would* touch me.

But he didn't lay so much as a finger on me. Instead, he stood there, continuing his ever so attentive study, as if he knew of my internal struggle. A part of me wanted to run screaming from the room, yet another part of me was anxiously waiting to be tied up.

"I wanted you to see this for yourself, if for nothing else than to ease my conscience that you know what you're getting into," Alexander said. He turned away and went back to the room that held his secret toy stash. When he came out, I was thankful to find him empty-handed. I wasn't sure if I could handle another lesson on bondage paraphernalia today. After locking the door again, he came back over to where I was standing.

"Why do you keep that door locked?" I asked curiously.

"I wouldn't want Vivian to come across my closet and get upset," he explained, flashing me a lopsided grin.

A surge of jealousy instantly surged through me. We had agreed to no strings attached, but I couldn't deny I needed some sort of explanation for this Vivian person. I wasn't the sharing type.

What if he's already in an arrangement with someone and just wants to add me to the ménage à trois?

The thought reminded me there was still so much for us to talk about. He had written down threesomes, but I had disregarded it as a typical male fantasy. But with Alexander, I was quickly learning how wrong it was to assume much of anything.

"Who's Vivian?" I asked suspiciously, with just a bit too much of an edge in my voice.

That I had caught him off-guard was all too apparent. He raised his eyebrows in a mock expression of surprise.

"Don't worry, Krystina. She's only my fifty-five-year-old

housekeeper," he clarified as if he had read my mind. "I prefer to limit who I share this with."

"Oh, okay," I said, instantly feeling relieved.

Good. I could handle old housekeepers.

He gave me a strange look but didn't comment on the housekeeper any further.

"Let's go back to the living room. We can talk more, and it might be less intimidating in there rather than in here," he suggested, motioning to the room around us.

"No… I'm fine here. I'm just…" I started.

How can I explain to him how I feel? This is all so twisted and bizarre, yet so unbelievably erotic.

"You're just what?"

"This room, that secret room of toys and whatever else you have hiding in there… it's strange. I don't know what to think," I said, my tongue feeling heavy in my mouth as I tried to overcome my awkwardness. "It's crazy because I feel like this is wrong in so many ways, yet I'm intrigued at the same time!"

"And what do you find the most intriguing?" he asked, his voice noticeably lowering to a deep throaty sound.

"All of it!" I blurted out, blushing profusely. "And, um… I sort of *really* liked being spanked last night. Is that weird?"

"I underestimated you, Miss Cole," he said, a shrewd smile curling the edges of his mouth. His blue eyes narrowed into dark slits as he studied me, the lust in them intensifying with every passing moment.

"I want to learn more about your world, Alex. I don't know why..." I trailed off again, suddenly very conflicted over the thoughts swirling in my head. "I didn't know this sort of thing would… well, interest me."

"This needs to be more than just a passing curiosity for you, Krystina. There is no halfway. I want you all in, or nothing. You should know only the strongest of individuals are able to give someone their gift of submission. I think you may possess that strength, but you have much to learn."

"I'm a quick study," I informed him confidently, but my mouth had become extremely dry.

He moved over to his dresser and flipped on the stereo. After a few moments, a distorted guitar sound filled the quiet bedroom of the penthouse, followed by the familiar voice of Brian Aubert of the Silversun Pickups. I listened to the lyrics of the song I already knew so well.

Catch and Release.

Alexander stood with his back to me.

I concentrated on the song.

He waited.

In just a few short seconds, the air in the room seemed to sizzle, like the wick of a time bomb waiting to go off. Alexander's ability to persuade me with music, yet again, was a true talent. He was the master at his craft—an artist—always seeming to know the right sound to ignite me in an instant.

When he turned back to me, there was a wicked gleam in his eyes.

"Are you ready for your first official lesson, Krystina?"

I watched his gaze skirt up and down my body, fanning the fire building in the pit of my stomach. I loved the way he looked at me sometimes, like he was picturing me naked beneath him, touching and exploring every inch of me.

My little devil had festooned a red feather boa around a pouting angel's neck and began kicking a lively Charleston around her. I was more than ready to dance. I nodded my consent.

"I need more than a nod, Krystina. I want you to say it out loud. Because once you agree to submit to me, there's no going back," he warned.

"I'm ready," I told him, forcing back the lump in my throat.

"If you're truly ready, then you need to pick a safeword," he told me, his deep blue eyes searing into mine.

"Sapphire," I blurted out without really thinking.

He cocked his head to one side, a curious expression on his face.

"Interesting choice of word. May I ask why you chose it?"

"It's a stone. And it... it matches the color of your eyes."

"It's perfect," he said, his voice thick as he moved around to stand behind me. "Now, raise your arms."

I hesitated to lift them, trying to predict what he would do, and he *tsked* at me.

"What?" I asked, worried I had already done something wrong.

"Lesson number one. Unconditional obedience. When we are together, you are to do exactly as I say. No hesitations."

I complied immediately and tried to will away my natural instinct to question everything. When he merely pulled my shirt over my head, I stifled a sigh of relief as my arms settled back down to my sides. I wanted this, yet I was still so afraid.

"Now what?" I asked, feeling extremely silly because I didn't know how to act. I wasn't an inexperienced virgin, but in Alexander's kinky world, I might as well have been.

"Relax, angel. I can feel how tense you are," he said, lightly massaging my shoulders. "Close your eyes. Listen to the music and feel my touch. Submit yourself to me, and I promise to give you more pleasure than you can ever imagine."

His voice was husky in my ear. Goosebumps of anticipation prickled me from head to toe as I did what he asked. He placed his hands on my shoulders and slipped his fingers under the straps of my lacy black bra. Then, sliding them torturously slow down my arms, he unhooked the clasp in the back and unceremoniously tossed the lingerie to the floor.

My immediate reaction was to cover myself, but he pulled my self-conscious hands away.

"Don't ever cover yourself. I want to see you," he said quietly, but there was a sharp authority behind his words, the way I imagined a Dominant would speak to a submissive.

When he circled his hands around me to roll my nipples between his fingers, I moaned under his touch, and my hesitations immediately dissolved.

"How does this feel?" he asked, pinching each peak harder.

A jolt of pleasure surged through my body.

"It's good...I love it," I breathed, as he continued to squeeze my tight points firmly between his fingers and thumb. He plucked for a moment longer before moving around to the front of me to capture one nipple in his mouth. I relished the feel of his tongue as his mouth sucked and his teeth nipped.

"Stay here," he told me.

I watched him make his way to his special closet, and the flames in my belly began to travel south, turning into a heated pulsing ache between my legs. I could only stand there in a state of restless agony, waiting for him to return.

When he came back a few moments later, he was carrying a coil of black rope.

Does he want to tie me up already?

My nervous jitters returned with a vengeance. I was scared I wasn't ready and almost told him so, but I sought the courage to trust him and didn't give voice to my fears. Instead, I watched him as he began to loop the soft nylon around my wrist. He bound them slowly and deliberately as if he sensed my unease. His movements were measured and gentle, his actions representing how he would introduce me to his world.

He tied each wrist together in front of me tightly, but not too tight. I found the rope to be surprisingly comfortable and not the rough feel I would have expected.

"Are you okay?" he asked.

"Yes. I'm okay," I said truthfully. Somehow, I knew Alexander wouldn't take me too far. Safeword or not, I didn't believe he would push me to use it.

His hands slid down my belly, making quick work of the button and zipper of my jeans. He coaxed the denim down my legs, and I sidestepped to help him remove them completely. I was left in nothing but a lace thong and felt vulnerable in the sheer scrap of material, my voluptuous behind exposed.

He slipped a hand down the front of my panties, through the patch of curls to meet my wet slit. The throbbing between my legs intensified.

"I love that you're already wet for me," he growled, circling the pad of his index finger around the pulsing little bundle of nerves.

He dipped his finger inside me then brought it up to his mouth to taste my juices. His eyes burned into mine as he rolled his finger around his tongue.

Holy shit—that's hot!

Little sparks of fire shot down to my girly parts, and I thought I might orgasm just from watching him.

A sly smile turned up the corners of his mouth as he moved his hands back down to my panties. He looped his fingers around the strappy sides and tugged hard. In one swift motion, he managed to effectively tear the thin material in two, leaving me completely naked before him.

I gave a little gasp in surprise.

Oh my God. How did he do that?

Shifting so he was standing behind me again, he leaned in close, his breath a soft feather whisper on my neck. I quivered from the goosebumps racing down my body.

"You can wear these thin little lacy things all the time, Krystina. I like that I can rip them off you so easily," he murmured into my ear. "But then again, I think I would much rather you didn't wear any at all."

He reached around my hips, hands caressing down my belly to part my slick and waiting lips. He slipped two fingers inside of me, and I moaned, completely enthralled in a sensation of pure bliss. Between the thought of going commando around Alexander and the feel of his expert fingers delving in and out of me, I was almost ready to come.

His fingers pushed deeper and harder while his other hand reached up to pinch and pull at the rigid peak of one of my breasts. In a matter of minutes, I was on edge and found myself pumping my hips against his hand, unable to control the burning ache building in my pelvis.

But he didn't let me come. Instead, he removed his fingers at a torturously slow pace and began a steady circular motion over my pleasure button. I throbbed under his touch, already swollen and sensitive, seeking that desperate release. Back and forth, in and out, his perpetual rhythm making me crazed with carnal need.

Oh, please...get me there!

He held me tight against him, and I could feel his manhood straining through his jeans against my backside. His motions intensified in speed, and I couldn't take it anymore. There was no holding back. My breath hitched, and my insides began to tremble and convulse, hitting an ultimate shattering point as a kaleidoscope of colors flashed before my eyes.

24

Krystina

It took me a few minutes to recover, my vision slowly returning to normal. I felt like I might fall over from the bombardment of tremors coursing through my body. Alexander moved around to the front of me, never relinquishing his hold on me but keeping me secure and upright before pulling me against his chest.

He tilted his head back and watched me intently. Even through my heavy lids, I could see his eyes were scorching. They revealed a dark primal need, sparking a whole new kind of fire inside of me.

"That was for you. Now, this is for me. Kneel, angel," he said, moving his hands to my shoulders and gently nudging me to my knees. I knelt before him on shaky legs, still lightly panting from my orgasm. "Are you familiar with the submissive position?"

"I…" I wavered, heat creeping up my neck and licking my cheeks. Unfortunately, it wasn't from arousal this time around.

"Be honest. You don't need to be embarrassed if you don't know."

"I recall reading the term, but…no. I don't know what it is," I admitted.

"Then here is lesson number two. Kneel all the way down, so you're sitting on your feet. Spread your knees, leaving your thighs open. I want all parts of you accessible to me."

I did as he instructed, enflamed once again in sexual anticipation as I shifted into position. Sitting this way made me painfully aware, every nerve ending standing at attention.

"Is this right?" I asked, desire making me eager to please him.

"Almost. Normally I would want your arms resting on your thighs, palms open to the ceiling. However, with the way I have your hands tied, you can't do that today. Just remember that in the future. For now, just bring your arms up around your neck and rest them there."

"Like this?" I asked, not quite sure how long I'd be able to stay this way before the blood drained from my arms.

"Just like that. You look beautiful like this," he appreciated. His hands moved over my face, fingers brushing softly over my lips. "Now I'm going to fuck your mouth."

He didn't wait for my consent, but I had no desire to protest either. I just stayed in the position he instructed and watched as he began to undo the buckle of his pants. His eyes never left mine as he reached into his pants to free the erection straining through his jeans. My eyes widened when I looked at the sheer size of him.

He wants to fuck my mouth with THAT?

I swallowed and licked my lips.

"You have the sexiest mouth," he growled.

He gripped the base of his cock with one hand, and the other hand moved to take hold of the back of my neck. He stroked his thick member and pulled me forward to position himself in front of my waiting lips.

I ran my tongue around the smooth crown, the tip already wet with pre-cum. He groaned, encouraging me to take in a little more of him. I wrapped my lips around his head, circling my tongue around the small opening at the tip. I opened my mouth wider and took more of him inside. He was thick and soft on my tongue as I sucked, his ridges sliding back and forth over my lips.

"Oh, yeah. Suck on it, angel," he said hoarsely.

He reached around and entwined both of his hands in my hair, thrusting himself deeper and forcing a steady rhythm. I opened my throat to accept him, sucking and twisting my tongue around his thick shaft as I began to pump faster.

I wanted to grab ahold of him but was prevented by the way my wrists were bound together. I felt desperate—as if I couldn't get enough of him. I swallowed and opened my throat even more, to take in every inch I could. I pushed my head forward, taking him deep with my swallow, and held him there. I pulled back and did it again, this time, my throat adjusting and taking him deeper than the last.

"Oh, fuuuck! Stop, Krystina! Stop!" he hissed, pulling back suddenly. His breathing was ragged, coming out in short successions. "I'll never last if you keep doing that."

"Maybe it will be *you* who can't handle *me*," I told him, feeling more than just a little bit smug at my accomplishment. I smirked at him and licked my lips.

"Cocky, are we? Maybe you need to be punished," he threatened.

"Yes, please, Master," I said mockingly, still feeling superior over the fact I almost made him lose control so soon.

"This is not a game. You are my submissive. It would be in your best interest to remember the unconditional obedience you promised me. Now, get up on the bed. Lay on your back with your head by the mirror," he ordered. His tone was stern, and I scrambled to my feet to do as he commanded.

Yes, sir!

Evidently, lesson number one was to be taken very seriously.

I must have positioned myself a little too high because he yanked me roughly by the ankles, shifting me closer to the foot of the bed. He moved his way up my body, straddling me with his still jean-clad legs, and pulled my arms up over my head. Before I could realize what he was even doing, he had my arms bound tightly to the rails of the mirrored headboard.

I tried to give them a slight pull just to see how much wiggle room I had. I could barely move an inch without pulling my entire body up.

"Be still. Don't struggle, or else I'll have to spank you."

Um, yes, please!

I stopped moving immediately, waiting in eagerness for what he would do next. He was still hovering above me, just watching me, his weight pressing down on my midsection. His gaze moved hungrily up and down my body.

"I want to taste your sweet pussy," he told me, causing me to tingle with delight.

He moved down my body and positioned himself between my legs. He lifted my one leg, then the other, and rested them over his shoulders. His hands slid slowly over my legs, spreading my thighs wider before coming to rest just inches away from my throbbing clit. He parted my folds with two fingers, effectively exposing my desire. I was drenched, and I arched my back up in longing.

"I told you to be still," he scolded, pushing my hips back down to the bed.

My teeth clenched as his tongue swept up my entrance and over my clit. He began lightly, teasing me almost, as he nipped and sucked along my tender flesh. My hands balled into fists, every muscle in my body shuddering. I knew I was supposed to be still, but I couldn't stop the slight pumping of my hips under his ruthless mouth.

His hands moved up to pinch my nipples while his tongue circled an unmerciful amount of pressure on my clitoris. My hands strained at the ropes as the tension continued to build in my stomach. He began to sucker harder as his fingers pinched and pulled on my erect nipples. I writhed under his merciless tongue, and all hope of keeping control was lost. I bucked under him, my hips lifting upward as my legs stiffened. In a blinding light, he pushed me over the edge again, leaving me shattered and breathless.

I lay there panting as he worked his way back up, leaving a trail of kisses along my belly and my breasts.

"I was too easy on you," he murmured into my ear. "But I'm not done with you yet, Miss Cole. I shouldn't have let you come again so soon."

"Hmm..." I murmured, still in a state of euphoria.

He called me Miss Cole.

I had no idea why that was such a turn-on. After having two mind-blowing orgasms, I should have felt spent. Yet, those two little words made me yearn for more.

"Turn on your stomach," he ordered.

My arms and legs were like dead weights. I couldn't even imagine moving at that moment. He must have known how I felt because rather than wait for me, he helped me turn. The way he had me tied, flipping me was effortless despite my Jello-like state.

I heard him moving around in the bedroom. The sound of clothing being removed and drawers opening then closing was faint in my ears. I wasn't sure what he was doing exactly, but I didn't particularly care at that moment. I was too busy basking in the aftermath of sheer ecstasy. I had no idea sex could be this good, and we hadn't even gotten to the actual act itself yet.

The tear of packaging had my ears perking up, effectively removing me from cloud nine.

Condoms. I'm glad one of us remembered.

I had been so caught up in the moment that I hadn't even given protection a passing thought. I reminded myself not to be so careless the next time.

When Alexander finally climbed back onto the bed, his naked weight pressed down on my backside, and his erection rested heavily between my thighs. I instantly became aware once more, yearning to be filled by him.

"Are you ready for me?" he asked, his voice a hoarse whisper in my ear.

"Oh, yes," I breathed.

One of his hands moved back down between my legs, sliding down my crack, past my puckered rear hole, before slipping his finger back inside my tender folds. Pushing my legs apart with his knees, he positioned himself just outside of my entrance.

"I'm going to take you now. Hard."

And with just that quick warning, he slammed into me. Deep and fast. There was nothing gentle about the way he pumped inside of me. This was a fuck. No doubt about it. I had never been taken this way—so brutally hard, yet it was as if I had waited for this moment my entire life.

Within moments, the buildup began again. His relentless rhythm repeatedly hit the pleasure point within my walls, pushing me closer to that glorious electrifying brink for the third time.

But right before I could go over the edge, he stilled.

"Alex, don't st—"

"Don't come yet," he ordered me, then started moving inside of me once again. But this time, it wasn't hard and fast—it was in long, agonizing strokes, burying his cock all the way to the hilt, only to slowly pull it back out again.

How am I supposed to stop myself from coming when you keep moving like THAT?

I literally just learned I *could* orgasm—how did he expect me to know how to prevent it? I pressed my face into the pillow, fighting my body, straining to do as he asked. I bit my lower lip so hard I could taste blood.

After what seemed like forever, I couldn't take his torture anymore. I couldn't hold back any longer.

"Alex, I have to come! Please, I can't take it anymore!" I screamed out.

"You did good, angel. You can let go now. Let me feel you tighten around my cock."

He took hold of my hips, fingers digging into my skin and gripping me hard, as he began pumping faster inside me. This was what I wanted. It was what I needed.

"Oh, yes! Alex, don't stop!"

My heartbeat began to roar in my ears as a burning knot in my belly tightened and quivered. In an instant, my vision became hazy as an explosion of incredible magnitude hammered me with pleasure. I felt my walls spasm and constrict around his steel-hard length, pushing him over the cliff into his own euphoria.

I heard Alexander gasp for a breath, then another, before his movements finally stilled. I lay there trembling and panting, my hands numb. I wasn't sure if they were numb from being tied up or from the multiple orgasms that had rocketed through me over the past hour. I was sure it was from the latter.

Oh, yeah. I could get used to Alexander's world really fast.

Alexander groaned and shifted off of me to lie at my side. He draped his arm heavily across my back, spent. After allowing himself a few minutes to catch his breath, he reached up with one hand to untie me. Once my hands were free, he began to massage my wrists.

"Are you alright?" he asked me, his voice groggy from exertion.

"Mmm...I'm great. Just great," I purred and turned on to my side to cuddle up next to him.

Alexander slipped his arm under my head, allowing me to nestle into the crook of his arm. We lay there quietly as he softly traced small circles on my shoulder with his fingers. I smiled to myself, feeling like the cat that swallowed the canary. If I was going to jump back into the swing of things, I couldn't think of a better man to do it with. Alexander made me feel alive.

I wanted to believe I could feel like this with any man had I chose to do so, but a part of me knew otherwise. Our chemistry was like a lightning bolt, sizzling and sparking with every look, with every touch. I couldn't deny the current of attraction charging between us.

There was a reason why I waited this long to be with someone again. I couldn't be with just *any* man. I needed a man like Alexander, and the thought scared the hell out of me. But what was even more frightening—the things he wanted to do. With me.

I thought about the neatly printed list Alexander had written out. Crazy things and terms—many of which I had never even heard of, much less contemplated ever actually doing. Even though Alexander's power of persuasion had been successful so far, we still needed to talk about his kinks. I wasn't convinced I could do most of the things he wanted, and there was no doubt he had gone easy on me tonight.

What would happen when he turned things up a notch?

After a while, Alexander's arm went limp, and his breathing became soft and regular. I chanced a glance up at his face and saw he was sleeping. If I stayed curled up next to his warm body much longer, I knew I would follow suit.

However, sleepovers were out of the question—especially if I wanted to keep this thing between us simple.

No strings.

I silently got out of bed, being extra careful not to stumble in the dim lighting. As noiselessly as I could, I collected my scattered clothing and got dressed—minus the torn underwear.

Once I was clothed, I allowed myself one more look at Alexander's glorious, naked body, the perfect specimen of the alpha male. My gaze traveled up over his muscular thighs to the rippled power of his rock-hard abs and across the broad width of his bronzed chest. His face, normally so controlled and acutely alert to his surroundings, was peaceful and relaxed while he slept. He no longer looked like the intimidating billionaire real estate shark who owned half of New York. He looked young. Innocent.

He was truly beautiful.

On a whim, I searched my purse for a scrap piece of paper and a pen. The only thing I could find was an old receipt from La Biga. That would have to do. I quietly moved over to the dresser and scribbled a quick note on the back of the register tape.

Thank you for the wonderful evening.
Your Angel

Tiptoeing to the bed so as not to wake him, I carefully laid the note on the pillow next to his head. Reaching over to the wall, I shifted the dimmer switch for the lights to the off position. Now, the only light in the room was cast from the half-moon shining through the windows. Lightning flashed in the distance, signaling an incoming storm. I knew I had better get going or risk getting caught in it.

I pushed aside the guilt gnawing at me over leaving without a word, then quietly slipped out of the bedroom and left the penthouse.

25

Alexander

The muscles in my legs burned from running for so long and so far. But she was right there. I could almost reach her. I only had to stretch a little further, and I could wrap my hands around that long black hair. Propelling myself forward, I latched onto her hair, finally catching hold of what I had been in search of for so long.

I spun her around to look at me. It had been forever since I had seen her face. But when she turned, she wasn't whom I thought.

The ebony black hair I had been chasing was now a curly auburn. And the eyes—eyes that should have been a deep crystal blue were instead a wide chocolate brown.

This wasn't right. How could this be?

Rage flowed readily through my veins, hotter than a Georgia night, and I reacted. Throwing her to the ground, I screamed in outrage.

"This is wrong!"

Those big brown eyes stared innocently up at me

"Alexander, I don't know what you mean."

I shook her by the shoulders violently, her head repeatedly hitting the pavement under her.

"You're not what I want! It wasn't supposed to be you!"

"I don't know what you mean," she said again. I continued to shake her, but she seemed unfazed. Blood was now pooling beneath her head, but she continued to repeat the same thing over and over again. "I don't know what you mean."

It was like a chant, every word pumping more lava through my veins, threatening eruption. She wouldn't stop. She had to stop.

Now.

I grasped her around her neck and pulled her upwards. Her face was inches from mine, her eyes wide and innocent as I squeezed. Blood streamed down from her hairline, dripping into her eyes that had suddenly filled with tears.

I looked at the hands wrapped around the slender neck. They were hard and calloused, with untrimmed fingernails full of black grime.

Not my hands.

Appalled, I dropped her to the ground, shocked at the sight before me.

Not my hands.

How did I let this happen?

I looked down at the beautiful woman on the ground, but I was too late. Her body had gone limp. All I had left was a cold, vacant stare.

I shook my fists at the sky and screamed, anguish ripping apart my soul.

I BOLTED UPRIGHT TO A LOUD BOOMING SOUND. COLD SWEAT drenched my body, and bedsheets twisted around me. Restricting. Almost suffocating.

A bright flash and another loud boom.

A thunderstorm had moved in. The rain was beating loudly against the windows, keeping in time with the thumping in my chest. I rubbed my hands across my face, up and down over the stubble of five o'clock shadow.

What a fucking nightmare....

I untangled myself from the sheets and got up from the bed. Moving over to the windows, I stared into the storm without really seeing it. I was too shaken to appreciate the beauty of nature's temper.

I knew it was only a dream, but it rattled me nonetheless. Memories that had long been buried had momentarily come to life while I slept.

It must be all the shit with Justine and Charlie.

But I knew that wasn't the most likely reason. The transition of my dream had said as much.

It was Krystina.

I was terrified she would push me for a truth I couldn't give her. And when I couldn't give it to her, she'd walk. Or worse, she'd run if I did.

Suppressed memories threatened to resurface.

I willed them away.

Don't go there...

But it was hard not to. The dream was like an unwelcomed punch in the face, a reminder of many childhood beatings. And about how the apple hadn't fallen far from the tree.

I stared back at my reflection in the window. I had inherited my mother's eyes and her dark waves. But my face mirrored my father's, a constant reminder of how much I was like him. Bile rose in my throat.

I am not my father.

Or so I had been telling myself for years. I had read all the psychobabble online stating there was no truth to the claim that BDSM stemmed from childhood abuse. But it was hard not to question the theory when I knew who I was.

And I knew where I came from.

My father was an abusive asshole with no particular preference as to who his target was. My mother was the complacent fool who let him use us all as punching bags—it didn't matter if it was Justine, her, or me.

I was not much different from him, and only I could justify my actions because I obtained consent before doing it. But the nagging voice of my conscience reminded me only a sadistic bastard got off from hitting women, and it didn't matter which way the story was told. Even though I would never get a high out of blackening a woman's eye, I did find it pleasurable to mark one with a whip.

I only share his face. I am not him.

An internal struggle began, so familiar, although I hadn't experienced it in years. The reality of what I was and how I came to be crashed down around me, the truth dating back to the first time I had sex—young, naïve, looking to get it on with Nikki Tyson, the hottest girl in school. That first experience was a fumble of awkward adolescent limbs but went off without much of a hitch—except for my overwhelming need to smack Nikki's behind a lovely shade of rosy red. The simple idea of doing precisely that scared the hell out of me. Ashamed of myself, I never spoke to Nikki again after that night.

At sixteen, I had already deemed myself to be unsafe.

I convinced myself of the inevitable and opted to tread a lonely path, choosing to keep away from girls altogether. I was too afraid I would one day bring physical harm to one of them, making me determined to stay the course. Until I met Sasha two years later, the mysterious girl with piercings and tattoos who lived down the block from me.

She was one merciless bitch.

I stared at the stormy skies, watching the lightning in the distance, remembering a time with a girl I hadn't thought about in ages. A bittersweet smile formed on my lips.

Sasha had pursued me, despite my resistance. But my eighteen-year-old cock couldn't keep her at bay for long. Once I caved, I could hardly believe my luck—I had met a girl who wanted her ass smacked. And more.

So much more.

Sasha had taught me about the world I had eventually adapted as my own. Because of that, I will always have an appreciation for her. She had unknowingly created an outlet I desperately needed during a time when life seemed to be spinning out of control. She showed me how to use pain and pleasure instead of allowing it to use me. She was the bottom who taught me how to top.

My time with her was twisted and had been short-lived, but she made me feel normal and put me back in control of my life and my emotions.

That's why I am NOT my father. I am in control.

I pressed the button on the wall that would lower the darkening screen. As I waited for the shade to move from ceiling to floor, I considered Krystina and where things were headed with her. Sasha had always kept things between us casual, and I recognized the importance of that after she walked away. There was a reason why I always kept women at arm's length. Keeping emotional attachments out of the equation made things safer. Easier. It was one of my rules—one that has always served me well.

I'm more than just bending them for Krystina.

I wanted to take her on as a regular sub. I wanted her for my own. I was contemplating the long term, becoming more involved with a woman and taking on the role of a true Dom in ways that went beyond the bedroom. I wanted to satisfy this compelling urge to take care of Krystina in all things.

The entire idea was a foreign concept to me, and I shuddered to think of all the things that could go wrong. She lacked the experience I would typically require of a submissive, and she continually tested my emotional limitations by challenging my every attempt at dominance. She was a spitfire who was only familiar with vanilla, and I was leading her down a very dark path.

Am I capable of keeping myself in check?

I didn't know the answer to that, and I never trusted the unknown. I only knew violence stemmed from emotion. And in the short time I've known Krystina, she had managed to spark several emotions I didn't think I was capable of feeling. I was afraid my father's legacy would come to fruition, proving I was no different from him. The mere idea of that happening caused a chill to race down my spine, despite the comfortable temperature of the room.

The bottom of the darkening screen touched the floor with a quiet thump, effectively blocking out all evidence of the lightning flashes. I turned around and navigated my way through the darkness to return to bed. I eased back down onto my back and rolled over onto my right side.

To hell with the rules—at least for tonight.

I may never tell Krystina the full extent of what happened all those years ago, but at that moment, I needed her as I'd never needed another human being. My dream had left me feeling cold—as if frigid ice water were pumping through my veins. I needed the press of Krystina's naked body against mine to make me feel warm again.

Through the dark night of the room, I reached for her. My grasp only came up with a fistful of sheets.

Krystina was gone.

26

Krystina

It was another glorious Fall day in New York, and I relished the feel of the sunshine on my face as I exited the subway terminal. Last night's storm had cleansed New York of the humid and sticky air, leaving a clean freshness in its wake. Shakira was blasting through my earbuds. And yes, my hips weren't lying as I sashayed into Wally's for my shift.

It was such a cliché, but I didn't care. I felt confident. Sexy. And lighter on my feet than I had in years. Nothing could ruin my mood today—not even the stress I felt over quitting my long-time job.

"Hey, Melanie!" I waved to a coworker working the register.

"Hi, Krys!" she called back while scanning groceries for a customer. "Mr. Roberts was looking for you a few minutes ago."

"Do you know where he is now?"

"I think he's back in his office."

"Thanks!" I said cheerfully with a beaming smile.

As I was making my way back to Mr. Roberts' office, I felt my phone vibrating in my pocket. I fished it out and read the incoming text. I smiled to myself when I saw it was from Alexander.

TODAY, 7:51 AM: ALEXANDER

My office. 3 PM.

Barking orders at me already?

Unconditional obedience or not, that wasn't any way to start a conversation—especially after the evening we had shared.

7:54 AM: ME

Good morning to you, too.

7:56 AM: ALEXANDER

You have to fill out some paperwork so that I can get you on the payroll.

Pleasure at night. Business by day. Check!

I knew this arrangement with Alexander was going to be a slippery slope, one I'd have to navigate carefully. I just didn't realize how icy it would be.

8:00 AM: ME

Sure. But I work until 5.

8:02 AM: ALEXANDER

Leave early.

Yes, Master! Geez... he's so demanding.

But rather than lash out and let his brusque temperament ruin my good mood, I continued to placate him the best I could.

8:04 AM: ME

I'll talk to Mr. Roberts about it. I'll text you if I can't get out early.

I waited for a response. When I didn't get one immediately, I pocketed the phone and continued to Mr. Roberts' office. I couldn't be sure whether this was Alexander's way of separating our business and personal lives, but if he thought he was going to snap orders at me like

I was some sort of dimwitted lackey, he had another thing coming to him. Hopefully, it wasn't the latter. Either way, I would deal with him later. I had more important business to get out of the way first.

I approached Mr. Roberts' open office door and gave it a light knock to signal my arrival.

"Hi, Mr. Roberts."

"Krys! Glad to see you. I was hoping you'd pop into the office. I have to talk to you about a few things."

"I needed to speak with you as well," I told him anxiously.

"You first. What can I do for you today?" he asked. He leaned back in his chair and offered me a warm smile, causing the wrinkles in the corners of his eyes to deepen.

He appeared to be in excellent spirits. It was a nice change, as Mr. Roberts' smiles had been few and far between, and I dreaded the idea I might ruin his good mood. However, I knew there wasn't going to be an easy way around this. Rather than beat around the bush with small talk, I blurted out my reason for coming to his office.

"I think you know already I received a job offer from Turning Stone Advertising. I've decided to accept it. This Friday will be my last day here."

"Yes, I know it is. That's one of the things I wished to discuss. I spoke to Mr. Stone about you in great detail this morning," he informed me, taking my announcement in stride.

It irked me to learn Alexander had taken it upon himself to talk to my boss about my end date, but a part of me wasn't the least bit surprised he had beaten me to it.

"I'm really sorry for the short notice, Mr. Roberts. It's just that Ale—er, Mr. Stone was insistent I start right away," I told him, glad I caught my slip up in time. If I had any hopes of gaining respect from my future coworkers, I had to be extra careful not to use Alexander's first name.

"Don't fuss over it. It's no big deal. Do what you have to do," he said easily with a sweep of his hand. But his easygoing attitude seemed false. I knew my boss pretty well, and despite the relaxed smile on his face, I could sense his wariness. And his disappointment.

"I can stay a bit longer if you need me to—maybe work in the evening when I finish for the day at Turning Stone," I offered, feeling terribly guilty. He had been under so much pressure, and I had just become an addition to his mounting troubles.

He got up from his chair and moved around the desk to where I was standing.

"Don't be ridiculous. I'm happy for you. Really, I am," he assured me.

I looked at him doubtfully.

"Are you sure? I mean, I could help you train my replacement."

Mr. Roberts took a deep breath and shook his head.

"Look, I don't mean to sound so dismissive. I thought if I acted like your departure was no big deal, it would make leaving easier for you. You're not one to make rash decisions, and I know your choice to leave Wally's wasn't something you'd considered lightly. Anyone with half a brain can see how incredible this opportunity is, Krys. But I will admit, it's going to be hard to lose you. You're like family."

I was immediately rendered speechless as memories of my time at Wally's flashed before my eyes. Mr. Seymour, the sweet older man I delivered groceries to. The company picnics. Mr. Roberts' funny antics and constant teasing jests. Even Jim McNamara's pestering. They were my work family, one of my few constants in a city full of chaos, and I would miss every last one of them.

I had spent the last six months worrying over bills and about getting a better-paying job. I hadn't even thought about what I'd be leaving behind. I fought back the sting of threatening tears, knowing that in the end, I was making the right choice.

At least, I hope I am.

"It's time for me to move on, but I will miss everyone at Wally's a lot," I told him truthfully. "I'll be back to visit—you can count on it!"

"You'd better—and often too. My wife and I will miss seeing

your face around here. I haven't spoken to her about this yet, but I know she'll share my sentiments."

Another pain of regret struck me when I thought of Mrs. Roberts. Both she and Mr. Roberts had been so kind to me over the years, and I should have told them both together.

"Please tell Mrs. Roberts I apologize for not telling you both at the same time. I just couldn't put this off. Mr. Stone actually wanted me to start sooner, but I had to tell him no. I didn't want to screw anyone here at the last minute."

"I appreciate that, and thank you for being so thoughtful," he said and gave my shoulder a reassuring squeeze. "Although, I'm somewhat inclined to push you out the door right now. Your talent is wasted on stocking shelves. I've always known that."

"I'm nervous about this new job. Thanks for your vote of confidence."

"You shouldn't be nervous. You're going to do great things, kid. I'm proud of you," he beamed. "But for now, while I still have you here, a lot of deliveries came in over the weekend, and the receiving department is a wreck. Could you head back there and help sort things out?"

"On it!"

I gave him a thumbs up and headed to the office to start my shift. Suddenly, I remembered Alexander's request, if one could call it such.

"I do have a small favor to ask before I get to work, Mr. Roberts," I said, turning back to him.

"Anything."

"I'm going to have to leave a little early today. Mr. Stone asked me to meet him at Cornerstone Tower at three o'clock so I can fill out a bunch of new hire paperwork."

"Not a problem at all. In fact, I have a two o'clock grocery delivery scheduled for Mr. Seymour. It's just a small one. You can take it to him, then be finished for the day. Just let me know if you need anything else this week."

Walter Roberts was usually pretty easygoing. However, with

the limited staff at Wally's, allowing me to leave a few hours early was a lot to give, even for him.

"Why are you so agreeable?" I eyed him suspiciously, pausing by the door.

"Krys, do you realize what Mr. Stone did for this company? For my family?"

"Um, no, not really. I mean, I know Wally's was in a tight spot financially, but I don't know the specifics."

"This past year has really taken its toll on the Missus and me. Haven't you noticed how much less hair I have now versus a year ago?" he joked. But his face quickly turned serious once more, his easy smile turning into a grim line. He looked tired and seemed to visibly age right before my eyes. "We were in jeopardy of foreclosing on most of our properties. Sales have been down, and operating costs have escalated. The cost of keeping the shelves stocked, payroll, and building expenses got to be too much on top of the loan payments. Safety, product, and labor laws had to be the priority. The mortgages became second. Unfortunately, that wasn't something the bank was willing to understand. So, to make a long story short, Mr. Stone stepped in, bought all of our buildings, and assumed the mortgages. He relieved a big portion of our overhead expense by doing this."

"I don't get it. How was taking on Wally's debt beneficial to him?"

"I don't know all the details on his end, but I do know he was able to renegotiate a few things with the bank, and now Wally's will pay rent to Stone Enterprise. He's not a stupid man by any stretch of the imagination—I'm sure he's making money off the deal. However, he looked at the bigger picture first when many turned their heads the other way. He considers Wally's to be a staple in this city and saved hundreds of jobs. And for that, I will forever be grateful. If Alexander Stone hadn't come along, many people, including me, would be looking for a new livelihood."

"He's a good man," I murmured. I smiled to myself, remembering all the articles I read about his charity involvements.

Wally's wasn't a charity, but Alexander was their benefactor in a roundabout way.

Mr. Roberts eyed me apprehensively, and he seemed to be contemplating his next choice of words.

"Yes, he is a very good man. But I'd be careful with him. He can be somewhat authoritarian, Krys. I'm not sure if he's the *right* man for you," he warned.

I stared at him in shock.

Am I really that transparent?

"Don't worry about me, Mr. Roberts. I'm sure I'll be able to handle Mr. Stone," I said, albeit halfheartedly. "Now, it's about time for me to get some work done around here."

I gave him a small wave and quickly headed out the door before he could give me any more insightful observations. This was not a discussion I would have with my boss, as he had no idea how loaded his words actually were.

27

Krystina

I had mused over Mr. Roberts' warning all day long as I cleaned and organized the receiving dock at Wally's. And by the time I arrived at Cornerstone Tower shortly after three o'clock, I wasn't entirely convinced Alexander was the right man for me either. In fact, he was *wrong* for me on so many different levels.

Levels.

I punched the button for the elevator in Alexander's building and repeated the word over and over again in my head. It was a reminder of the unfinished business between Alexander and me —the list. I could never give him all the things he wanted. I may be open to some, but definitely not all. I had to be upfront with him before things went any further.

When I reached the top floor, I found Laura Kaufman sitting behind her desk. She shot an icy glare in my direction when she saw me, and I felt a little ashamed. The last time I was in this building, I left in a rush and had rudely ignored her. I politely smiled when I approached her, attempting to make up for my abrupt departure.

"Hello, Laura. I'm here to meet with Mr. Stone," I said, reaching out to shake her hand.

"Yes, he's been expecting you. Down the hall, first door on the left," she said dismissively, completely ignoring my outstretched hand.

Okay, maybe I deserved that.

"Er...yeah. Thank you."

Obviously having no chance at polite conversation, I turned and made my way to Alexander's office. It was easy enough to locate, as the etched gold nameplate on the frosted glass door was a gleaming beacon to all who passed.

ALEXANDER STONE
Chief Executive Officer

I gave three short raps on the door before pushing down on the handle to let myself in. Alexander, appearing every bit the part of a polished businessman, sat behind a desk of black mahogany surrounded by enormous windows that revealed astonishing city views. He was leaning to one side of his high-backed chair, chin resting on his fist. He actually looked more suited for the pages of a Giorgio Armani catalog rather than a CEO of a multibillion-dollar corporation.

"Hey, good-lookin'. Sorry I'm a few minutes late."

Alexander glanced in my direction and tossed me a single nod.

"I'll get you the paperwork in a minute," he said before turning back to his computer. He seemed to be in the middle of something. Rather than disturb him, I made myself comfortable in the chair across the desk from him. I waited for him to finish what he was working on and used the opportunity to look around at the surrounding space.

Like his conference room, the office was sophisticated in style, boasting a posh interior design with every modern amenity one could want in a workspace. It made me eager to see the offices at Turning Stone Advertising.

"You have a really nice office," I appreciated.

His only response to my compliment was a slight grunt. I frowned curiously at him, wondering what was up.

The phone on the desk buzzed, and Alexander quickly snatched up the receiver.

"You better be calling me with a date and time, Steve," he said irritably into the phone. After a moment, his face turned sour. Whatever the person on the other end was saying, it couldn't have been good. "I don't care what the excuse is. Find another underwriter to get it done. And if you don't, then I will. I want this deal closed by the end of the week."

He forcefully put the receiver back onto its cradle, turned back to his computer, and began furiously typing on the keyboard. After a minute, he stopped and appeared to be studying whatever was on the screen. His jaw ticked while his thumb tapped a steady beat on the desktop. I had never seen him look so agitated.

"Is everything okay?" I asked cautiously.

Alexander looked up from his computer in surprise, almost as if he'd forgotten I was there.

"Everything is fine. I just hate delays." And with that, he picked up the receiver again and dialed a number. "Laura, get ahold of Joshua Swanson. Tell him to check his email. I want a progress update by the end of the day."

He's on the warpath over something...

"What happened?"

He eyed me strangely but didn't answer my question. Instead, he got up from his desk and went over to a file cabinet.

"Here's the salary and benefit information for you to look over. It includes a severance deal as well," he said coolly, unceremoniously tossing a manila folder onto the desk. "After you read it, you'll need to sign a few things near the back."

He sat back down and returned to whatever task he had been so engrossed in. I was somewhat taken aback, his frosty reception perplexing. I squirmed uncomfortably in my seat. Between Alexander and Laura, I was beginning to think there was something seriously wrong with the water at Cornerstone Tower.

"I think I offended Laura the last time I was here," I stated casually, trying to do something—anything—to break the tension in the room.

"Don't worry about her. She can be fickle sometimes, but she's extremely efficient, which is why I keep her around," he absently waved off, not looking away from the flat-screen monitor.

Something wasn't right, and it wasn't just his frustration over a delay. He was acting differently toward me—cold almost.

Is this the way he planned on separating our personal lives from work?

I watched him for a moment longer before picking up the folder, the click of the mouse the only sound heard in the room. I opened it and pretended to peruse the contents, but I wasn't really seeing them. I flipped through the pages, chancing furtive glances at him in an attempt to decipher the real reason behind his mood.

"Alex, what's wrong?" I finally asked.

"Nothing is wrong," he dismissed, again not bothering to glance up. More silence. Another click-click.

Maybe he got what he wanted last night, and now he's done with me.

I fought the familiar internal battle between my insecurities and basic common sense. It was a real struggle not to imagine the worst.

I'm not my mother. It's better to ask than assume.

"Look, I understand our arrangement, but do you really need to act so rigid toward me? I mean, we're not exactly strangers anymore." I received no answer, just a few more clicks. After several minutes of listening to nothing but his tapping on the mouse, my patience slowly diminished, and self-doubting instincts began to override all rational thoughts. In the end, conjecture won out. "I'm sorry, but am I interrupting something of vital importance here? Or is it because last night you got your quick fuck, and this is your way of saying *sayonara*?"

He looked up sharply, eyes piercing through me like knives.

"First of all, you're not a quick fuck. I don't want to hear you say anything like that again. Ever," he spat out. "Secondly, you left last night."

Ohhhh, so that's what's got his panties in a bind!

"So, what if I left? I had to work today, and I didn't have any clothes with me. I had to go."

And that was the truth. Partially.

"You leave when I say you can leave."

"Oh, is that how it is? Well, let me tell you—" I started before he abruptly cut me off.

"There were important things that needed to be discussed last night. I only dozed off for a few minutes. That did not entitle you to make an impromptu exit," he boomed. I felt myself wince. Alexander was not the type to shout, as his quiet authority was enough to get any point across. He must have realized how loudly he was talking because when he began again, his voice had noticeably lowered several decibels. "Did you talk to your roommate last night when you got home?"

"Um...no. She was asleep when I got in. Why?" I asked, completely thrown for a loop by his question.

"That's one of the things I wished to speak with you about last night. Imagine my surprise when I woke up to find you were gone," he added with a frown.

"You wanted to talk about Allyson?"

"Not Allyson. My privacy. Remember what I said about keeping my affairs quiet? You cannot tell your roommate about us."

"It's going to be sort of hard to hide, Alex. I do live with her after all."

"I don't mean about the two of us being together. You can obviously tell her that much, at least. I'm referring to what we do behind closed doors."

I raised one eyebrow at him in surprise.

If I told Allyson the truth about you, she'd haul my ass to a shrink so fast my head would spin. She would think I had lost my damn mind.

I loved my friend, but I knew she'd never understand. Allyson could not know about Alexander's naughty bedroom antics.

"Oh, no worries there. I won't tell Ally," I quickly assured him. But after I spoke the promise, I immediately felt a small pain of guilt over not being truthful with my best friend.

"Nobody else can know either. I'm very serious about this. I am often in the public eye. What I do—what I like—can be viewed as dirty laundry by most people. I would prefer not to have it aired."

"Oh, and here I thought I might call the gossip columnist from —" I stopped short when I saw his face pale. "Alex, I'm only kidding. I'm not the kiss and tell type. Even with Ally. My sex life is nobody's business. You can relax."

"Don't joke about this, Krystina."

I put my hands up in mock surrender.

"No more jokes. I promise."

He leaned forward on the desk and pressed his forehead against his palms. Shaking his head as if to clear it, he eventually looked back up at me. He seemed calmer, yet there was a certain level of torment in his eyes.

"I'm not one to lose my head like that, Krystina."

"It's fine, Alex. You seem like you've had a rough day. Don't think twice about it," I blew off.

"No, no. It's just that I tend to forget myself with you sometimes. In all honesty, I don't think you'll go running your mouth about us. I'm just pissed off because you left last night. I wanted you to stay. I'm sorry for raising my voice the way I did," he apologized, catching me by surprise with his admission.

"I suppose I owe you an apology as well. I'm sorry I slipped out on you. And since we're being honest with each other, it wasn't that I didn't have a change of clothes—although that was a small part of the reason. I'm just trying to keep this thing between us as simple as possible. I thought staying at your place would only complicate things."

"Only if you allow it to, Krystina." He smiled wryly at me. "If you're going to be my submissive, you'll be doing overnights."

Whether or not I was going to do overnights was subject to debate, one that I didn't want to get into at that particular moment. I had just gotten him to calm down, and I didn't want to rile him again. Besides, it was my submission, or rather his freaky-deak ideas about what he expected me to do, that really needed addressing.

"Yeah, about that. I'll try to keep an open mind about overnights," I began. "But first, we need to go over the list you wrote. However, I'm not sure if this is the most appropriate place for talking about it."

"For Christ's sake, Krystina. Forget the stupid list! That's negotiable and doesn't even begin to explain what I expect from you." He got up from his chair and came around to where I was sitting. He pulled me up to my feet and placed his hands firmly on my hips. His heated eyes zeroed in on mine. "The list is only words on paper. Being in a Dominant and submissive relationship means more than textbook terms. It's a lifestyle—one I want to teach you. For your sake, I'm going to take it slow. As for the overnights, you'll have to stay at my place if you want to learn. And I'm serious when I say that you'll have to stay over often."

"I don't see why I have to spend the night with you to learn anything, Alex."

"It's my job as your Dominant to see to your every want and need. I can't very well do that when you're not with me. We got off to a more conventional start than what I am used to. But that ends now. You're staying the weekend with me."

"It would have been nice of you to ask, rather than order—"

He placed a finger over my lips to silence me.

"Remember lesson number one? Unconditional obedience. You want to learn, don't you?" he asked, but it wasn't really a question. It was more like a challenge.

I could feel the heat coming off of him, his body so close to mine, yet not quite touching. His eyes burned into me, blazing with desire. I slowly let out the air in my lungs I hadn't realized I'd been holding.

"Yes," I finally answered hesitantly.

"Good. Then here's another lesson for you. When you are in my home, you will be naked. Always. Unless I command you otherwise. Since you're so focused on my list, you'll remember nudity was written on there. I want you easily accessible to me at all times."

My eyes widened, and I couldn't respond to him if I tried. All words had escaped me. I wanted to argue and say I couldn't *always* be naked, yet a part of me relished the idea. It was so easy to get wrapped up in his words. His fantasies. It was so simple to get lost in the haze, my thoughts constantly muddled in the depths of those sapphire eyes.

I shook my head to clear the fog, the practical side of me winning out yet again.

"Look, I know you said to forget it, but we really need to discuss that list. Last night was beyond amazing, but I know you went gentle on me. I'm afraid of what's coming next. If I'm going to do this, it's important that we talk about it."

"I knew that's how you would feel," he said, shaking his head in resignation. He stepped away from me, leaving a cold and vacant space that was once fiery hot just seconds before. He leaned over his desk and plucked out a sheet of paper buried under a pile of folders. "That's why I brought the damn thing with me today. I figured I wouldn't be able to convince you to drop it."

"You brought the list *here*?"

"Are you surprised?"

"Well...yes. I mean, what if someone saw it!" I exclaimed, mortified at the thought of Laura stumbling across a list of taboo sexcapades.

"Don't worry, Krystina. Nobody enters this office without my knowledge," he said, laughing at my outward shock.

"I just assumed, considering your privacy concerns, we would keep our personal stuff a little more discreet."

"And we will, for the most part. Come on. Let's sit down and get this over with." He motioned me to follow him to the cushy leather loveseat at the far end of the room. Once we were comfortably seated, he spread the list out on the low glass table in front of us. "We'll go through this together, one thing at a time. You can cross off anything off-limits, then we can discuss anything you would consider."

"You want to go through this here? Right now?"

"I do. Then, when we are finished, we put this away for good, and you're all mine. Deal?"

"Why are you doing this? You clearly have certain expectations. Why would you consider altering them for me? What if I say I can't do *any* of these things?"

He looked up sharply, tearing his eyes from the paper and fixing me with his steely gaze. For a moment, I could see right through him, and all of his turmoil and indecision were transparent. He wasn't used to changing his ways. Yet, there was a certain amount of savagery in his expression as well, and I believed it to be the driving force behind sorting out his uncertainties.

"There's something about you, Krystina. I don't really know what it is—I only know from the first moment I saw you, all I've thought about is burying my cock inside you. If I have to make a few adjustments, trust me when I say I'm willing to do so. However, you get today only. After we go through this, I won't coddle you anymore."

His tenacity was inspiring, and I was suddenly overcome with a feeling of determination. I had to do this. I didn't want to be a scared, timid girl, afraid of the shadows lurking in the night. I wanted to explore the dark edges of desire—with him—and I wanted to please him.

"Do you have any highlighters around here?" I asked.

"Ah, I might?"

The perplexed expression on his face was almost comical, forcing me to clarify my obsessive need for organization.

"My OCD is kicking in. I mean, I'm not *really* OCD. I just need to color code this stuff, okay?"

His confusion was slowly replaced by amusement, making me fully aware of how silly this all was, despite my crazy need to have some sort of framework outlined for this relationship.

"Let me see what I can find," he obliged with a slight chuckle.

Alexander went back over to his desk and began rifling through a drawer. I took a minute to scan the list again. I thought about the night before and the way he had worked magic on my body. I certainly enjoyed last night, ropes and all. I was sure it was only a sampling of what he could make me feel.

I need to keep an open mind—with both pain and pleasure.

28

Alexander

As I rifled through one of my desk drawers, searching for highlighters, I was dumbfounded over how quickly Krystina was able to diffuse my temper. When she came into my office, I had every intention of solely focusing on business and calling it quits on the other half of the deal. After all, she had left me alone last night.

When I needed her.

But then she walked into my office. Just the sight of her stopped me in my tracks. As much as I tried, I couldn't concentrate on the business in front of me. Gone was the thought of ending the personal side of our agreement. Instead, I could only focus on her alluring face and the memory of her head thrown back in passion. And although she was now clothed in tight jeans and a Wally's T-shirt, I couldn't help but envision the sight of her perfect breasts molded in my hands, responsive to every touch.

I walked back to where Krystina was sitting and held out my hand to show her the findings—a red marker and a yellow and green highlighter.

"I thought you could use the red Sharpie to cross off any

definite 'no,' the yellow highlighter for a 'maybe' and the green one for a 'yes.' Is that OCD enough for you?"

"Don't make fun of me, Alex. But, yes—this will work just fine," she bit out, snatching the colored markers out of my hand.

I watched her run her finger down the list, immediately taking the red marker to cross off caning.

"Remember what I said, Krystina. I won't hurt you," I said, interrupting the striking of her script.

"I know you wouldn't," she said, and I was curious as to why she was suddenly so certain of that. Perhaps I was finally beginning to gain her trust.

"I'm glad you're starting to have a little bit of faith in me. Keeping that in mind, you shouldn't cross things off so quickly."

"This particular thing, it's not about trust or faith, Alex. It just sounds so medieval. The whole idea is a turn-off."

I simply nodded and allowed her to go back to the list.

She highlighted spanking in green, having already experienced the feel of my hand on her ass, but hesitated over flogging and whipping. She almost color-coded them red but picked up the yellow marker instead. However, before she could mark them, I stopped her hand.

"Remember the soft feel of the flogger in your hands from last night. Trust me, Krystina."

I saw the question in her eyes, deep and probing. But after a brief moment of indecision, she coded both green.

"Okay. I can make sense of most of the bondage part of the list, but you'll have to explain suspension to me," she said, needing more clarification.

"It's just like it sounds. I suspend you from the rails of my bed, leaving your body free for me to do whatever I'd like."

Her head snapped up to look at me. Those big browns went big as if she were picturing herself suspended in the air. My cock twitched, and I shifted slightly in my seat, the image filling my own head.

Krystina—spread out and on display. We are never going to make it through the list if I keep picturing all of this stuff.

I hoped she wouldn't continue to question every little thing. Detailed descriptions of what I wanted to do to her were killing me. As it was, I wanted nothing more than to strip her naked and embed myself in her satin heat. Right here, right now. On the couch in my office.

Patience. Get through the list first. Gain her acceptance.

In the end, she highlighted suspension in green, and I breathed a small sigh of relief when she moved on to the next thing.

"Hogtie?" she mused the question out loud, but thankfully I didn't have to give her an explanation that would torture my groin further. Her scarlet cheeks told me she knew the answer almost as soon as she voiced the question.

"I'm going to ask you not to go through and highlight the list of enhancements. Over time, I will get to know your body better than you do, and I'll know how far you can be pushed. Will you just let me use my judgment on those?" I asked her.

"I don't see why not. There isn't anything too crazy on here," she observed, scanning the rest of the list.

"See? This stuff isn't as bad as you originally thought, is it?"

She almost nodded in agreement, but then her eyes rested on something that had her head shaking back and forth.

"Wait, hang on. I don't know about anal bea—"

"Do you trust me?" I asked again, cutting her off.

Trust.

There was that word again, one I had thrown out a countless number of times. I could tell she was thinking the same, as her eyes were looking searchingly into mine. I wanted her to open up to me, but I understood her hesitation. My world was unknown to her, and she was bound to make countless mistakes on the unfamiliar path. She needed to trust me to guide her way.

"I trust you," she finally said.

"Good. Then we are finished with this," I said with an air of finality. I leaned forward and took her chin in my hand. "All of this talking about bondage has made my cock rock hard, and we need to decide how we are going to rectify that situation."

Krystina

I FELT MY SKIN PRICKLE IN ANTICIPATION AS HE MOVED HIS HAND UP to tuck a stray curl behind my ear. I shifted my eyes to Alexander's big mahogany desk before looking back to meet his sapphire blues. They were filled with heat and desperate need. I could tell he wanted me. My nipples hardened instantly, longing to be touched.

At the office? Seriously, get yourself in check, Cole. That's so unprofessional.

We could never do it *here*.

"Surely, you don't mean to do it right now?" I questioned, horrorstruck and thrilled over the idea all at once.

He didn't answer me but leaned in closer. I began to pant softly as the pad of his thumb traced the outline of my lips.

"I love the heart shape of your upper lip and the way your lower lip is fuller than the top. It's pouty, always teasing me, taunting me to kiss you. I'll be kissing these lips quite often, Krystina."

I closed my eyes and breathed in his scent. He smelled so good, a natural aphrodisiac provoking my wild desire for him. I exhaled slowly and licked my dry lips.

"Is that a promise, Stone?" I breathed.

He groaned, cupped the back of my head, and sealed his lips over mine. His kiss was firm and demanding, yet perfect as always, with just the right amount of pressure. He tilted his head from one side to the next, deepening the kiss with his tongue. His strength of purpose provoked a tightening hunger in my core.

I reached my hands up to run them greedily through his silky waves, pulling his powerful frame in closer to me, causing my passion to build to a fanatical need for more. I distantly realized we were no longer in a sitting position but had become horizontal on the loveseat. Alexander's body pressed down onto mine. Instinct had me scissor one leg around his waist. I arched my hips up against him, appreciating the feel of his manhood through our clothing. I kissed him back with a fierce urgency, wanting him desperately without any regard for our surroundings.

But then I remembered Laura was just down the hall, her severe scowl popping uninvited into my brain.

"Alex, wait! We can't," I started, pushing against his chest. "What if Laura comes in?"

"Hmmm...she won't. She knows better," he said, moving his mouth down to nip at my neck.

"What is that supposed to mean? Do you do this sort of thing often?" I asked accusingly, wiggling my way out from under him and moving to a standing position.

He looked up at me through glazed eyes, hair sticking up all over, and his clothes disheveled. His tie had loosened at the neck, and his shirt had pulled free from the waistband of his pants. I couldn't be sure if it were him or me who ran amuck on his attire.

Damn, if he doesn't look sexy like that...

"No, Krystina. It means I'm very busy, and I don't like disruptions," he said, sounding exasperated. "She knows to either buzz my phone or knock first."

I immediately chastised myself for always being so suspicious.

"Sorry—paranoia can get the best of me sometimes. I just got nervous about someone catching us. That's all," I admitted, pushing aside the thought I might not have been the first woman to be kissed on that couch.

He stood up and began tucking his shirt back into his pants. Then, after his tie was straightened, he reached for me and pulled me against him.

"I'm the one who should apologize, but I can't say I'm all that sorry," he murmured into my hair.

"What do you mean?"

"I shouldn't have done that. At work. In the office. Believe it or not, I do hold myself accountable to a certain level of professionalism. I should have restrained myself, but I..." he hesitated. "It was all that talk. And your damn highlighters. I had to have just a little taste of you."

"It's okay. I kind of liked it," I said, resting my head against his shoulder. He pulled back and studied me.

"Yeah, me too," he thoughtfully agreed. He sounded somewhat surprised by that fact.

"What's the matter, Stone? Did you break another one of your rules?" I asked, playfully slapping him on the arm.

"I did, actually," he admitted with a frown. "And if we keep this up, we'll never get any work done. I still have a lot to go over with you today."

Reluctantly, I removed my arms from his waist and took a step back.

"You're right. So, what's the next order of business?" I asked, focusing on why I was here in the first place.

"For starters, you still need to sign the salary and benefit information."

He went over to his desk and retrieved the folder I had left there.

Taking the paperwork from him, I took a seat in front of his desk and got to work on reading over the necessary information. When I flipped to the second page, I let out a gasp of astonishment.

"Alex, this salary would feed a small country for a year. It's too much!"

"Well, that's a first. I don't usually have people tell me I pay them *too* much," he said with a laugh, taking a seat behind his desk. "Don't sweat it, Krystina. I can afford it."

"If you say so," I mumbled, perusing the rest of the documents. Everything looked to be in order, including the health insurance and 401k benefits neatly outlined in detail. Only the salary was over the top. I picked up a pen from the desk and began scrawling my signature over the required documents.

When I was finished, he handed me another folder.

"Your first assignment," he told me. I peeked at the contents, anxious to see where I would begin.

"Wally's?" I asked in surprise.

"Yes. The grocer needs help boosting their sales. This

campaign is pro-bono, at least for now. I took a big risk with them, which is something I don't normally do, but I think it will be extremely profitable in the long run. Make sure you do it justice."

"Of course, I will!" I exclaimed, eagerly looking through the information in front of me. The chance to help out Wally's was exciting, but at the very least, it might help me move past the melancholy feelings I had over leaving.

"Wally's is personal to you. That alone will be beneficial. I'm confident you'll do well with it."

I looked up, beaming at Alexander for the opportunity, and saw him holding yet another folder out for me to take.

"What's that?"

"Last folder, I promise," he said, placing it in front of me. "This is my clean bill of health, as you required on *your* list. I don't suppose you scheduled a doctor appointment for yourself yet?"

Shit. I knew I forgot to do something.

I was mentally going through my schedule for the week, trying to figure out when I might be able to squeeze in the appointment when I heard my phone buzzing in my purse.

"No, sorry. I didn't schedule one. I meant to, but it slipped my mind," I absently apologized while I dug through the contents of my purse in search of my cell.

"That's what I thought, considering how this thing with us happened rather suddenly. So I pulled your doctor's contact info from your phone and took the liberty of scheduling an appointment for you. You'll go on Thursday, ten in the morning."

Too busy reading the incoming text, it took me a minute to process what he had said. Once it registered, I wasn't sure if I had heard him correctly.

"Wait. You scheduled a gynecologist appointment for me?" I asked, completely aghast. I wasn't sure if I should be pissed off or embarrassed.

"Don't be mad, Krystina. You set the stipulations, and I couldn't agree more. Besides, I'm anxious to ditch the condoms. I want you cleared and on some sort of birth control so I can feel that silky pussy of yours without any barriers," he said huskily, unabashed arousal in his eyes.

Oh no, buddy.

His sexy eyes and suggestive wiles weren't going to work. He had just crossed more lines than I could count, impeding on *my* privacy.

A woman's gynecologist was supposed to be *personal.*

"You overstepped your bounds, Stone. My doctors are private. You had no right to do that," I said through gritted teeth.

"Krystina, do you really want to go a round about this? Because I don't. You would have made the appointment anyway. So, what if I did it for you? Think of it this way—we'll have no worries come the weekend."

"First of all, depending on the form of birth control *I* choose, we may not be in the clear in time for the weekend. Second of all, you're assuming I'm going to spend the weekend with you."

"I'm not assuming anything. I know you are. Just you and me, angel. Flesh on flesh. And your unconditional obedience," he finished shamelessly.

Like I really needed another reminder of lesson number one.

I scowled at him.

Yes, we had an agreement—one I was determined to meet. I had said I would give him my submission, or at least try to, and I wasn't the type of person to take failure lightly. I certainly wasn't about to start now. Unfortunately, the pride I felt over maintaining my independence kept getting in the way. If this was going to work, I needed to loosen the reigns a little bit. However, I made a mental note to make an entirely new list—one outlining the definition of my supposed obedience.

Just take a step back and give him some measure of control. At least for now. That's all he really wants.

"Fine. You win this round. I'll stay the weekend," I said begrudgingly. "But in the future, I'd appreciate it if you allowed me to schedule my own appointments."

"Fair enough, as long as you remember that it's my job as your

Dom to take care of you—in all matters. I can see that's going to be a struggle for you."

"You think?" I sarcastically replied.

He got up from his seat behind the desk and came to stand behind me. Placing his hands on my shoulders, he began to massage, kneading small circles with his thumbs over my neck.

"In time, you'll learn to understand how this works, Krystina. In fact, once you learn your role, you'll welcome it."

"I don't know about welcoming it, but I'll try," I said, softening under his miraculous hands. I might be able to withstand his crafty way with words for a time, but I was a pile of mush under his touch.

"I want an entire weekend with you tied up and naked," he said, leaning down to nibble on my ear.

"Mmm...actually, since we're talking about the weekend, do you have any particular plans for Friday night?" I asked, tilting my head to the side so he could sample his way down my neck.

"I have several plans, many of which include you tied to my bed."

"Stop it," I lightheartedly scolded. "You really are the devil! I'm serious now."

"Me too. I want to start checking off all the things you highlighted green on your little list," he added suggestively, hands moving down to cup my breasts.

"Alex!" I shrugged his hands off. "I'm not kidding around. Melanie, a girl I work with, just texted me. A few people at work are planning a get-together at Murphy's Pub on Friday. It's sort of a good-bye party for me."

I looked up at him, only to see his eyes had darkened.

"Murphy's? I don't think so, Krystina. But you should go to it. Hale can drive you there, then pick you up after if you'd like."

"Why don't you want to come? It will be fun," I tried to persuade him. I was curious about the strange expression on his face. "Don't you like Murphy's?"

"I just don't fit in well at parties."

"Please," I pouted.

He frowned, then moved around the desk to grab his suit coat. "We'll see. As for now, I'm starving. Let's go grab some dinner."

"Um…sure. Where do you want to go?" It was pretty clear he was trying to change the subject, and I was interested in why.

"Do you like Thai?"

As if on cue, my stomach growled at the mention of one of my favorite foods, reminding me I had skipped lunch.

All right, you get a pass this time. My hungry belly is calling to me.

"That sounds so good right now, and I haven't had Thai in ages."

"Then Thai it is. We'll get takeout and bring it to my place. Then we can start on your list," he added, flashing me a sexy lopsided smile.

"You want to start checking things off right away, do you?"

"We could jump right to the yellow highlighted things," he suggested.

"You're too much," I said, shaking my head. My stomach rumbled again. "Food first, then we'll see where the night takes us."

"Oh, don't worry, Miss Cole. I plan on taking you to many places tonight."

I could only hope I was up for the challenge.

29

Krystina

Alexander dumped the bags of takeout on the dining room table.

"Make yourself comfortable. I'm going to round up some utensils and plates," he told me, heading to the kitchen.

I kicked off my shoes and went to work on emptying the contents of the Thai takeout. When I opened the container of red chicken curry, steam wafted from the entrée, causing my mouth to water. I dipped my finger into the sauce to have a taste.

"You're still dressed," Alexander said from behind me, causing me to jump out of my skin. I guiltily sucked the remaining sauce off my finger.

"Why wouldn't I be?" I asked, confused at first, but then I understood his meaning. When he told me to make myself comfortable, it was really a guise for wanting me to strip. "You didn't actually expect me to be naked while we eat, did you?"

"I said *always*, Krystina."

"Sorry, Stone. A girl has to eat. I need substance before I can begin your shenanigans."

"You agreed to try," he pointed out.

He looked frustrated with me for not cooperating. I wasn't confident I could bring myself to eat dinner without any clothes, naked under his scrutinizing gaze.

Oh, to hell with it.

It wasn't like he hadn't already seen every part of me.

"Fine," I spat out, aggravated because I was famished. "Where should I go to *prepare* myself to your liking?"

He frowned at me, his impatience abundantly clear.

"It's not supposed to work like this, Krystina." He ran a hand through his hair in frustration. "Forget it. Just sit and eat."

He hastily sat in a chair and began ripping through the remaining contents of the takeout bag. If I didn't know any better, I would think this was Alexander's version of a temper tantrum. I ignored him, too hungry to care, and dug into my food. The silence stretched on for a good ten minutes before he finally spoke.

"You're a pain in the ass. Do you know that?"

"So, I've been told from time to time. But in my defense, I did warn you I'd be too much work for you. This is all new to me. I didn't know you literally meant *always* naked. That's just not realistic. Either way, had I known, I would have mentally and physically prepared myself for it. I'd want a minute to freshen up before you jump on me."

"Jump on you? Is that what I do?" Alexander asked, amusement alight in his eyes.

I merely smiled in return before taking another forkful of the curry.

"So, I was thinking about a few things earlier today," I started.

"Uh, oh," he feared mockingly.

"Cut it out," I said. I balled up my napkin and threw it at him. "I was thinking about how I know pretty much nothing about you. I mean, my original thought was to keep personal details out of this, but it makes it tough to have a meaningful conversation, at least one not based around sex."

He smirked at me.

"I don't have any issues with our topics of discussion. Do you?"

"Not at all, but you know all sorts of stuff about me. I think it's only fair you give me a little something in return."

"What do you want to know?" he asked, albeit cautiously.

"Well, I told you about where I grew up. What about you?"

"I already told you I lived in New York my whole life," he told me, evading specifics and shifting his gaze back to his plate.

"Details please, Alex. It's like pulling teeth with you sometimes," I muttered.

He silently chewed his food, eyes weary. I could almost see the struggle inside of him. Seeming to come to a decision, he put down his fork and leaned back in his chair.

"You know I have a sister named Justine. Our childhood was spent in a rundown house in the Bronx. Definitely not a good neighborhood for kids, that's for sure. But we survived. We lived there until I was fifteen, then we moved in with my grandparents."

My fork froze midway to my mouth, shocked he had willingly divulged so much in just a few sentences, although he had barely said a thing. For me, it was like he had opened up Pandora's box, causing a million and one thoughts to twist around in my mind. I had trouble deciding which question to ask next.

"Why did you move in with your grandparents?"

"Now that, my sweet angel, is the million-dollar question—one I'm not going to answer. My parents are off-limits, remember?"

"Okay," I acceded. I didn't want to risk pushing him too far. I wanted him to keep talking. "Are your grandparents a safe topic?"

His face noticeably softened then, revealing a small smile.

"I can tell you about them. They were good people. My grandmother was a very kind woman. There wasn't a nasty bone in her body. My grandfather was a stubborn Englishman, but he had a tender heart, and he loved my grandmother fiercely. I've never witnessed such devotion between any other couple."

"That's so sweet," I awed, smiling at his brief synopsis. My bitter heart softened a bit. It was nice to know some people could live a life surrounded by the coveted white picket fence. But then again, his grandparents were from a different generation, from a time when commitment actually meant something. It was a shame knowing the world had changed so much.

"When my grandfather passed away, my grandmother was never quite the same after. She died in her sleep a few months after his passing. My sister says she died of a broken heart."

"How long ago did they die?"

"A little over ten years ago. I was in college. I wouldn't have what I have now if it wasn't for them."

"Were they well off?" I asked, assuming he was referring to his wealth at such a young age.

"Not so much, but my grandfather was a smart investor. That, combined with a substantial life insurance policy, my sister and I inherited a decent chunk of change. My sister's ex-husband gambled hers away," he told me, his face momentarily turning into a scowl. "As for me, I bought my first apartment building when I was twenty-one. After six months, it paid for itself, and I found I had a knack for scoping out profitable real estate. I bought a second building later that year. The rest, as they say, is history."

"You're either extremely fortunate or brilliant," I remarked after he finished his tale. I was awestruck by how easily he was able to obtain his fortune.

"I'd like to think both," he surmised with clever eyes, his mouth tilting up in a sexy lopsided grin. "Real estate is like a game of chess. You need to be able to read your opponent and know how to achieve checkmate. I'm good at winning, Krystina. And I always get what I want."

"Apparently, you do," I agreed, choosing to ignore his double meaning. I didn't want to acknowledge how quickly I surrendered in this complex game of strategy.

"You've finished your dinner."

"I have," I agreed, eyeing him curiously.

"At the risk of sounding cliché, I'm ready for dessert. You can use the master bathroom to freshen up before I jump on you—as you so aptly put it earlier. But, when you've finished, I expect you to come out of the bathroom naked."

My stomach constricted nervously. I should have seen this

coming. His body language had changed a few moments before, and his statement about winning had been a subtle clue as to where his mind was headed. So caught up in the story about his grandparents, I had forgotten about how he expected me to sport my birthday suit at the dinner table.

A mischievous glint flashed in his eyes before evolving into something deeper. Darker. I knew in an instant that Alexander would not hold back tonight.

He was going to test my limits.

"Okay..." I said, my voice coming out shaky. "Do you want me to come back out here? To the dining room?"

Naked.

"No, you can stay in the bedroom. Do you remember the submissive position I told you about?"

"Yes."

"That's how I want to find you, Krystina. On your knees."

Collecting my courage, I swallowed the lump in my throat, and I stood from the table.

"I'll go get ready. Give me a few minutes, okay?"

"Take all the time you need, angel."

I made my way to the bedroom and into the bathroom. The walk seemed torturously long, as my feet felt like they had lead weights attached to them.

When I entered the dark master bath, the only thing I could see at first was the marble countertop gleaming under the moonlight flooding in through the skylights.

I flipped on the light switch. It was no shock to see how impeccable the space was. There was not a thing out of place—no toothpaste smudges in the sink and not a speck of dust on the mirror. With its massive walk-in shower and whirlpool tub large enough to fit a small army, it was like I had walked into a modern-day Roman bath. I half expected a servant to come scurrying from some hidden corner and offer me grapes and a robe.

If only I could be afforded the luxury of a robe right now...

I unfastened the button of my pants and began to undress. I gathered my clothes at a painstakingly slow pace, trying to buy more time. Once folded, I laid the pile carefully on the counter, then turned to face the large oval vanity mirror.

I took in my reflection. Like all girls do, I began to critique the imperfections of my body. When my gaze eventually traveled up to my face, I froze. I looked terrified.

Naked and kneeling. That's how he wants me.

I struggled to erase the fear in my eyes as I smoothed out my unruly hair back into a ponytail. I was afraid for so many reasons. It wasn't sex that scared me. After all, it wasn't like this would be our first time together. I already conquered that challenge. I was petrified of putting myself on display for Alexander.

What if I did it wrong? What if he pushed me too far?

I worried I'd have to use my safeword. The fear of disappointing him consumed me.

Digging around in one of the vanity drawers, I located a tube of toothpaste. Using my finger, I brushed my teeth as best as I could. I took extra care to wipe out the sink, leaving it just as spotless as I had found it.

Then I looked in the mirror again. I didn't look quite as terrified as I did a few moments earlier. I couldn't stall any longer.

Committed to getting the first wave of awkwardness out of the way, I exited the bathroom. There was no sign of Alexander. However, he must have been in the bedroom while I had been undressing. The lighting had been adjusted to cast a muted glow about the room. Music filled the space, a dark vibe filled with raw emotion that was hauntingly beautiful. An assortment of objects had been placed on the edge of the bed, as well. One of them I recognized as the flogger. My breath hitched upon laying eyes on it, and my heart attempted to beat a hole through my chest.

The angel who had been conspicuously absent came to the forefront of my mind once again, reminding me it was not too late to back out of this. I dismissed her warnings with surprising ease and gave myself a pep talk.

I can do this! Don't be such a scaredy-cat!

I inhaled a lungful of air to steady my racing pulse. Walking to the center of the room, I kneeled in the instructed position. Thighs spread, palms to the ceiling.

I stayed like that for what seemed like ages, but it was realistically only a few minutes before Alexander finally entered the room. My skin instantly flushed, threatening to break out in a cold sweat at any moment.

He paused in the doorway, eyes filled with appreciation when he saw me. His approval made me relax a bit, and I gradually exhaled the air I'd been holding.

He moved toward me, making a slow circle around where I was kneeling, sizing me up.

"You look beautiful like this. You're like an angel. My angel," he said, stopping in front of where I was kneeling. Using his foot, he nudged my thighs further apart. "Tell me your safeword."

"Sapphire," I blurted out automatically.

Like I would forget it.

That word was my only protection in this little adventure into kink.

"Remember to use it if you feel like you're being pushed too far. But you need to trust I'll know your limitations. If you use your safeword too soon, the mood will be broken, and everything stops. Do you understand?"

"I understand."

He leaned down to skim his fingers softly along my jaw. My entire body came alive with pleasure at his touch.

Continuing on their path, those same fingers reached down and latched on to one of my nipples. My breath caught in my throat, and my head lolled to the side as I enjoyed the sensation of him twisting and squeezing the hard nub.

He squatted down further until we were almost eye level, and his other hand moved slowly down my belly until he reached my sweet spot. His finger worked through my folds, lightly grazing over my clit. Electricity flowed through me, causing every nerve ending in my body to stand at attention. He teased me for a minute or so before pushing two fingers partially inside of me.

"Oh, angel. I can feel how wet you are already," he said, voice edged with arousal. "But you're not allowed to come until I say so. Understand?"

I nodded my response, trying to decide if I should be proud or embarrassed by how quickly I was turned on. We hadn't even done anything yet, and I was dripping.

He pushed his fingers deeper inside of me, making a circular motion around my walls, while his other hand continued to pinch and pull at one of my nipples. Plumping my breast in his hand, he captured one hard point between his teeth.

I moaned, fighting the instinct to cry out, as he relentlessly worked me closer to the breaking point. I didn't want to lose control yet—not this soon. Regardless if he wanted me to come or not, I wanted to savor this sensation for as long as possible. But everywhere he touched left a trail of fire, making it impossible for me to control my own body.

"Alex, you have to stop. I-I'm..." I faltered over my words, my breath hitching as he increased the pulsing motion of his fingers. "I'm so close. I don't know if I can hold back."

But he continued his rhythm, using his hands and mouth to torture me by keeping me right on edge. His proficiency at knowing how to keep me there was mind-blowing. I wanted to scream out and absently found myself wishing Alexander had gagged me.

Eventually, he slowed his pace and removed his hands and mouth from my body. My shoulders dropped, sagging from pure pent-up frustration.

"You're ready for me. I could feel your pussy clenching around my fingers," he murmured into my ear.

"I want you, Alex. Desperately," I breathed, tilting my head back to invite his mouth to sample my neck.

"All in good time, angel. I have other plans for you first," he told me, pushing himself up to his feet. "Stand up. I want you on the bed, assuming the same position."

He held his hand out and pulled me up from the floor. Guiding my way, Alexander led me over to the black satin-covered bed. I crawled over the cool spread and positioned myself the way he'd instructed.

Climbing up onto the bed next to me, Alexander leaned in to take one of my nipples between his teeth. He pulled back and blew, causing the already erect peak to pucker into a hard point. I sucked in a breath sharply. Squeezing it firmly between his fingers, he reached into his pocket and produced what looked to be a small and round metal clamp of some sort.

"Alex, what—"

"Shhh," he silenced me. "Be patient. You'll like this."

He moved meticulously, placing the circular clamp around my areola and cranking its clasp tight, so it stayed firmly in place. The clamp was cold to the touch, only serving to enhance the rigidity of my nipple. He repeated the process with my other breast, each motion intensifying the volatile pulse between my legs. I had never been more turned on in my entire life.

After both clamps were firmly secured, he moved off the bed and began to undress. Once he was completely in the flesh, I found myself staring at him in awe. I had seen him naked before, but never quite without an unobstructed view.

Now here he stood before me, in all his glory, the perfect specimen of everything a girl could ever fantasize about. From his dark silky waves, flashing eyes, and perfectly chiseled jawline; to the contours of his honed shoulder muscles and washboard abs, highlighted by the shadows in the room, coming to a V just above his pelvis. He was the flawless male any Renaissance sculptor would have died for. The sight of him naked made my mouth water.

"I want you on your hands and knees, Krystina," he said huskily, and I reluctantly tore my eyes away from his impeccable form. "I want to see that beautiful ass of yours in the air."

I rolled over onto my hands and knees, feeling extremely self-conscious in the vulnerable position.

A few seconds later, his hands were on me once again, molding and kneading my behind. Moving at a leisurely pace, his hands and mouth worked their way up my spine, causing a shiver of goosebumps to dance over my flesh. I could feel his hard erection pressing into my thighs.

"I could rub my hands and lips over you all night. I love your body, the way it feels beneath my hands, the way it responds to my touch...you drive me wild, Krystina."

He worked his way back down, teeth lightly nipping my skin all the way to my behind. I desperately ached for him—for the release I had been craving—and my body hummed from the way he so reverently worshipped me. I no longer just felt alive, as the expression seemed too blasé for how I actually felt. I was phenomenal in the supernatural sense—as if I could be anything he wanted me to be, do anything he wanted me to do.

"Alex, I don't want to wait anymore...just take me!" At my plea, he pulled away. I arched, opening myself to him, just waiting to be filled.

"You need to tell me if you're not ready for this, angel. I didn't want to rush you into this too fast, but I can't keep holding back. Are you sure you can take it?"

"Please, I'll do anything!" I cried out. I surrendered fully, not caring about anything other than satisfying my burning need. So lost in my own excitement, I didn't realize he had the flogger in his hand.

30

Krystina

S*NAP!*

The crack of the flogger hit my behind, a violent shock to my system, and I cried out. It hurt like hell, and it was unexpected. My natural instincts compelled me to yell out my safeword. Pure stubbornness ended up being the only driving force stopping me from doing just that. There was no way I would forfeit that quickly. However, as much as the sting hurt, the pain was fleeting. Now I only felt a slight tingle on my backside.

He ran the ends of the flogger up my back, causing a shiver of goosebumps to spread all over me. I breathed a sigh of relief, thankful there wasn't more to this.

I can handle this.

I barely had time to process the thought when another blow from the flogger came across my behind. This time it was harder but in a different place. Fire spread over my ass. That one had hurt more—a lot more.

"Feel the burn, angel. Embrace it while you focus your attention on the weight of the nipple clamps."

I did as he said, and this time when the strap hit me, I felt an entirely new sensation. My nipples hardened, straining through the clamps. They ached but in a good way. A moan escaped my lips, rather than the cry of shock like the previous two times I had felt the bite of the leather.

A fourth crack of the flogger.

I didn't even feel the sting this time around because my mind was too focused on my breasts aching for attention. Another lash, then another, never in the same place twice. Eventually, an unbearable throbbing had begun between my legs. I wanted him now, in the worst way. I ached for him to give me some sort of release. I squirmed a little, hoping the friction would alleviate this longing to be touched.

As if he sensed my need, he reached his hand under me, softly rubbing his fingers through my folds. He teased small circles around my clit, exerting just the right amount of pressure to ease my ache but not enough for a full release.

"Oh, baby...you're drenched," he said, his voice low and husky. He placed feather-light kisses over my reddened backside before he began to work me over again, one lash after another. "You like this, don't you?"

Adrenaline pumped through my veins until I floated into a dream-like state, completely detached from reality. I sluggishly processed his words.

"No—yes, I do," I breathed out, confused by desperation. "Alex...just...make me come. Please!" It came out like a broken sob, giving a voice to how much I was truly suffering.

I needed it. I needed him.

Please. Now.

"I'll get you there. Have patience," he assured. He rubbed the flogger softly over my back, its feathery touch reminding me the tool was not only used for pain but pleasure. After a moment, I felt the bed shift as he moved to position himself under me, head between my parted legs. "Spread your legs wider. I want to taste you. I want you to come all over my tongue."

If his words weren't enough to send me over the edge, the first gentle flick of his tongue was. The orgasm crashed over me like a giant tidal wave, surprising me with its intensity. His tongue became more aggressive, the sucking of his mouth more demanding. He kept me at my peak like he was dying of thirst, seeking to drink every last drop.

My leg muscles had tightened from euphoria, trembling involuntarily and out of control. I couldn't stay on my knees much longer, and I was almost grateful when he moved out from under me, allowing me a moment to slump down onto the cool bed sheets. Entirely spent, I listened to the sound of my pulse thudding in my ears. However, the telltale sound of foil ripping for the condom reminded me Alexander was not yet finished with me.

"Roll over. I want to see you when I take you," he said huskily.

My strength had left me, and it was a struggle to do as he requested.

When I eventually managed to turn onto my back, he pulled my legs up and spread them wide, effectively exposing my swollen clitoris slick with his saliva. He hungrily drank in the sight, his palpable desire causing my pulse to quicken once again. Nestling his cock near my entrance, he slowly and deliberately pushed his way in.

I gasped when he began to move, never having come down fully from my orgasm. And just when I thought I couldn't go any higher, he brought me to a whole new height. Pounding fast and hard, he brought a thumb to my clit, massaging the now oversensitive bundle of nerves. I wrapped my legs around him, giving him better access to drive even deeper. It was too much, the pleasure unbearable.

"I-I can't!" My words rushed out in a faltering cry.

"You can, and you will. Feel it, Krystina. Feel me, all of me."

He stopped circling my clit, and instead just applied a small amount of pressure, intensifying the throb of the blood flow while his cock continued to thrust deep. With his other hand, he began to flick at one of my nipples, still rigid and straining through the clamp. The combination drove me mad.

I was wild for him.

"Oh, yes! I'm there. I'm there!" I cried out.

Wave after wave of pleasure crashed over me, full of pure and unadulterated ecstasy, as Alexander pushed me over the edge once again.

"You're so tight, angel. I could spend the rest of the night buried in your heat," he said in a guttural tone. "I want you to come for me again but wait for me this time. I want to come with you."

I was still buzzing, almost delirious from the last one, panting and gasping for breath.

One more?

I wasn't sure if I could do it again.

Alexander shifted his position upward. His fingers curled around my hips, and he pounded forward fast and deep, pushing into me with a brutality that took my breath away—possessing me further and harder than I thought possible, repeatedly hitting the pleasure point in my core.

"Oh, Alex. You feel so good," I moaned.

My words seemed to drive him crazy, and he hammered home with an animal-like force. Within minutes, I felt that familiar ache, the build-up a steady roar in my ears until I finally released into a moment of astounding rapture. A muffled cry escaped my lips as something inside me snapped. The room around me became a blurry haze. My body involuntarily bucked upward as I began to pulse and clench around him again. Almost simultaneously, I felt him shudder.

"Ah, fuck—Krystina," he grunted, pumping faster, milking his own release with every thrust.

He slumped down on top of me, blanketing me with his heat. We were both sticky from exertion, but I didn't care. I wanted to savor his occasional twitch inside of me, the final echo of his release, prolonging those final few flutters of my own staggering climax.

When it seemed we'd both caught our breaths, he reluctantly and carefully pulled out, leaving me practically purring like a kitten.

"Stay here," he said.

I glanced to my right and saw him walking into his master bathroom. I heard a few cabinets opening and closing, then the water running for a few minutes. While he was gone, I had a vague awareness of the music still playing. The songs no longer spoke of wild passion and desire and were more soothing and fitting to my current state of being.

When Alexander returned, he began to wipe a warm washcloth between my legs, removing the remnants of our lovemaking. The tenderness and intimacy of his actions were surprising. And for the second time since meeting Alexander, I felt a little crack in my carefully built walls.

Careful now...it's just the aftereffect of sex.

I had to watch my step before I was left with nothing but a pile of rubble.

However, I wanted to enjoy this moment, at least for another minute. And as he climbed into bed, I pushed away the nagging worry that perhaps I liked this all a little *too* much and allowed him to pull me close against him.

I nestled my head against his chest.

Only for a minute, Cole.

Because a minute was all I could afford to give.

Alexander

I HELD KRYSTINA TIGHT AGAINST ME, WITH HER HEAD RESTING UNDER my chin. Using my index finger, I traced the line of her spine and the shape of her shoulder blades. She hummed under my touch, satiated from the throws of passion.

I brushed my lips over the top of her head, breathing in the scent of her hair. Her intoxicating smell caused my desire to surge, blistering hot through my veins.

Goddamn, but I want her again.

I closed my eyes and took a few measured breaths, fighting off the urge to take her once more. I couldn't, at least not just yet. If we were going to venture into a true BDSM relationship, there were certain things I had to attend to first. In the past, I had always felt it was the submissive's responsibility to attend to their personal needs after playing. However, Krystina was different. If I ignored certain aspects of my world, it would be a huge mistake we would both regret.

"Sit up, angel. I need you to drink a glass of water," I told her, shifting us both into a sitting position. I reached onto the nightstand to get the vanity cup I had filled while in the bathroom.

"Thanks. I'm parched," she said groggily but eagerly took the glass to quench her dry mouth.

"Easy, not too fast. You need to hydrate, not make yourself sick."

"I'm thirsty, Alex. Don't worry. I don't think water will make me ill," she laughed, but her words were still sluggish. I didn't like the coloring of her skin. I could see her cheeks were flushed through the dim lighting, but the rest of her was ghostly pale. I closed my eyes briefly. Guilt swelled in my gut.

I was too hard on her. Dammit!

I knew better than that. Going too rough on a first-timer could have devastating results.

"I'm serious, Krystina," I insisted. I moved to position myself behind her and began to massage her shoulders lightly. "It's important you take care of your body after a scene like we just had."

"What do you mean?"

"I didn't hold much back with the flogger. At any point, tonight, did you find you lost your focus at all? Almost as if you were in a trance?"

She turned her head to face me, brows furrowed in question.

"Actually, I did. Why?"

"It's a natural occurrence for a submissive, and part of the reason why I want you to stay overnight with me tonight," I explained, continuing to knead and press my thumbs into the muscles of her shoulders. "It's important you are cared for properly after feeling that way. What you experienced is something called subspace, and it's not something that should be considered lightly."

Her nose pinched up in confusion.

"Subspace? Isn't that something from *Star Trek*?"

The purity of her question was so unexpected and completely disarming. A low chuckle emerged from me. I was amazed at how easily I was able to laugh with her. To simply be me.

"Possibly, I guess. I'm not sure. I've never seen *Star Trek*," I admitted.

"You're kidding! Everyone has been a Trekkie at one point in their life—it's like a rite of passage. You must have had a very boring childhood," she scoffed. Her words were beginning to sound a little more energized, and her skin coloring was returning to normal.

Good. She's coming down.

"Well, perhaps it's in a science fiction movie, but I assure you—what I am referring to is anything but fictional. It's a very real thing."

"How do you know so much about this stuff?"

"Time. Practice. I learned a lot from the clubs. What I didn't learn from there, I read about. Besides, it's what I like. Why wouldn't I make it my business to know a lot about it?"

She got quiet then, her expression thoughtful as if she were mulling over my words. After a minute, she cast her gaze down and started fiddling with the sheets tangled around us.

"Water, back rubs, sleepovers...do you take care of all your submissive women this way?" she questioned timidly. It was almost as if she were afraid of the answer.

"No. You are the first," I openly admitted.

She slowly looked back up, eyes round and disbelieving.

"Really?"

Her insecurity hit me square in the chest.

Angel, don't you know? You're not just another random girl in my bed.

To see such fragility beneath her iron core resolve threw me off-kilter, and I struggled to find my balance. I reached up to tenderly push a stray curl away from her face, tucking it behind her ear.

"Yes, angel. Really. Except for my first stint with BDSM, my experience has been limited to one or two night affairs. Until I met you, I've never taken the chance with a more long-term arrangement."

She turned back around and settled herself against my chest once again.

"Who was your first? I mean," she paused, giving herself over to a yawn. "You told me you've been into this for years, but I guess what I really want to know is if all of your relationships have been this way."

Whether it was her captivating curiosity or the docile way she lay in my arms, I couldn't stop the words from flowing if I tried.

"I was eighteen. I was seeing this girl from my neighborhood. We were only together for a couple of months, but she was into it. When I look back, what we did was like playing in the minor leagues, but it sparked more than just a simple curiosity for me. As I got older, I learned money had a way of talking. I started traveling in different social circles, particularly in circles that included a few millionaires with diverse tastes. Eventually, I was propositioned about joining a club. Everything just fell in line after that."

"So, it's that easy? You just go to a club and pick out a random girl?" She posed her question indifferently, but I could hear a small measure of disgust hidden beneath her tone.

She doesn't understand.

I had to rein her in before the conversation went south.

"It's not quite as simple as you're making it sound, Krystina. There is a process involved—it's not a difficult one, but steps are taken to make sure all parties are safe and discreet. That's why I typically favor the club scene. The women there know the rules, they have the experience, and they can keep emotional attachments out of an arrangement."

"Hmm...I think I'd like to go to your club one day," she mused.

Oh, hell no.

Knowing Krystina's inquisitive mind, I should have predicted she'd want to go to the club once she knew about it. I cursed myself for not considering the possibility. The thought of her being inside Club O made me feel sick, but I couldn't tell her without an explanation.

She didn't know what went on there, despite the controls put in place. She would be vulnerable to any number of controversial behaviors, depending on who was in attendance. As it was, she had already been rattled by what she had found on the internet. Seeing it in person would be an entirely different experience—one I didn't think she could handle. And I'd be damned if I would be the one to expose her to the depth of licentiousness that could happen.

"I don't think that's a good idea."

"Why not?"

"It's not the sort of place you'd like," I tried to dismiss.

"Either way..." she paused, giving herself over to another yawn. "I'd like to go someday to see for myself."

I could tell she was fighting off sleep, so I quickly took advantage of her exhaustion to dispel any thoughts she may have about pushing the subject further.

"You need sleep, angel. We've talked enough tonight, and you have to rest. Just close your eyes."

Unsurprisingly, it didn't take much convincing. Within minutes, Krystina's breathing was soft and even. It was all I could do not to breathe a sigh of relief. I knew if she had her full wits about her, I wouldn't have been let off the hook so easily. My involvement with her was moving rapidly, and I often found myself inadvertently giving away too much information. I had to remember how green Krystina was to my scene and disclose information at a more measured pace. If I continued to give her too much all at once, I'd risk pushing her away.

I shifted her weight to the side to lay her down beside me. She barely stirred as I slid the covers up over her body. Propping a pillow under my elbow, I rested my head on my hand and stared down at her for a long while. Her lips parted ever so slightly with each breath she took, her alluring face soft and tranquil. She was beautiful when she slept.

I couldn't help but think about how perfect she looked here—in my bed—as if she were destined to be there. I was surprised by how easily I had adapted to the idea of having her here regularly. The feelings she stirred were unfamiliar, but I couldn't say they were unwelcomed. Being with Krystina made me realize how empty my life had been. She was unknowingly filling a void I hadn't known existed before.

However, I could not ignore the steadfast pull in my gut, the constant reminder I shouldn't get too close. I knew if I wanted to keep Krystina around, I needed to find a way to balance the past with the present before I got in any deeper.

Giving in to a yawn, I fought against my eyelids that had suddenly become heavy. It was barely ten o'clock, but I felt exhausted.

I can't fall asleep...not yet.

I didn't think Krystina was going anywhere anytime soon, but there was no way I would chance her slipping out on me again. I had to keep the sandman away for just a little while longer.

I got out of bed and went over to the far side of the room to hit the dimmer switch for the bedroom lights. Moonlight shone through the glass wall, casting dark shadows over the walls. I was considering pouring myself a nightcap when I heard Krystina mumble incoherently.

"I'm sorry. What did you say?" I asked, moving back toward her.

"Alexander," she murmured.

"Yes, angel."

No answer.

She must be talking in her sleep.

I smiled at that, finding the sound of my name on her lips to be endearing, even during sleep. Forgetting the drink, I climbed back into bed and settled in alongside her.

"I...no, I shouldn't. I have to go," she mumbled, words barely audible. Through the glimmer of the moonlight, I saw her brow crease up as if she was tormented over some thought or another.

"Shh, Krystina. You don't have to go anywhere," I whispered to her, but she didn't respond.

I pulled her tight against me and stroked the top of her hair.

You're staying right here, angel—where you belong.

31

Alexander

As my body clock dictated, I woke up before sunrise to the feel of Krystina still in my arms. She was pressed up against me, her naked body warm and inviting. Almost too inviting. I slowly rolled onto my back before a particular part of my anatomy decreed Krystina wake up too.

Reaching over to the nightstand, I grabbed my smartphone to begin the usual routine of checking emails and looking at the schedule for the day ahead. Before I opened my inbox, I saw I had a slew of text messages Matteo had sent the previous night.

YESTERDAY, 8:30 PM: MATTEO DONATI

What are you doing? Want to meet up for drinks?

I sent Bryan a text. He's in. Meeting at Social Lounge in an hour.

I scoffed after reading that.

Of course, Bryan was in.

My accountant was always up for a party—especially if it was at a hot pickup joint.

10:02 PM: MATTEO DONATI

Where are you?

You're always glued to your phone. I hope you aren't answering because you're getting laid. How is the girl, by the way?

I had to stifle a laugh after reading his last text, or I'd risk waking Krystina. Matteo was anything but subtle.

Smart-ass.

After thinking about how I should respond, I began typing out a reply to my friend.

TODAY, 5:37 AM: ME

I just saw your message. The girl is fine. When I get laid is none of your business. I hope you guys had fun. Sorry I missed it.

I fired off the quick response to Matteo and opened my inbox.

There was an email from Kimberly Melbourne giving me a status update on the Turning Stone office remodel. According to her projections, the remodel would be completed as scheduled.

Good.

There was an email from Bryan stating the groundbreaking ceremony had finally been scheduled for Stone Arena.

It's about damn time.

Obtaining all the required building permits had been a considerable holdup. The delay had cost Stone Enterprise a pretty penny, which had skyrocketed my accountant's blood pressure. He was not happy about my endeavor with the soccer complex or the price tag for the naming rights. But despite his reservations, Bryan had practically moved mountains to cut through all the red tape. I owed him and a few other key staff members a thank you at the very least.

TO: Bryan Davenport
CC: Stephen Kinsley, Laura Kaufman, Hale Fulton
FROM: Alexander Stone

SUBJECT: Re: Stone Arena

As you know, this venture is personal to me, and I appreciate all of your efforts on the project. Stephen will work out the remaining legalities with the arena board members. However, I will break the mold with this and not hire out the usual planning firm for the groundbreaking. Hale will be heading up security, and I want Laura to act as lead coordinator on the event details and PR. Every board member for the arena must be present when we break ground—this is not negotiable. We've received a lot of pushback on this deal, and I'm sure the press will swarm us. I want a united front.

Keep me apprised of the planning process.

Alexander Stone
CEO, Stone Enterprise

I sent the email and moved on to the next.

I was surprised to see a message from an old friend from college. I hadn't spoken to him in a few months, but the title of the email had me arching my eyebrows in curiosity.

TO: Alexander Stone
FROM: Burke Dalton
SUBJECT: Desperate

Alex,
I'm in charge of a convention for Boston Lifestyle and Investments. Our keynote speaker canceled on me at the last minute, and I'm in a bind. You would be a perfect fill-in. It's a two-day event, this week Thursday and Friday. I know this is last minute, but I'll owe you big if you can make it happen. See what you can do. Your help is much appreciated.

Regards,
Burke

The last thing I wanted to do is go to Boston this week, and I wasn't sure if I could squeeze it in. I quickly forwarded the email to Laura to see if she could make it work. The woman had the ability to make miracles happen, but I didn't want to confirm anything with Burke until I got with her on it.

Once that was sent, I read Laura's daily correspondence, the one summarizing my schedule for the day. I smiled when I saw I had a fairly light agenda planned. All in all, the day was already shaping up to be a successful one, even if I did have a potential monkey wrench for later in the week.

I glanced down at Krystina, who was still sound asleep beside me.

When was the last time I took a morning off?

Today's schedule would allow me to go into the office a little later than usual, and the idea of spending the morning with Krystina was appealing. On impulse, I sent Laura a very uncharacteristic message.

TO: Laura Kaufman
FROM: Alexander Stone
SUBJECT: Re: Today's Schedule

Laura,
I'll be in the office later than normal today. You can expect me in by 11 a.m. However, I'll need an immediate response regarding Boston. Let me know as soon as you have it figured out.
Also, I need you to get in touch with Vivian ASAP. She will need to pick up breakfast fixings before getting here (she'll know what to buy).

Alexander Stone
CEO, Stone Enterprise

I hit the send button and climbed out of bed. After allowing myself a good stretch, I threw on jogging pants and a T-shirt. The next order of business was a note for Vivian. I retrieved a notepad and a pen from my study and made my way to the kitchen. I jotted a quick note outlining my requests for the day and placed it on the counter for her to see when she arrived.

I really wish that woman would stop being so resistant to technology and get a cellphone.

However, I quickly dismissed the passing thought since she was so good at her job. I could rely on Vivian for almost anything and had committed to concede this one thing for the housekeeper long ago. There would be no changing it now.

You can't teach old dogs new tricks.

I headed back into the bedroom to grab my sneakers and to check on Krystina. She was still sleeping like a baby, with her arms curled around a pillow and her mass of curls fanned out behind her head. The sun was just beginning to lighten the night sky, casting a luminous glow over her skin.

I moved to lower the darkening screen in the room so the light from the pending sunrise wouldn't wake her. Satisfied she would stay asleep for a while longer, I left her alone so that I could grab a quick workout in my personal gym.

Krystina

A RUSTLING SOUND CAUSED MY EYES TO FLUTTER OPEN. AT FIRST, I was disoriented, my surroundings unfamiliar. It took me a good thirty seconds to realize I was in the penthouse. In Alexander's bed. The sunlight peeking out from behind the window shade told me I had been here all night.

Shit!

I hadn't planned on staying the entire night.

"Good morning, Krystina. Sleep well?"

I rolled over onto my back to see Alexander standing at the foot of the bed, completely in the buff and utterly shameless. He had obviously just showered and was towel drying his wet hair. Droplets of water rained down from his head and glistened on his shoulders and chest. He was a magnificent sight, and I sighed inwardly.

Does he have to look so flippin' beautiful all the time?

I gazed at him for a moment before chastising myself for ogling.

Focus—you need to get home!

"Very well, actually. What time is it?" I asked, looking around the room in search of a clock. Allyson was probably worried sick. I never stayed out all night.

"It's just after seven."

"I have to go."

"Oh, no, you don't. Not before you eat something. I'm generally not good in the kitchen, but I can make a killer omelet."

"No, I really should. Ally is probably crazy with worry right about now. I don't make a habit of not coming home."

"You're always in such a hurry to leave me. You have to stop doing that. Besides, you're a grown woman, Krystina. I'm sure Allyson will understand," he said, slipping into a pair of jeans. "Just text her and tell her where you are if it makes you feel better."

"Fine. A quick breakfast then," I conceded. Holding the sheet up to cover my chest, I sat up. Alexander may have been okay with parading around naked, but I wasn't entirely comfortable with the concept yet. "Would you mind grabbing my clothes from the bathroom? I left them there last night."

"They aren't there. I sent your clothes out with Vivian for laundering when she was here this morning to drop off groceries. Your clothes should be back in about an hour. Until then, you can just wear one of my T-shirts. Unless you're ready to take another crack at the naked thing..." he trailed off, throwing me a suggestive smile.

I frowned at him.

"I'll stick with the T-shirt if that's alright with you."

Alexander shook his head at me and moved over to his dresser.

"Have it your way," he said, tossing me a shirt he had pulled out from the top drawer. "But the next time you come over, bring some clothes that you can leave here."

And with that, he left me alone in the room to contemplate his suggestion. He posed it very casually, but the idea sounded way too permanent for my tastes.

Deciding not to put too much thought into it, I pulled Alexander's T-shirt over my head. I breathed in the scent of it as it slipped over my shoulders. A mix of laundry detergent and male, the shirt was all Alexander and potent to my senses.

I rolled out of bed and made a quick pit stop to the bathroom to freshen up and take care of business. When I eventually sauntered my way into the kitchen, I found Alexander already working on our breakfast. Bacon sizzled in a frying pan while he expertly cracked two eggs into a bowl.

"Do you want help?" I offered. I felt useless just watching him while he diced up ham and bell peppers for omelets.

"No, I've got this. Just have a seat. There's coffee over there with your name on it," he said. He interrupted the making of his egg creation to point to the small breakfast table at the far end of the kitchen. A cup of steaming hot coffee was waiting for me.

Drawn to the aroma of a dark roast, I made my way over to the table and took a seat. I shifted uncomfortably in the chair, realizing for the first time how sore my behind was from last night. I hadn't realized he worked me so hard.

Ignoring the troublesome concern over that fact, I took a sip of coffee.

"You make one hell of a cup of coffee. Aren't you going to have some?" I asked after seeing only one mug had been poured.

Alexander looked over his shoulder at me and wrinkled his nose in distaste.

"I don't drink the stuff."

"That's a crime in my books. It's like sanity in a cup," I said and took another drink, savoring the bittersweet taste on my tongue. "I can't live without it."

"My sister is the coffeeholic. I never acquired a taste for it," he told me. Walking over to the table, he placed two plates of piping hot eggs and bacon on the table for each of us.

Suddenly feeling ravenous, I speared a piece of omelet with my fork and blew on it for a minute to cool it down before taking a bite.

"Wow, this is no joke. You really do make a killer omelet," I appreciated.

He merely nodded, seeming confident in his superb breakfast-making skills, and dug into his own food. We sat there and ate in quiet for a while, both content to enjoy our start-of-the-day meal. After a while, Alexander started perusing the front page of a newspaper on the table. The entire scene was very domestic, and it made me uncomfortable. Rather than mention it, I continued to eat my food quietly, suddenly eager to get the meal over with.

"Do you know you talk in your sleep?" Alexander asked, looking up from his readings and breaking the silence of the kitchen.

I felt my face flush in embarrassment. I had been dreaming about Alexander while I slept.

"So, I've been told by my mother and Frank. It used to drive Frank crazy because he's a light sleeper. Hopefully, I didn't say anything too crazy."

"No. You just said you shouldn't do something or another. It wasn't clear. You were kind of mumbling."

"Hmm...I'm not sure what it was about. I rarely remember my dreams once I wake up," I lied.

The truth was, I remembered the dream very clearly. I had dreamt about the wild images I found on the internet, and Alexander doing many of those things to me. I had been gagged and spread out in my dream, tied down with black rope while Alexander reigned a riding crop over me. Even in sleep, I knew I shouldn't want it, but I did. I tried to leave, but I couldn't. I wanted him to push me to see how much I could take. I had a vague recollection of waking up at some point during the night, wishing Alexander would do those things to me in life.

The fact I may have revealed myself while I slept was absolutely mortifying.

"You talk about your mother and stepfather a lot, but what about your real father?" Alexander asked.

I suppressed a sigh of relief at the opportunity to change topics, as I found last night's self-discovery of my inner freak to be very disturbing.

"I don't know him. The sperm donor left my mother when I was just a baby," I said flippantly, using the term I had adapted whenever I referenced my biological father.

"That had to be tough on her—and you for that matter."

"Honestly, I don't really have an opinion about him one way or another, except when I think about my mom. That's when I get a little mad. She struggled pretty badly trying to make ends meet. There were many nights when I woke up to hear her crying in the kitchen. I would come in, see the pile of bills… but I was young, and I didn't really understand."

I felt a small lump begin to form in my throat as I thought back to all of those nights, my mom rocking me to sleep, telling me it would be okay. She said her job was to worry about the grown-up problems, and it was my job to be a kid.

"So, when did your stepfather come into the picture?" Alexander asked, pulling me away from the memories of my youth.

"She met Frank when I was around eight or nine. They were married just after my tenth birthday. After that, my mom didn't have to worry about money anymore. Frank takes care of everything," I finished with a shrug of indifference. I didn't elaborate further, as my feelings on the subject were mixed. Frank was a good man, but I had often wondered if my mom married him out of necessity or if she married for love.

"Hmm," he mused with a frown. "That's interesting. From everything you've said in the past, you seemed to be a lot like her. But now, I think you're very much the opposite. You're too independent."

"Well, I try," I said with a sardonic grin. I squirmed in my chair, and not because of my sore bum. I simply did not want to get into a discussion about the differences and similarities I had to my mother. "Do you mind if I grab a shower?"

"Help yourself," he said, accepting my dismissal in stride. "Towels are in the linen closet."

"Thanks."

After clearing my plate, I got up from the table and made my way to the bathroom, eager to get away from our very unusual breakfast exchange.

This conversation is way too deep for this time of the morning.

Between the recollection of my dream and the chatter about my mom, I was ready to climb back into bed and hope for a do-over.

32

Krystina

I had been in Alexander's bathroom before, but I never noticed the details in the grand shower stall. Floor to ceiling tiles lined the walls, with an intricate mosaic overlay in the middle of one wall. There was a built-in bench lining two of the walls as well, with various jets cleverly placed around the area. I reached for the knob to turn on the water and was pleasantly surprised to see the waterfall stream raining down from the ceiling.

Once the water was to temp, I stepped back to strip out of Alexander's T-shirt, looking forward to enjoying his luxurious shower. Just when I was about to get in, Alexander slithered up behind me. I jumped, having been caught off guard.

"Oh, you scared me! I didn't hear you come in!"

"Mmm…" he murmured into my ear. "Watching you walk away in my T-shirt…I couldn't resist. You have amazing legs. Do you know that?"

He ran his hands over my shoulders, down my arms, then back up to cup my breasts. Grabbing a handful of curls, he pulled my hair aside and started nibbling his way down my neck.

"I'm never going to shower if you keep that up," I chided halfheartedly. A shiver raced down my spine, and a small moan escaped me.

"I could just turn around and go back to the kitchen. Is that what you want?" He teased. He slid his hands down my belly but deliberately stopped short at my pelvic bone.

"No," I breathed, frustrated he didn't continue traveling south.

"Well then, Miss Cole. Do you mind if I join you?" he propositioned.

"Why, not at all. *Sir*," I played in return. I was about to make a jest about calling him sir but was abruptly silenced when he spun me around. In one swift motion, he picked me up under the arms and had my legs scissoring around his waist. Before I knew it, I was in the shower, back pressed up against the wall, his mouth pressed against mine.

"Mother of God, you're perfect. The things I want to do to you..." he trailed off, moving his lips down my neck. I pressed my back against the wall, pushing my hips up hard against him, only to discover the rough feel of denim.

"Alex! You still have your jeans on!" I exclaimed in shock.

"I guess I do," he said impishly. He spun us so he could lower me down onto the shower bench.

After unbuttoning his fly, he pushed the wet material down his legs. I giggled when I saw him struggle. His movements were typically so graceful. To see him wrestle with the soaking wet jeans was quite comical.

"You should have thought things through a little better before you assaulted me," I laughed. He ignored me, so concentrated on the task of removing his pants from around his ankles. Once they were completely off, he tossed them out of the shower into a wet heap on the bathroom floor. Turning back to me, his eyes were dark.

"I'm going punish you for mocking me," he promised. "I'm going to make you crazy with need, so much, so you won't even be able to think straight. But you're not allowed to come. Do you understand?"

"Yes," I whispered. A tightening in my belly formed, turned on by the idea of being kept on the edge.

"Spread your legs. I want to see your sex wide open for me. And no matter what I do, you're not allowed to move unless I tell you to."

My breathing quickened in anticipation as I did what he asked.

Alexander pulled down a detachable showerhead from the wall and performed a slow dance down my body. Starting with my head, he moved the water flow down each arm and over each breast until the pulse of the spray stopped over my mound. He rested the showerhead on the bench, keeping the water flow shooting against my now throbbing clit. However, the jet was just enough of a tease, lacking enough pressure to get me off.

It was outright torture.

Standing up, Alexander retrieved a bottle of body wash. Squirting some of the soap onto his hand, he made quick work of building a soapy lather. He began massaging my shoulders, fingers slipping up and around my nipples until eventually working all the way down to my feet. When he moved up on me again, his hands slowed to knead my upper thighs, making his way ever so torturously over my pulsing clitoris, still aching for release from the subtle pressure of the showerhead.

"I'm going to shave this glorious pussy of yours. I want to see your juices glistening all over your lips."

What?!?!

I supposed it wasn't that out of the ordinary. A lot of women shave or wax it. But it was one thing to take care of business yourself and another to let someone else do it for you. I couldn't help the foreboding thoughts over allowing another person to put a razor on the most sensitive part of my body.

"Um," I hesitated.

"Do you trust me?" he asked, exerting just a little more pressure onto my clit. I leaned my head back and moaned, savoring the way he fondled, pinched, and flicked at the swollen nub.

"Yes," I sighed.

"Then close your eyes. I just want you to feel."

When the shaving cream hit my mound, I found myself spreading my legs even wider to give him better access to apply the cream over the tender folds. When I felt the initial swipe of the razor move across my skin, I gasped with pleasure over the unique sensation.

Alexander was careful, moving the blade with calculated precision, intent on the task at hand. My initial anxiety was replaced by pure desire. It was the most erotic turn-on that was unexplainable and indescribably intimate.

"You're so wet," he said, sliding his fingers along my cleft. "Slide down a little on the bench."

Once I shifted my position, he took hold of both my legs and placed them over his shoulders. Spreading me wide, he ran the razor across the newly exposed areas, stretching me open so as not to miss anything.

When he finished, he gently massaged the freshly shaved lips while rinsing away the remaining cream. Without warning, his finger pushed against my puckered rear hole, the sudden pressure catching me by surprise.

"One day, I am going to claim this ass, Krystina." My pulse accelerated at the mention of the taboo act, my breath hitching irregularly. "Relax your body. Let me show you something new."

When his finger tried to push into my tight entrance, I tensed in response to the foreign intrusion. I tried to relax, but my body fought it. He moved the spray over me again, letting it pulse on my clit. I gave in to the pleasure and felt myself melting under the beating force of the water.

Taking advantage of my distraction, he persisted and managed to push his finger inward to the first knuckle. I felt my tight opening greedily clench around him as he began to twist and stroke. Giving in to the moment, I allowed myself to feel the unfamiliar touch. He pushed in a little deeper and continued to prod and caress. Before long, I was twitching with need.

When he paused in his stroking and pulled his finger out, I gasped in dismay. It was almost shocking. I actually wished he would put it back, which was the complete opposite of what I wanted five minutes before.

"Oh, please..." I arched against him, feeling wanton for craving his finger once more.

"My angel likes this," he observed and pushed into me once again. But this time, I was ready and relaxed enough to take in more of him. "That's a good girl. Feel my finger while I taste you."

His tongue swiped against my swollen labia. Once. Twice. And on the third time, I cried out.

"I'm going to come!"

"Oh, no. Not yet. This is your punishment, remember?"

Suddenly, he stopped everything. He had removed his finger, and gone was his tongue. All of the air in my lungs left with a solid *whoosh*, my frustration reaching the ultimate peak. I was desperate, and my body begged for release.

"Please, Alex! Just...just take me. I'm yours," I panted, barely able to get the words out.

At that, he pulled me into a standing position and spun me around, so I was facing the bench.

"Bend over. Place your hands on the seat."

I did as he instructed without delay, and within half of a second, I felt his cock plunge deep, stretching the tissues still swollen from the night before. He splayed his palms across my backside, running his fingers down the seam of my ass. Using his thumb, he pressed against my rear hole without quite inserting it.

"Yes, please..." I begged, not giving the specifics of what I desperately wanted.

"You want something?" he asked.

"Yes, I want it," I said, surprised at how bold I suddenly was. The thought of both holes filled at the same time was a sinful sort of thrill, causing a dark shiver of desire to snake through my veins. My little devil applauded me for being so scandalous.

"Tell me specifically, Krystina. I want to hear you say it."

"Your thumb!"

"Here?" he taunted, circling the rim of my tight entrance. He stood completely still and unmoving, only allowing me to feel the rotation of his teasing thumb and his throbbing cock still buried deep.

"Alex! Please," I whimpered, straining my hips and pushing against him.

"I don't think you've earned it yet. You can't keep still. I told you not to move, remember?" I immediately stopped thrashing, although it was a difficult thing to do. My body had a mind of its own at that moment, writhing and twisting on its own accord. "That's better. Now, tell me what you want."

"I-I already told you!" I stuttered, wholly overwhelmed and half-crazed with need.

He gave my behind a light smack.

"Stop being shy, damn it! I want to hear the words, Krystina. Where do you want it?" he demanded.

I snapped, pure desperation forcing away all inhibition.

"In my ass, Alex! Now!"

Without delay, he pushed his thumb into my eagerly waiting ass, satisfying my libidinous need. After a moment, he began to move, rewarding me with the tight sensation of being completely filled. He pounded into me repeatedly, his powerful drive matching the rhythm of his thumb. I met him thrust for thrust, pursuing the feel of my orgasm, not caring I was supposed to keep still.

"Give it to me, angel. Come for me."

"I'm almost there! Just don't stop!"

I was astoundingly aroused. The dual sensation made my vision hazy, like a high I had never before experienced. A fire spread through every fiber of my being, and I began to shake uncontrollably. My knees threatened to buckle as the orgasm crashed around me in a massive everlasting explosion. I cried out, the sound echoing off the shower walls, completely lost in the throes of my climax.

Alexander stilled, allowing me a moment to catch my breath. Once I came down, I was able to feel his erection pulsing with unsatisfied need. I began to slowly move back and forth, milking his swollen cock with the quivering walls of my vagina.

"No, fuck—Krystina!" Alexander gasped and took a step backward, his thumb and cock unexpectedly leaving my body, making me feel shockingly empty. I turned around, half expecting him to chastise me for moving too much, only to find him half slumped against the shower wall, his face pinched with torment.

"What's the matter?"

"No condom," he explained.

Once again, I had carelessly forgotten.

"Oh," I said, feeling deflated.

"Let's move this party to the bedroom," he said. His voice sounded strained as he reached to take my hand.

I smiled coyly at him, a different solution to the problem presenting itself.

"I have a better idea."

Alexander

I WATCHED KRYSTINA COME TOWARD ME, HER EYES DARK AND smoldering with promise. She dropped to her knees, took the full weight of me in her hands, and wrapped her perfect lips around my cock. In an instant, any thoughts I had about taking her into the bedroom and tying her to my cross disappeared. I was surprised at how easily I allowed her to take control of the scene, but I certainly wasn't going to argue with her.

"Oh, angel...you do that so good," I whispered. I grabbed the back of her head and pushed deeper into her throat.

I glanced down and found myself completely taken by the sight before me. Her mass of curls was wet and plastered to her head, dripping water down her backside and over the curve of her ass. She was using one hand to brace her position by holding firmly onto my hip. The other hand was secured around the base of my cock, while she used her mouth to perform miracles of epic proportion. The vision she presented was hotter than all the flames in hell.

She looked up at me, her eyes burning with a secret only she had the key to, and I wanted nothing more than to unlock this woman's mysteries. She pulled back and ran a torturous tongue over the length of my erection, never once breaking eye contact with me. Then she did it again and again, flicking her tongue over the sensitive tip after every swipe.

I should punish her for that.

She was deliberately teasing me, showing me she was now the one in control. It was a bold power play on her part, but it made me want her even more. I had lost. I was without any defense. Relinquishing all control over to Krystina, I leaned my head back against the shower wall and moaned. I could feel her smile form over my dick. Triumphant in her victory, she tightened her suction around me once more.

Her passion was unbreakable, taking me deep into the back of her throat over and over again. I was coming apart, knowing I wouldn't be able to hold back much longer. I palmed her forehead to steady her, forcing her to look up at me.

"I'm going to come," I warned her, my words sounding hoarse. "It's up to you whether or not you want it in your mouth."

She seemed to think about it for a brief moment, then without saying a word, she pulled back and began pumping me with her hand.

Her movements were precise, fingers sliding deftly over the length of my shaft. A feeling of heightened awareness began to spread through me, intensifying the connection to the fiery woman on her knees before me. Then all at once, everything erupted into a moment of perfect clarity. Within seconds, my seed spurt out all over her chest, coating her nipples before being washed away by the water flow of the shower jets. It was a glorious sight to behold.

Energy spent, I lowered to sit on the floor beside her. Together we slumped against the wall, both utterly sated.

"That was pretty amazing," she eventually said after we had caught our breaths. I reached up to push a wet lock of hair from her face and kissed her softly on the forehead.

"You are amazing, Krystina. Just when I think I might be pushing your limits, you ask for more."

Her already flushed cheeks turned a deeper shade of crimson, spreading to the tips of her ears. I could tell she was remembering how she had practically begged me to put my thumb in her ass. I had to suppress a smile. I never thought she'd be open to any sort of anal—at least not right away. Given Krystina's limited experience, I figured it was something I'd have to work up to eventually. But now that the door was open, I found myself wondering if I had underestimated Krystina's limits. Perhaps I could push her further than I had initially thought.

"Don't you ever run out of hot water?" she asked.

"Tankless water heater. I have an unending supply."

"Brilliant," she mused. "I'll keep that in mind the next time I decide to shower here. But now, as much as it pains me to think about getting up from this floor, I really should be heading home. I never ended up texting Ally. My phone battery was dead."

"Well, if we stay here much longer, we'll end up shriveled like prunes. Come on. Up you go," I said, getting to my feet and pulling her up alongside me. I leaned down to kiss her softly, my lips molding seamlessly to hers. "Thank you for a perfect morning, Krystina."

"Mmm...," she murmured, wrapping her arms around my neck. "It was kind of perfect, wasn't it?"

Her naked body pressed up against me, warm and slick with water from the shower still running. My dick twitched, preparing for round two.

"We really have to get out of this shower, or I'll never get any work done today," I told her. After allowing us another moment amidst the steam, I reluctantly pulled away and shut off the shower valve. Reaching outside the stall, I retrieved a towel from a nearby bar and began to dry her from head to toe. She didn't argue over my lavishing, for once accepting my painstaking efforts to take care of her.

"I just remembered my clothes. Do you think Vivian has returned with them yet?" she asked.

"It's been well past an hour, so I'm sure you will find them in my room."

"Oh no!" she exclaimed, eyes suddenly filled with terror. "You don't think she heard us, do you?"

I chuckled at that.

"You worry too much, Krystina."

The truth was, there was a very good chance Vivian had heard us, but I wasn't going to let Krystina stress about it. Vivian knew not to ask questions, so there was no real harm. Then again, I used to say that about the rest of my staff too, but they've all been full of second-guessing and scrutinizing stares as of late.

Once we were both dressed, I grabbed my phone off the dresser and saw I had a response from Laura regarding Boston.

"It looks like I have to take an unexpected trip to Boston for a few days."

"Oh? What for?" Krystina asked offhandedly.

I looked up from reading the email to see her standing in front of the full-length mirror in the corner of the room. She had removed a brush from her purse and was combing out her long mane of curls.

"A friend of mine needs a favor. I'll be speaking at a conference, which I'm sure will be dreadfully boring," I paused as an idea came to mind. "Why don't you come with me?"

"Alex, I can't go to Boston," she said. "I have to work."

"I'm sure I could make a call to Walter and work something out."

She stopped brushing her hair and stared pointedly at me through the mirror.

"No. Don't you dare do any such thing!"

"Okay," I begrudgingly conceded, hands held up in surrender. "Have it your way. But if you aren't willing to come with me, I do want you to stay the night with me again tonight."

"Again?"

"Unconditional obedience," I reminded her.

She scowled.

"We need to come to some sort of an agreement about that. I'm all for following orders in the bedroom, as I've recently discovered. However, it's never going to work when it comes to the rest of my life. You can't keep throwing the assumed unconditional obedience in my face."

I shook my head, frustrated I was still failing miserably at managing a regular Dominant and submissive relationship. If only Krystina understood what her obedience would get her. I was a man of means, and the world was at her fingertips.

Why can't she just accept what I have to offer?

Knowing I would get nowhere by snapping orders at her, I changed tactics. Walking over to where she was standing, I removed the brush from her hands and took over where she left off. I combed through her hair, smoothing out the tangles, appreciating the soft feel of the damp curls against my fingertips. I found the simple act of brushing out Krystina's hair to be surprisingly calming. I could only hope it had the same effect on her.

"I don't want to fight. Just stay with me," I eventually said after a few minutes. "I'm going to be away for a few days, and I want to see you again before I go. It's that simple."

She seemed to soften at that.

"We'll see. I'm not making any promises. I need to get home and touch base with real life for a minute before I can commit to staying here again."

"Alright. I'll just sit here and twiddle my thumbs in anticipation of your answer," I joked.

"Oh, stop that!" she laughed. The sound was thrilling to my ears. "Fine, I'll stay. And, if it makes you happy, I'll even pack an overnight bag."

I smiled wickedly, satisfied I had gotten my way so easily.

"Oh, but Miss Cole, now that you've agreed to stay, I should warn you. You won't be needing clothes for what I have in mind."

"Good. I was hoping you'd say that."

33

Krystina

When I got home, I found Allyson standing in the kitchen with her hands on her hips and eyes full of accusation.

Shit.

I had hoped she would be at work, giving me time to avoid the inevitable for the afternoon at the very least. She was mad, and rightfully so.

"Is your phone broken? I've been texting you since last night!" she snapped at me.

"Sorry. My phone was dead, and I didn't have a charger on me."

Weak excuse, Cole. Real weak.

"That sounds like something I would say, not you. Besides, remember our deal? No all-nighters? I was really worried, Krys!"

I winced at her reminder, and a guilty stab of pain knifed at my gut. The last time one of us stayed out all night unannounced, disaster struck. I was living my darkest hour and needed Allyson desperately, but I didn't know where to find her. After that night, we made a deal. Neither of us would stay out all night without letting the other one know where we were.

"I know, I know—and I'm super sorry. I should have found some other way to reach you. I've just had a lot going on over the past few days. I didn't mean to worry you."

"Yeah, right," she harrumphed.

"I apologized! I don't know what else to say, Ally. I didn't intend to stay out all night."

"For starters, where in the hell have you been?"

"With Alexander," I said with an air of nonchalance.

The hands that had been planted firmly on her hips fell to her sides. Her jaw dropped open, and she began mouthing words that wouldn't come out. For once, I made her speechless, and her disbelieving stare made me laugh.

"Oh, no—don't laugh," she said, shaking her head back and forth. "We never finished our talk from the other night. I mean, I don't want to keep being all mother hen-like, but I don't think Alexander Stone is the kind of guy you want to tango with."

"It's fine, Ally. I can handle him," I told her confidently. "Just let me go change into comfy clothes, then I'll tell you everything. Okay?"

"Now that I know you're not dead in a ditch somewhere, a few details would be nice."

I ignored her sarcastic comment and retreated to my bedroom to get more comfortable. Wally's clothes two days in a row sucked, even if Alexander did have them laundered. I quickly changed into sweats and came back out into the kitchen. Allyson had made coffee and pulled out cinnamon rolls for us to eat.

"Oh, no. I'll take the coffee, but I can't eat that. I'm still full from this morning," I told her. She eyed me suspiciously, forcing me to explain further. "Alexander made breakfast."

"Oh?" she asked, cocking up one perfectly shaped eyebrow. "So, he cooks?"

"No, not really. Just breakfast. But hang on—let me backtrack to the beginning."

I poured myself a cup of coffee and went on to tell her the

interesting tale of Alexander Stone. It was a complicated story to tell, as I had to leave out a certain amount of sensitive information. When I was finished, Allyson had a look about her that said she wasn't satisfied with what I had to say.

"That's it?" she said. It was like she could see right through me, reminding me of her canny ability to read between the lines. I tried to be more convincing.

"There's really not much more to it."

Liar!

My pestering angel was back, and she was frowning her disapproval.

"What about the whole Dominant thing?" Allyson asked.

"Oh, that!" I feigned innocence. "He only meant he had a dominant sort of personality."

She looked at me with troubled eyes, forcing me to look away. I began stirring my coffee needlessly with a spoon.

"Are you sure it's smart to get into a relationship with someone like that?" she asked quietly after a few moments.

"I know what you're thinking, but I assure you it's fine. I like him," I paused, suddenly realizing exactly how much I liked being with Alexander. Uneasiness sprang into my chest, and I looked warily at Allyson. "I like him a lot, actually. But I won't let myself get in too deep. Besides, he knows where I stand on this. I flat out told him he could not control my life, and I wanted to keep things with us casual. I'm proud of who I am now, and I won't jeopardize that. You don't have to worry."

"I can't help it. I watched you go through hell and back, Krys. I mean, the flashbacks I had this morning when I saw you never came home..." she trailed off for a minute, eyes looking far away. "It was insane. I kept picturing you in that damn hospital bed with your ribs all taped up. I don't want to see a repeat of that. Ever."

Torment over the terrible memories made her voice crack and almost brought me to tears. It pulled at my heart and brought forth my own painful recollections. However, I couldn't allow myself to get lost in the past.

Not anymore.

"Do you remember our last talk? You said to let go and have a little fun, remember?" I reminded her. "Well, I realized it was time to take your advice. I can't dwell on the past or worry about what may or may not happen in the future. In fact, when I see myself in the future, do you know what I see? My mother. I love her, but I don't want to *be* her. My scars have made me bitter for far too long. I need to focus on the present, live for today, and take it as it comes."

Her face noticeably softened at my words. And while I may have only given her a half-truth about Alexander, I meant every word about putting the past behind me.

"That's probably the best thing I've heard you say in a long time," Allyson said. Her eyes shined with tears as she stood up to hug me. "I guess if you're happy, then I'm happy. It's good you're ready to move on. I don't mean to sound like I'm trying to stop you. I just worry, you know? Promise me you'll be careful."

I blinked back my own threatening tears. However, they weren't from sadness but joy. I was so glad to have her as my friend, knowing I could count on her no matter what.

"I promise," I said, hugging her in return. Pulling away before things got too out of control mushy, I asked her the question that had been on my mind since I got home. "So, how come you're not working today?"

"Photoshoot in Paris came up unexpectedly," she said, sitting back down. "Today is considered a travel day, so I don't have to go into the office. My flight leaves at five o'clock this evening."

"Paris!" I screeched. "That's so exciting! When do you get back?"

"Late Thursday night...sometime around midnight, I think. But the nice thing is I get to take off on Friday and enjoy a long weekend."

"I'm off on Friday too. The only thing I have going on is a goodbye party at Murphy's in the evening. In fact, you should come. You know most everyone from Wally's. Plus, Alex might be there, and you could meet him."

"Count me in. I'm anxious to meet this mystery man of yours," she said with a wink. "But let's plan something for the afternoon too."

"We could do a spa day," I suggested.

"That's a great idea! We haven't done that in ages!"

"Because neither of us could afford it before!" I laughed. "But now that we both have fatter paychecks going forward, I think we can splurge a little."

"For sure! We should go to one of those high-end places. You know, the ones we could only dream about before?"

"Ooh! The Mandarin. I'll call and set it up," I offered, suddenly giddy over the pending girl's day out. I had been so wrapped up in Alexander, and it would feel good to have one-on-one time with Allyson.

"Okay, you call while I go take a shower. I still have to pack for my trip too."

"Sounds like a plan," I said, unable to contain my grin. "Oh, and one more thing. You're not a mother hen. I know why you worry, and I appreciate that more than you know. Thank you for being there, Ally. I don't know what I'd do without you."

"I'm here for you, babe. Always."

Alexander

I COULDN'T STOP THINKING ABOUT THE LOOK KRYSTINA THREW AT ME when I mentioned she should keep some of her clothes at my place. Her expression was bothering me, so much so, I couldn't concentrate on business negotiations throughout the day. I tried leaving the desk work behind and went down to check on the construction of Turning Stone Advertising, except even that wasn't enough to distract me.

I knew Krystina would never willingly hang a single stitch of material in my closet anytime soon, but I didn't understand why it troubled me so much. The only solution I had was to take the liberty myself.

When I announced to Laura I would be leaving the office for a few hours to go on an impromptu shopping trip, the expression on her face was almost comical.

Yes, Laura. Believe it or not, I do know how to shop.

I dismissed her protests about calling Gabriella, my preferred sales rep over at Duncan Quinn, to order the things I needed. Gabriella was an expert in men's fashion, and she also had contacts at several high-end women's boutiques. However, making a simple phone call to order clothing for Krystina seemed too impersonal. This was one spending excursion that required my individualized attention.

I called Hale's cell to tell him to bring the Porsche Cayenne around to the front of my building.

"I'll have it there within five minutes," Hale assured. "Where are we going?"

"Fifth Avenue. We're going shopping."

"Yes, sir," he said.

And if I wasn't mistaken, I thought I heard a hint of amusement in his voice.

34

Alexander

Surprisingly, shopping for Krystina had been rather enjoyable. From sweaters and skirts to jeans and boots—the possibilities with women's clothing seemed endless. Looking at various styles and picturing certain items on Krystina was an experience unlike any other. I was careful with my selections, keeping her tastes above my own. I wanted her to be pleased with my choices and know I'd had her interests in mind. And most importantly, I wanted to show her how much I wanted to take care of her yet still allow her to maintain her individuality.

I knew I was taking a risk. Krystina might be downright furious once she saw everything I bought. But I also knew she might be more apt to accept my gifts if she knew I'd personally selected each item.

When I arrived home shortly after six, I was pleased to see the packages from the day's spree had been delivered. Vivian had already organized my spacious walk-in closet to accommodate the purchases. It was strange to see the colorful array of cotton, silk, and cashmere hanging next to the line of utilitarian-colored suits.

Yet, I also derived a certain amount of satisfaction at seeing it, as if I had achieved some kind of great accomplishment.

As I closed the closet doors, the intercom to the penthouse buzzed. I assumed it was Jeffrey letting me know Krystina had arrived, and it irked me that he hit the call button to announce her arrival. I had given him explicit instructions to simply send her up whenever she came to my home.

"Yes!" I snapped into the intercom.

"Mr. Stone. Ah...I, um Miss—" Jeffrey started.

Just what I thought.

"Allow Miss Cole into the elevator, Jeffrey. Now please."

"Yes, sir. Sorry, sir. She's on her way."

I walked away from the intercom speaker, not bothering to thank him. Whatever patience I had for the bumbling doorman was starting to run thin.

I waited in the entryway for the elevator to arrive. When the doors opened, my breath caught in my throat. No matter how many times I saw Krystina, her beauty took my breath away. Her hair was in a loose ponytail at the nape of her neck, allowing a few stray curls free to frame her delicate face. Her tight jeans and scoop-necked sweater accented every flawless curve of her body.

She was perfect, like a goddess from the heavens. Little had I known this woman would turn my world upside down when she slipped and fell that day at Wally's. I wanted her then, and I want her even more now—more than I ever wanted any other woman in my life. She was an angel.

My angel.

I closed the distance between us in less than a second, then scooped her up under the legs to cradle her in my arms.

"Alex! Put me down!" she half scolded and giggled at the same time, swatting at my arm. I ignored her and breathed in the sweet smell of her hair.

"Mmm...not a chance. I missed you," I murmured into her ear.

"Already?" she laughed.

"Very much," I admitted before kissing her softly. "You've been on my mind all day, angel."

"Oh, have I? I can only imagine all of the wicked things you were thinking today."

"Miss Cole, you have no idea."

I ran my nose down the length of her cheek to nuzzle the sweet spot below her ear. She hummed and closed her eyes, angling her head to the side. I moved back up, savoring the softness of her skin, nipping along the line of her jaw. My teeth grazed her parted lips, and I kissed her again, but this time it was long and possessive. She surrendered and gave into my tongue, allowing me to revel in her taste.

"I could get used to greetings like that," she murmured once I gave her a chance to come up for air.

"My girl likes to be swept off her feet, I take it," I joked.

I felt her stiffen in my arms.

"I guess I do," she said with a small smile. However, her grin didn't quite reach her eyes, and I knew she was thinking metaphorically about what I had said.

"I was only messing around, Krystina. After all, I did quite literally sweep you off of your feet."

"I know," she said, planting a placating kiss on my cheek. I set her down, and if I wasn't mistaken, I thought she looked relieved. Her sudden change of demeanor was perplexing.

"You okay?"

"I'm sorry," she said sheepishly. "I think I'm just tired, that's all. Somebody wore me out last night."

"I didn't hear any complaints," I said with a wink.

"Oh, not at all. But I must admit that the day is finally catching up with me. I'd love to just lounge on the couch for a little while. Maybe watch a movie? What do you say?"

A movie?

Lying on the couch and watching a movie with a woman was foreign to me, yet it provoked some very interesting ideas. The thought of getting Krystina horizontal had me readily agreeing.

"I'm game for that. But first, I have something for you. Come with me."

I took her hand and led her into the bedroom. When we

reached the closet doors, I paused before opening them. I was thrilled at the chance to give Krystina her surprise, but I was nervous about it too.

What if this is a mistake?

I thought of the way her new clothes looked hanging next to mine. For me, it was simply a gift—one I was anxious to give her. However, Krystina tended to look too much into things, and I was afraid of how she might perceive the appearance of my closet.

Maybe I shouldn't show her this. Not yet.

"What is it?" she asked.

Her question tore me away from the indecisive meanderings.

I shook my head to clear it, feeling uncomfortable with how I seemed to be questioning my every move as of late. I have always been confident in my choices, yet I seemed to stumble over the smallest of decisions surrounding Krystina, and it was starting to wear on me. I didn't like it. Not one bit.

Get your shit together and just give her the damn clothes!

"It's here. In my closet," I told her.

I opened the doors and gestured her inside. She stopped when she reached the threshold, not having to venture any further to see what was plainly before her. I saw her visibly blanch, in what I could only assume shock, before she slowly turned to face me. Our eyes locked, and hers were flashing with accusation.

I should have waited.

"Alex, you said you had some*thing* for me. These are *things*. As in plural. Very plural."

Her voice was strained, and I could tell she was trying to keep her temper in check.

"I just wanted you to have a choice, that's all," I tried to shrug off.

She got quiet, unusually so. From the way she shifted her weight from one foot to the other, she appeared agitated. She attempted to tuck a curl behind her ear, but it sprang free again. I reached up to do it for her, but she jerked her head away. I dropped my hand to my side, knowing she was just as angry as I feared she would be.

She cast her eyes down, seeming to stare at some invisible speck on the carpet. Occasionally, her eyes would dart back up to her new wardrobe, but then down again as if she couldn't bear the sight. Her silence was vexing, but I held my tongue, waiting for her to break it first.

"I wish you didn't do this," she eventually whispered.

"I wanted to," I stated simply.

She looked up at that, sticking out a stubborn chin.

"What if I don't want to accept?"

I pursed my lips in annoyance, trying not to feel insulted over her rejection. I took a deep breath, reminding myself Krystina responded best to brutal honesty.

"You're not getting it, Krystina. I want to buy you things. I want to take care of you. It's a need I can't explain," I told her, trying to sound as earnest as possible. "It makes me happy to do so, as I so discovered today. This is just something you'll have to get used to."

"Look, I appreciate it, but it's you who isn't getting it. A week ago, we were both saying no strings attached. All of this is a whole lot of strings," she said, motioning to the clothes with her hand.

I chuckled at her unintentional pun, trying to keep the mood light. I was just grateful she was talking again.

"Angel, it's only clothes."

"It's more than clothes to me. It's what it symbolizes."

"I understand your hesitation. And to be perfectly honest, I don't know what possessed me to do it. I've never personally gone shopping for a woman before, not even for my sister. It was just..." I struggled to try to find the right words to explain my compulsion. "It was just something I wanted to do. Accepting would make me very happy."

Her face looked pained as if she were suffering from some sort of internal battle. She looked at me, eyes full of uncertainty, before walking into the closet and running her hand up and down the sleeves of the hanging blouses.

"You shopped for all of this by yourself?"

"Sort of. Hale may have had a thing or two to say about some of the stuff I bought."

Her head snapped around so fast that it threatened whiplash. Her eyes were round with apparent disbelief, but then she let out a loud and genuine laugh. The sound was infectious and music to my ears.

"You two must have been such a sight!"

I crossed my arms and smirked at her.

"Are you laughing at me, Miss Cole?"

"I would never dare," she retorted.

Her eyes twinkled, a sure sign I was on my way to securing the win.

"Does this mean you'll accept my gift?"

"I suppose I could," she mused the consent.

I hesitated before dropping the next bomb on her.

"I hope so because this isn't all of it."

Her shoulders slumped, and she shook her head back and forth.

"No more gifts, Alex," she implored.

"You said you'd accept. What's next is just part of the package."

"Please. No," she tried to deny, but I ignored her pleas.

I went over to the dresser and picked up the small gift-wrapped box I had left sitting there. When I turned back to face her, there was no describing the look of horror spreading across her face. She couldn't tear her eyes away from the package in my hand.

I looked from her to the box, then back up at her. Then it dawned on me.

"Chill out, baby. If I were going to propose, I'd do it better than this," I said dryly. "Just open it."

I thrust the cube-shaped box into her hand, annoyed this was going so badly.

A blush crept over Krystina's cheeks. I was reasonably certain her embarrassment over jumping the gun was the only thing keeping her mouth shut while she went to work on opening the package.

Carefully, she pulled at the satin bow and slid her fingernail across the tapeline to unwrap it. Inside the box, nestled in a royal blue pillow, lay the necklace I had a local jeweler custom craft for her.

"Alex, it's beautiful," she said in awe. She ran her fingers across the platinum interlocked spiral emblem and over the three smooth sapphires placed in the surrounding circle. She looked up at me and smiled.

Ding, ding, ding! We have a winner!

Confident she wasn't going to argue with me about the necklace, I released a sigh of relief.

"It's a triskelion—or at least a variation of one," I told her. "Some people call it a triskele."

"What's a triskele?"

"It's a symbol of the BDSM community."

"Oh. Well, um..." she hesitated, and her smile faltered. "Am I... to wear this? I mean, don't get me wrong—it is truly a beautiful necklace. I'm just not too keen on advertising my newfound interests."

"Don't worry," I lightly laughed. "The triskelion symbol has many meanings depending on who you ask. Most people you encounter will think it means something entirely different. I personally believe it may be why the BDSM community adapted it. Look it up one day, Krystina. You may be intrigued by its history."

"How so?"

"BDSM may be a subject never talked about, but many aspects of it are often in plain sight. Here, let me put in on you."

I reached to take the box from her hands. I could still see the apprehension on her face, but she didn't argue when I secured the clasp around the back of her neck. The emblem rested perfectly against her smooth skin, accenting the flawless swell of her breasts.

"Well, whatever the symbol is, you have impeccable taste. I love it, Alex. Thank you."

"I'm glad you do. That will make it easier to give you the last surprise."

"Alex," she said in a warning tone. "I said thank you for the necklace, not the clothes. I'm still not sure what to think about those, let alone a third surprise."

"It's nothing, really. This one is more a joke than anything else. Open the top drawer of my dresser."

She eyed me suspiciously but did as I instructed.

"What's this?" she asked after she peered at the contents.

"Replacement underwear for the ones I ripped off of you. Remember?"

I flashed her a devilish smile, recalling the night I tore the black lace from her hips. The image of doing it again caused a stirring in my groin.

"Oh, I can certainly remember! But this is more than a replacement—there must be at least ten pairs in here!"

"A dozen, to be exact," I moved over to her and circled my arms around her slim waist. I leaned down to whisper in her ear. "So that means I get to rip them off of you twelve more times."

I felt her shiver in my arms, and I knew I had truly won. I reached down to cup her behind, pulling her hips tighter against me.

"Twelve more times, huh?"

Her words sounded breathy already, and I hardened in response.

"Yep," I confirmed, nipping at her ear. I trailed a line down her neck, feeling the beat of her pulse beneath her skin. My hands found the hem of her sweater, and I slid them up her back to undo the clasp of her bra.

"Well then," she started but then paused to moan when I found one of her nipples. "We should, ah...we should get to work on that."

"I thought you wanted to watch a movie."

I rolled her taut peaks around between my thumbs and forefingers, flicking them softly while I did so.

"The movie can wait," she breathed.

"Yes, it can," I agreed, relishing in every response she had to my touch. I stepped away and reached into the drawer to retrieve one of the lace thongs. I looped it around my finger and held it out for her to take. "I think you need to go put on a pair of these so we can test their durability."

"I'll be right back," she promised, taking the panties from me.

After Krystina disappeared into the bathroom, I went to the stereo to select a playlist for inspiration.

Something darker, I think.

I wanted to show Krystina something new tonight, to take her to a place she hadn't been. Selecting music I thought was appropriate for what I had in mind, I turned back to the bed. Reaching up, I began to unlock the latches holding the crossbars in place for the St. Andrews cross.

Once I was satisfied everything was secure, I fished keys out of my pocket and headed over to my private closet to retrieve the leather cuffs I would need. However, I stopped midstride when I heard Krystina cry out from the bathroom.

"Oh, no!"

She exited the bathroom, looking like she might cry.

"What? What's wrong?" I asked, completely alarmed by her outburst.

"I have my period."

35

Krystina

Alexander started laughing like it was the funniest thing he'd ever heard. I, on the other hand, was thoroughly annoyed.

"This isn't funny, Alex!"

"Well, it does put a damper on my plans for you, but it's your reaction that's making me laugh."

He laughed harder when I scowled at him. I reached for one of the satin throw pillows on the bed and threw it at him.

"You're such an ass," I told him, although my words didn't carry any true venom. I, too, was fighting off a smile.

"I take it you're surprised by your monthly friend?"

"Sort of. I started getting a headache this afternoon. That's usually a warning it's coming." I frowned, feeling somewhat chagrinned over my negligence to the matter. "I really should keep better track, but since I wasn't having sex until recently, I guess I didn't see the necessity. I'm sorry."

"Don't apologize for nature, Krystina. It's not your fault."

"I suppose, but it doesn't change the fact our night is ruined. No point in me staying over now."

"Don't be ridiculous!" he exclaimed as if it was the most absurd thing he had ever heard. "There are other things we can do besides have sex."

"Like what? That's the only thing we do!"

I tried to say it with a laugh, but it sounded forced. I was all revved up with nowhere to go. I wanted nothing more than to sit in a corner and pout for the remainder of the night.

This sucks.

Alexander came over to where I was standing, his expression stoic as he pulled me into his arms.

"You really should give us a bit more credit, Krystina. Do you still have a headache now?" he asked.

"Yeah, just a little one, though."

"Well, let's see what we can do about that. Shall we?"

He released his arms from my waist and took hold of my hand. Leading me into the bathroom, he opened up the linen closet and began searching for something. I expected him to pull out aspirin for me, but instead, he produced a bottle of bubble bath and scented oil.

"What are you doing?" I asked curiously.

"My grandmother used to say the best cure for a headache was a hot bath. So, my angel, that's what you're going to have."

He went over to the massive, sunken marble bath and began to run the water. Unscrewing the cap for the bubbles, he slowly poured the thick soap into the water, mixing it with the scented oil. Before long, a soft smell of lavender and vanilla filled the room.

"You know, if you're trying to warm me up to the idea of you taking care of me, it's working."

He flashed me one of those sexy grins I loved so much.

"I must say—you certainly make me work for it," he said lightly. He leaned in to plant a tender kiss on my forehead. "I'll give you a minute of privacy so you can get into the bath. I'll be back in a few minutes."

Once I was alone, I had a minute to digest the unexpected. The impromptu bath Alexander had drawn for me was sweet—

remarkably so. It was the exact sort of thing Alexander said he wasn't capable of and the same thing I told him I wasn't looking for.

Teddy bears and roses.

If the perfumed bubble bath wasn't the definition of teddy bears and roses, then I didn't know what was.

An uncomfortable feeling began to form in my stomach, and I tried to ignore it as I undressed. After removing my clothing, I wrapped myself in a towel and stood in front of the vanity mirror. My cheeks looked flushed from the swelling steam in the bathroom, and my hair was growing bigger by the minute. I hastily pulled it up into a messy bun on top of my head and secured it with a rubber band I had around my wrist.

Satisfied my hair would stay put, I made my way over the bath. Seeing it was almost filled, I reached down to turn off the faucet.

Once the noise of the running water was silenced, I noticed music coming from somewhere. I looked around and saw tiny speakers strategically built into the walls of the bathroom. The sound was soothing, fitting to the serene environment Alexander had created for me.

However, despite the luxury surrounding me, I still felt anxious, and I wasn't sure why.

It's because he's breaking down your defenses.

I dismissed the bothersome voice in my head immediately, determined to just enjoy the moment.

It's like I told Ally—live for today. Just take it as it comes.

I stepped into the bath fit for a god and sunk into its sweet foam. Leaning back, I appreciated a few minutes of uninterrupted relaxation.

When Alexander returned, he was carrying two glasses of wine and was wearing nothing but a towel around his waist. The lines of his abs rippled when he bent to set the glasses down on the ledge of the bath. I wanted to reach out and run my hands over his muscular contours but stopped myself when I remembered why I couldn't.

"Alex, I'm sorry. But if you have plans to join me, I can't when I have my—" I started.

"Relax, Krystina. I have no expectations. Tonight, it's all about you. Now slide up in the tub," he ordered.

I hesitated for a moment but then did as I was told.

Alexander dimmed the lights, so there was only a soft glow about the room, adding to the tranquility. When he shamelessly dropped his towel, I found myself blushing for some unknown reason. I cast my eyes down, not wanting to brazenly ogle while he climbed in behind me.

Once he had settled, he procured matches from somewhere and lit the candles placed in the corners of the marble surround. Pulling me back against him, I had little choice but to settle in.

After a moment or two, he began to massage the muscles in my shoulders. A sigh of appreciation escaped me as I sipped on a delightfully sweet white wine and absorbed the music. I literally felt like a pampered queen.

"This song that's playing—it's really good. Who is it?" I asked, curious about the female artists' sensual lyrics and textured contemporary sound.

"It's called "Breathe" by Of Verona. It's on one of the playlists I made for you."

"Oh, I didn't realize. But then again, I haven't had a chance to listen to all the songs yet."

"That's a shame, but it might explain why I still have to try so hard to coerce you," he laughed.

"What do you mean?"

"This particular song is on the Surrender playlist."

"I see," I mused, suddenly very intrigued by what Alexander hoped to accomplish with his playlists. "I'll make a point to listen to them all soon."

"Actually, it's okay if you don't. I like seeing your reactions when you hear a song you like. You're very responsive to music."

"I know. It's hard to explain. It's like I can feel music—if that makes any sense," I told him.

Alexander shifted his position slightly, causing his manhood to brush against my backside. The seductive music alone was doing a fine job of provoking my already heightened sexual ache—the last thing I needed was to feel *that*. A shiver of desire raced down my spine.

"Is the water too cool?" Alexander asked, seeming oblivious as to why I had quivered. I gave myself a lecture in an attempt to ignore the longing I felt.

Focus on the massage. Tune out the music. Just disregard the feel of his body.

That's wet and warm.

And slick with bath oils.

"No, the water is fine. Perfect actually," I said, my voice sounding slightly higher pitched than normal. It was a real struggle to focus exclusively on the kneading of his phenomenal hands on my shoulders.

"Hmm, yes. This is nice," he agreed easily, but he seemed distracted.

I glanced up at him. He looked lost in thought and totally unaware of the torment I was experiencing.

"What are you thinking about?"

"Actually, I was thinking about this weekend. If the weather holds out, I thought maybe we could go out on my boat on Saturday."

"You have a boat?" I asked, seizing the opportunity to break the progression of my salacious thoughts.

"Yes, I do. It might be the last chance we have to use her too. I don't expect to have many more days of good weather."

"I don't think I'd be much fun out on your boat. Frank used to take me fishing on Rensselaer Lake when I was a kid. I would always get seasick."

I could feel his chest vibrate with a low chuckle.

"I'm sure my boat and the water conditions are quite a bit different than being out on Frank's fishing boat. But don't worry. I can get you a bracelet for seasickness if you need it. And there's always a motion sickness pill, although I'm not a huge fan of them."

I watched the steam furl in the air above the tub and contemplated the likelihood of getting seasick. After a while, the lazy swirls were mesmerizing, and I began to fully relax for the first time since Alexander joined me in the tub. It seemed silly to fret over whether I may or may not get sick aboard his boat.

"Whatever you say," I agreed readily.

Content to just appreciate the moment, I closed my eyes and breathed in the soft scent of the billowing moist air surrounding us.

Alexander continued to knead the muscles in my neck and shoulders. When his hands moved down to massage my arms, I was starting to get drowsy with sleep. However, my eyes snapped open when I felt his fingertip brush over one of my nipples. I couldn't be sure if it were by accident or not. However, when he skimmed over it a second time, I sharply sucked in a breath, knowing it wasn't merely happenstance. My nipples hardened in response, just aching to be touched, a painful reminder of what could not happen.

Slipping both hands under my arms, he captured both breasts, and I realized how heavy they felt. Yet, despite their fullness, his gentle rolling of the ultra-sensitive points began communicating to another part of my body. Unfortunately, that area was currently wearing a do not disturb sign.

It was like torture of the worst kind.

"Oh, *why* couldn't my period have come tomorrow?" Frustration gripped me and made the rhetorical question sound like a whine.

"Shh…don't talk, Krystina."

He tilted his head forward and began trailing kisses up and down my neck. His teeth tugged at my earlobe, causing a shiver to race down my spine. I could feel his erection growing and pulsing against my lower back, a sure sign he would soon have frustration to match my own.

"Alex, you're making this worse," I moaned. He moved his hands down my belly, coming precariously close to the mark before I stopped him by squeezing my thighs together.

"Open your legs for me, Krystina."

"You know I can't."

"You can," he persisted. Shifting his legs, he locked his ankles around mine. In one swift motion, he spread our legs out together. Water sloshed out onto the floor.

"You're making a mess," I scolded, hoping to distract him from whatever it was he had planned.

"You really are a terrible submissive," he murmured into my ear. Moving his hand back down to my waist, his finger circled my belly button before traveling farther south to find my sweet spot.

"Or maybe..." I began, trying one last time to divert him from the inevitable. "Maybe I just have a bad teacher."

"Hmm," he growled. "Don't remind me."

Without warning, he pressed down on my clitoris. I could feel the nub instantly begin to pulse beneath his finger, and I cried out. I arched my back, trying to squirm out of his reach, but my efforts were in vain. He still had my legs trapped and one arm secured tightly around my waist. There was nowhere for me to go.

"Alex..." I tried to plead. However, my attempt to stop him was halfhearted. Despite my reservations, I craved his touch with every fiber of my being.

"Trust me for a minute and just let yourself feel, Krystina."

Ever so gently, he began to flick back and forth, teasing my pressure point. I was amazed at how quickly Alexander had learned my body. He knew all the places that brought me the greatest pleasure, and he used the knowledge to make me crazy with need time and time again.

Angling my head up, I looked at him. His blue eyes were blazing with so much heat that I had little choice but to surrender. I reached to pull his head down to meet mine and gave myself over with abandon.

I LAY CURLED UP AGAINST ALEXANDER'S SIDE, LISTENING TO HIS EVEN breathing while he slept. However, sleep evaded me as the past few hours played like a tiresome broken record over and over again in my head.

Overall, our evening had been amazing in inexplicable ways. Alexander had unselfishly satisfied me without taking anything for himself. From the erotic pleasures he rewarded me with in the bath to the way he carried me to bed for the night, he was true to his word and made our night together all about me. I couldn't have asked for anything more perfect.

But despite the seamless end to the evening, I couldn't help but remember how it started. Alexander was slowly tipping the scales in his favor—and it was terrifying.

I was apprehensive about the slew of woman's clothing hanging in his closet, clothes I could not bring myself to think of as mine. I had concerns over accepting the necklace, which I was sure cost a small fortune. And while the clothes and the necklace may simply be material things, it was hard not to think of them as something more.

I glanced down at the emblem still hanging around my neck. The sapphires sparkled, reflecting the moonlight streaming in through the windows. It was a beautiful piece, but I knew it would probably be best to give it back to him. It may be a symbol of the BDSM world, but to me, it was more like Alexander was putting his stamp on me. It served as another reminder of how fast we were taking things. We were moving at a breakneck speed, and it was more than just a little bit troubling.

Just that very morning, I promised Allyson I wouldn't get in too deep. In fact, it wasn't just an assurance I gave to Allyson, but it was a personal vow I had made to myself. Yet here I was, ready to blindly fall. I couldn't shake the nagging worry I still may be subconsciously clinging to the hope of someday finding that white picket fence.

The idea made me feel edgy. Restless.

I rolled over, facing myself away from Alexander. He stirred but didn't wake. I punched at the pillow, but my efforts to get comfortable were not working.

Happily ever after will never happen, Cole.

After all, I was the one to set the rules. I had been blatantly clear about no strings attached. The time I spent with Alexander was supposed to be a small step to putting the past behind me, not some massive leap that would leave me fumbling to find my footing again.

I flipped over onto my back and stared at the ceiling.

There was still too much Alexander didn't know about me, and I barely knew a thing about him. He lived in a clandestine world of kink and sex clubs, where everything was one giant secret that I couldn't be privy to. He spoke of domination and said it was my duty to submit to his every need. But what he said he wanted was confusing to me, as his actions showed differently. He catered to my every whim, striving to please me at every step, while I gave him nothing but push back out of fear he would eventually change me.

However, I saw the shift in Alexander during the short time we were together, and I was very conscious that it was me who was unintentionally changing him. Whether he was aware of what was happening or not, no good could come from it either way.

What had begun on shaky ground was shaping up to be something more—something I didn't want. And I was fairly certain Alexander didn't want it either. I felt like I was being pushed, lost in a colossal storm of emotions I wasn't ready to feel. I knew it was time to take a giant step back. If I didn't, I sensed it wouldn't be long before I slipped and fell from the ledge.

36

Alexander

It had been a stimulating morning, making the letdown for the next two days that much worse. Before dawn, I awoke to the feel of Krystina's warm body spooned tightly against mine. Never one to miss an opportunity, I seized the moment and made sure to leave her with a farewell neither of us would forget about during my absence. Unfortunately, there was no sex for obvious reasons. Instead, we kissed and caressed in ways that were surprisingly fulfilling. It was another first for me and a completely unique experience in itself.

The early morning hours I had spent with her almost seemed surreal as I climbed aboard the Airbus ACJ318. Hale was already on the private jet when I arrived, neatly stowing our travel bags into an overhead compartment.

"Morning, Hale."

"Good morning, sir."

"If my speech is in with those bags, take it out for me. I want to review it one more time before we get to Boston."

"Already done. It's in a folder right over there," he said,

pointing to a corner end table in the spacious lounge area of the plane. "I think Laura made a few adjustments to it."

I went over to the table to review the contents. Laura had made quite a few changes, and I was thankful for her sharp eye. The speech was a couple of years old and needed updating. If I had more notice, I would have written a new one.

Satisfied Laura had done it justice, I tucked it back inside the folder and turned back to Hale.

"I assume the flight will be leaving on time?"

"Yes, sir. I just confirmed it with the pilot. The trip to Boston should be a smooth one. However, we may encounter an issue on the return flight. There's a bad storm moving in on the overnight. It's remnants of a hurricane that's traveling up the coast."

"Monitor the situation and make other travel arrangements for the return trip home if needed. I want to be back no later than eight o'clock Friday evening."

"Yes, sir."

"Did you have time to arrange the delivery I emailed you about this morning?"

"Vivian will be setting it up this afternoon," Hale informed me. "You should get an email confirmation as soon as it's received."

"Excellent. Oh, and I meant to ask you. How is your mother settling in?"

"Very well. I appreciate your help in securing her placement. After the fall she took, I can rest easier knowing she's getting the proper care. Thank you again."

I acknowledged his gratitude with a nod, glad that things had worked out. Before reaching the age of sixty, Hale's mother was diagnosed with early-onset Alzheimer's. It had come as quite the blow to my security detail. When I heard he couldn't afford the cost of a reputable nursing facility, I immediately made calls to get her the best care in New York and covered the expenses. Hale protested, of course, but I would hear none of it.

The pilot came over the intercom system, interrupting our conversation to let us know it was almost time for takeoff. I settled into my seat and looked out the window. Cumulus clouds dotted the bright blue sky, making it hard to imagine we were under a severe storm alert.

I heard the soothing hum of the plane engine as it came to life, and I rested my head back with the hopes of catching a quick snooze on the flight. My mind quickly filled with images of Krystina.

I wish she had agreed to come with me.

I opened one eye to look at Hale. He sat across from me, already engrossed in the *New York Times.*

Hale accompanied me on nearly all of my business trips. He was a good traveling companion and was always willing to discuss whatever I had a mind for. Usually, the topic was business.

That's me. Always business.

"Hale, let me ask you something," I said on a whim. He looked up from the newspaper, his expression attentive. "Do you ever regret not settling down?"

"Sir?"

Yeah, I know. The question sounds crazy to me too.

"I mean, with a woman," I clarified. "Do you have any regrets?"

If he was surprised by my inquiry, he didn't show it. Instead, he looked thoughtful.

"My mother always wanted grandchildren. When I think of how happy it would have made her, I do have regrets. However, now that she's sick, it doesn't really matter. Either way, I've never met a woman who I wanted to spend the rest of my days with."

"Or maybe it's because I keep you too damned busy to meet anyone," I joked.

The corners of his mouth turned up in a rare smile.

"I believe we all have our own calling. So far, mine has been the service of your employment, and it has suited me well. If I were meant to settle down before now, I would have done so."

"Hmm, perhaps," I mused.

"Sir, permission to be frank?"

I laughed at his seriousness.

"You're not in the military anymore. Speak what's on your mind, Hale."

His lips tightened into a thin line as if he were concentrating on selecting the right words. He looked pointedly at me.

"Miss Cole is a lovely young woman. Don't let her be *your* regret."

Krystina

I HAD DELIBERATELY PACKED MY SCHEDULE, SO I HAD MORE THAN enough reasons to deny Alexander's multiple requests for me to accompany him to Boston. Because of that, the next couple of days went by quickly. I worked out my remaining shifts at Wally's, went to my gynecologist appointment, and caught up on lost gym time. Keeping busy allowed me not to dwell on the fact I felt unexpectedly lost without Alexander.

I didn't like that I missed him, and the time apart made me realize we needed separation more often. I had become entirely too familiar with his presence. With that in mind, I didn't answer his calls and kept all communication strictly texting. I knew just the sound of his voice would cause me to fold.

By the time I arrived home Thursday evening, I had realized Alexander and I would have to negotiate some sort of compromise. If we continued the way we were going, I would end up with very little time alone, especially come Monday when I started the job at Turning Stone. I had never agreed to give up every night and weekend for him, despite his original wishes. Yet somehow, I ended up doing precisely that.

I went to the fridge to see what I could use to throw together a quick dinner for myself. Settling on a green salad with various fixings, I pulled out the ingredients I would need. I went to work on slicing up chicken into thin strips and contemplated how I should approach the subject of maintaining my personal space with Alexander.

Boundaries. We need to establish some boundaries.

The sound of my phone vibrating on the counter tore me away

from my thoughts. Setting the knife down, I picked up the phone to see there was an incoming text from Allyson.

TODAY, 6:34 PM: ALLYSON

My flight is delayed. What's up with the weather in NY?

I looked out the window at the storm that was getting worse by the minute. Wind slashed at the windows, and the rain appeared to be going sideways.

6:36 PM: ME

Tail end of a hurricane that moved north.

6:40 PM: ALLYSON

I'll be lucky to get in by late Friday at this point.

6:41 PM: ME

Stuck in Paris. Gee, I feel so bad for you...

6:43 PM: ALLYSON

Ha-ha. Not funny. I'm miserable. It's nearly 2 AM, and I'm holed up in an airport indefinitely.

I paused my texting to glance at the clock. I had forgotten about the time difference.

6:45 PM: ME

Sorry, that sucks.

6:50 PM: ALLYSON

Can you reschedule our spa day? Maybe for Saturday if you're free?

Alexander planned on taking his boat out on Saturday, but by the looks of the weather forecast, that wasn't going to happen.

This is my chance to create a little space.

It took me about half a second to make the decision.

6:53 PM: ME

Saturday it is. I'll change the reservation.

6:55 PM: ALLYSON

Great! Hopefully, I'll be home by then. I'll text if there's another delay.

I looked up the number for the Mandarin. It was no trouble switching our reservation to Saturday. However, I knew rescheduling with Alexander would not go off quite as easy, and I dreaded the conversation.

I went back to preparing dinner and layered arugula with sliced chicken, walnuts, and feta cheese. I was about to pour a balsamic over the top when a knock at the door interrupted me.

My stomach grumbled in annoyance over the second disruption as I went to answer it. I peered through the peek hole to see who it was, but there wasn't anyone on the other side of the door.

That's weird.

I opened the door anyway and found a flower delivery on the floor in front of the threshold. Unsure as to whether the flowers were for Allyson or me, I picked up the beautiful arrangement of blue delphiniums and baby's breath and brought them to the kitchen. Placing the bouquet on the counter, I removed the envelope from the vase. The card was addressed to me.

"I have found that among its other benefits, giving liberates the soul of the giver." - Maya Angelou
Looking forward to the weekend.
Alex

I smiled after reading the quote, appreciating Alexander's attention to detail by citing my favorite poet.

I was about to put the card back into the envelope when I noticed a blue velvet satchel tied around the vase's neck.

What's this?

However, I predicted the answer to the question almost as soon as I thought it. Knowing Alexander wouldn't take back his gift of the necklace, I had decided to forgo any sort of argument by simply leaving it on his dresser the morning he left for Boston. Apparently, this was his way of turning the tables on me.

Loosening the drawstring tie from the cloth bag, I dumped the contents into my palm. Just as I expected, out poured the platinum triskelion and chain. It was then that I understood the reason for the Maya Angelou quote—Alexander wasn't only referring to the flowers, but all of his gifts.

In the face of his sweet gestures, I couldn't help but feel a little sad about it. It would be so much easier to simply accept everything Alexander had to offer, but I didn't feel right about it. I sensed he wanted more from me, but there were some things I couldn't give—at least not without compromising my standards.

I'm at a crossroads.

One path would have me push Alexander away to create more distance between us. He may not like it, and it could potentially lead to our demise. It would be a risky choice because I knew I wasn't ready for things to end.

But if I chose the other, I would become deeper involved. I'd expect more from Alexander and would want him to be more open about the secrets I knew he was carrying. From the history of his parents to his underground life, everything was a mystery to me. I knew I wouldn't be able to continue without answers. However, that path had its risks, too, as it may force me to reveal my own truth.

The prospect of facing that pain frightened me, for giving up my secret would hurt me in ways physical submission never could. The choice should have been an obvious one, knowing I didn't have the strength to handle the latter. However, I couldn't decide what to do—for emotional surrender was my only true hard limit.

37

Alexander

The conference was going relatively well, even if it was boring as all hell, and I arrived back at my hotel room shortly after dinnertime. I considered going out to the Faneuil Hall area with Burke in search of a bite to eat but decided on the solitude of room service instead. I didn't feel like keeping company with my old friend but rather wished I had pushed Krystina harder about coming to Boston.

A short rap on the hotel room door signaled the arrival of dinner. I opened the door to find a pretty brunette balancing two platters. I was absently wondering how she managed to knock with her hands full when I noticed the trays balancing precariously in her small hands.

I was dangerously close to wearing stuffed flounder and hollandaise sauce.

"Here, let me take one of those," I offered, removing a tray from her wavering grasp.

"Thank you, sir," she appreciated.

We both entered the room and set the trays on the small dinette set in the suite's living room.

"Do yourself a favor and use a cart of some sort next time," I told her, fishing out my wallet to get her a tip.

"Oh, yes," she readily agreed. "I'll make sure to use one the next time I come up. Will you be staying here long? Um, Mr...."

She sounded giddy, almost schoolgirlish. My head snapped up to look at her. I was all too familiar with the tone she took. She was watching me with a pair of innocent doe eyes, but this girl was anything but naïve and was obviously looking to score more than a tip.

I pursed my lips in annoyance, choosing not to answer her. I handed her a twenty.

Be on your way, doll. That's all you're going to get.

"Thank you," I told her, albeit dismissively.

She looked momentarily disappointed but took the dismissal in stride and left me alone to enjoy my dinner in peace. The transparency of some women floored me at times, and I suddenly had a newfound appreciation for Krystina's ambiguous personality.

I wasn't impressed by the hotel fare. The flounder was overcooked, and the sauce was flavorless. I began to regret my choice not to accompany Burke to one of the more notable seafood restaurants in the city. As I swallowed the last bite of the rubbery fish, my phone pinged with the notification of a new email. I pushed the plate away and pulled out my cell.

It was a confirmation notice stating the flower delivery was received. The time stamp on the message told me it was just after seven, which meant Krystina should be home from Wally's.

I'll try calling her now. Maybe she'll actually pick up this time.

Exiting out of the email, I dialed Krystina's number.

"Hello, angel," I greeted after she answered. It felt so good to hear the sound of her voice.

"Hey. How's the trip going?"

"Incredibly boring."

"That bad, huh?"

"Next time, you're coming with me," I told her.

"We'll see," she murmured on the other end of the line. She

seemed distracted. I had been so pleased she finally answered her phone that I hadn't picked up on how distant she sounded until that moment.

"Is everything okay?"

"Everything is fine. Oh, and thank you for the flowers, by the way."

I noticed she didn't mention the returned necklace but decided not to bring it up. I missed her, and I didn't want to spoil our conversation by risking an argument.

"Are you sure you're alright?" I asked again instead.

"I'm good, really I am. I'm just tired and a little sore. It's been a long day."

She does sound tired.

Perhaps that was truly all that was wrong.

"I thought Walter would have gone easy on you since today was your last day."

"Oh, work was alright," she assured me. "I'm just worn out because I was up early and at the gym by six o'clock this morning. I couldn't get an evening appointment with the trainer I like to work with, so I had to go in early if I wanted to meet with him."

Him?

The idea of Krystina having a one on one training session with another man made me uncomfortable.

Extremely uncomfortable.

Am I jealous? Since when do I get jealous?

"I didn't know you had a trainer," I tried to say indifferently.

"It's pricy, so I don't do it often. But Eric is a good motivator, and I needed him to get me back into a routine."

Eric? So, the asshole has a name.

I pictured Krystina in spandex shorts, possibly a sports bra. With her midriff slick with sweat and face flushed from exertion, she would have been a provocative sight to behold. Hopefully, she had the sense to cover up with a T-shirt.

Either way, I didn't like the situation one bit. I made a mental note to set Krystina up with my personal trainer—someone I knew and trusted to keep his sweaty paws off her.

"Routine is good, but don't overdo it. You need to save some energy for the weekend," I joked lightly, suppressing the uncharacteristic jealousy that wanted to come lashing out.

"Actually, I wanted to talk to you about that—the weekend that is," she said a little too quickly.

"What about it? I mean, I've been keeping up with the storm, and I know flights into New York have been delayed indefinitely. But I'll make sure I'm back in time for the party at Murphy's."

"Oh, it's not that. Although, I'm glad you decided to come. This is about Saturday."

"What about it?"

She went on to tell me about her planned girls' day out and how flight cancelations forced them to reschedule for Saturday. Then she proceeded to talk non-stop about how poor the weather would be for boating, barely pausing to take a breath. She sounded nervous, almost as if she was afraid to tell me about the change of plans.

"I'm sorry. I know I promised you the weekend," she finally finished.

Amused by her ramblings, I decided to go easy on her.

"That's fine. It's only for the earlier part of the day. If you'd like, I could have Hale drive you and Allyson to and from your appointment."

"Allyson would get a kick out of that for sure," she laughed. And if I wasn't mistaken, she almost sounded relieved.

"Consider it a done deal. Just email me the reservation details, and I will forward it on to Hale."

"I'll do it in the morning. Right now, I'm going to change into pajamas, eat my dinner, then collapse on the couch. Maybe I'll catch up on a few shows I had set to DVR," she considered.

"That sounds exceedingly dull," I teased.

"Oh, not to me. A stormy night, house to myself...I can't think of anything else I'd rather be doing."

"I could think of a few things," I said suggestively. I could hear rustling in the background. "What are you doing?"

"Exactly what I said I was going to do." Her voice echoed as if she'd switched me over to speakerphone. "I'm changing my clothes."

An image of her slipping out of her bra and panties caused a stirring in my groin.

"What are you wearing right now?"

"Um, a tank top," she said, sounding slightly confused.

"Anything else?"

"Just my..." she paused. "My underwear."

Sweet Jesus...nothing but panties and a tank top.

I suppressed a groan as the image of Krystina's lithe, naked legs clouded my vision. I stood up and began pacing the room in an attempt to work off the restless energy that had suddenly come over me.

"Are you trying to torture me?" I asked.

I could hear her fumbling with the phone, switching it off of speaker mode.

"No, I'm not," she tried to convince me. However, her words sounded raspy, a sure sign she was connecting the dots, and her mind was beginning to gravitate to the same dark place as mine.

"I don't believe you. In fact, I may have to leave Boston right now just to come home and punish you."

"Oh, really?"

"You sound excited by the possibility, Miss Cole."

"Maybe I am," she teased.

"You're asking for it," I warned.

"I'm not asking for anything. But now that you mention it, how would you punish me exactly?"

Oh, game on, baby.

It was time to enlighten Krystina on the many ways I could punish an obstinate submissive.

"I would bind you face down, with your arms and legs spread to all four corners of my bed. You won't be able to move," I told her. There was dead silence on the other end of the line. I waited a moment before continuing, hoping she was forming a visual. "You will be blindfolded so you can't see what's coming. You remember the bite of the flogger, don't you?"

"Yes," she whispered.

"It will be different this time. I'm going to run it torturously slow down the length of your body, over and over again until you beg me to mark you with it. But even then, I won't. The more you beg, the more I'll introduce new tortures, ones that will bring you near to the edge of your breaking point and keep you there."

"What kinds of tortures?"

I smirked at the way she provoked me, knowing she didn't have an inkling of knowledge about the torments I could introduce her to.

If you want to play femme fatale, let's see how you react to this.

"You've felt my finger, but just wait until you feel a plug stretching you impossibly wide." I heard her breath suck in sharply. "Yes, Krystina. You know what I'm talking about. Close your eyes. Picture it. Now imagine the plug, with me standing over you and finally giving you the flogging you begged for. But even then, I won't let you come until you've earned it."

Her breathing became heavier, the sound a turn-on that left my head spinning. I leaned back against the wall of the hotel room and stared at the ceiling. If only I could reach through the phone and touch her. I wanted nothing more than to leave the mind-numbing conference, go home, and plunge into Krystina's satin heat.

"When will I have earned it?" she prodded me further.

I suppressed another groan.

Oh, angel...keep pushing me, and I'll be on a plane within the hour.

"That depends on how quickly you begin your penance." I continued the game but decided to add a twist.

"Penance?"

"Go to the full-length mirror in your bedroom. Stand in front of it," I told her. "Are you still just wearing panties and a tank top?"

"Yes, why?"

"Don't question. Just let me know when you're in front of the mirror."

"I'm here," she said after a few seconds.

"Good girl. Now, look at yourself. See what I see when I look at you. Follow the long lines of your legs to the curve of your hips. Notice the swell of your perfect tits…I imagine your nipples are poking through your tank top. Am I right?"

"Y-yes. They are."

Her stutter sounded hoarse.

"That's because you're incredibly turned on. Now I want you to feel what I would feel. Touch yourself, Krystina."

"Alex…" she hesitated.

"Earn it, angel. Slip your hand down the front of your panties. Feel how wet you are."

"I-I can't do that. I'd rather wait for you."

I could hear the shyness in her voice, but I could also hear the longing. I only had to push her a little further.

"Not following my directions will only make your punishment worse. How much do you think you can take?"

"I don't know. I guess I'll find out when I see you next. Until then, goodnight, Alexander."

At that, the line went dead.

Goodnight!

I banged my head back against the wall.

Once. Twice.

She must be freakin' kidding me!

I had a hard on rivaling any other, yet she left me hanging.

It took me a solid five minutes to steady my racing pulse. My only consolation was that I knew her frustration surely matched my own.

I stepped away from the wall and rubbed the back of my now sore head. I stared down at the phone, resisting the urge to chuck it across the room. Instead, I pocketed the cursed thing and went to the bathroom to take a shower.

A very *cold* shower.

THE WIND AND RAIN SLAPPED AT MY FACE, BUT THE STORM WAS NO match for the resolve running hot through my veins.

I had to find her.

I will find her.

I just wasn't searching in the right places.

Out of the rain and into a dark building. It smelled musty in here, like unwashed hair and dirty laundry.

I stepped into a room that had long been neglected, abandonment taking its toll over time. I knew this place all too well—the curtains that hung from the windows, the tattered couch against the wall. Cobwebs covered the lampshades on the end tables.

I hadn't been here in so long...

I glanced down at the throw rug in the living room and saw a large brown stain of blood. Bile rose in my throat at the sight, and I quickly turned away.

How did I end up here?

I knew she wasn't here. I had come to the wrong place again.

"Alexander."

I heard my name, but the voice was wrong. It wasn't the voice I had been searching for. It belonged to someone else—it was the voice that had the ability to soothe and frighten me all at once.

"Krystina?" I called out.

"I'm here," I heard her say from another room.

I ran through the dingy apartment in search of her. She didn't belong here, not in this dirty, tainted place.

How did she find out about it?

How did she know to find me here?

"Krystina, where are you?" I yelled.

I tore through the hallway, searching room after room. But it was as if every time I closed a door, another would appear. The dim lights began to flicker until eventually they went out completely, and I was left in nothing but darkness.

"I'm here," she said again. With only her voice to guide me, I stumbled into another dark room.

"Where? I can't see you?"

"Here," her voice came from somewhere behind me.

I turned to go toward the sound, but my feet came out from under me, and I was falling.

"Krystina!" I yelled through the air that whipped past my ears. "Help me!"

"I can't," I heard her say, but her voice seemed to be farther away now. So much farther...

Falling.

Falling.

I couldn't let her slip away. She was my only hope. I grappled for something to hang onto, anything to keep me from plummeting to the ground.

"Krystina!"

"Alexander," her distant voice echoed through the endless abyss that threatened to swallow me whole.

I SAT UP LIKE A SHOT, SWEAT-DRENCHED AND SHAKING. THE SOUND of rain lashing at the windows caused me to become disoriented, and it took me a moment or two before I remembered where I was.

Boston. The hotel. Only a dream.

But I could still smell the damp air. I still had that sinking feeling in my gut from falling—the kind you get on a roller coaster after it goes over the first crest.

It was the second time in a week a dream had shaken me up. I could blame the dreams on my heightened emotional state since meeting Krystina. Or maybe it was an underlying fear my sister's ex-husband would dredge up the long-buried past. Or perhaps tonight, it was simply because I had bad fish for dinner.

I lay back down against the overly soft pillows and tried to shake off my unease.

A shrink would have a field day with me.

I rolled on my side in an attempt to get comfortable again, but my efforts were futile. I couldn't downplay certain elements of the dreams. They left me with a feeling of emptiness that made my heartache. I could not ignore the fact while I was sleeping, I had been searching for my mother.

38

Krystina

Murphy's was as loud as ever when I walked in to meet my friends from Wally's. I pushed my way through the crowd of people and scanned the room for a familiar face. I wasn't sure if anyone else had arrived yet.

"Hey, baby. Fancy meeting you here," I heard from behind me. I spun around, shocked and pleased to hear the familiar voice.

"Alex!" I impulsively threw my arms around his neck. Resting my head against his chest, I breathed in his scent. He may have only been away for a few days, but it seemed like a lifetime.

"Glad to know you missed me," he said with a laugh.

I pulled back, feeling apprehensive over how elated I was to see him. I convinced myself the previous evening that I could manage to keep Alexander at arm's length. But after taking just one look at him, my optimism began to fade rapidly.

So much for taking the road that would create a little distance, Cole.

My chest tightened at the thought of facing the alternative option.

"What happened?" I asked, trying to shake off my unease. "I thought all flights into New York were still backed up."

"I have my ways. Besides, I told you I'd be here. So, here I am."

"Well, I'm happy you made it," I said.

"So am I, angel. I'm glad to see you wearing the necklace I bought you too."

I reached up to touch the emblem around my neck and felt my cheeks flush.

"I started thinking about the quote you sent me with the flowers. That was sneaky of you, by the way. But, if it makes you happy for me to wear it, then I don't see the harm."

His eyes glimmered wickedly dark as he circled his arms around my waist.

"What do you say we ditch this joint? I want to go home and see you wearing nothing but that. And maybe those fuck-me shoes that you have too," he whispered into my ear.

"As enticing as it sounds, I can't really ditch my own party before it even starts," I declined begrudgingly. I pulled away to scan the crowd. "I'm not sure if anyone else is here yet, though. Let me go and ask Will. Come on."

I removed Alexander's arms from my waist and took hold of his hand.

"Uh, no. Krystina, I'll just wait here," he said, pulling free of my grasp. His face looked conflicted.

"What is it?"

I watched his brow crease until he seemed to come to a decision.

"Nothing," he finally said. "Just lead the way."

I frowned, perplexed over his hesitation, but then dismissed it with the thought that perhaps he was just tired from traveling. Pushing our way through the crowd, I stepped up to the bar. When Will eventually made his way over to us, I smiled at the pub owner.

"Hey, Will. How's it going?" I asked.

"Why, hello there, little lady," Will greeted me with a smile. "I hear you're the guest of honor at a party here tonight."

"It's just a small goodbye party with the people from Wally's.

Oh, and Alex too," I said, turning around to motion Alexander forward. "Will, I'd like you to meet Alex."

When the two men locked eyes, there was no denying they already knew each other. I felt Alexander's body stiffen beside me, almost as if he was bracing for a fight. Will's eyes flashed with distinctive anger.

"Will," Alexander said, reaching his hand across the bar to shake his hand.

Will simply nodded his response and returned the handshake. If I wasn't mistaken, they both seemed to be squeezing hands a little too hard. However, to the average outsider, their exchange was nothing but cordial.

"Your party is waiting for you at your usual table, Krys. I'll send Lisa over with a round of drinks on the house," Will told me with a dismissive wave. And at that, he turned his attention to another patron who was waiting to be served.

I looked back and forth between Alexander and Will. It was probably the most bizarre interaction I had ever seen between two people. As soon as we were able to walk out of earshot of Will, I pounced on Alexander.

"What was *that* all about?"

"What?" He feigned innocence.

"Oh, come on! You two obviously know each other."

"Yeah, we do. He isn't one of my biggest fans—I'll say that much."

"Will is normally so down to earth. I've never seen him act like that. What happened between you?"

"It doesn't matter, Krystina," he said with a shake of his head. "Let's just go meet your friends."

Another secret.

I felt my stomach plummet.

However, there was a certain amount of finality to his tone, warning me not to press the issue. I was contemplating if I should or not when I spotted Melanie waving to get my attention. I raised my hand, signaling I would be there in a minute.

"I'm not sure what's going on, but you seem uncomfortable. We can go if you want to," I offered.

"Don't tempt me, angel," he said with a wink. "I believe you still have a punishment coming to you."

I knew he was trying to steer me away from the conversation to avoid giving me the truth once again.

"I'm serious, Alex. I'll just make an excuse, and we can go."

"That would be foolish. These people are here for you, and we shouldn't keep them waiting any longer."

Alexander linked his hand in mine and led me to the back of the pub, successfully drawing the matter to a close.

For now, at least.

His constant vagueness drove me to the point of insanity but pushing for answers in the crowded pub would not earn me a favorable result. Whatever the story was behind Alexander and Will, I would get to the bottom of it after we left Murphy's.

Alexander

THE GET-TOGETHER WITH KRYSTINA'S CO-WORKERS WAS PRETTY low-key, and I was thankful the celebrations ended early. I wasn't sure if I could handle another minute of watching Jim McNamara gawk at Krystina. The way he obnoxiously stared at her throughout the night was nauseating—especially when he didn't stop after I put my arm around her waist to stake my claim. Krystina was oblivious as usual, not understanding the effect her simple beauty had on the opposite sex.

However, McNamara wasn't the only reason why I had felt edgy most of the evening. It was awkward being inside the pub tonight and seeing William Murphy. I expected as much and should not have gone in there. Personal issues aside, it's never easy to run into a club member outside of the scene. Both parties wonder if the other will slip up, break the assumed code of secrecy, and shatter the other person's need for privacy. It was a dicey situation, and I was relieved the evening went off without too much of a hitch.

Arms loaded with parting gifts, Krystina and I waited at the bar's front door for Hale to arrive. When the Porsche pulled up to the curb, we made a mad dash for the SUV, fighting the rain whipping at our faces. Once we were seated inside, I noticed Krystina was unusually silent, and I half wondered if she was still thinking about the interaction between William Murphy and me.

"You okay?" I asked once we were situated in the back seat.

"I'm fine." Her tone was clipped.

"You don't sound fine. Is it because of the thing with Will?"

"Yes. No...I don't know, Alex. Honestly, it was the whole night."

"What about the whole night? You seemed like you had a nice time."

"I guess I'm a better actor than you are," she commented sarcastically. "It was pretty damn obvious you weren't enjoying yourself. I know you said you don't fit in well at parties, but geez! You looked like you'd rather be anywhere else!"

"Sorry, but sitting there watching Jim McNamara look like his puppy just died every time you spoke was a little much," I said dryly.

"You could have ignored him. Oh, wait. You did, along with everyone else who was there. You barely spoke a word all night."

"They are your friends, Krystina. Not mine," I pointed out.

"So, what if they aren't your friends? And what about that thing with Will? How do you guys know each other?"

She was making my head spin with the way she fired off one question after another in such rapid succession.

I sighed. Krystina had her fighting gloves on, and I didn't want to go a round with her. I had missed her, and I wanted nothing more than to get her back to my place, naked and tied to my bed. To hell with her cursed time of the month. If she was still on her period, I didn't give a damn. I was desperate to be inside her again.

Maybe I should finally introduce her to my cross...

I temporarily shelved the idea when I noticed she was staring me down, still waiting for a response.

"He belongs to the same club I do," I finally answered.

"Club? Like one of *those* clubs?" she asked incredulously.

"Yes, Krystina. One of those clubs. My club. Anyway, we had a disagreement some years back. Let's just leave it at that."

"Will? I mean, I never thought..." she trailed off. "I just didn't think he'd be the type to be into your sort of thing."

"It's your thing too now. Remember?" I asked, pointing to the necklace secured around her neck.

"Oh, well, isn't this just dandy!" she exclaimed, throwing her hands in the air. "I researched this, Alex. Based on what you're telling me now, I'm pretty sure Will doesn't think I'm wearing a Celtic symbol around my neck!"

"Trust me—I think Will is just as shocked as you are over the situation."

"This is so embarrassing," she mumbled. She put her head down and began rubbing her temples.

Krystina was in a foul mood, and I couldn't say it was all because of my behavior at the party. There was truth to her words. I had been somewhat standoffish throughout the night, but it merely was because I felt out of my element amongst her peers. There was something else eating at her, but I couldn't pinpoint what it was.

"What else is bugging you?"

"I've been walking around all day with this necklace on, advertising I'm a part of a world I truly know nothing about. The only experience I have is with you!"

"What's your point?" I asked somewhat irritably. I was beginning to lose my patience with her little temper tantrum.

"You're so tight-lipped about your past. Hoping for a straight answer from you about anything is like wishing for snow in July. Then there's this whole business regarding your alternative lifestyle—that's an entirely different beast. I know there's more you're not telling me, and it's probably nothing I can read about on the internet," she paused to take a breath, then looked me square in the eyes. "I need answers. I want to go to your club."

So that's it...she wants to go to Club O.

I wondered why she suddenly decided to press the issue. Whatever the reason was, I knew I couldn't take her there—at least not anytime soon. Krystina had yet to fully understand the meaning behind a true Dom and sub relationship. It was built on trust and honesty. They went hand in hand, and neither of us had fully given that to each other as of yet. There were too many secrets between us—a fundamental fact neither of us could deny. The club would only complicate our already fragile start.

"Krystina, I already told you. I don't want to take you there. You're not ready for it."

"And who are you to decide what I'm ready for? I don't need you to be my protector. I can handle it, and I want to see and learn for myself. It's barely after ten. I'm sure it's not too late to go now."

Now! As in tonight! She's out of her fucking mind...

There's a certain mindset a person needed to have before walking through the doors of Club O, and Krystina had anything *but* the right frame of mind at that moment.

"Not a good idea—especially not tonight. I think it's been a long week for both of us. Let's just go back to my place and relax."

"No, I want to go home," she said, folding her arms across her chest in defiance.

"Krystina, we agreed you would stay the weekend with me."

"Or what? You'll threaten to punish me for not giving unconditional obedience again?" she barked.

My head jerked back, shocked by her outburst. It was probably better she did go home—at least until the bug decided to crawl out of her ass.

"Fine." I leaned forward to hit the button that would lower the privacy glass. "Hale, Krystina will be going back to her own apartment tonight."

"Yes, Mr. Stone," Hale acknowledged.

Once the glass raised back to its original position, I heard Krystina sigh.

"I'm sorry, Alex. I shouldn't have snapped at you," she said in a resigned voice. "I just think we've been spending too much time together, that's all."

What is this now?

I was completely flabbergasted.

"What are you talking about? I just got back into town!"

"Yes, I know. And I appreciate the surprise. But honestly, I have an early morning spa day planned with Ally, and then I'll be by your place after to spend the night. I think one weekend night is enough."

She's pulling away from me.

I leaned forward and hit the privacy glass again.

"Change of plan, Hale. My place."

"What? I said to take me home!" Krystina demanded.

"No. Not until we sort out whatever issue it is you seem to be having. You're all over the board tonight, and I want to get to the bottom of it."

39

Krystina

I paced Alexander's family room, trying to calm my mounting fury. I didn't know who I was angrier with—him for bringing me to his house despite my protests or myself for acting like an inconsolable teenager.

Alexander wanted answers for my behavior, and rightly so. But if I couldn't explain to myself how I was feeling, I had no hope of explaining it to him rationally. I had been back and forth for days—one part of me wanted to put some space between us, yet another part of me wanted all in. Space was a safer choice, but I didn't know how to separate my emotions. The alternative would force me to open my heart and bare my soul, an option that could potentially cripple me.

"Krystina, sit down, please. You're going to wear a hole through my carpet."

"I'm fine standing," I told him but stopped pacing. I rubbed my temples in an attempt to ward off the imminent headache.

"Would you like something to drink?"

"Wine would be great right now," I accepted without hesitation.

I would need it to get through what I was about to do. It was time to choose my path. To do that, I would have to lay it all on the line. Alexander's response to what I had to say would determine my chosen direction, as I had proved to be inept at maintaining a half-in relationship status. I would either be all in or not at all.

Alexander opened the bottled wine refrigerator and quickly made a selection. Popping the cork, he poured me a glass of white. I took a huge gulp and another until the glass was drained. I handed the glass back to him. He merely raised one eyebrow at me, then refilled it.

"What's wrong, angel? Tell me."

Angel.

I liked when Alexander called me that, but I knew only people who were dating typically used pet names. I wasn't sure how we had gotten to that point since I couldn't even say we were an official couple.

"I'm miserable because I feel like I constantly have this battle going on inside my head," I confessed. "I've been thinking a lot over the past few days, and I've come to a conclusion. This thing between us cannot continue like it is. Something needs to give here."

He cocked his head to one side, a look of confusion plain on his face.

"What are you trying to say?" he asked cautiously.

"Look, I've tried keeping separation between us, but it isn't working. I had this fantastic idea I could somehow just have sex with you and want nothing more. It was a foolish notion on both of our parts. Your history with one-night stands probably worked to keep out emotional attachments in the past—but that isn't what we are. It's not who we've become. We've far surpassed that, and the more time goes on, the more I want. It doesn't matter how much I fight it."

"So, don't try to fight it then," he stated simply as if it were so easy.

"You don't want me to? I mean, you want more than just the sex, too?"

"You're not the only one navigating unfamiliar territory," he ironically admitted. "Long-term has never been in my vocab until I met you. At first, I thought I could manage a steady Dominant and submissive relationship with you. But you're not built for it, and it's not what I want anymore. My ideals have changed. I told you I don't do teddy bears and roses, yet I had flowers delivered to you just yesterday. I've never done that for any woman before. I suggest we put away the idea of what we *said* we wanted and focus on what we want now."

"I can't do that," I gravely said, shaking my head back and forth in denial.

"Then what's the point of having this discussion?"

"Trust. I can't focus on moving forward in this while we are both clinging to secrets."

Alexander moved over to the couch and sat down. He ran his hands through his hair in a display of evident frustration.

"Krystina, as hard as I try, I don't understand you. I know there are things in your past you aren't telling me. But whatever it is, it's getting in the way of us. Sure, we are certainly unconventional compared to most, but that doesn't explain why you continually push me away. If we have any shot at making this work, you need to either tell me or get past whatever it is that's holding you back."

"That's not fair. What you're saying goes both ways."

"You're right, and I knew you'd say that. But you have to understand there are some things I can't tell you because they involve others. I can't tell a story that isn't completely mine to tell. I think you're only hell-bent on unlocking my past because you are desperately clinging to yours."

"I am not," I said stubbornly.

"Really? Then why can't you let go enough to tell me?" he challenged.

I walked over to where he was sitting and looked down into his eyes. As I stared into those vibrant blues, I knew he was right. To build any sort of foundation, he needed the truth. And perhaps, if I gave in first, he would open himself up to me.

I took a shaky breath, trying to gather the courage to dispel my apprehension.

"Alright," I gave in. "I'll tell you. But I can't say knowing it will make any bit of difference. In the end, my past defines who I am today. I can't change that."

"Go on," he encouraged patiently.

"When I was still in college, I dated this guy for a couple of years. I've mentioned him before. His name is Trevor."

"Yes. I remember," he told me. His lips pinched into a thin line. I could tell he was trying to contain his irritation upon hearing my ex's name, but I ignored it. This was far too important for me to waste time worrying about whether or not Alexander would be insulted.

"Well, he was super controlling, and that's putting it mildly," I continued. "I won't bore you with the details, but you have to know I easily gave in to him. I gave up a lot to cater to his every whim, completely sacrificing who I was. It was one of the biggest mistakes of my life. That's the reason why I'm so adamant about maintaining independence. I won't let it happen again."

"Well, we've already established you are a terrible full-time submissive," he laughed lightly, then sobered when he saw I wasn't finding his comment funny. "Seriously, I'm not asking you to give up everything. I thought you understood that. There's no need to rehash what we've already discussed."

"Wait, there's more. A lot more. I'm not sure if you want to hear it."

Alexander reached up and tugged at my hand to pull me down onto the sofa. I broke free of his grasp and shook my head. I didn't want to sit, as I found it easier to talk while standing, and I began to pace the floor again.

"Krystina, just tell me," he prodded.

"Trevor was abusive—not at first, but over time. It started more verbal than anything else, and I easily ignored it. He shoved me a few times—once in front of Allyson. I fought with her a lot over that. She called Trevor out on his shit pretty regularly, and he hated her for it."

"Ally sounds like a smart girl," he said dryly.

"She saw what I couldn't see. So, Trevor did everything he could to keep Ally and me apart. I let him."

"Everything is okay with you and her now, though, isn't it?"

I caught Alexander's eye and smiled wistfully.

"Yes, Ally and I are fine. She saved me."

I saw his brow furrow in confusion.

"Saved you?" he asked.

"From Trevor."

As much as I told myself I wouldn't cry, I felt a tear slide down my cheek. I hastily wiped it away, annoyed I was showing signs of weakness.

"Krystina, it's okay," Alexander assured as he came over to where I stood. He wrapped his arms around me and held me tight to his chest. "It was a long time ago. He's not worth it."

I looked up and saw the hurt in his eyes.

He thought I was crying over Trevor.

"I'm not upset over him. I'm upset because of what I have to say next. I'm sorry, but I've never talked about this in detail, not even to Ally. She only knows what she knows because she's smart and connected the dots. I don't think you know how hard this is for me."

His face paled, and I could see panic begin to set in.

"Christ, what the hell happened? You're starting to scare me, Krystina."

I removed myself from his embrace, unable to meet his eyes while I told the ending of my tale. For some reason, I was awash with humiliation, even though I knew I had nothing to be ashamed about.

"For the first time, I stood up for myself," I continued. "I decided to leave him after he cheated on me. Well, he was having none of it. You want to talk about fatal attraction—I lived it."

"You don't have to tell me anymore if you don't want to," Alexander said. His voice wavered uncharacteristically. It was as if he was afraid to hear the rest.

But what Alexander didn't understand was I *had* to tell him.

This wasn't only about building trust between the two of us. It was more about me. If I truly wanted to move on from my haunting past, I had to admit certain things to myself. I needed to speak the words aloud, something I had never done before.

"No, I have to get this out. For me," I added. He nodded his head once, accepting my need to finish. "About a month after I left Trevor, he showed up at my apartment. He had been drinking a lot before he came. I should have just slammed the door in his face, but I was worried because he had driven to my place. I didn't want to send him off to get behind the wheel again, so I let him come inside. I figured once he had time to sober up a bit, I'd tell him to leave.

"One thing led to another, and we started to argue. Eventually, I lost patience with him and stormed off into my bedroom. I hoped he'd sleep off his drunken stupor on the couch and be gone by morning. But he followed me instead," I paused and took a shaky breath.

Don't cry. Don't cry.

My vision narrowed, and I felt like I was in a trance, as if I were looking down on the scene taking place in the penthouse. I didn't even notice Alexander was right by my side until I felt his hand on my cheek. Using his thumb, he brushed a tear away.

"You don't have to finish," Alexander said beseechingly.

I looked up into his beautiful eyes, so full of patience and understanding. A weaker version of myself may have folded right then and there, seeking the comfort of his embrace to protect myself from the rest of the world. However, I wasn't that person anymore. I knew I was stronger than that. Determination settled in my bones with a renewed confidence that turned my spine to steel.

You can do this.

I squared my shoulders and took a deep, self-assured breath.

"He came at me, but I was no match against him. He beat me," I paused, struggling to get the rest out. "And he forced himself on me."

"He raped you?"

I winced at hearing Alexander voice the brutality I refused to acknowledge, even after all this time.

"Yes, he raped me."

Uttering those few words made me feel as if I was being ripped apart from the inside. The pain was tremendous, yet I felt a certain amount of relief through the hurt. It was as if the weight of the entire world had been removed from my shoulders.

"Fuck, Krystina," Alexander swore, his voice full of venom. "I... I knew there was something. But I had no idea."

He pulled me close to him, but this time I welcomed his embrace. His touch seeped a little bit of warmth into my blood that seemed to be flowing arctic cold.

"I tried to reach Allyson, but I didn't know where she was, and she wasn't answering her phone. I waited for her all night," I choked on the last sentence as the memories from that fateful day began to take their toll on my strength. "When she finally came home the next morning, I was a mess. I couldn't even speak. I just remember crying uncontrollably. Honestly, the entire thing is kind of foggy even now. One minute I was home, and the next, I was in a hospital bed. Doctors and police officers were asking me questions, but I couldn't get the words out."

Alexander pulled back suddenly, alarm spreading over his handsome features.

"I hope you don't think...I mean, when I talk about punishing you, you know it's different than—" he started, but I cut him off before he would finish.

"I know it's different. At first, I worried what happened might get in the way. But you convinced me to trust you in that regard. You unknowingly taught me the difference between pleasure that comes from pain and pain that comes from violence."

Alexander squeezed me tighter to him.

"I've always underestimated your strength, but I can't help but apologize. I would have done things differently with you had I known this earlier," he murmured into my hair.

"Don't be sorry. I'm glad you didn't know because I wouldn't want to change anything. In fact, I always worried people would look at me differently if they knew what happened with Trevor. I couldn't even talk about it to the therapists I tried going to. I was serious when I said I never told anyone the details of that night up until now."

"Nobody?" he asked.

"Like I said, not even Allyson."

He abruptly pulled back to look at me. All of the compassion was gone, and I was alarmed by the amount of anger flashing in his eyes.

"You said there were police at the hospital. Are you saying you never even told them? He walked?"

"Alex, I was in so much pain that day—emotionally and physically. I was too weak to admit the truth to myself, let alone to a stranger in a uniform. So, yes. I let him walk."

He searched my face carefully, although I wasn't sure of what exactly he was trying to find.

Is he looking at me now with different eyes? Will he still touch me the same way?

After a moment, I tore my gaze from his. I didn't want to entertain the many ways my revelation could change our relationship. However, he took my chin in his hand and turned my head back to look at him.

"Do not blame yourself," he said vehemently.

"What makes you think I'm blaming myself?"

"Because you said *you* let him walk. And I'm familiar with the look on your face. My mother wore that look."

I froze.

"Your mother?"

"Yes. My father was an abusive man, and she always blamed herself. Don't be that woman, Krystina. Don't allow yourself to be the victim. You're tougher than that. Your admission today tells me as much. By overcoming what happened and moving on from the horrors in your past, you become the champion. The minute you stand proud and strong, Trevor becomes nothing but a weak little man."

While I knew there was truth in his words, I couldn't help but zero in the mention of his parents.

"What happened to your mother and father, Alex?"

He tilted his head up to the ceiling and closed his eyes. When he looked at me again, his expression was pleading.

"Angel, please don't ask me that. I'm sorry, especially after all you have told me about yourself tonight. But I...I can't tell you."

It hurt that he wouldn't open up to me. Only the torment written on his face stopped me from pushing him further, despite the fact I was dying to know the truth. Alexander had his own demons he was battling. It wouldn't be fair for me to pressure him if he wasn't ready. Because if there was one thing I learned tonight, revealing the deepest and darkest parts of your soul was a decision one had to make on their own.

"It's okay," I told him. "When you're ready to tell me, you'll know it."

He looked doubtful, but he didn't truly understand. For me, I felt the truth had quite literally set me free. And as I stood in the penthouse with Alexander, the remarkable, alluring, and captivating man he was, I realized something else. Our time together thus far may have been short, but it felt like we had known each other for a millennium. He wasn't really the stranger I thought he was, but familiar to me in ways rooted deep and unexplainable.

There was a silent understanding between us as I took hold of Alexander's hand and led him to the bedroom. There would be no barriers between us tonight, as the past was finally behind me, and there would be no looking back.

40

Krystina

I tightened the belt of the plush robe I wore and followed a petite Asian woman down the main corridor of the Mandarin Day Spa. Allyson and I had only made it halfway through the day, and I was already feeling like a pampered princess. My face felt revitalized after an herbal facial, and my bones were like liquid after the therapeutic oil massage. Next up was a hot stone pedicure, and I could hardly wait.

"This is our Serenity Suite, Miss Cole," the Asian woman said once we reached our destination. "Please, take a moment to relax here while you wait for your friend. Miss Ramsey should be joining you momentarily. There is bottled water for you on the buffet, both sparkling and still. Feel free to help yourself to whatever you'd like."

"Thank you," I graciously accepted.

After getting a bottle of mineral water, I made myself comfortable on a sprawling chaise lounge. I lay back and closed my eyes, taking note of the soft music playing from a hidden source within the suite. It sounded like a bamboo flute, the melody almost hypnotic.

I could go to sleep right here.

"Oh, I don't think I've ever felt so good!" I heard Allyson exclaim through the tranquility of the room.

Or not.

I opened one eye to peer at her.

"Good massage, I take it?"

"That masseuse was gifted the hands of a God!" she swooned. She tossed a wicked smile at me. "And he kind of looked like one too."

"You're bad," I laughed, shaking my head. I sat up and gave in to a good stretch. "Things not going well with Jeremy?"

"Oh, Jeremy is fine," she said offhandedly. "However, we're not til' death do us part or anything. I'm still allowed to look."

The Asian woman who brought me into the room came in quietly behind Allyson. Her peaceful demeanor versus Allyson's boisterous entrance was almost comical.

"Would you like to relax here for a bit? Or are you ladies ready for your pedicures now?" she asked Allyson and me.

"It's up to Krys. I'm up for whatever."

"We could go now," I said.

"Then please, follow me this way," the small woman said, motioning for us to follow her.

"This place is amazing," Allyson appreciated, taking in every detail of our surroundings as we walked. "I agree," I concurred, sharing in her sentiments. "It's just what I needed. It's been a complicated couple of weeks."

We took our seats in the cushy chairs that would serve as our personal thrones during the pedicure. I relaxed back, trying to find that quiet place I had in the Serenity Suite, while I enjoyed the feel of various oils and stones being rubbed over my feet and legs.

"You okay?" Allyson asked after a while.

I turned my head to look at her, confused by her question.

"Of course, I'm okay. How could I not be when I'm getting pampered like this?" I laughed, pointing to the tub of swirling hot water in which my feet rested.

"I was only checking. I thought you might still be stewing over the fact Alexander picked up the tab for all of this," she said, motioning to our surroundings.

"It was unexpected, but that's just how he is. I shouldn't have been the least bit surprised," I said with a frown.

"Well, if you're sure everything is okay..." she trailed off. "You just seem sort of quiet today, that's all. I mean, you took some major steps recently. I just want to make sure you're handling it all right."

"I'm fine, Ally. Just taking it one day at a time..." I trailed off, closing my eyes again.

I wished I could tell Ally exactly how significant those steps were, and for the first time in our friendship, I felt lost. She knew I had a secret, but she had respected my boundaries over the years. It pained me to think of how hurt she would be if she knew I had opened up to Alexander before her.

But I couldn't explain my reasoning for telling Alexander without filling her in on the rest of it. She wouldn't understand the complicated layers that made up my relationship with him, as her worry for my wellbeing would overshadow all else. Telling Alexander was a giant leap of faith, one I had to take if I wanted to continue the path I was on with him.

Trust and honesty.

That's what he told me. Without that, we would never stand a chance.

I heard someone say the word Alexander, and my ears naturally perked up. I peeked around my chair to see two women walk into the room and take seats behind Allyson and me. They both looked familiar, but I couldn't place either of them.

Maybe customers from Wally's.

I dismissed the notion I knew them from somewhere and tried to resume relaxing. However, it was difficult because neither woman would shut up.

"Suzy, I trust him, and so should you," said one of the women.

"I'm sorry if I have a slight trust issue when it comes to him," the other woman spat out.

"Ugh. You need to get over it. It was a long time ago. Besides, it never would have happened."

"I know better than anyone. The man will never commit to anyone."

I heard Allyson groan beside me, and I looked at her.

"Those two sound like a couple of cackling hens. I wish they'd pipe down," she complained, motioning her head back to where the two chatty women sat.

"Yeah, tell me about it," I agreed. "But we are almost done anyways. Lunch should be waiting for us once our pedicures finish."

"Good, because I'm famished. I discovered I'm not a big fan of French food and feel like I haven't eaten in days. I never want to hear the words *haute cuisine* again!" Allyson finished with an exaggerated French accent that made me laugh.

"No, I kept it light, with your appetite for American-fare in mind. We're just having finger sandwiches and a green salad. Nothing too exotic."

"Sounds perfect," she said, settling back against her chair and closing her eyes.

I did the same, wanting to cherish the last few minutes of self-indulgence.

However, as hard as I tried, I could not tune out the two women. They were still adamantly going at it.

"But Justine, how can you be sure what he did will work?" I heard one woman ask the other.

Justine. I know that name.

I turned again to take a closer look at the two women. Sure enough, there was no mistaking that glossy black hair. It was Alexander's sister. The other woman was a redhead, the same woman I saw photographed with Alexander in the article I had read online.

What was her name? Suzanne Jacobs...I think?

It was strange to realize I had only done the research a few short weeks ago. I quickly spun back in the chair, unsure of what to think about the unusual coincidence.

I glanced at Allyson, still resting back with her eyes closed. By some miracle, she had managed to block out the two women. But now that I knew exactly who they were, any hope of ignoring them would be fruitless.

"I know it will work because Alex said it would. His people are all over it. I can't keep making myself sick about it," I heard Justine say.

"Charlie is nuts. I just hope Alex and his cronies know what they're doing."

"Please, Suzy. Don't you think I know that? And Alex knows too. Why do you think he's building the women's shelter?" Justine spat out bitterly. "I'm sure he's hoping one day our mother will waltz through the doors, then we can have a big ole' happy family reunion."

Wait. What? His mother?

The room felt like it was buzzing, feeling overwhelmed with shock by the fact Alexander's mother was alive. He had told me his parents were dead.

I respected his decision not to divulge his story to me, but telling an outright lie was another thing.

Why did he lie about it? Is his father alive too?

I tried to listen to the two women again, but the pedicurist announced we were finished and began draining the footbath. She started talking nonsense about our lunch, and I had to fight the urge to shush her. I just wanted to scream.

Be quiet! I'm trying to listen!

"Krys, what's wrong?" Allyson asked.

I blinked once. Then twice, forcing myself to focus on the people standing in front of me. Allyson and the pedicurist were looking at me with concerned expressions.

"Nothing. I'm fine. It's just a little warm in here," I lied.

Allyson shot me a look that might as well have said I sprouted another head but said nothing as I got up from my seat. The quiet Asian woman appeared again out of nowhere and motioned for us to follow her.

As we exited the room, I chanced a glance back at Justine and

Suzanne. Unfortunately, they were no longer talking but sitting back and enjoying their spa treatments. A part of me wanted to go up to them and demand an explanation, but I thought better of it. This wasn't the sort of place to risk making a scene. It would be best if I just waited and confronted Alexander about it later.

Allyson and I sat down to lunch. She chattered endlessly about her time in Paris. I listened and nodded at all the appropriate times, but I wasn't fully into the conversation. I kept thinking about what I overheard in the pedicure room as a million questions swirled in my head.

What was Alexander's relationship with Suzanne Jacobs? Why didn't she trust him?

Who is Charlie?

And what about Alexander's mother and the woman's shelter?

Should I demand truth from Alexander? Or should I wait for him to come to me?

My stomach was tied up in knots, causing the food to taste like cardboard. It was a real struggle pretending to enjoy the tiny sandwiches.

My cell pinged with a text notification, distracting me from my thoughts. Allyson continued talking while I looked at my phone.

"I wish I had time to go and see the Eiffel Tower," she said wistfully. "That would have made the trip worthwhile, at least. But I was there for work purposes after all, so I guess—"

"Oh, no! Not now!" I exclaimed, unintentionally interrupting her.

"What do you mean not now? What happened?"

"It's my mother. She told me a while back she was planning a trip to the city sometime soon. Apparently, that time is now. She just sent me a text to let me know she's here."

"So, what?" Allyson asked. "It's not like this would be the first time she's shown up unannounced."

"True, but I had plans for the rest of the weekend. Now I either have to cancel them or tell my mother about Alexander."

"Oh...I didn't even think of that," Allyson said.

Her eyes were round and full of dread, for she knew once my mother found out I was seeing someone, all hell would break loose.

41

Krystina

When Allyson and I arrived home, we found Frank and my mother already inside our apartment. My mother was ordering Frank to bring a bunch of packages into the guest bedroom, and neither noticed we had come in. By the looks of things, she had apparently been shopping.

The living room was littered with bags from various retail shops throughout the city, making a disaster area out of the normally tidy apartment. I had half a mind to ask my mother to return her key. However, I knew I couldn't do that as long as Frank was paying the rent. So, I defaulted to politeness rather than throwing a fit about the mess my mother had made.

"Hi, mom," I greeted.

My mother was the only woman I knew who could pull off such casual elegance by simply wearing a cardigan and a pair of trouser pants. She appeared to be examining her nails for a chip and looked up when she heard my voice.

"Oh, good! You're home! I didn't hear you two come in!"

"Hello, Mrs. Long," Allyson said.

"Allyson, you look marvelous as always," my mother swooned.

Her silver bracelets jingled as she came over to give Allyson and me a hug. "I'm so happy to see you both. It's been too long since my last visit."

As far as I was concerned, it wasn't long enough. It wasn't that I wasn't happy to see her, but I didn't have the patience to deal with her today. After my day at the spa, I now had more pressing matters to attend to.

"When you told me you were planning on a visit, I thought you would have given me a heads up," I said, perhaps a little bit too harshly.

"I'm sorry, honey. But you know Frank's schedule. Things come up at the last minute with the dealerships, which makes long-term planning tough. The weekend was free, so we decided early this morning to take the drive in."

"Krys!" I heard from behind me. I looked over my shoulder to see Frank coming out of the guest room. I smiled when I saw him and was happy to see him looking so well. He was a little grayer than when I had seen him last but still looked trim and fit despite the fact he was pushing sixty.

"Hey, Frank," I said.

"Come here, girl. I missed you," Frank said, pulling me into a fierce bear hug. "Thank goodness you're home. I think your mother had me walk half the streets in the city in just a few short hours. We only came back here to drop off packages. It's your turn now."

"I'm up for a shopping trip," Allyson chimed in.

"That's a great idea!" my mother exclaimed. "The three of us girls can shop, then Frank can meet up with us for a late dinner afterward."

My mother's face lit up like a Roman candle at the idea, and I dreaded being the one to extinguish it.

"I'm sorry, mom. But I can't go shopping tonight."

"But, dear, why not?"

"I have plans," I said, deliberately evading the specifics. I looked to Allyson in a silent plea for help.

"That's okay, Mrs. Long. The two of us can go," Allyson offered.

"Besides, I'm way overdue for a new pair of boots."

I was grateful to Allyson for jumping in to take the reins, but there was no fooling my mother. She saw the look passing between Allyson and me, and her eyes narrowed in suspicion.

"What sort of plans do you have tonight, Krys?" my mother asked. She tried to pose the question as being off the cuff, but I knew her too well.

"There's just something I have to do, that's all," I tried to shrug off. "If you're up for more shopping tomorrow, I can go with you then."

My mother wasn't falling for it, so she turned to Allyson instead.

"Has she met someone?" my mother asked.

Here comes the third-degree interrogation...

"I'm standing right here, mom. You don't have to ask Ally."

"So? Have you?" she asked, staring pointedly at me.

Allyson began to rummage through her purse with the pretense of looking for something, while Frank made a loud show of clearing his throat.

"Um, I'm going to check the car to see if there are any more bags," he announced. Moving quickly to the door, Frank made fast work of slipping his shoes on, and out he went.

Thanks for the support.

I knew there would be no putting this off. I had barely been home for five minutes, but my mother's radar was already honed in.

"I am talking to someone, but it's nothing serious," I admitted.

"Krys, you barely just broke up with Trevor. You don't need the distraction of another guy right now. You should be focusing on building a career."

I closed my eyes and tried to count to ten. Just once, I would like to have a normal mother-daughter visit, one where I didn't have to face a lecture or jump on the defense about my personal business. From the way my mother acted, you'd never know I was a recent college graduate. She still treated me like I was in grade school.

"Actually, it's been two years since Trevor. And for your information, I found a job. It's a good one, too. I start on Monday," I said proudly.

"I'm glad about that, but it's even more of a reason why you shouldn't be wasting your time on dating. You should be directing your attention to getting ahead in life."

I should have known she'd focus on the guy thing rather than be happy I'd landed the job she had been hounding me about. I pursed my lips in annoyance.

"I'm sure I can manage to juggle both a career and a relationship," I said dryly. It was a good thing she didn't know my new boss *was* the relationship.

"Krys, I wish you would just take my advice for once. It's like I've always said, you should wait to—" she started, but I interrupted her.

"Yeah, yeah. I know. I should wait until I'm established in a career before I think about getting serious with anyone. I know your stance on the matter, mom."

Allyson, knowing the situation was starting to spin out of control, decided to speak up.

"Mrs. Long, would you like something to drink? Why don't you sit down and relax for a bit? I'm sure you've had a tiring day, with the drive and full day of shopping and all."

"I'm fine, dear. But thank you," my mother dismissed. Then without skipping a beat, she came at me again. "Krys, I just don't want you to make the same mistakes I did."

"Mom, I'm not you," I said in a warning tone.

"I know that, and I'm not comparing. I'm talking in general here. Too often, women rely on men for support, only to be left high and dry when things don't work out. I don't want that for you."

"It won't be," I said through gritted teeth.

"How can you be so sure? You never know if—"

"I know because I refuse to spend my life dwelling on the what-ifs!" I lashed out. "I refuse to walk around bitter at the world for things out of my control. I don't want to grow old only to look back and see I spent my life being a spiteful and untrusting human being! I can't hate a person strictly because they have a penis! That's who you are, and I don't want to be like you. I want to be happy!"

Her head jerked back as if I'd slapped her. I watched all the color visibly drain from her face.

"I have a good life, Krystina Lynne," she said quietly, using my middle name she typically reserved for times when she was truly angry. Or hurt. Her eyes began to glisten with tears. "I gave you a good life. I don't want you ever to forget where you came from."

Seeing her tears made me instantly regret losing my temper. I was in a foul mood because of the recent shock about Alexander and the confusion I had surrounding our relationship. She didn't deserve me taking it out on her.

She just made it so hard.

She was constantly on my case, riding me about one thing after another. We have had more arguments than I could count in the past, but this was the first time I truly spoke back. I knew this day would eventually come, and I thought I would feel better for it. Instead, I felt terrible.

"Look, mom—" I stopped short when a knock at the door sounded, and I could hear Frank calling from the other side to be let in.

"I'll get it," Allyson offered.

However, when Allyson opened the door, Frank wasn't alone. Alexander was standing there with him.

I suppressed a groan.

Great. Just what I need right now.

Alexander

To say there was tension in the air would be an understatement. It was more like the aftershock of a nuclear explosion.

A leggy blond, who I assumed to be Krystina's roommate, stood in the kitchen with her brow furrowed in consternation. I guessed the other woman to be Krystina's mother because of their striking resemblance, although her eyes were red-rimmed with tears while Krystina's face was flushed in anger.

I looked to Frank Long, but he just shrugged and shook his head. The poor man looked like he'd rather be anywhere else. Having little choice in the matter, I did what I did best. I put on my game face and took control of the situation.

Leading the way, I entered the apartment with Frank in tow.

"Good evening, ladies," I greeted. Stepping up to Krystina, I planted a kiss on the top of her head and motioned over to Frank. "Look who I met in the elevator?"

"Alex, I thought Hale was coming back for me later, and I was going to meet you at your place," Krystina said. Her voice sounded strained.

"After he dropped off you and Allyson, I gave him the rest of the night off. I happened to be out, so I decided to come by to pick you up instead," I said easily. "How was your day at the spa?"

I heard the subtle sound of one clearing their throat from somewhere behind me. When I turned to look, I saw the blond watching me carefully.

"You must be Allyson," I assumed. I flashed her my most disarming smile, but she wasn't taking the bait. She only narrowed her eyes suspiciously.

"And you must be the infamous Alexander Stone. Krystina's told me a lot about you."

Hopefully, not too much.

"Sorry, I'm being rude. I forgot you haven't met," Krystina apologized. "Alex, this is Allyson Ramsey."

"Don't believe half of what she says about me," I joked to her roommate. She smiled at me in return, but her grin didn't quite meet her eyes. "I'm happy to have finally met you. Krystina speaks very highly of you. The two of you seem close."

"Of course, we are. As they say—opposites attract," Allyson said.

I tilted my head to the side in confusion.

"She's Aries, I'm Cancer," Krystina explained. "Ally's really into stuff like that."

"Sorry, ladies. I don't know too much about zodiac signs," I laughed.

"It just means we balance each other out," Allyson said. "And the ram is usually very protective of the crab."

"I'll keep that in mind," I responded, completely unruffled by her discernible warning. I smiled politely. If Miss Ramsey thought she could intimidate me, she would be sadly disappointed.

"Alex, you've already met Frank, my stepfather," Krystina continued her introductions, seeming oblivious to the undercurrent flowing between the roommate and me. "This is my mother. Mom, this is Alexander Stone."

Krystina motioned to her mother, who had been noticeably quiet since I had come in. Turning to face her, I extended my hand.

"Yes...um," she stuttered, seeming to be caught off guard. "I'm Elizabeth. Elizabeth Long."

"It's a pleasure to meet you, Mrs. Long."

"Please, call me Elizabeth," she offered.

"Your daughter never mentioned you would be in town this weekend," I remarked courteously, throwing a sidelong glance at Krystina.

"They showed up unexpectedly," Krystina clarified. "Had I known, I—"

"If you two have plans, don't let us get in the way," Elizabeth Long cut in. "Go on ahead, honey. I'll just go shopping with Allyson. Besides, Frank is wiped out. I think there's a football game he wants to watch anyway. We'll catch up later on, or perhaps tomorrow."

"Michigan State, my alma mater," Frank chimed in. "They're playing Iowa tonight."

"Wait, you want me to go out?" Krystina incredulously asked her mother. She seemed utterly floored.

"Why wouldn't I?" Elizabeth responded innocently—a little

too innocently in my opinion, and I was curious about what went down before I arrived.

"Because you just said..." Krystina trailed off. She looked at me, seeming completely at a loss. It was as if she was torn between visiting with her family and spending time with me. However, I sensed there was more to it than just that.

Much more.

"Krystina, if you want to go shopping, that's fine with me," I offered, trying to lighten her burden of making a choice. "I can stay here and watch the game with Mr. Long until you get back."

She looked absolutely appalled by the idea, and I had to stifle a smirk.

"No, that's okay," she vehemently shook her head. "We can still go on as planned."

"Whatever works. But in the meantime, I have a suggestion. The night is young," I stated, turning to address everyone else in the room. "Assuming it won't impede on the shopping trip, why don't the five of us share a pre-dinner cocktail? I'm sure these ladies keep a decent stock, and I've been told I can mix an excellent Manhattan."

Everyone just stared at each other awkwardly for a minute upon hearing my proposition. Frank was the first to speak up.

"I think that's a great idea, don't you, Lizzie?" he said to his wife. "We've come all this way, and I'd like to get to know this gentleman Krys has taken a liking to."

"Sounds like a good plan to me," Allyson agreed. She was still carefully scrutinizing me, and I knew she was seizing the opportunity to get to know me as well.

Deciding not to wait on the approval from mother and daughter, I went to the kitchen and began pulling out glasses from a cabinet.

"Allyson, could you point me in the direction of your liquor stash?" I asked, using the occasion to engage Krystina's roommate. Allyson wasn't the only one with an agenda. My hope was, after a drink or two, she would begin to warm up to me.

"I'll show him," Krystina offered, jumping up to assist me instead.

Once we were out of earshot from everyone, Krystina swooped in like a vulture.

"What are you doing?" she hissed.

"Well, as soon as you get me the things I need, I'll be mixing drinks."

She smirked at me and handed me a bottle of red vermouth she retrieved from a nearby hutch.

"You know what I mean, Alex."

"Relax, angel. Everyone's wound a little tight. I'm just helping to ease the tension in this place." I took the liquor from her and leaned down to whisper in her ear. "Because when we are done here, I thought we might hit a *club* tonight."

To my satisfaction, her eyes grew big. She had caught my meaning.

"A club?"

"Yes, assuming you're up for it," I taunted.

"Well, yes...yes, it's fine," she stammered, sounding fairly stunned.

"Good. I was hoping you'd say that." I finished pouring the whiskey and topped off each of the five drinks with maraschino cherries. Handing two glasses to Krystina, I gave her a smile of reassurance and said, "Now, let's go entertain your guests. Shall we?"

42

Krystina

Alexander and I stepped out of my apartment building and into the foggy night. The storm had fully passed, leaving a damp feel to the air in its wake.

"You were great with my mother and Allyson tonight. Thank you for that," I appreciated. "Those two can be tough. The fact you got them laughing within twenty minutes was no small feat."

"Piece of cake, angel," he told me with a wink. "Besides, Allyson made it easy when she spilled her drink all over your stepfather's lap."

"That was funny," I agreed. I was grateful for Alexander's ability to diffuse the precarious situation with my mother. He even managed to put Allyson's watchful eye at ease.

However, none of it negated the fact my head was still reeling from what I had discovered earlier in the day, and I contemplated how or if I should bring up what I had learned of his mother. I had hoped to figure out a way to approach Alexander about it when I got home, but I never had the chance in all the chaos with my mother.

Alexander opened the passenger door for the Tesla. Once I

was securely buckled, he went around to the driver's side and got in.

"Do you have any preference in music?" he asked, navigating expertly through the elaborate touch screen of the car.

"No, you pick," I told him absently.

"Uh-oh," he said, shaking his head. He stopped tapping on the screen to look at me. His face appeared troubled. "You've got that tone."

"What tone?" I asked defensively.

"The tone that says you're thinking seriously about something."

"No, not really," I lied, but only because I hadn't had a minute to process my thoughts.

"Is it the club?" he pushed. "I thought you wanted to go, but if you're having second thoughts, then we can always do something else."

"No, I want to go. But I have to ask—what made you change your mind about taking me?"

"A couple of reasons actually," he admitted. "For one, you seemed like you could use a distraction. I'm not sure what was going on before I arrived, but it didn't look pretty."

"It was just my mother being...well, my mother. I don't feel like rehashing it."

"That's okay. I'd rather you didn't, at least not tonight anyway. I don't want to see you get all worked up again."

"So, what's the other reason?"

He sat back in his seat and stared thoughtfully out the windshield.

"You gave me a lot to think about last night. Your opening up made me realize I needed to give you something in return. And while I can't give you the truth you're after, I can give you this. You were right, Krystina—there's a lot we don't know about each other. If going to my club gives you better insight into my life, then we'll be better off for it."

I sat there quietly and contemplated his words. My instinct was to confront him about what I heard his sister talking about at the Mandarin, but what he had to say made me think twice about doing it. In his own way, Alexander was trying. It may not have been in ways I envisioned, but it was something at the very least.

Respect his limits. Let him be the one to tell you.

However, there was another thing that left me wondering as a result of my eavesdropping.

"Who is Suzanne Jacobs?" I asked.

Alexander turned to look at me peculiarly.

"She's a friend of my sister's. Why do you ask?"

"I stumbled upon an article about you and the redhead online," I told him, deliberately evading the whole truth.

"Oh, yes. That's right. I remember you bringing this up once before," he recalled with a frown. "I can't imagine the article was very lengthy. There isn't much to tell. She accompanied me to a couple of political functions a while back. Long story short, she read too much into it and wanted things I couldn't give her."

Alexander turned his attention back to the car and started the ignition. The vehicle hummed quietly to life.

"So that's it?" I pushed.

He pursed his lips in mild annoyance.

"That's it," he said, looking pointedly at me. "Now, we can do one of two things. Either remain sitting here at the curb so you can continue with this unwarranted cross-examination, or you can pick out music for the drive. You choose."

"I didn't mean to sound like I was giving you the third degree. Just go ahead and pick out a song. Something upbeat," I conceded. Until I could wrap my head around the events of the day, it was better just to let it go.

A punchy drum pattern combined with a bluesy guitar riff filled the quiet space of the car. Alexander tossed me a roguish smile before pulling out into traffic.

"You can never go wrong with The Black Keys. Cause, baby—I'm howlin' for you!" Alexander said, then followed up with a long wolf cry.

I busted out into a fit of laughter.

"You're crazy!" I exclaimed. Alexander grinned and rapped his thumb on the steering wheel to the beat of the music.

"Angel, you bring out sides of me I never knew I had."

I laughed again, then sat back to appreciate the tune sure to lighten my dismal mood.

When the car came to a halt a short while later, I was surprised to see we were in front of Alexander's penthouse.

"Why are we here?" I asked in confusion.

"You'll need to change. You can't go to the club wearing jeans and a sweater," he paused to give me a devilish look. "And I have just the thing for you."

Alexander

KRYSTINA LOOKED NOTHING SHORT OF AMAZING IN THE OUTFIT I HAD bought for her, and I was glad she didn't protest over wearing the black leather pants and emerald green silk halter. The thin top was cut low in the back, forcing her to go braless. When she moved the right way, I could see just a hint of her nipples swaying beneath the shirt, something that was sure to drive me insane with lust for the rest of the night.

She had taken it upon herself to touch up her makeup, darkening her eyes and donning siren red on her lips. Although the shades were darker than what I was used to seeing on her face, I couldn't say I didn't like it. In fact, she was downright sexy as all hell, with her mane of curls cascading down her back. I had half a mind to turn the car around and bring her back to my place.

However, I noticed how she kept looking at her reflection in the side-view mirror as we made our way to the outskirts of the city. It was as if she wasn't confident in her appearance. Her hands hadn't stopped fidgeting since we got back into the car, and they would move up to rearrange her hair every thirty seconds needlessly. She seemed nervous.

"You look beautiful, angel," I told her. "Just relax."

She gave me a small smile.

"Am I that obvious?" she asked wryly.

"You can't seem to sit still."

"I'm just anxious, that's all," she admitted. "I've been pushing you about this, but..."

"But what?"

"It's nothing. My imagination gets the best of me sometimes. I'm just hoping this place isn't too terribly scary," she admitted with a halfhearted laugh.

"You'll be fine."

I hope.

We pulled up to a black iron gate, and I lowered the car window to insert my key card into the access slot. The gate opened, and we drove through.

"What's with the key card?" Krystina asked.

"It keeps out voyeurs."

"Voyeurs?"

"Yeah, you know—peeping Toms. Everyone who comes here has to go through screening to be allowed admittance," I told her.

"What about me? I haven't gone through any sort of screening process."

"You're with me. That's all the screening they need," I said, not bothering to disguise any arrogance in the matter. I flashed her a cocky grin and circled the car around a long and winding bend.

When the massive stone building housing Club O came into view, Krystina gasped in astonishment.

"Wow!" she said in awe. "From the view of the street, I would never have thought this was hidden here. You weren't kidding when you said a person couldn't accidentally stumble into one of these places."

I pulled into a parking spot and stepped out of the car. I surveyed the lot as I walked around to the passenger side of the vehicle and took note of the long line of expensive cars filling the parking spaces.

It's a full house tonight.

It wasn't unusual for the club to be busy on a Saturday night, but the number of cars in the lot was well above the norm. It had been a while since I had last visited the place, and I wracked my brain trying to think of a particular event that may be going on. Considering it was nearing late October, there was a good chance the club was hosting its annual Halloween party. Uneasiness seeped into my bones when I thought over the potential risks.

I stretched my neck from side to side in an attempt to shake off my apprehension.

Krystina's nerves must be wearing off on me.

I opened the car door and made room for Krystina to step out.

"You ready?" I asked, extending my elbow to her.

"As ready as I'll ever be."

She took hold of my elbow, and we made our way up the stone walkway to the mansion. Pushing through the massive wooden double doors, I motioned Krystina inside.

Here goes nothing.

43

Krystina

Alexander stepped aside so I could enter into an elegantly decorated vestibule, complete with a breathtaking rock garden and tranquil waterfall. It was not at all what I was expecting. I had envisioned pulsing neon lights for a place like this, and certainly not the aristocratic interior before me.

The walls were covered with shades of blue and green mosaic tiles, giving the entire entryway an almost underwater effect. Next to the waterfall stood a marble statue that looked like it had been transported in time from two thousand years ago. The figure was of a woman wrapped in a loosely draped cloth, with one breast revealed. Her sculptor captured an alluring expression of mystery, presenting a certain degree of erotic beauty.

"That's a beautiful statue, Alex."

"It's a rendition of Venus, the goddess of sexuality," he told me.

"I thought Aphrodite was the goddess of sexuality."

"Aphrodite is a Greek. Venus is Roman, even though some people consider them to be virtually the same. I prefer Venus because I find her attributes slightly more appealing – beauty, persuasion, seduction, and sex," he explained.

"That's interesting. I didn't know that," I mused, reaching up to slide my fingers over the cool marble arm of the statue.

He chuckled at my fascination and took hold of my elbow.

"This way, angel."

He ushered me ahead into another room, where the old world feel flowed seamlessly from the entryway. Except in here, it looked like a Halloween cocktail party was taking place. Everyone was stylishly dressed in costume, conversing casually and sipping fancy colored drinks.

"It looks like a Halloween party in here."

"That's because it is. I'd forgotten tonight is Club O's Annual Halloween Masquerade," he paused and frowned. "But even if I had remembered, I'm not into the costume thing. Come on. Let's go get a drink."

Alexander led the way over to a long mahogany bar at the far side of the room. While he worked on getting the attention of the bartender, I surveyed all the people present. Every last one of them was in a costume of some sort. It made me feel self-conscious about my very ordinary yet extremely provocative attire.

"Are you sure we won't stand out? I mean, look at everyone," I whispered.

"Grey Goose with a splash of cranberry and a glass of Chateau Ste. Michelle Riesling. I'll also need a red bracelet." Alexander told the bartender before turning back to me. "Don't worry about it, Krystina. This is only a small part of the club. I'm sure there are people without a costume downstairs."

"Downstairs?" I asked.

"Yes. Now here, put this on your wrist," he told me, handing me a red silicone wristband the bartender had passed to him.

"What's this for?" I asked.

"The red signifies you are strictly here for observation, and you're not available."

"Available for what?" I asked in confusion.

"For another Dom. The club utilizes a color system as a protocol for their guests. Red means you are only available to me and will prevent any unwanted advances," he explained. "If you were wearing blue, it would mean you were available with my permission. Those wearing green send the message they're free to any Dom."

I considered his words as he handed me the drink he had ordered.

"Would you ever have me wear another color?" I asked in honest curiosity.

"Let's just get through tonight, shall we? I know you have questions but be quiet for a few minutes. Right now, I just want you to watch."

"What am I watching?"

"The people."

I scanned the room. There was a soft, almost whimsical, sort of music playing overhead. Some people were standing and talking while others mingled together on various settees and chairs.

My gaze moved to the right and settled on three people sitting on a leather couch. There were two women dressed as sexy felines, and they sat on either side of a man dressed as a vampire.

His costume was fitting for him because he looked like he wanted to take a bite out of one or both women. I watched him place a hand on the side of one women's neck while the other woman ran a hand suggestively up his thigh. She didn't quite reach the mark before moving her hand back down to his knee. I felt myself blush, suddenly realizing why Alexander told me to watch. The scene playing out before me was one of seduction.

I brought the glass of wine to my lips and took a long swallow.

I could feel Alexander's eyes on me as I watched them. After a moment longer, the three people got up and left through a side door.

"Where are they going?" I asked.

"Either upstairs to the common room and private suits or down to the dungeon."

"The dungeon!" I exclaimed. I had read about what went on in BDSM dungeons. Images of women and men dressed in skintight vinyl, all tied up and gagged in cages, popped into my head.

"Shhh, Krystina! Lower your voice. It's not what you think."

"Well then, what is it?" I hissed.

"It's like a dance club down there—sort of. Come on, I'll show you," he said, taking hold of my hand.

He led me to the door the three people went through, taking me down a long narrow corridor. The lighting was dim, but I thought it was meant to give a cozy and inviting feel to the hallway. I knew the sinister feel was strictly conjured up in my head.

We rounded a corner, and I stiffened in my tracks. The hallway had split. To the left, there was a staircase I could only assume led up to the private suites Alexander had mentioned. Several people were traveling up and down the wide set of steps. To the right, there was a black door with a massive gargoyle head above it. A sign reading "The Dungeon" hung over the monster's head.

I was seriously starting to get creeped out.

"Do you want to go down, or do you want to go back to the lounge?" Alexander asked.

"What about the common room you mentioned?"

"Oh, no. You're not ready to go up there," he paused and looked thoughtful. "Actually, I don't think you'll ever be ready for that."

"Why not?"

"Trust me on this one. Unless you have a sudden interest in orgies, I don't think you'd like it."

"Ah, no...um, we can go on ahead...to the Dungeon, I mean," I stumbled in my attempt to mask the hesitation I felt. I didn't want him to think I was a chicken. After all, I was the one who pushed to come here in the first place.

"You're very skittish tonight, but there's nothing to worry about. I'm here with you," he said reassuringly, rubbing my shoulders. "But I have to warn you, just about anything goes down there. I'm not sure what we'll find here tonight."

"I'm good. Let's go."

Alexander opened the black door, and a set of long winding stairs came into view. The pulsing bass of house music assaulted my ears. It was shockingly loud, as I hadn't heard a single trace of it when we were in the hallway or back in the subdued lounge area.

When we reached the bottom of the staircase, an entirely new world opened up before me, revealing a twisting sea of dancing bodies. Some were in costumes, and just as Alexander had predicted, some were wearing normal attire. I also saw a few individuals dressed in leather and studs. However, I knew enough now to know those people were not dressed for Halloween fun but for the lifestyle.

My gaze traveled up from the dance floor to the high vaulted ceilings. The ceilings were extremely high for a basement, easily eighteen feet tall. Around the edges of the room, there was a caged platform filled with more dancing men and women. My foot started tapping in time to the pulsing music. The urge to dance swelled in me, and I reached for Alexander's hand.

"Let's go dance," I said, urging him toward the dance floor.

"Definitely not. You are *not* going out on that floor to dance."

"Why not?"

"A girl like you won't be doing much dancing out there," he said dryly, nodding in the direction of the dance floor. I pinched my face in confusion.

"What's that supposed to mean?"

"Never mind. We can go up there instead," he said, pointing to the caged platforms.

We made our way up the short metal staircase leading to the platform. Alexander elbowed his way through the crowd of dancing people until we reached someplace a little more secluded. He turned me around and pulled my back close to his chest. I thought he wanted to dance with me from behind, but when I started to grind myself against him, he made me be still.

"Hang on. I want you to see something first." I could barely hear him over the music, and I reached a hand up to my ear, gesturing for him to talk louder. He leaned down closer and said, "Look down there. Do you see why I didn't want you to dance there?"

I looked to see where his finger was pointing. I couldn't stop the gasp from escaping me. Down below, in the middle of the dance floor, there was an elevated stage I hadn't noticed before. Two men were strapping a naked woman to a St. Andrew's Cross.

Once she was secured, one of the men leaned in to say something to her. Whatever it was, she nodded, and the man stepped back to speak with the other man. They moved out of my line of sight for a second or two before the crowd separated to create a large circle around the stage and the woman on display. The music was suddenly lowered to dull background noise and replaced by a booming male voice.

"Ladies and gentlemen! In honor of the Halloween festivities, Kendra's Master has decided to grant her wish of a public flogging!"

What? Is this actually for real?

The crowd cheered while I stood there feeling like I had just gone back in time to Colonial America. I scanned the room, half expecting to see stocks and pillory at the ready.

"Alex, this is really messed—"

SMACK!

I jumped mid-sentence as the first lash of the flogger rained down on the woman.

"It's all just part of the show, Krystina."

"Yeah, but..." I trailed off as another thought occurred to me. "Have you ever participated in something like this?"

"Me? No," he said with a shake of his head. "I told you – I'm not an extremist. Some people get off on public displays. To each his own, I guess. But that's not my style."

"Then why do you come here?" I asked.

"I come for the social aspect of meeting like-minded individuals. Dramatic scenes of this magnitude don't happen that regularly. The club usually reserves them for special occasions, like tonight, for example. If I had realized today was the Masquerade, I probably wouldn't have brought you here. It can be a little intense, especially for a newcomer."

SMACK!

The sound of another lashing forced me to look back at the

bound woman. I was curious to learn why someone would want to be whipped like that in public. I tried to keep an open mind rather than view it as nothing more than a crude spectacle.

After every few lashings, the man I assumed to be her Dom would pause to massage oil over her reddened backside and limbs. She would thank him profusely, and then he would resume again with the flogger.

SMACK!

The woman threw her head back and let out what I had initially thought to be a cry of pain. However, after seeing her expression, I realized the woman was actually crying out in pleasure. It was fantastically absurd, in a twisted sort of way, yet there was something unbelievably erotic about it as well. Eventually, I lost count of how many lashings she took, but from the way she writhed on the cross, it was apparent she was desperate for release. I wondered how long the man would make her wait.

"How long will this go on for?" I asked Alexander.

"It depends. Only her Dom knows her limitations. Although, I expect he'll most likely push her close to her breaking point."

"Then what?"

"If he thinks she's earned it, he'll allow her to orgasm in front of the crowd, or he may choose to take care of her in a private suite," he told me with a shrug. His indifference to the scene baffled me.

Heat moved into my cheeks.

"In front of everyone?" I asked incredulously.

"You're blushing, Krystina. Are you enjoying this?"

"I don't know...I mean, an orgasm is *so* personal and intimate. I can't imagine having one in public," I said honestly. "And I can't say a public display of dominance does anything for me either."

I heard the woman cry out again, and simple curiosity had me turning to see what was happening. She had been repositioned while I was talking to Alexander. She was no longer strapped to the cross but bent over an elaborate spanking bench of sorts. Her ass was high in the air, exposing her sex for all to see. I should have felt embarrassed for the bared woman, but the reverence her Dom showed her made me feel differently. It was as if he were worshipping the sexuality of the female's body.

He ran the flogger up and down her back, slowing over her sweet spot to graze it softly. Occasionally he would lean down to whisper words only she could hear, and her body would twitch in response. This went on for what seemed like eons, but it was probably only a few minutes before he finally showed her some mercy. For when he leaned down to her ear for the final time, he reached beneath her to pull at her erect nipples. That simple action sent the woman reeling.

Her orgasm rocked her entire body, and the air seemed to hum. Every individual who was present in the Dungeon could feel the sheer magnitude of her pleasure. My surroundings seemed surreal. I looked back to Alexander only to see his eyes full of concern.

"Are you okay, angel? You have a strange look on your face."

I wasn't sure what to say, unable to find the words to describe what I was thinking. The scene I had just witnessed left me feeling relatively stunned. Yet, I was turned on in the most indescribable way. The intimacy and trust shown between the couple on the platform was a level of epic proportions. She was the definition of the ultimate surrender and had given complete charge of her body over to the man in ways I had never given to Alexander. And for the first time, I realized what Alexander meant about trust being the root of BDSM.

"Honestly, Alex? I think it's just the environment we're in. It's muddling my thoughts. The whole place reeks of sex."

He laughed and wrapped his arms tightly around me.

"I was a little nervous, but you handled that better than I thought you would," Alexander admitted. He pulled back to look at me, only a slight hint of concern still visible in his striking blues. "Why don't we get down from up here and go grab another drink? You look like you could use one."

The loud music of the club returned, the sound almost deafening compared to moments before.

"That sounds like a good idea. I think one show was enough for me."

We headed down the steps to the ground floor of The Dungeon and made our way to the crowded bar. There was a wooden sign above the bar labeled "Obsequious Cantina." However, we bypassed that particular bar and went on to the next. This area was by far the swankier of the two, with plush furniture and mini tables cordoned off into more private sections with billowing black sheers. This bar had a metal sign reading "Sovereignty Cocktails."

I snickered after realizing the meaning behind the signs.

"What's so funny?" Alexander asked.

"The names of the bars in this place," I told him and laughed again. "They have one bar for the master and another for the servant. I just find it funny."

"Don't forget that one over there," he said, pointing another bar across the way. I looked over and saw a sign that read "Queen's Landing." After looking at the patrons, it wasn't hard to figure out why it was called that.

"You don't want to go over to that one?" I asked with a wink.

Alexander's mouth turned up in a crooked smile at my teasing.

"Angel, there are just certain things I *don't* do. Now, go see if you can spot an open table while I try to track down a bartender."

I scanned the area for available seating, but there didn't seem to be anything open given the crowd in the club.

When Alexander returned with our drinks, I told him as much.

"We can go over to the VIP lounge?" he suggested. "It's a bit quieter in there."

"That's okay. Standing is fine with me. Besides, this way, I can dance with you." I wiggled my eyebrows and swayed closer to him. Placing one hand on his hip while balancing my drink with the other, I moved my hips in time with the music. "Thank you for bringing me here tonight. This place is definitely...well, different. But I think I'm starting to understand what you mean about trust being the foundation for everything."

"Hmm," Alexander murmured into my ear. "I'm glad about that. But personally, I can't wait to get home so I can tie down those swivel hips."

I shivered in anticipation.

"I hope you don't expect me to call you my Master," I joked. "We still have a long way to go before I can do that."

Alexander's hand suddenly stiffened on my shoulder, making me think I had said something wrong. I stopped dancing to look up at him. Whatever was behind me had caught his attention, and his eyes flashed angrily. I turned to see what he was looking at and saw a beautiful redhead walking toward us. I groaned inwardly.

Ugh! Another redhead?

"Hello, Alex," she purred when she reached us.

"Beat it, Sasha," Alexander snapped. I could feel his tension mounting, his grip becoming tighter on my shoulder.

The girl circled slowly around me, sizing me up. I felt like I was being stalked. Her hand reached up and wrapped around my neck, taking me by surprise. Her grip was soft yet firm at the same time.

She's a Dominant.

I stood frozen, not sure what to do. I wanted to slap her hand away, but I certainly didn't want to make a scene. From what I saw on the dance floor, this might have been just another normal behavior in The Dungeon.

"That's enough," Alexander said, pushing her hand away. "We're not here for this. We're only here as observers."

"Alex, don't be rude. She's clearly your sub. It's only polite for you to share her with a fellow Dom," she said sweetly, reaching to cup my breast. I let out a gasp of surprise when she pinched my nipple through the thin material of my blouse.

My breathing sped up, and my cheeks flushed, shocked by her brazenness.

"No," he reaffirmed through clenched teeth.

I looked back and forth between the two of them. She looked like the cat that swallowed the canary, while Alexander looked as though he might rip the woman's throat out. I had never seen him look so visibly angry.

"Why don't you let her decide? Look at how flushed her cheeks are. She seems to be enjoying herself," she challenged.

Alexander looked at me, his blue eyes silently questioning. I wasn't sure what to do. My sudden arousal was unexplainable. Maybe it was from watching the woman on the cross. Or perhaps I was hyped up from the blatant sexuality prevalent in every corner of the club. Whatever it was, there was no denying Sasha's touch was a complete turn-on for one reason or another.

I returned Alexander's stare, trying to decipher what he was trying to tell me when I suddenly remembered a particular word I had once highlighted in red.

Threesomes.

It felt like a lifetime ago Alexander and I had sat in his office and went through a list of limitations. Having a threesome was among my list of hard limits. But then again, so was anything anal. It was unsettling to realize how quickly I changed my mind about things I once said I would never do.

"Have you shared a submissive with others before?" I asked. His eyes seared into me, but I could feel his hesitation. He looked conflicted, almost as if he were deciding on how much to reveal.

"Yes," he finally responded.

I took a closer look at Sasha. She wasn't as pretty as I had initially thought. Her natural hair color was blond, as I could see the roots beneath the artificial fiery red. Cold gray eyes sat too small in her face and were smudged heavily with liner black as midnight. Her mouth was turned up in an arrogant sneer, giving her an air of malevolence.

I turned back to Alexander, conflicted about the unexpected and not so welcomed proposition.

"Do you want me to do this?" I asked him. He didn't answer, but he didn't have to. I could see the burn in his eyes.

"Since this is her first time, I'll go easy on her," she said smugly to Alexander. She grabbed hold of my shirtfront and pulled me close. I briefly caught the triumphant gleam in her eyes before her tongue swiped up my neck. Her teeth grabbed hold of my earlobe, and her breath was hot in my ear as she whispered, "So fresh… what shall I make you do?"

Suddenly, I was afraid. Very afraid.

Oh my God. I didn't agree to this! How did it get to this point?

It had all happened so fast. I had little time to process the situation, but I knew this woman wasn't messing around. Before I could even think of how to react, she was pulled abruptly away from me. Alexander stepped between the two of us.

"Get the fuck off her, Sasha. You're not going to taint her with your twisted ideas about domination," Alexander growled ominously.

"Such a spoilsport," she pouted and *tsked* at him. "And here I thought we could have a little fun with this one."

"Go find someone else to harass. We're done here."

"Oh, Alex. Haven't I taught you anything?" she purred.

"You taught me enough," he spat out. "And some lessons I'll never forget."

What are they talking about? Who is this woman to him?

A knowing smile plastered across Sasha's face. On the other hand, I felt like my head was spinning, and I could barely keep up.

"Oh, come on now!" she went on. "Don't tell me you're still sore over the whole thing with Will."

Will?

Alex took a step closer to her. He was mere inches away from her face, jaw twitching and fists clenched tight in anger. His eyes flashed with pure loathing, and for a moment, I was scared. I thought he might actually hit her.

"Don't push me," he hissed. "I told you to get lost. I'm not going to repeat it."

"Very well then. It's your loss. Maybe next time," she stated matter-of-factly.

Seeming completely unruffled by Alexander's wrath, she easily sauntered away with her hips swaying seductively in her wake.

"What in the *hell* just happened here?" I demanded, alarmed after witnessing Alexander almost lose total control. He was raking his hands through his hair, appearing thoroughly rattled by the confrontation.

"I'm sorry, Krystina. Sasha's a sadistic bitch, and I shouldn't have let it go that far."

"It's not hard to imagine that woman with whips and chains. With all the leather she was wearing, she looked like she could be the poster girl for Dominatrix R Us," I said sarcastically.

"Actually, she's a flipper."

I rolled my eyes in exasperation.

"I don't even know what that means!" I shouted, altogether incensed over everything that had just happened. I lowered my voice to a level that could barely be heard over the loud music. The last thing we needed was to draw any more unwanted attention. "Explain, please."

"It means she can play both. I told you about my first submissive. Well, Sasha was the one who filled the role."

"Okay, so what does that have to do with Will? I'm assuming she was referring to Will Murphy."

"Yes," he said in a resigned voice. "Will used to be her sub, at least until she got bored. Then she planned a little *ménage à trois*, completely without the knowledge of Will or me."

My eyes grew wide as the pieces of the puzzle began to come together.

"You and Will? Did you...um, you know," I started.

"Hell, no!" he exclaimed, sounding completely aghast. "It never went that far. Didn't I just say there are certain things I *don't* do?"

"I'm sorry! I'm sorry!" I apologized quickly. "I didn't mean to imply anything."

"Yeah, well...William Murphy, on the other hand, is a switch hitter. And I also happen to know his Irish family is hardcore Catholic. His bedroom antics are not something he wants to be made known. Needless to say, things have been very awkward between us ever since. Plus, he blames me for Sasha leaving him."

"Gotcha," I said, having a better understanding as to why things between Alexander and Will had been so tense.

Alexander pinched the bridge of his nose and shook his head back and forth in aggravation.

"I don't know about you, but I've had enough for tonight. I'll be right back. I'm just going to hit the restroom, then we're leaving," Alexander announced.

I couldn't agree more as I watched him walk away. The atmosphere had become strained, and I grappled with trying to absorb the completely obscure turn of events. I was beginning to question why I ever wanted to come here in the first place.

I looked around at the people in the club. Some were dancing, mingling, and talking, while others groped and fondled. Most were scantily dressed. Whether they were in costume or normal attire, there was no modesty whatsoever amongst the crowd.

I noticed a man seated with two women at a table not more than ten feet away. One woman wore a masquerade mask and corset that left her breasts completely exposed, showing off nipples pinched tight by jeweled metal clamps. The other woman wore devil horns and sat with her legs apart. The table hid very little, and I was able to see the man had his hand shoved up her tiny excuse for a skirt. Having noticed I was watching them, the horned woman's eyes locked on mine, and she smiled suggestively.

I quickly turned away and began to feel sick to my stomach.

Why am I here? This is not who I am.

"Well, well. This is the last place I thought I would see you," said a familiar male voice from behind me. I froze at the sound.

It can't be. No...please no.

I turned around, praying I was mistaking the cocky, assured voice. But I wasn't mistaken.

It was Trevor.

44

Krystina

I felt my insides twist and the sickening in my stomach intensified. I swallowed the bile welling in my throat. It was all I could do to stop myself from vomiting all over the floor. My heart was racing, and my breathing became irregular. I hadn't seen or heard from Trevor since that terrible day nearly two years prior, but I never thought I would feel this way if our paths crossed again.

It was as if the floor had come out from under me, and I was falling into an endless pit of nothing but blackness. I could feel the panic rising to meet me, so I quickly turned my back to him in an effort to pretend he didn't exist.

Deep breaths. In and out. You're fine.

"Oh, come on, Krys. Can't you even say hi? Or even better, how about we head upstairs for a quick fuck. You know, for old time's sake."

You son of a bitch!

Angry heat instantly flooded my cheeks from his audacity. I spun on my heel to face him, all of my anxiety replaced by pure and unadulterated rage.

"YOU! You are *not* allowed to talk to me. Ever!" I spat out through clenched teeth. I wanted nothing more than to claw the smug look off of his face.

"Don't be like that," he said in a placating way. "It's been a long time. You look good, Krys."

I ignored his poor attempt at flattery and narrowed my eyes. Staring him down, I tried to appear unaffected by him and come off as arrogant as he was.

"I can't say the same for you. You still look like the same old filthy swine to me. It shouldn't surprise me you're into a scene like this now. At least here, you get permission to abuse women," I said. My voice threatened to waver, but I was controlled enough to laden my tone with sarcasm as I motioned to the club around us.

"I always was into this," he said knowingly. He eyed me up and down as if seeing me in a whole new light. "I must say, though, if I had any idea we shared similar interests, I might have thought twice about banging Lisa."

Images of a college dorm room flashed before me. The long-legged blond I caught him with had been tied up to the cheap metal bed frame.

How come I didn't remember that before now?

I shook my head to clear it.

"Go away, Trevor," I seethed.

"You're still mad at me. But that's okay—I like mad. It means I'll get more of a fight from you the next time."

The trembling I had managed to keep at bay up until that point came on full force. The fog that was my memory started to shift, and the long-suppressed details hit me square in the chest. I felt like the wind had been knocked out of me, a pain so familiar it forced me to remember what happened. My muddled memories suddenly became clear as day.

I did fight back. I always knew I must have, as I had bruises and broken bones to show for it. But I never fully recalled all of the details.

I remember now.

I had scratched, clawed, punched, and kicked. But every

attempt I made earned me another blow from his fist.

And the lamp. It had been knocked off of my nightstand. He used it. That's how I received two broken ribs. It was the lamp.

I couldn't move after he hit me with it, the pain so unbearable I could only lie there like dead weight while he tore into me. I winced from the recollection, the hurt as fresh as it was two years ago.

I vaguely realized Trevor was laughing, forcing my attention back to the present. His easy dismissal of the violence I had endured caused my fury to mount to an astonishing level. I needed him gone before I did something drastic.

"I said go away, Trevor. That's the last time I'm going to say it." My voice shook, making the discernable warning sound pathetic.

"Or what?"

I squared my shoulders and looked him straight in the eye. I would not allow myself to be intimidated by him again.

"I'm here with someone. Trust me when I say you don't want to be here when he gets back."

"Maybe he could join us," he suggested with a wink, reaching for me. When his hand made contact with my arm, I felt like I had been burned.

"Don't touch me—*ever*!" I exploded, pulling away from him. "Don't look at me! Don't talk to me! Just get away from me!"

Trevor jumped back, startled by my outburst. Given a chance, I would have thrown something at him—anything to inflict some sort of damage to the face I hated above all others. However, a member of club security showed up out of nowhere and stepped in between Trevor and me.

"Is there a problem, Miss?"

"No problem at all," Trevor answered for me, hands held up in mock surrender. "Just a misunderstanding."

"Are you sure you're all right?" the security guy asked me again. He was a big, beefy man with small eyes. He wore a black T-shirt with yellow lettering boasting his title of Floor Security Manager. He didn't look trustworthy to me, so I just nodded my response and turned away.

"I think you'd better be on your way," the manager suggested to Trevor.

"Sure thing. I was just leaving. I already tapped that one anyways. She's a terrible fuck," I heard Trevor say.

I glanced over my shoulder only to see Trevor glaring at me, but he backed away and disappeared into the crowd.

I couldn't speak. My nerves were shot, and I was trembling so bad my knees threatened to buckle. I needed to sit down somewhere. But most of all, I needed to leave this place.

What is taking Alexander so long?

I contemplated just leaving without him but found an open bar stool and sat down instead. I scanned the sea of people around me, but I wasn't really seeing them. I felt like I was in a bad dream —as if my surroundings were just an illusion. And for the second time that evening, I questioned why I wanted to come here so badly. With my history, a place like this should have terrified me. Everything about the club screamed of domination—the very thing I had shied away from for years.

So why do I want it from Alexander? Or don't I?

Perhaps there was something mentally wrong with me. I had read about women who continued making the same mistakes, about the ones who jumped from one abusive situation to the next. They neurotically seek relationships that mirror previous ones with the hope they will somehow turn out differently.

Is my traumatic history making me choose the wrong things?

The club's loud music pulsed in time to the rapid beating of my heart as I considered the possibility. I thought I enjoyed the things Alexander and I did together, and my relationship with him was different than my relationship with Trevor. However, I now found myself questioning whether or not they were actually one and the same.

Am I just fooling myself?

I began to analyze every emotion I had surrounding Alexander, not knowing if what I felt was real or if it was just something twisted in my psyche. However, I knew I was shaken from a bizarre sequence of events that took place over the past few hours. Between my mother, the club, Sasha, and seeing Trevor, it was near impossible to think clearly and rationally.

But no matter what the cause was for my angst, the damage was done. The lines were now blurry. I didn't know who I was anymore or what I wanted.

I only knew it was time for me to reevaluate everything in my life, including my current relationship with Alexander.

Alexander

I SPLASHED COLD WATER ON MY FACE AND LOOKED AT MY REFLECTION in the mirror. A tired bastard stared back at me. The strain over what happened with Sasha had exhausted me, and I regretted my decision to take Krystina here.

The look on her face when Sasha had practically assaulted her was one that I wouldn't forget anytime soon. She appeared confused and terrified all at once, but it was the look of accusation that would haunt me for a while to come.

I knew I was to blame. Krystina wasn't worldly to people like Sasha, and I should have protected her better. My only defense was I didn't realize how much Krystina would stick out in Club O. Her naivety and thirst for knowledge were like a bull's-eye for every predator in the joint.

Given that and my newfound knowledge of her traumatic past, I should have followed my original instincts. My club was not a place for her, and it was high time I got her out of here.

I pushed through the door of the men's room and headed back to where I left Krystina. However, I was instantly alarmed when I spotted her. She was sitting on a bar stool with her arms hugged tightly around her body. Her eyes were as wide as saucers, and she was a ghastly shade of white.

"What's wrong?" I asked once I reached her. I put my hand on her shoulder, only to feel her trembling. "Why are you shaking so bad?"

She looked up at me with a blank stare.

"I just want to leave, Alex. Please, take me home."

"Okay. Angel, I'm so sorry," I apologized, rubbing my hands up and down her arms. "I should never have brought you here. This was a huge mistake. When we get back to my place, I will draw you a hot bath and—"

"No, Alex. I want to go *home*. To my apartment, not yours," she said, cutting me off midsentence. I stopped rubbing her arms and looked deeper into her eyes. Her beautiful browns, normally so expressive and full of life, appeared shockingly empty.

Whatever she was thinking about was not something I wished to discuss in a noisy, sex-laden club. I quickly gave in to her request with the idea I could change her mind about going home once we were out of the building.

"If that's what you want to do," I told her.

We made our way up the stairs and back into the main lounge area. When we walked through, I tried to put my arm around Krystina's shoulders, but she jerked away from me. Her rejection stung, but it was understandable. She had a right to be angry.

I'm such an asshole for exposing her to this.

I was about to tell her as much when a man stepped in front of us and blocked our path to the door. He was of average height with sandy blond hair, but he had suspicious eyes. I felt Krystina stiffen beside me.

"It was good seeing you again, Krys. Enjoy the rest of your night," he said easily. However, his tone was almost mocking, and there was something shady about the way he leered at her.

I instantly hated the man.

Cocking my head to one side, I stared pointedly at him.

"And you are?" I inquired coolly.

"An old friend. Right, Krys?" he replied, tossing Krystina a wink.

"Let's go, Alex," Krystina said. There was no denying the fact this guy was making her nervous for some reason.

Is he the cause for her upset?

Perhaps it wasn't the incident with Sasha at all.

Krystina hurried past whomever the jackass was, not bothering to wait to see if I was following. I was torn. A part of me wanted to stay behind and slug the stranger over the mere fact he was bothering Krystina. However, after deciding it was best not to leave her alone anymore that evening, I threw a menacing glare at the guy and hurried to the exit.

When I exited the club, I saw Krystina was already halfway across the parking lot, and I had to run to catch up with her.

"Who was that guy?" I demanded after reaching her.

"Nobody," was all that she said.

"Bullshit. Who was he?" I asked again. She continued to walk in silence but didn't answer me. She was starting to seriously piss me off. Finally, I grabbed hold of her arm and spun her to face me. "Who was that guy, Krystina?"

She glanced down at my hand that was squeezing her arm, then up at my face. Her expression was full of fury, and her eyes were glassy from unshed tears.

"Let go of my arm. Now," she said icily.

Shocked that I had lost my temper, I instantly let go and took a step back. I intended to simply get her attention, and I hadn't meant to grab her that way.

That's the second time I lost my cool tonight.

We walked the rest of the way to the car without speaking. Once we were seated inside, I cranked on the heat to ward off the chill. I was about to throw the car in reverse but decided against it. I wanted to talk first.

"Are you going to tell me who that guy was now?"

"No," she stated, expression completely deadpan.

I pursed my lips in annoyance. Of course, I would find out regardless, but it would be less of a headache for me if she just told me herself.

"Fine. Then at least tell me what you're thinking."

"Me and you," she paused to motion her hand back and forth. "And our relationship. It isn't normal."

"Normal is only how an individual defines it, Krystina."

"No. It's that we aren't healthy for each other," she said quietly.

"What's that supposed to mean?"

Krystina closed her eyes for a moment, then opened them again to look at me. She didn't seem angry anymore but resolved. My heart started to hammer inside my chest. I knew what she was going to say next. She was going to try to end us before we really even had a chance to start.

I fucked this up.

I held my breath and waited for her to speak.

"You know my past," she began. "You know I've experienced violence of the worst kind. And although you haven't shared your story with me, I know you have your own demons that stem from an abusive father. Those two things combined...well, let's just say a psychiatrist could write a book about us."

Her expression was cold and distant, her words sounding like she had been practicing them in front of a mirror for days. It wasn't her talking. This bleak and flat-tempered person was not my angel.

"You're just shaken up after what happened with Sasha," I tried to dismiss. "I can't apologize enough for that. It's making you talk nonsense."

"You really believe that's all it is?"

"Yes, I do."

"We both have serious trust issues," she ascertained.

"Krystina, trust isn't going to happen overnight. It takes time," I tried to tell her patiently.

"Hmm," she mused. "I'm just wondering how much time would have passed before you told me your mother is alive."

I stilled as if jolted by an electric shock upon hearing she knew of my mother. The fact she waited until this moment to share her knowledge had me on guard, and my friend Matteo's words resounded in my head.

Secrets never stay hidden forever.

"Where did you hear that?" I asked after several moments.

"Does it really matter, Alex? Because even now, you still aren't admitting it."

She was right. I couldn't tell her. And I probably never would. There was too much at stake.

"What's your point?" I snapped, feeling my temper start to rise again. "I don't know what you're trying to accomplish with all of this."

"I've said it before, and I'll say it again. No matter how hard we try, our past has shaped who we are today."

"Dammit! You're so hell-bent on talking about the fucking past. You are you. I am me. End of story. Why do we keep doing this?"

"Because I have to!" she yelled. "Don't you see? It's an endless cycle. I went from one controlling guy to another. I refuse to wind up a statistic, Alex!"

"What are you talking about?"

"You! For all I know, you could turn out just like your father! Then where will that leave me?"

I felt all the blood drain from my face.

Just like your father...

"Don't," I tried to warn. I shook my head, unable to think of anything else to say, completely devoid of all other words.

"No, really, I have to worry about these things. Studies show people who have suffered from extreme situations of violence are more likely to become...."

She went on and on about some crap she had read. She began to quote articles about abused children growing into adulthood and women who lose their identity by getting lost in an abusive relationship.

However, I wasn't listening to anything she was saying. My ears were ringing, like the aftershock of being too close to a grenade detonation. Her original words just kept playing over and over again in my head.

Just like your father...

Krystina had unknowingly voiced my worst fear and crossed a line she hadn't known was drawn. I felt like I was free-falling into a pit of nothingness, just as I had in my dream.

I said the only thing I could think of to make her stop talking.

"Sapphire."

45

Krystina

"What?" I asked, confused by Alexander's use of my safeword.

"Sapphire. I've had enough."

I looked at his face. It was twisted in pain, and the magnitude of hurt showing in his eyes was shocking. I tried to keep my heart tightly guarded, but now it felt like it was splitting into a thousand pieces. Because of that pain, my decision to do what needed to be done solidified.

"We are a lethal combination, Alex. We can't work."

"I want us to work."

"Me too," I sadly admitted.

I reached up to touch his cheek. His eyes were full of regret.

"I tried to warn you. I said I wasn't good for you," he reminded me.

"You're right," I agreed and smiled wistfully, thinking of the job interview that seemed to be forever and a day ago. "You did try to warn me. I should have listened to you. But then again, I was never very good at that."

I traced the lines of his face with my finger, committing every detail to memory. The strong contour of his jaw. His chiseled cheekbones. The perfectly shaped mouth that, even at that moment, I wanted to kiss. And his eyes—the beautiful sapphires that had lit up my soul. I would miss his eyes the most.

I reluctantly pulled my hand away and climbed out of the car.

"Where are you going?" he asked in alarm.

He seemed shocked as if he couldn't see the inevitable. But then I realized, perhaps he did see it and was only trying to deny it.

"I'm going to get a cab."

"Angel, don't do this," he pleaded.

I looked down at him. Pain lanced at my chest, but I was resolute in my choice.

"Goodbye, Alex."

I closed the car door and began to walk down the long winding driveway that had brought us to Club O. Alexander didn't follow me, but that was okay. I knew it was for the best. I was making the right decision.

Then why does it hurt so bad?

Deep down, I knew the answer. It hurt because I had allowed myself to become vulnerable. I had given Alexander an essential part of myself. Not only did I give my trust, but I also gave him a piece of my heart I knew I would never get back.

When I reached the end of the drive, I slipped through the pedestrian gate that would take me to the street and phoned for a cab to pick me up.

After ending the call, I looked down at my cell.

Alexander's first gift.

I reached up to finger the triskelion emblem hanging around my neck—another gift and a reminder of a life that would never be.

His world—not mine.

Memories of the past weeks flooded me, drowning me with their intensity. On impulse, I opened up the music folder on the phone and scanned the song titles in each of Alexander's playlists.

Choosing a Metric song fitting for my mood, I sat down on the curb to wait.

A tear trickled down my cheek, but I didn't bother to wipe it away. Tears were not bad. They were healthy and good, just so long as I picked myself back up.

And do that, I would.

To be continued...

MUSIC PLAYLIST FOR HEART OF STONE

Thank you to the musical talents who influenced and inspired *Heart of Stone*. Their creativity helped me bring Krystina and Alexander to life.

Listen on Spotify!

"Wait Up (Boots of Danger)" by Tokyo Police Club *(Champ)*
"Hurricane" by Thirty Seconds to Mars *(This Is War)*
"Rocky Road To Dublin" by Dropkick Murphy's *(Live on St. Patrick's Day)*
"Stompa" by Serena Ryder *(Harmony)*
"Blue Jeans" by Lana Del Rey *(Born to Die)*
"Samba Pa Ti" by Tadeusz Machalski, self-released *(Guitar Collection)*
"Do I Wanna Know?" by Arctic Monkeys *(AM)*
"Sweater Weather" by The Neighbourhood *(I Love You)*
"Closer" by Nine Inch Nails *(The Downward Spiral)*
"Catch and Release" by Silversun Pickups *(Swoon)*
"Hips Don't Lie" by Shakira *(Oral Fixation, Vol. 2)*
"Desire" by Meg Myers *(Make a Shadow)*
"BTSK" by MS MR *(Secondhand Rapture)*
"Seven Devils" by Florence + The Machine *(Ceremonials)*
"Breathe" by Of Verona *(The White Apple)*
"Sanya Seiran" by Riley Kelly Lee *(Shakuhachi Honkyoku - Japanese Flute)*
"Howlin' For You" by The Black Keys *(Brothers)*
"Beauty of Sadness" by Spiky *(Whimsical Fantasy)*
"Silence" by Delerium (feat. Sarah McLachlan), DJ Tiësto *(The Best of Delerium)*
"Breathing Underwater" by Metric *(Synthetica)*

FOLLOW

SUBSCRIBE TO DAKOTA'S NEWSLETTER

My newsletter goes out twice a month (sometimes less). It's packed with new content, sales on signed paperbacks and Angel Book Boxes from my online store, and giveaways. Don't miss out! I value your email address and promise to NEVER spam you.
SUBSCRIBE HERE: https://dakotawillink.com/subscribe

BOOKS & BOXED WINE CONFESSIONS

Want fun stuff and sneak peek excerpts from Dakota?
Join Books & Boxed Wine Confessions and get the inside scoop!
Fans in this interactive reader Facebook group are the first to know the latest news!
JOIN HERE: https://www.facebook.com/groups/1635080436793794

OFFICIAL WEBSITE

www.dakotawillink.com

ABOUT THE AUTHOR

Dakota Willink is an award-winning *USA Today* Bestselling Author from New York. She loves writing about damaged heroes who fall in love with sassy and independent females. Her books are character-driven, emotional, and sexy, yet written with a flare that keeps them real. With a wide range of publications, Dakota's imagination is constantly spinning new ideas.

Dakota often says she survived her first publishing with coffee and wine. She's an unabashed *Star Wars* fanatic and still dreams of getting her letter from Hogwarts one day. Her daily routines usually include rocking Lululemon yoga pants, putting on lipstick, and obsessing over Excel spreadsheets. Two spoiled Cavaliers are her furry writing companions who bring her regular smiles. She enjoys traveling with her husband and debating social and economic issues with her politically savvy Generation Z son and daughter.

Dakota's favorite book genres include contemporary or dark romance, political & psychological thrillers, and autobiographies.

AWARDS, ACCOLADES, AND OTHER PROJECTS

The Stone Series is Dakota's first published book series. It has been recognized for various awards and bestseller lists, including *USA Today* and the *Readers' Favorite* 2017 Gold Medal in Romance, and has since been translated into multiple languages internationally.

The *Fade Into You* series (formally known as the *Cadence* duet) was a finalist in the *HEAR Now Festival Independent Audiobook Awards*.

In addition, Dakota has written under the alternate pen name, Marie Christy. Under this name, she has written and published a children's book for charity titled, *And I Smile.*

Also writing as Marie Christy, she was a contributor to the Blunder Woman Productions project, *Nevertheless We Persisted: Me Too*, a 2019 *Audie Award Finalist* and *Earphones Awards Winner*. This project inspired Dakota to write *The Sound of Silence*, a dark romantic suspense novel that tackles the realities of domestic abuse.

Dakota Willink is the founder of Dragonfly Ink Publishing, whose mission is to promote a common passion for reading by partnering with like-minded authors and industry professionals. Through this company, Dakota created the *Love & Lace Inkorporated* Magazine and the *Leave Me Breathless World*, hosted ALLURE Audiobook Con, and sponsored various charity anthologies.

ACKNOWLEDGMENTS

To my children, for your endless patience with having to "be quiet" while mom works. There were some long (and silent) days in our house... you don't know how much your understanding means to me. I love you both so much.

To Linda and Alicia, for being my first unofficial audience, and for giving me much needed criticism and feedback when it mattered most.

And finally, to my husband...for so many things. I wouldn't be where I am today without you. You believe in me when I am in doubt (even if it means you have to stay up until 2 A.M. reading my latest chapter edits). Your support has been immeasurable and *Heart of Stone* would still be a dream if you hadn't pushed me to write. You are my love and my soul – my white picket fence. I love you, babe!

Made in United States
North Haven, CT
29 March 2023

34693783R00264